NECROPOLIS

RUSSIAN LIBRARY

R

The Russian Library at Columbia University Press publishes an expansive selection of Russian literature in English translation, concentrating on works previously unavailable in English and those ripe for new translations. Works of premodern, modern, and contemporary literature are featured, including recent writing. The series seeks to demonstrate the breadth, surprising variety, and global importance of the Russian literary tradition and includes not only novels but also short stories, plays, poetry, memoirs, creative nonfiction, and works of mixed or fluid genre.

■ □ ■

Between Dog and Wolf by Sasha Sokolov, translated by Alexander Boguslawski

Strolls with Pushkin by Andrei Sinyavsky, translated by Catharine Theimer Nepomnyashchy and Slava I. Yastremski

Fourteen Little Red Huts and Other Plays by Andrei Platonov, translated by Robert Chandler, Jesse Irwin, and Susan Larsen

Rapture: A Novel by Iliazd, translated by Thomas J. Kitson

City Folk and Country Folk by Sofia Khvoshchinskaya, translated by Nora Seligman Favorov

Writings from the Golden Age of Russian Poetry by Konstantin Batyushkov, presented and translated by Peter France

Found Life: Poems, Stories, Comics, a Play, and an Interview by Linor Goralik, edited by Ainsley Morse, Maria Vassileva, and Maya Vinokur

Sisters of the Cross by Alexei Remizov, translated by Roger John Keys and Brian Murphy

Sentimental Tales by Mikhail Zoshchenko, translated by Boris Dralyuk

Redemption by Friedrich Gorenstein, translated by Andrew Bromfield

The Man Who Couldn't Die: The Tale of an Authentic Human Being by Olga Slavnikova, translated by Marian Schwartz

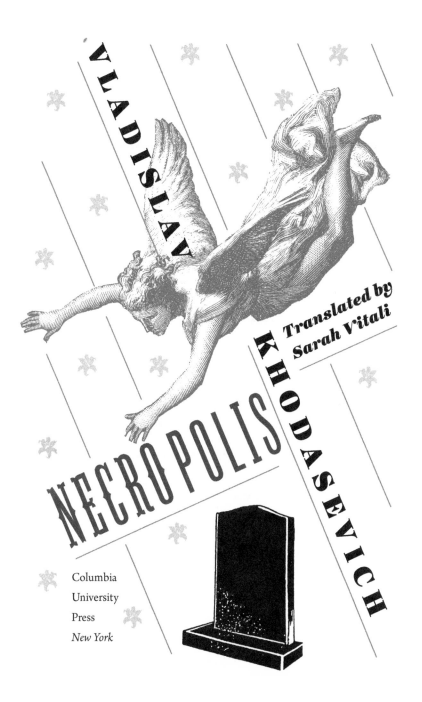

VLADISLAV

KHODASEVICH

Translated by
Sarah Vitali

NECROPOLIS

Columbia
University
Press
New York

Columbia University Press
Publishers Since 1893
New York   Chichester, West Sussex
cup.columbia.edu

Published with the support of Read Russia, Inc.,
and the Institute of Literary Translation, Russia

Library of Congress Cataloging-in-Publication Data
Names: Khodasevich, V. F. (Vladislav Felitsianovich), 1886-1939,
author. | Vitali, Sarah, translator.
Title: Necropolis / Vladislav Khodasevich; translated by Sarah Vitali.
Other titles: Nekropol'. English (Vitali)
Description: New York : Columbia University Press, 2019. |
Series: Russian library | Includes bibliographical references
and index.
Identifiers: LCCN 2018038861 (print) | LCCN 2018047136 (e-book) |
ISBN 9780231546966 (electronic) | ISBN 9780231187046
(cloth : alk. paper) | ISBN 9780231187053 (pbk.)
Subjects: LCSH: Authors, Russian—20th century—Biography. |
Symbolism (Literary movement)—Russia.
Classification: LCC PG3476.K488 (e-book) | LCC PG3476.K488
N413 2019 (print) | DDC 891.71/3—dc23
LC record available at https://lccn.loc.gov/2018038861

Printed in the United States of America

Cover design: Roberto de Vicq de Cumptich
Book design: Lisa Hamm

CONTENTS

TRANSLATOR'S ACKNOWLEDGMENTS

I would like to begin by thanking Polina Barskova, who first inspired me to undertake this project. I also owe a tremendous debt of gratitude to Stephanie Sandler, without whose encouragement and guidance this manuscript might never have left the proverbial desk drawer. I am grateful, too, to Justin Cahill, Ainsley Morse, and Maria Vassileva for generously offering their advice at vital moments along the way.

My thanks go to the wonderful board and staff of Columbia University Press's Russian Library project and, especially, to Christine Dunbar for her excellent editorial work and insights. The administrative support of Christian Winting, as well as the keen eyes of copyeditor Jane Paulsen and project manager Ben Kolstad, have been invaluable to this project. Many of the notes to this work have drawn on the excellent research of N. A. Bogomolov, who wrote the commentary to *Necropolis* in the four-volume collection of Khodasevich's writings recently released by the Soglasie Publishing House in Moscow, and to whom I am extremely grateful. I would also like to express my sincere gratitude to the anonymous reviewers of this manuscript and to Michael Wachtel, whose incredible eye for detail and generosity of time and expertise have greatly enriched the finished product.

Finally, I would like to thank my husband, Daniel Green, for his unflagging support and patience while I was off traipsing through Khodasevich's city of the dead.

INTRODUCTION

DAVID BETHEA

y the time he was forced into exile by the Soviet regime
in June 1922, the Moscow-born Vladislav Khodasevich
(1886–1939) was already an important poet and literary
figure. He had written four books of verse, two of which, *Grain's Way*
(1920) and *The Heavy Lyre* (1922), established his status among the
cognoscenti as indisputably "major." Indeed, with its startling fusion
of Symbolism and post-Symbolism, Pushkinian lapidary simplicity
and ever-questioning irony, *The Heavy Lyre* would go down as one
of the truly great poetry collections in the modern Russian tradition. The musical instrument that is handed out of nowhere to the
poet to give the collection its title (in the poem "Ballad") is weighty
because he, a modern Orpheus, still manages to make mesmerizing
sound out of the direst existential circumstances. Moreover, Khodasevich's prosodic conservatism (e.g., his use of the iamb as a kind
of classical amphora for the storage of semantic vitriol); his strange
visions of a fiercely private *psikheia*, or "psyche"; his willingness to
weigh his own words "on Pushkin's scales"; and his impeccable taste
and stern standards in matters of artistic conscience were all qualities that set him apart in the swirling context of revolutionary and
postrevolutionary literary trendsetters. In this respect Khodasevich
was never a joiner; he was always "*sam po sebe*," "all by himself." Similar things can be said of the poet's many-faceted service to Russian

literature in the years leading up to his exile: whether the words belonged to the critic, translator (especially of Polish classics and modern Hebrew poets), literary historian, or Pushkinist, Khodasevich's verbal traces were always of a piece, deeply organic, emanating from the same integral source. Andrey Bely helped to make his reputation with important articles on him in 1922 and 1923. Other accolades, from sources as varied as Maxim Gorky and Osip Mandelstam, followed.

This, for example, is how Nabokov recalls the Khodasevich of his émigré years in *Speak, Memory*:

> I developed a great liking for this bitter man, wrought of irony and metallic-like genius, whose poetry was as complex a marvel as that of Tyutchev or Blok. He was, physically, of a sickly aspect, with contemptuous nostrils and beetling brows, and when I conjure him up in my mind he never rises from the hard chair on which he sits, his thin legs crossed, his eyes glittering with malevolence and wit, his long fingers screwing into a holder the half of a *Caporal Vert* cigarette.[1]

Necropolis, the book of memoirs published by Khodasevich on the eve of his passing, is a gift to historians and scholars of the so-called Silver Age of Russian literature for a number of reasons. First and foremost, it is written in the words of a poet who has turned to prose and who is remembering figures that in several cases he knew intimately (Valery Bryusov, Bely, Gorky, Mikhail Gershenzon, Muni [Samuil Kissin], Nina Petrovskaya). This simple statement of fact conceals layers of meaning that require their own unpacking. Like no one else before or after, Khodasevich was putting the Symbolist epoch in high-resolution historical perspective and explaining to the reader the causes of its rise and fall. He was doing so both as a participant/actor, as we see in his memoir of Muni, and as a survivor/audience, as we see in his memoir of Bryusov. The goal was sobriety after the literal and figurative madness of the period. Speaking procedurally, Khodasevich's business was to present eye-witness accounts that did not ignore his own role in the proceedings but still placed the accent on his subject's actions and (to the extent that they became obvious) motives, and in the final reckoning attempted to capture the very core of each individual's personality. And to do this the memoirist had to, if not remove himself, then at least bracket any tendency toward personal animus. Thus, despite the author's reputation for tetchiness, none of the portraits in *Necropolis* is about score-settling, even the history of Khodasevich's complicated relations with Bryusov, of whose domineering affect and cynical manipulation of younger poets such as Viktor Gofman, Nina Petrovskaya, and Nadia Lvova he clearly disapproved.

To get a clearer picture of Khodasevich's approach to memoir writing, let us perform a brief experiment comparing like sources. First, there was the passing of the baton between generations: inasmuch as poetry writing was the Silver Age's privileged genre, and inasmuch as the poet embodying "life creation" (*zhiznetvorchestvo*) was the era's cultural hero par excellence, it was an event when a leading poet from a younger generation paid tribute to a departed poet from an older generation. Second, the reason that "life creation," the urge to translate the arc of one's life into a plot that appeared shaped "from beyond," was such a crucial theme in *Necropolis* was that the dynamics surrounding this urge constituted the very essence of Symbolist overreach, and the figures it destroyed, among them Alexander Blok and Bely, were Symbolism's greatest heroes—virtual brothers, spiritual extensions of each other. Khodasevich's book of memoirs tells this story through primary and secondary characters, keeping the focus all the while on the body count, the lives drawn into Symbolism's powerful undertow and then drowned and left behind on the shore.

Now for the experiment. The only poet equivalent to Khodasevich in stature who occupied the same exilic status (and thus was free of Soviet censorship) and who penned analogous valedictory pieces on departed colleagues was Marina Tsvetaeva. Recall, for the sake of comparison, her farewell to Bely ("Captive Spirit," 1934), which was dedicated to Khodasevich. Here, for example, is a well-known passage describing Tsvetaeva's meeting with Bely:

> "And so, you are kin? I always knew you were kin. You are the daughter of Professor Tsvetaev. And I am the son of Professor Bugaev. You are a daughter, I am a son."
>
> Overcome by irrefutable fact, I remain silent.
>
> "We are professors' children. Do you understand what that means, professors' children? After all it means an entire circle, an entire credo. (A deepening pause.) You can't understand how happy you've made me. I don't know why but all my life I *alone* have been a professor's son, and for me that was like a label. O, I don't want to say anything bad about professors—but still, it's lonely, no? [...]
>
> But let's leave aside *professors'* children, let's leave aside just the *children* themselves. We're, as it turns out, children (in an elevated tone)—it's all the same whose! And our fathers have died. And we're orphans. And you also write verse, don't you? Orphans and poets, wow! And such happiness that we're at one table, and that we're able to order coffee, and that they'll bring it to us both, coffee from the same pot, in two identical cups. Well, doesn't that make us related?[2]

Bely's manic speech patterns, his associative leaps and febrile wordplay, come through as if transcribed. Tsvetaeva follows up her description of the meeting with documentary evidence reinforcing the older and younger poets' kinship: a letter left behind by Bely after he had spent the night reading Tsvetaeva's poetry collection

Parting (1921) and showing him to be profoundly struck by the book's melodics (*melodika*)—the contrast between rhythm and meter that very much interested Bely at the time. The point is that Tsvetaeva keeps the essence of Bely's "captive spirit" *and* her poetic reaction to the encounter within the frame.

Now, the opening paragraphs of Khodasevich's memoir of Bely:

> In 1922 in Berlin, Andrei Bely presented me with a new edition of *Petersburg*, inscribed: "With feelings of concrete love and lifelong connection."
>
> In ideology, in literature, and in life, fate pushed us along in opposite directions—if not for our entire lives, then for nineteen years at least. I did not share the greater part of Bely's views, but he exercised a greater influence over me than any other person I have known. I didn't belong to the same generation as Bely, but I first came into contact with his generation when it was still young and active. Many people and circumstances that played a conspicuous role in Bely's life turned out to do the same in mine.
>
> For various reasons, I cannot relate everything that I know and believe to be true about Bely at this time. But even in the context of this short narrative, I would rather preserve a few truthful sketches for the benefit of literary history than satisfy the curiosity of the contemporary reader. After all, literary history has already begun to demonstrate an interest in the era of Symbolism in general and in Andrei Bely in particular—with time, this interest will only grow more acute. I feel compelled to be exceptionally fussy with the truth. I consider it my (far from easy) obligation to omit any hypocritical thoughts or euphemistic language from this account. You mustn't expect me to offer up an iconic or canonical image of my subject. Such images are harmful to history. I am certain that they are immoral as well, since only a complete and truthful image is capable of revealing the finest attributes of a truly remarkable person. By its

very nature, the truth cannot be low because there is nothing higher than the truth. It seems appropriate to counter Pushkin's "uplifting deception" with an equally uplifting truth: we must learn to respect and love a remarkable person together with all of his weaknesses, and occasionally even because of them. Such people require no embellishment. They require something far more difficult from us: our total understanding. (49–50)

Khodasevich's viewpoint is retrospective. Six years older than Tsvetaeva, he is closer to Bely in age (Bely's dates are 1880–1934) and thus closer to the entire Symbolist ethos. He says as much when he writes that he "first came into contact with [Bely's] generation when it was still young and active." While Tsvetaeva cites the letter Bely leaves behind in praise of her *Parting*, Khodasevich mentions the signed copy of *Petersburg*, Bely's great novel, which his friend presents to him "with feelings of concrete love and lifelong connection." He also admits that no one "exercised a greater influence over [him]" than Bely. But it is not his role in the memoir to probe that influence, to speak about how their work may have intersected on a poet-to-poet basis. Rather, in the aftermath of Symbolism, "for the benefit of literary history," he wants to try to help the reader understand by pitting the truth as he sees it and *lived* it against a Pushkinian "uplifting deceit" that brushstrokes out the human toll of Symbolist excess and endeavors to keep the "Heroïca" of the era intact, uncommented upon.

As mentioned, Khodasevich's chief aim in writing *Necropolis* is to capture the essence of each subject's personhood before that personhood, as a combination of art and life, joins forever the world of shadows, hence the title with its reference to the city of dead. Although each chapter in the book can stand alone as a portrait of a significant figure of the age, different themes intertwine to give the whole a sense of coherence and integrity. The first of these is the life and death of Symbolism/Decadence, which stands at the center of the stories of Nina Petrovskaya, Bryusov, Bely, Muni, Blok-Gumilyov (these two are linked), and Sologub. The pieces on Esenin and Gorky also have to do with the twilight of those subjects' lives, but in their cases the emphasis is more on their biographies as functions of, perhaps even prisoners of, their artistic credos and personal myths. The eminent Pushkinist (author of *The Wisdom of Pushkin*, 1919) and intellectual historian Gershenzon is a case apart, a clear bright spot: an individual who belonged to the era and who lived for ideas, but who, thanks to his sturdy ethical (and ethnic, Jewish) moorings and essential modesty, was memorable for how he steadfastly plied his craft in straitened circumstances and looked after fellow writers in need.

Khodasevich knows he is a unique narrator, both an actor and an observer, a fact that colors everything he writes. Indeed, it is this "straddling" stance, which understands implicitly what it means to be positioned experientially within the work of art (the dictates of inspiration, as it were) and outside it at the same time ("literary history"), that qualifies the speaker in this special way. No poet of Khodasevich's generation speaks more intelligently about the relationship between artistic form and artistic content than he: the two cannot be separated because together they represent creative life itself—they are not discrete entities or essences, but meaning-laden extensions of each other. What lasts in literary history is a good poem, and for this memoirist and his generation its survival is not simply a matter of taste. Rather, it is a distillation of lived experience, sensitivity to words, awareness of prosodic history, and sheer creativity in the moment that constitutes its own ontological reality. The tradition sorts out what deserves to be remembered, although mistakes and lapses take place. This holistic perspective frames each of the character studies in *Necropolis,* as Khodasevich relates to the reader the human being in his or her context who produces the work of art, oftentimes interleaving the narration with quotes from the subject's own work (Esenin and his *Inonia* is a good example of this).

In this respect, it should come as no shock that Khodasevich was critical of both the formalists for foregrounding artistic expression at the expense of content and of the "proletarian" writers (the future socialist realists), whose model was Gorky, for focusing exclusively on message. Figuratively speaking, there is a relationship between form and content that is "organismic," like a body pulsating with life within and between its different "plasmic" layers: cell, organ, organism, environment. To push the poem too far in one direction, to destroy the "Pushkinian" homeostatic balance that is everywhere its "mind," is to create something ugly or monstrous, not worthy of survival. The poet and his poem together are the culture's individual organism that seeks "life" (survival) by finding a provisional perch between tradition and innovation, personal biography and literary history, words as inherited and words as one's own. Khodasevich understood all this with consummate sensitivity, in large part because he was living out his own and his tradition's extinction in the last two decades of his life, as he stopped writing verse and described the dying out of the art and artist once intensely alive in *Derzhavin* (1931) and *Necropolis,* his masterly swan songs in prose.

The three main actors in the history/story (the two are hopelessly blurred) of Symbolism are Blok, Bely, and Bryusov. Khodasevich knew the latter two intimately, and the former he observed closely in the last months of his life. Again, Symbolism was not simply a literary movement, it was an attempt to translate art (mythopoetic "plot") into life ("life creation"), not only on a personal level but on a national one as well, hence its fatal embedding in revolutionary politics and apocalyptic thinking:

The Symbolists had no desire to separate the writer from the human being, the literary from the personal biography. Symbolism was not content to be merely an artistic school, a literary movement. It was constantly striving to become a means of life creation, and therein lay its deepest and perhaps most unmanifestable truth. However, to all intents and purposes, its perpetual striving toward that truth formed the backdrop to Symbolism's history. This history consisted of a series of attempts—at times, truly heroic ones—to discover the proper alloy of life and art: a philosopher's stone of art, if you will. (3–4)

In Khodasevich's telling, Blok and Bely were the movement's sincere, and for that reason ultimately tragically defeated, adepts, while Bryusov, more aligned traditionally with Decadence, was its manipulative magus. Instead of defining the difference between Symbolism and Decadence as one of aesthetic affect or attitude, which is typically the position of literary historians, Khodasevich presents it as a high-modern morality play, a love story gone wrong. Symbolism was infected with "decadent" poison in its bloodstream from the beginning, although unaware of it. Its "fatal sin" (*smertnyi grekh*) was a function of its own impossible romanticism, its urge to engage in life creation as though there were no tomorrow. Love, or rather a maximally high-pitched falling-in-love, which inevitably led to sex, something still shocking for this late Victorian period, was elided with intricately interrelated acts of artistic creation in a repeated pattern that left the participants burned out and psychically demoralized. Symbolism's "fall," however, did not come until it became conscious of its bad faith, its "infection," which according to Khodasevich emanated from Bryusov and his use of others to advance his own place in the literary dominance hierarchy. Decadence in essence became itself when, through Bryusov, it caused Symbolism's lapse into history:

> Decadence is a relative concept: a fall is defined by its starting height. Bearing this in mind, it is meaningless to apply the term "decadence" to the art of the early Symbolists: this art didn't, in and of itself, represent a fall in relation to the past. But the sins that grew up and developed *within* Symbolism represented a decadence, a fall in relation to those early years. It seems that Symbolism was born with this poison in its blood. It ran in the veins of all Symbolist figures to varying degrees. To a certain extent (or at a certain point), each one of them was a decadent. (8)

Of these three central actors, Blok was the one who most embodied the "heroic" in Symbolism. He was, in Akhmatova's famous phrase, the "tragic tenor of the epoch." It could be argued that the life-art residue surrounding Blok, his verbal-cum-personal charisma, is what has been most lost to history as the study of modern Russian poetry has turned the bulk of its attention to the four great post-Symbolist poets who emerged in Blok's wake—Akhmatova, Mandelstam, Tsvetaeva, and Pasternak—even though at the time these very poets would not have denied Blok's unique preeminence. Nabokov, the other great, though slightly younger, post-Symbolist, was himself "infected" by Blok's magic in his formative years. This is what he writes Edmund Wilson as the latter is introducing himself to the poet: "I am glad you are studying Blok—but be careful: he is one of those poets that gets into one's system—and everything else seems unblokish and flat. I, as most Russians, went through that stage some twenty-five years ago."[3] In other words, there is something truly dangerous about "absorbing" Blok. One cannot look at things the same way after the virus has spread.

At this point a brief aside is needed. Blok's courtship of Lyubov Dmitrievna Mendeleeva is the stuff of Symbolist legend, and scholars have pored over the facts of that relationship ever since to arrive at an accurate picture of events, although it is unlikely objective reality can ever be constituted in this case. "Objective" here veers too closely to the subjective. In any event, this is where the story really starts. "Sasha" and "Lyuba" were both beautiful and gifted young people, he playing Hamlet to her Ophelia in adolescent stagings, and in the first blush of their love they existed in a prelapsarian atmosphere of distinguished parentage, estates in sylvan settings, and Solovyovian premonitions of a new dawn (the great philosopher-poet Vladimir Solovyov being the universally acknowledged godfather of Symbolism). This new dawn came with the new century and with expectations that "She," the Beautiful Lady, Blok's version of Solovyov's Sophia (Holy Wisdom), would materialize as a world transformed for the better. But Blok always had his doubts, which were hinted at in his *Verses on the Beautiful Lady* (1901–02) from the beginning. He believed his own blood (from his father's side) was tainted with madness and male violence, and thus sex, the source of fearful procreation, was always a negative, something attractive but dark and haunted, in his mind, not something appropriate for either his mythopoetic Beautiful Lady or her flesh-and-blood avatar. Blok and Lyubov's marriage remained long unconsummated, a complication not helped by Bely's arrival on the scene and his courting of Lyubov, itself deeply myth-enshrouded though also in the end unconsummated (see below). In his middle period Blok turned to prostitutes and taverns to satisfy his urgings and to simultaneously humiliate himself ("The Stranger," 1906). This is when playacting turned to self-mockery and the undermining of earlier chivalric codes in the famous Meyerhold-directed *Fairground Booth* (Balaganchik, 1906). Eventually the hopes for a renovated Russia morphed into a full-scale *cris de coeur*, with prophetic warnings that history would violently repeat itself ("On the Kulikovo Field," 1908) and with articles in the periodic press lashing the liberal intelligentsia for its cravenness and bad faith ("Intelligentsia and Revolution," 1918).

For Nabokov, as opposed to Khodasevich, Blok was eventually seen as a kind of evil genius or "dark bloom," as in the English anagram. Think of the Baudelaire of "Harmonie du soir" or, closer still, since this is where Humbert Humbert's troubles begin, the Poe of "Annabel Lee," whose dark, haunting sounds become an imprisoning echo chamber ready to fetishize a prior "beautiful lady" and engulf "lucidity." By telling Wilson to be careful, Nabokov is suggesting that Blok is ethically and aesthetically the opposite of Pushkin, the bright genius of *The Gift*, whose hero bears a surname (Godunov) thick with Pushkinian notions of genuine fatherhood versus imposture. What is lost again to the prose writer's belatedness, however, is the *heroic* quality of Blok's quest: his struggles feel larger than life, more than personal fantasy, and the unreproduceable sound of the verse and the biographical death that mysteriously followed the end of the "music" were all the proof necessary of their authenticity. Last but not least, that Nabokov was reading Blok's Florence cycle to his mother on the night his father was assassinated must have confirmed this demonic connection. Nabokov and his mother (both superstitious) loved these poems, were intoxicated by their sounds; yet perhaps there was something "indecent" or "uncontrollable" in their charm.

Now, back to Khodasevich and his take on the Blokian phenomenon. In the year of Blok's death (1921) a celebration of Pushkin was organized in Petrograd, soon to become Leningrad. Such occasions, which were intended to keep alive the poet's bright legacy, took place on or close to the day of Pushkin's death (February 7 new style, January 26 old style), itself a highly symbolic gesture, as it turned out, since in later Soviet times these holidays were switched to the day of Pushkin's birth. This particular celebration, so freighted with meaning at this juncture in literary history, was repeated three times in the following weeks. It was here that Khodasevich read his famous Pushkin speech "The Shaken Tripod" and Blok his "On the Poet's Calling."

The manner in which Khodasevich captures this innerly (and soon literally) dying Blok is remarkable. On the one hand, the beautiful young Hamlet has become, physically, somehow merged with his severe northern climate and maritime setting:

> Blok went on last with his inspired Pushkin speech. He wore a black jacket over a white turtleneck sweater. Wiry and desiccated, with his weather-beaten, reddish face, he looked like a fisherman. He spoke in clipped tones and in a slightly muffled voice; his hands were stuffed into his pockets. (102)

On the other hand, the words he is pronouncing, so slowly and deliberately as though from the bottom of a barrel, might come from Pushkin, except that they contain knifelike thrusts directed at the pain of the present moment and its historical significance. The individual is dying, the tradition is dying, the extinction of a poetic species, as it were, is taking place before everyone's eyes:

> "Peace and free will. The poet needs both of these things in order to liberate his harmonies. But his peace and free will are being taken away. Not his peace in the superficial sense, but his artistic peace. Not his childish will, not the freedom to play at being a liberal, but his artistic will, that secret freedom. And the poet is dying because there is nothing left for him to breathe: his life has lost its meaning." (111–112)

The portrait is concluded with a reminiscence of a sit-down Blok and Khodasevich had backstage before their February 26 performance:

> On that evening [...] he was more melancholy than ever. He spoke about himself at great length. It was as if he were talking to himself; he became deeply introspective. He spoke very restrainedly, sometimes in allusions, sometimes vaguely and confusedly, but one

could sense a stern, sharp honesty behind his words. It seemed as
if he were seeing himself and the world around him with a tragic
rawness and simplicity. And this honesty and simplicity forever
remained connected in my mind with memories of Blok. (104)

But the point for us and for the readership in posterity is that the
poetry as living speech and the person as mortal vessel go hand
in hand—they cannot be separated. In these pages Khodasevich
recalls one of Blok's final public readings of his verse.

Blok went on during the second act. [...] He read only a few poems,
but he did so with a poignant simplicity and profound gravity that
are best described using Pushkin's phrase: "with solemnity." He
pronounced his words very slowly, joining them together into a
barely distinguishable melody, which was perhaps only intelligible
to those capable of discerning poetry's internal movement. He
read clearly and distinctly, articulating every letter, but, at the same
time, he moved only his lips, without ever unclenching his teeth.
When he was met with applause, he neither expressed gratitude nor
affected disregard. His face remained motionless; he would lower
his eyes, stare at the ground, and wait patiently for silence. The last
thing he read was "On the Stand" ["Pered sudom," 1915], one of his
most hopeless poems:

Why do you cast down your eyes, embarrassed?
Look upon me in your former way.
So this is who you are today—made humble
In the uncorrupted light of day!
Nor do I shine with my former glory:
Out of reach, proud-hearted, perfect, mean.
I now observe more kindly and forlornly
Our simple and insipid life routine. (110–111)

It is, I would suggest, this special blend of seeing and hearing that is Khodasevich's signature. The picture of the man and the sound of his words go hand in hand. Myth and history, the sacral and the secular, words that are spoken once in time and words that are spoken in eternity: this is the "seam" that Khodasevich apprehends and wants to preserve for posterity. His postmortem on Blok is one for the ages: "But what did he actually die of? No one knows. He somehow died 'in general': because he was sick all over, because he could no longer go on living. He died of death" (112).

Perhaps because Khodasevich knew Bely and Bryusov better, his recollection and analysis of their roles in the Symbolist plot differ dramatically from his evaluation of Blok. The older Bryusov, born in 1873, had been a mentor for Khodasevich as the latter began to make his way as fledgling poet, and the incandescent Bely, as already mentioned, spent long periods in close quarters with Khodasevich and influenced him more powerfully than any other contemporary writer/thinker. In the Symbolist plot, Blok stands more as a hero apart, distanced, with one foot already in mythical space, while Bely and Bryusov stand squarely in the foreground, their stories set closer to everyday space and enmeshed in literary politics and petty squabbling. Thus, in terms of the Christian myth-cum-fairytale gone wrong, Blok begins by waiting for the Beautiful Lady to come (which she doesn't) and by avoiding sexual congress with the maiden he thinks, or hopes, will turn into his ideal (she also doesn't). Bely, in contrast, sees himself from early on as "Andrew the White" (his pseudonym), a Christ-like knight on a white horse (Revelation 19), who has arrived to marry the Women Clothed in the Sun (Revelation 12) in a history-ending hierogamy. Khodasevich, for his part, does not dwell on this Symbolist apocalypticism originating in Solovyov and lived out by Blok and Bely. He is more interested in what happens to the principals once they are caught in the undertow of Symbolism's "mortal sin," "life creation." Finally, the Symbolist plot needs more than abstract biblical stage machinery. To come alive for the participants it needs Eros, bodies aroused through words. It likewise needs something earthbound, calculating and malevolent, to give it psychological traction. This is, in Khodasevich's telling, Bryusov's cue to enter the picture.

The fates of Bryusov and Bely are tightly interwoven in the different storylines constituting *Necropolis*. Other figures with chapters devoted to them, such as Nina Petrovskaya and Muni, whose stories Khodasevich doesn't want to be forgotten by literary history, exist in the penumbrae of Symbolism's principal plot. While the two figures seemed to be drawn to each other as foils—recall that the Bely–Nina Petrovskaya–Bryusov triangle was playing out in a Decadent key what the Blok–Lyubov–Bely triangle was playing out in a Symbolist one—Bely was by far the more consequential in terms of philosophical and artistic fireworks. Just as Khodasevich was the first critic to fully appreciate the budding genius of Sirin-Nabokov, so too was he the first to fully articulate the different forces that made up Bely's outsized Symbolist persona. In this respect, anyone wishing to penetrate the frenetic artistry of *Petersburg*, a novel Nabokov places on par with a small cadre of the twentieth century's greatest prose works, should begin with Khodasevich's chapter on Bely in *Necropolis*.

The first quality that Khodasevich isolates in the young Bely is the "light" of his physical and mental presence. He is Symbolism's child of the sun:

> The little boy had golden curls that reached down to his shoulders and his eyes were deep blue. He rolled a golden hoop along a golden path with a golden stick. Eternity, "that child at play," pushes the golden circle of the sun along in precisely the same fashion. The image of Bely as a young child is closely linked with the image of the sun. (50)

The golden curls and the blue eyes were the physical manifestations of an inner luminescence under whose sway all seemed to fall. As Khodasevich describes his friend in 1904,

> Andrey Bely was still very young, with golden curls, blue eyes, and a tremendous amount of charm. [. . .] People would go into raptures over him. When he was around, it was as if everything was instantly transformed, shifted, or encircled in his light. And he truly was radiant. It was as if everyone, even those people who envied him, was a little bit in love with him. (10)

But as with the youthful Blok and his prelapsarian premonitions, there was a snake in Bely's light-filled garden, which Khodasevich traces with great imaginative empathy and insight to his friend's troubled relationship to his parents—the one a genius-level mathematician but physically unattractive, absent-minded and socially awkward in the extreme, and the other a worldly beauty who hated mathematics and loved poetry and music. Formed by primal scene battles staged between father and mother and by the striking contrasts defining their personalities, Bely's potent psyche became a cauldron of repressed patricidal urges and filial self-loathing that he then projected onto the country's political and social tensions in epoch-defining works of art and criticism. (As an aside, here we see, to take the most obvious example, the autobiographical links between the hero, Nikolai Apollonovich, and his father, Apollon Apollonovich, and mother, Anna Petrovna, in *Petersburg*: "As time went by, it became progressively clearer to Bely that everything 'positive' and dear to his father was dear to him as well, while art and philosophy must be reconciled with hard knowledge—'otherwise, it would be impossible to live' [54].) Bely came to see himself as hopelessly "torn" (*razdiraemyi*) by these unpredictable electrical storms, which he carried with him into the future (54). Others would impute a kind of hypocrisy, or "two-facedness" (*dvulichie*), to Bely, as he would attack a well-meaning friend out of the blue or become reconciled to an adversary suddenly for no good reason. But Khodasevich knew better what was going on: "[Bely] came to love the reconciliation of the irreconcilable, the tragedy and complexity of internal contradiction, the truth in untruth, and, perhaps, the good in evil and the evil in good. [...] But there was no guile or opportunism at the base of his two-facedness; there was nothing like that in its nature" (53–54).

Thus it was these inner storms, coupled with his persona as "Andrew the White" and apocalyptic heir apparent, that Bely brought with him when he came to St. Petersburg to meet and befriend his greatest contemporary Blok and Blok's wife, Lyubov. It was a volatile situation just waiting to detonate.

> His [Bely's] tactics would always be the same: he would charm a woman with his near-magical charisma, appearing to her surrounded by his mystical halo, as if to nip any thoughts of sensual pursuit in the bud. Later on, he would start to force his attentions on her, and if she, struck (and sometimes offended) by the unexpectedness of these attentions, didn't respond in kind, he would fly into a rage. [Again, compare this description of Bely to that of Nikolai in his behavior toward Sophia Petrovna, followed by the "rage" of the "red domino" episode, in *Petersburg*—DMB.] On the other hand, every time he did manage to achieve his desired result, he would feel besmirched and defiled, and would likewise fly into a rage. It also sometimes happened that, at the very last moment before the "fall," he would manage to escape, like Joseph the all-comely—but in that case, he would be twice as indignant: both because a woman had almost seduced him and because she hadn't quite managed it. (55)

In other words, sex was never simply sex, or even open-ended romance, but predetermined by the larger plot.

However, this pattern met with a worthy opponent when Bely began to fall in love with Lyubov. The sort of erotic teasing that Bely couldn't help but that was both intensely infuriating and humiliating for the potential lover involved exploded in a way that changed everything:

> All things considered, this love affair [between Bely and Lyubov] seems to have proceeded in the following manner. Apparently, the young lady received the brotherly feelings that Bely initially extended to her favorably. But when Bely, as was his wont, progressed from such brotherly feelings to feelings of a different nature, his task became immeasurably more complicated. Perhaps it would have been entirely insoluble if it hadn't been for his dazzling charm, which, it seemed, was genuinely irresistible. But every time his romantic pursuit was nearing the point of success, Bely's unavoidable ambivalence would bubble up to the surface, just as it always did. He was mad enough to convince himself that his actions had been taken the wrong way, "sinfully"—and he said as much to the lady in question, who, in all likelihood, had undergone significant sufferings before offering up her consent. The consequences of Bely's backpedaling aren't difficult to imagine. The woman he loved was seized with wrath and contempt. And she got her own back. [...] And as for Bely? I can say with great certainty that, from that moment onward, he actually began to love her genuinely, with all his soul, and, I am deeply convinced, forevermore. He experienced both other loves and fleeting infatuations later in his life, but this love remained throughout it and above it all. She was the only woman he ever truly loved, she and she alone. (58)

Bely's story was far from over at this point. He was someone of immense stamina and manic, inexhaustible energy. But despite the ongoing surge of novels, essays, philosophical excursuses, and memoirs up ahead, something was broken. Khodasevich, probably as close to Bely as anyone during these years, follows this arc on its way down as well. He was present, for example, during Bely's Berlin period when his crazy, drunken dancing was misinterpreted by both the local and the émigré populations, a context that also happened to provide the setting for one of Khodasevich's most terrifying and brilliant poems, "An Mariechen" (1922):

> He [Bely] moved to the city [Berlin] that autumn [1922]—and all of Russian Berlin bore cruel and curious witness to his hysteria. They saw it, they delighted in it, and far too many of them mocked him for it. I will describe this hysteria in a few brief words. It manifested itself primarily in the drunken dances he gave himself over to on various Berlin *Dielen*. It wasn't that his dancing was bad; it was that he was terrifying when he did it. He brought his own "variations" to the monotonous crush of foxtrots: it was a funhouse mirror image of the unswerving originality he displayed in everything else he set his hand to. When he danced, his performances would turn into monstrous mimed dramas—sometimes even obscene ones. He would ask ladies he did not know to dance. The bolder women would accept him to amuse themselves and their companions. Others would decline—in Berlin, this was almost an insult. Still others were forbidden by their husbands and fathers. Bely's performances were not just the stumblings of some drunk: they were, in the end, a symbolic violation of that which was best in himself. (71–72)

And so Bely continued on to the end, paranoid, half-mad, "torn." He returned to Russia in 1923 "to mount the cross" for his friends, a number of whom he had denounced to the authorities at the Soviet embassy in order to convince them of his loyalty, which was itself another instance of his "two-facedness." He died in 1934, with tragic poetic justice, of a sunstroke. But as Khodasevich had captured Blok's demise with epigrammatic precision, so too did he understand Bely's perhaps better than anyone:

> Still, I did learn one thing from all of his hysterics in those days: that his new pain, the one he was experiencing at that time, had woken up his old pain, and his old pain turned out to be even more painful than the new one was. An idea occurred to me then that, later, taking into account a number of different factors, turned out to be correct: everything that occurred in Bely's love life after 1906 was simply an attempt to heal the wound he had incurred in Petersburg. (74)

The wound would never heal.

Now for Bryusov, our third lead actor in the period dramas involving "life creation." Khodasevich's recollections of Bryusov, who was thirteen years his senior, are, as noted, complicated by different factors than those relating to Blok and Bely. On the positive side, it was the older poet, so influential in Moscow literary circles at the turn of the century, who gave the neophyte versifier his start. Khodasevich was friends with Bryusov's younger brother Alexander, and through the latter became acquainted with the larger Bryusov household and their crowded abode on Tvetnoy Boulevard. Bryusov controlled the fates of younger poets at the time, schooling them in the culture and techniques of European Modernism and, for those who passed muster, granting them access to prestigious publishing houses and bellwether journals (e.g., "The Scales"). He was an exacting, immensely erudite mentor, conquering culture the way he dominated human relations. It was also Bryusov who, not without significance, served as best man at Khodasevich's wedding to his first wife, Marina Ryndina, in April 1905 and who was the primary influence on his first book of verse, *Youth* (1908). To be fair, in addition to introducing into Russian literary space topoi and poetic devices from world culture that seemed new and exotic, Bryusov was somewhat shocking, *outré*, in his public assault on the intelligentsia's propriety (think Poe, Baudelaire, scenes of trysts in crypts and acts of necrophilia), which appealed to the younger generation's need to challenge authority:

> Later, looking back on the young Bryusov, I realized that the acuity of his poetry from this period lay precisely in that combination of decadent exoticism with the most artless of Muscovite petty bourgeois attitudes. It was an extremely potent mixture; it represented a very sharp break, a trenchant dissonance, but that is precisely why Bryusov's early books (up to and including *Tertia Vigilia*) are, in fact, his best: they are the sharpest. (19)

Hence Bryusov's leading position as *littérateur*, both man of letters and cultural impresario, went far beyond Blok's and Bely's inclinations in this regard. Possible competitors who shared Bryusov's exotic thematics and prosodic range, such as the Decadent movement's acknowledged "songbird" Konstantin Balmont, lacked Bryusov's organizational talents. And, to be sure, there was a definite aura surrounding Bryusov: after he published *Urbi et Orbi* in 1903, Blok, for example, wrote him that "I have no hope of ever finding myself next to you,"[4] while Bely stated in an article of 1905 ("Apocalypse in Russian Poetry") that, after Pushkin and Lermontov, Bryusov was one of the greatest Russian poets, on equal footing with Nekrasov, Tyutchev, and Fet.[5]

Still, this urge to cultural (and personal) domination had a definite negative side, which Khodasevich eventually realized and detailed in *Necropolis*. Whether presiding at a meeting, making a public entrance or exit, or even shaking hands, Bryusov had a way of conducting himself that put others on the defensive. And he took pleasure in this. He was both highly formal and deliberately unpredictable. Coming from a merchant background that was only recently removed from the peasantry, he was hard-nosed and self-contained in his dealings with others, yet had a domestic ("bourgeois," *meshchanskoe*) streak that seemed at odds with his literary adventurism and scandalous affairs of the heart.

> The concept of equality was entirely foreign to Bryusov. Incidentally, it is altogether possible that Bryusov's petty bourgeois background played a role in this. The bourgeois has a much easier time bowing and scraping than, for example, the aristocrat or worker does. By the same token, the desire to humiliate others when given the chance overwhelms the happy bourgeois with greater force than it does the worker or the aristocrat. (25)

All of this would have made no difference in the long run except that, as Khodasevich portrays the Decadent subplot in its juxtaposition to the primary Symbolist storyline, people's lives were ultimately at stake. When Bryusov told Khodasevich in December 1903, on the occasion of his thirtieth birthday, "I want to live my life in such a way that two lines about me will appear in a general history of literature" (30), he was saying that literature mattered to him more than anything else and that, if it came to it, life itself should be sacrificed on the altar of art (see, e.g., his programmatic poem "To the Poet" [1907]: "Perhaps everything in life is only the means for vividly sonorous verse").

It is a subtle difference but an important one: Blok and Bely believed in, or wanted to believe in, their apocalyptic visions but never consciously used others as "life creation" material to achieve their ends. As romantic and maximalist (and in Bely's case, at times mad) as they were, their tragedy was that life did not ultimately respond to their premonitions. Recall what Khodasevich says of Bely, that "there was no guile or opportunism at the base of his two-facedness." Bryusov is a different story, however. Three of Khodasevich's friends from these early years, Viktor Gofman, Nina Petrovskaya, and Nadia Lvova, all came to tragic ends because of their contact with Bryusov. In each case Bryusov schooled the aspiring poet in a live-life-on-the-edge worldview that promoted "lyrical improvisation" and the expanded "moment" (*mig*: Bryusov borrowed the motif from Fet, an influential precursor whose aestheticism was central to the Decadents) at the expense of *durée* or continuous everyday time.

> The business of the poet was to "take" these moments and "annihilate" them, that is, experience them as keenly as possible and then, having exhausted them, move on to the next ones. [. . .] The process of accumulation ran quite chaotically, and without spiritually enriching anyone, it simply wore out and undid one's nerves in the extreme. Life turned into a constant state of intoxication, a sort of gnawing of emotional sunflower seeds, the more of which are eaten, the harder it is to stop, while the hunger does not lessen, and the heartburn intensifies.[6]

Gofman's end came after his access to Moscow journals was blocked by Bryusov, his once promising poetic career fell apart, and, arriving in Paris in 1911 a broken man fearing for his sanity, he put a gun to his head. A similar fate befell Lvova, who worshiped the much older Bryusov, wrote verse under his tutelage, but then couldn't come to grips with the reality that the decadent *maître* also enjoyed his home life and his wife's carrot pies. After Bryusov systematically prepared her for the denouement to her story, Lvova ended by shooting herself in 1913 with the same revolver that Nina Petrovskaya had once used to take her revenge on Bely for throwing her over (luckily the gun misfired). The Browning had been a gift from Bryusov (36).

But the Decadent version of "life creation" reached its greatest fever pitch in the notorious love triangle involving Bryusov, Bely, and Petrovskaya. One reason, perhaps the primary reason, both Blok and Bely feared consummating their love for the Beautiful Lady/Woman Clothed in the Sun was that each believed in his core that Symbolism's "higher reality," the poetic word, Logos, had the potential to transform biology and turn procreation into a higher form of creation (the legacy of Solovyov), and neither wanted to be the one to commit the act that betrayed that legacy, that returned them to their own difficulties with biological parents and literal bloodlines. Bryusov had no such scruples. In "The Fiery Angel" (1908), his *roman à clef* about necromancy and witchcraft in sixteenth-century Germany, there is a thin veil of fiction drawn over the real-life triangle: the hero, Ruprecht (Bryusov); the possessed heroine, Renate (Petrovskaya); and the rival, Count Heinrich von Otterheim (Bely), who Renate believes is the incarnation of the "fiery angel" Madiel, the object of her love since childhood. Needless to say, the angel and the count are not a seamless fit, which is Bryusov's irony. In the fictional world of Renate's obsession, the ideal of the light-bearing spirit never dovetails with the reality of the inconstant lover. For his part, Ruprecht helps Renate look for Heinrich, and together they go so far as to engage in black magic to hasten his return (a motif replicated in life), but to no avail. In the meantime they too become lovers. Renate's obsession is fatal, however. In the end, accused of becoming a witch by the Inquisition, she dies in the arms of Ruprecht, believing that the fiery visitor whose essence she could not make her own in this world has released her from her sins.

Khodasevich calls his opening chapter in *Necropolis* "The Death of Renate" (literally "The End of Renate") because he wants to draw attention to the discrepancy between the fictional character's plot-ending death and the historical person's life that continued on for more than two decades. The idea of "life creation" had its own embedded plot potential, and it had to go somewhere. Unfortunately, Petrovskaya's life of heightened moments and lyrical improvisations descended into deepening circles of alcoholism, drug use, and extreme poverty until she finally, after threatening to kill herself for years, turned on the gas in a sordid Paris hotel room in 1928. Before she died she managed to stay in touch with Khodasevich, sometimes visiting him and writing him letters:

> She came to hate Bryusov: "I felt breathless in my wicked luck, knowing that he couldn't get at me now, that now it was others who were suffering. How was I to know who those others were; by that time, he had already finished off Lvova . . . I continued to live, taking revenge on him with every movement, every thought." (15)

Khodasevich's book of memoirs ramifies out in many directions and touches on its primary and secondary subjects in myriad ways. In the chapters on Gershenzon, Esenin, and Gorky, for example, there are no obvious links to Symbolist "life creation," as these figures had different interests and career arcs. Still, as we attempt to summarize these introductory remarks, *Necropolis* is an apposite title not only because it is the city of the dead and each of the inhabitants recollected has passed to the other side. It also bears this name because the theme of death is virtually omnipresent and the body count involving suicides alone—Petrovskaya; Lvova; Muni; Sologub's wife, Anastasia Chebotarevskaia; Esenin—is striking. Khodasevich's principal concern throughout, however, is that each individual's story be told honestly, in light of what the author knows and experienced personally, and that in telling the story the mainspring, the irreducible quiddity, of that person's character be revealed. To repeat what Khodasevich wrote regarding his Bely portrait, "I feel compelled to be exceptionally fussy with the truth. [. . .]

By its very nature, the truth cannot be low because there is nothing higher than the truth."

Space does not permit a full accounting of the other portraits in *Necropolis*, but in closing let us say a word about each individual's special nature and his (the remaining cast of characters is male) connection to the times. Muni was Khodasevich's closest friend and "poetic co-conspirator." Although a minor literary figure who would be forgotten otherwise, he possessed an echt-Symbolist sensibility that breathed the air of the time and saw everywhere the eerie play between coíncidence and coincídence. Khodasevich could not be there to save his friend from suicide when the latter became isolated and despondent at the front, but he did write one of his most beautiful lyrics, "Look for Me" (1918), to commemorate Muni's passing and to suggest that their spiritual closeness was still alive. Nikolai Gumilyov is treated in tandem with Blok because their deaths in August 1921, Blok's from illness and Gumilyov's from execution at the hands of the Cheka, shocked the literary world and were universally perceived as a dark watershed. Another protégé of Bryusov, Gumilyov resembled the master in his organizational skills (his role in founding Acmeism) as well as in his passion for conquering culture (the African theme). The special trait of Gumilyov's that Khodasevich preserves for posterity is the childlike quality with which he carried on with his associates (his love of organized play). As fate would have it, Khodasevich was the last person Gumilyov saw before he was arrested. An intellectual historian and Pushkin scholar of the first order, Gershenzon combined a meticulous parsing of primary materials with an approach that, according to Khodasevich, was essentially creative, intuitive. Indeed, Gershenzon's errors were often more revealing that other scholars' accurate breakthroughs. When Khodasevich would challenge his kind yet stubborn friend with the query that Pushkin himself might not agree with a proposed reading, Gershenzon would counter, "Who cares what 'Pushkin himself...'? Perhaps I know more about Pushkin than he knew about himself. I know what he wanted to say and what he wanted to hide—and what he said without understanding it himself, like the Pythia" (129).

With regard to his final three subjects, Khodasevich isolates a different tragedy, or rather perception of tragedy, in each. In the case of Sologub, he interweaves quotations from the verse with reminiscences of personal encounters and suggests why the man behind the expressionless mask seemed to withdraw into himself in public. The son of a tailor and a cook, the village schoolmaster Teternikov was from the beginning thrust into a life so raw and bleak that, regardless of imagined worlds of amoral beauty and pleasure with their exotic toponyms (Mair) and upper-case deities (Lucifer), there was no evolution, no development, in his art. That art was circular not only because of Decadent stage props and Nietzschean notions of eternal return but also because the man creating it never felt a connection to the real world as something meaningful, as having plot potential in its own right. The story of Esenin is both different and analogous. As discussed, the Silver Age was rife with utopian strivings and apocalyptic forebodings. A great lyric poet but a poor student of history, Esenin plied his peasant roots to construct a utopian vision, beginning with his poem *Inonia* (1918), that rewrites Christianity and its notion of redemption through Christ's suffering into the coming of Socialism—a world "named Christ," but "without the cross," "a bright city erected by the peasant." Khodasevich, who met Esenin in 1918, plots the latter's decline into drunkenness, "holy foolishness," and ultimately suicide to this tipping point. Finally, Maksim Gorky, an individual Khodasevich knew as intimately as he did Bryusov and Bely, and with whom he lived on a daily basis for equally extended periods, was perhaps the single most significant literary figure in the conceptual birth of Soviet literature and its programmatic brainchild Socialist Realism. His reputation on the world stage was huge. In terms of their artistic interests and genealogies, Gorky and Khodasevich could not have been more different. But before Gorky returned to the Soviet Union to take his place at the apex of the cultural hierarchy, both he and his friend made multiple efforts to create a genuine dialogue between the authors writing abroad and those writing at home (see, e.g., the story of their ill-fated publishing venture *Colloquium* [Beseda]).[7] Khodasevich's unlocking of the riddle of Gorky's personality is as penetrating as his analyses of Bely and Bryusov, for in this last chapter of *Necropolis* the author returns brilliantly to the same problematic issue of Pushkinian "elevating deceit" with which he framed his opening comments on Bely. Ultimately, in the careful dance he performed with the Soviet authorities as he negotiated his return from the safety (but potential lack of relevance) of emigration, Gorky gave in to a self-deception he could not do without. He needed to stay wedded to his "stormy petrel of the revolution" sobriquet not because he desired wealth or the trappings of fame. Instead, loving the idea of the rebel as trickster and brazen rule breaker, from the petty swindler who cheats to the revolutionary who defies the law, he became a prisoner of his official biography and the lie pretending to be reality embedded in it.

Eyewitness, participant, friend, and confidant, creative force in his own right, Khodasevich brings us in contact with his age and its leading actors with unparalleled vividness and lucidity. Now the general reader has the happy prospect of encountering this remarkable book of memoirs in the fine translation by Sarah Vitali. Nabokov once wrote on the occasion of Khodasevich's own passing in 1939, when it seemed too painful to contemplate the loss of the person, "Let us turn to the poems." Now let us turn to the poet's prose cenotaph; he is gone, but his words live after him.

NECROPOLIS

FOREWORD

The reminiscences collected in this book about certain authors from the not-so-distant past are based solely on events that I have borne witness to myself, the direct testimony of those involved, and published or written documents. I have omitted any information that has come down to me second- or thirdhand. The two or three minor exceptions to this rule have been noted in the text.

THE DEATH OF RENATE

On the night of February 22, 1928, in a wretched little hotel in a wretched little neighborhood in Paris, the writer Nina Ivanovna Petrovskaya turned on the gas and took her own life. When the newspapers reported her death, they called her a writer. Somehow, though, the appellation doesn't quite suit her. To be frank, her writings were insignificant, both in quantity and in quality. She didn't know how to—and, more importantly, certainly didn't want to—"waste" what little talent she possessed on literature. She did, however, play a conspicuous role in the life of literary Moscow between the years of 1903 and 1909. Her personality exerted an influence over certain circumstances and events that might seem entirely unconnected to her name. Before I offer my account of her, however, I am obliged to touch upon what is often called the spirit of the era. Without such explanation, Nina Petrovskaya's story would be incomprehensible, and perhaps even uninteresting.

■ □ ■

The Symbolists had no desire to separate the writer from the human being, the literary from the personal biography. Symbolism was not content to be merely an artistic school, a literary movement. It was constantly striving to become a means of life creation,[1] and therein lay its deepest and perhaps most unmanifestable truth. However, to all intents and purposes, its perpetual striving toward that truth formed the backdrop to Symbolism's history. This history consisted of a series of attempts—at times, truly heroic ones—to discover the proper alloy of life and art: a philosopher's stone of art, if you will. The Symbolists stubbornly sought out the genius in their midst, the one who would be capable of fusing life and art together into one. We now know that such a genius was never to appear and that such a formula would never be discovered. In short, the story of the Symbolists turned into a story of broken lives, and their art remained, as it were, incompletely manifested: only a fraction of their artistic energy and inner experiences was manifested in their writings, while another part remained incompletely manifested and leaked out into their lives, just as electricity leaks out when it lacks sufficient insulation.

The extent of such "leakages" would vary from case to case. The "person" and the "writer" would wrestle with one another for supremacy within the individual. Sometimes one side would emerge triumphant, sometimes the other would prevail. In most cases, victory would go to whichever side was stronger, more gifted, more resilient. If one's literary talent turned out to be stronger, then the "writer" would triumph over the "person." If one's talent for living outstripped one's talent for literature, then the literary activity would fade into the background, subjugating itself to an art form of a different, more earthly order. It might seem strange at first, but it is, in fact, entirely logical that, at that particular time and among those particular people, the "gift for writing" and the "gift for living" were considered to be of nearly equal value.

In the first edition of *Let Us Be Like the Sun*, Konstantin Balmont wrote (in the dedication, no less): "To Modest Durnov, an artist who has fashioned an epic poem from his own personality." At the time, such words were far from empty. They were deeply ingrained with the spirit of the age. Modest Durnov, an artist and versifier, did not leave his mark in the world of art. A few feeble poems here, a few inconsequential covers and illustrations there, and it was all over. But his life, his personality, were the stuff of legend. The artist who created an "epic" not in his art, but in his life, was a legitimate phenomenon at the time. And Modest Durnov wasn't alone. There were plenty of others like him—and Nina Petrovskaya was among them. Her gift for literature wasn't great. Her gift for living was immeasurably greater.

> From a poor and chance existence
> I fashioned flutters without end . . .[2]

She had every right to say this about herself. She really did make an endless flutter of her life, though she made nothing of her art. She composed the "epic poem of her life" with greater skill and decisiveness than anyone else could have. It must be said that an epic poem also sprang up around her. But I will come to that later.

■ □ ■

Nina concealed her age.[3] I think that she was born around 1880. We met in 1902. When we first became acquainted, she was already an aspiring fiction writer. I believe that she was a bureaucrat's daughter. She had graduated from gymnasium[4] and then taken courses in dentistry. She had been engaged to one man and married another. Her youthful years were accompanied by a drama she did not care to recall. As a rule, she didn't like to look back on her early youth, the time that had come before the "literary period" of her life. Her past seemed poor to her, pathetic. She found herself only after falling in with the Symbolists and the decadents, the Scorpio and Griffin circles.[5]

Yes, they led a singular sort of life there, unlike the one that she had previously known—perhaps unlike anything else at all. They were attempting to transform art into reality and reality into art. As a result of the blurriness, the tenuousness of the lines that delineated reality for these people, life events could never be experienced as life events, pure and simple: they would immediately become a part of one's inner life, a part of one's art. Conversely, anything written by anyone at all would become a life event for everyone else. Thus, reality and literature were both shaped by what seemed to be collective forces. Though at times these forces appeared antagonistic to each other, they were united even in their antagonism; they were the forces of all those who had wandered into that unusual way of life, that "symbolic dimension." It seems to have been a genuine instance of collective art.

They lived in a state of furious exertion, in eternal agitation, aggravation—they were constantly moving at a fever pitch. They lived on several planes at once. In the end, they became entangled in a collective web of loves and hates, both personal and literary. Soon, Nina Petrovskaya became one of the central knots, one of the primary loops that constituted that web.

I am incapable of "making a sketch of her inherent character" as a memoirist ought to do. Alexander Blok, who came to meet the Moscow Symbolists in 1904, wrote to his mother that Petrovskaya was "very sweet, rather smart."[6] Such labels don't even begin to describe her. I knew Nina Petrovskaya for twenty-six years: I saw her kind and cruel, yielding and stubborn, cowardly and brave, submissive and willful, faithful and false. One thing remained constant: in both her kindness and her cruelty, in her truths and in her lies, always and in everything, she wanted to take things to their limit, to their very edge, to achieve a certain sort of fullness—and she demanded the same thing of others. Her motto might have been "all or nothing"—and that was to be her undoing. But this quality was not born in her of its own accord; it was instilled in her by the era.

Earlier on, I referred to the attempt to fuse life and art together as Symbolism's "truth." This truth will live on after Symbolism is gone, though it does not belong to Symbolism alone. It is an eternal truth that just happens to have been experienced most deeply and vividly through Symbolism. But the major fallacy of Symbolism, its deadly sin, was also rooted in this truth. Having established its cult of personality, Symbolism did not set itself any task apart from "personal development." It demanded that such development take place, but how, why, and to what end, it did not specify, did not wish to specify, and, in any case, would not have known how to specify. All that was required of each person entering the order (and Symbolism was, in a certain sense, an order) was a ceaseless burning, a ceaseless flow of activity—it made no difference what the burning and activity were for. All paths were open to them, and there was only one requirement: to go as fast and as far as one could. This was Symbolism's exclusive, fundamental doctrine. One could exalt both God and the Devil alike. One could be obsessed with anything at all, so long as the obsession was absolute.

Hence the Symbolists' feverish pursuit of emotion of all sorts. All "experiences" were venerated as blessings, just so long as they were plentiful and strong. Hence, in turn, the coherence and practicality of these experiences became a matter of indifference. The "personality" became a piggy bank for experiences, a sack into which one could pour one's indiscriminately hoarded emotions—"moments," as Valery Bryusov called them: "We gather moments in their loss."[7]

The eventual consequence of this emotional tightfistedness was the deepest imaginable void. The miserly knights[8] of Symbolism died of spiritual hunger while sitting atop sacks of hoarded "experiences." But this was only the final consequence. The most immediate consequence, the one that made itself known much earlier, practically right from the start, was a different one. The constant striving to reorganize one's thoughts, life, relationships, and even one's very manner of being in order to rack up yet another "experience" forced the Symbolists into constantly posing for themselves—into playing out their own lives as if they were performing in a theater of fervid improvisation. They knew that they were acting, but the act became their life. The reckonings, however, were far from theatrical. "I am bleeding cranberry juice!" Blok's jester cried[9]. But sometimes the cranberry juice turned out to be real blood.

Decadence is a relative concept: a fall is defined by its starting height. Bearing this in mind, it is meaningless to apply the term "decadence" to the art of the early Symbolists: this art didn't, in and of itself, represent a fall in relation to the past. But the sins that grew up and developed *within* Symbolism represented a decadence, a fall in relation to those early years. It seems that Symbolism was born with this poison in its blood. It ran in the veins of all Symbolist figures to varying degrees. To a certain extent (or at a certain point), each one of them was a decadent. Nina Petrovskaya embraced only the decadence in Symbolism—and she was not alone. Nina immediately conceived a desire to act out her life—and to this (essentially false) mission, she remained faithful, true to the end. She was a genuine victim of decadence.

■ □ ■

To the Symbolist or decadent, love opened up the most efficient and direct line of access to an inexhaustible warehouse of emotions. All one had to do was be in love and he or she would be furnished with all the objects of primary lyrical importance: Passion, Desperation, Exultation, Madness, Vice, Sin, Hatred, and so on. And so everyone was always in love, and even if they weren't actually in love, they at least convinced themselves that they were; if they discovered the tiniest spark of something resembling love, they would fan it with all their might. It is no coincidence that even phenomena such as the "love of love"[10] were so highly praised at the time.

Genuine feeling can run the gamut from eternal love to fleeting infatuation. The very idea of an "infatuation" was revolting to the Symbolists. They were obligated to derive the maximum number of emotional possibilities from each and every one of their loves. According to their moral and aesthetic code, each love had to be fateful, eternal. They sought out the superlatives in everything. If they didn't manage to make a love "eternal," they could fall out of it. But each time they fell out of love and back into it again, the process had to be accompanied by profound upheavals, internal tragedies, and even a complete revision of their worldviews. In fact, that was precisely why they did it all in the first place.

Love and all of its attendant emotions were to be experienced with the utmost intensity and to the absolute fullest, without gradations, unintentional impurities, or hateful psychologisms. The Symbolists wanted to feed on the strongest essence that a feeling had to offer. A real feeling is personal, concrete, inimitable. A contrived or overwrought feeling lacks such qualities. It becomes its own abstraction, the *idea* of a feeling. That is precisely why the Symbolists so often wrote this word with a capital letter.

Nina Petrovskaya was not attractive. But in 1903 she was young— and that makes quite a difference. She was "rather smart," as Blok said, and she was "sensitive," as they might have said if she had lived a century earlier. Most importantly, she was very good at "matching pitch." She immediately became the object of a number of loves.

The first person to fall in love with her was a poet who fell in love with absolutely everyone, without exception.[11] He offered her a headlong and ruinous love. It was absolutely impossible to refuse him: her flattered vanity (for this poet was fast becoming a celebrity), her fear of appearing provincial, and, most importantly, the lessons on "moments" that she had already deeply assimilated each played their part. It was time for her to start having "experiences." She convinced herself that she was in love, too. This first love affair flared up and went dark, leaving behind an unpleasant residue in her soul, something analogous to a hangover. Nina decided to "cleanse her soul," which had, in fact, been somewhat contaminated by the poet's "orgyism." She renounced "Sin," donned a black dress, and repented. Practically speaking, repentance was appropriate to the situation. But hers was more of an "experience of repentance" than the genuine article.

In 1904, Andrei Bely was still very young, with golden curls, blue eyes, and a tremendous amount of charm. The journalistic back alleys were in stitches over his poetry and prose, which were striking in their novelty, audacity, and occasional flashes of true genius. How and why this genius later came to ruin is a different matter. At the time, no one had anticipated that particular misfortune.

People would go into raptures over him. When he was around, it was as if everything was instantly transformed, shifted, or encircled in his light. And he truly was radiant. It was as if everyone, even those who envied him, was a little bit in love with him. Even Bryusov occasionally fell under his spell. It was only natural that Nina Petrovskaya should succumb to these general raptures as well. Before long, these feelings would evolve into infatuation, and then into love.

Oh, if only it had been possible in those times to simply love, to love for one's own sake and for the sake of one's beloved! But in those days, one had to love for the sake of some abstraction, against the backdrop of it. In this particular case, Nina was obliged to love Andrei Bely for his mystical vocation, which both she and he forced themselves to believe in. And he was required to appear before her in nothing less than the full splendor of his halo—I won't say that it was a counterfeit halo, but perhaps a symbolic one. They adorned their tiny truth, their human, simply human love, in the garb of a truth that was immeasurably larger. A black strand of wooden prayer beads and a large black cross appeared over Nina Petrovskaya's black dress. Andrei Bely wore a cross of the same sort . . .

Oh, if only he had simply fallen out of love with her, simply betrayed her! But he didn't fall out of love; he "ran from temptation." He ran from Nina so that her all-too-earthly love would not besmirch his spotless raiment. He ran from her to shine all the more dazzlingly in the presence of another, one whose name and patronymic, and even whose mother's name, came together to make it symbolically obvious that she was the harbinger of the Woman clothed with the Sun. And his friends, those lisping, badger-legged mystics, would visit Nina to reproach, denounce, and abuse her: "Madame, you have nearly defiled our prophet! You are driving knights away from the Woman clothed with the Sun! You are playing a very dark role! You have been motivated by the Beast that ascendeth out of the bottomless pit!"[12]

And so they played with their words, mangling meaning, mangling lives. Later on, they would also mangle the life of that very same Woman clothed with the Sun and the life of her husband, one of our most cherished Russian poets.

Meanwhile, Nina found herself cast off, and, what's worse, insulted. It became all too clear that, like many cast-off women, she wanted both to take revenge on Bely and to win him back at the same time. But their story, having fallen into the "Symbolist dimension," was destined to continue and develop in its depths.

■ □ ■

One day in the autumn of 1904, I chanced to tell Bryusov that I saw a great deal of good in Nina. "Is that so?" he snapped. "She's a good little housekeeper, is she?"

He pointedly refused to take notice of her. But he changed his tune just as soon as her break with Bely became public knowledge because he could not, in his position, remain neutral.

He was an ambassador of demonism. It behooved him to "languish and gnash his teeth" before the Woman clothed with the Sun. Thus, it was at this moment that Nina, her rival, was transformed from a "good little housekeeper" into something significant, clothed in a demonic aura. He proposed forming an alliance against Bely. This alliance was immediately shored up by mutual love. Again, this is all quite understandable and true to life: this sort of thing happens all the time. It is understandable that Bryusov, in his own fashion, should begin to love Nina and it is also understandable that Nina should unconsciously look to Bryusov for consolation, a balm for her injured pride, and, through their alliance, a way of "taking revenge" on Bely.

In those days, Bryusov took an active interest in occultism, spiritualism, and black magic—probably without believing in any of these things as such, but rather feeling that the acts themselves were gestures that gave expression to a specific spiritual current. I think that Nina felt precisely the same way. It is unlikely that she believed that the experiments in magic she was carrying out under Bryusov's guidance would actually restore Bely's love to her. But she experienced them as if they represented a genuine association with the devil. She wanted to believe in her own sorcery. She was the hysterical type, and perhaps this was what had attracted Bryusov to her in the first place: of course, he knew from the latest scholarly sources (he always held scholarship in high regard) that, in the "great age of sorcery," hysterical women had been considered—and had considered themselves to be—witches. If, "in the light of scholarship," the witches of the sixteenth century had turned out to be hysterical women, in the twentieth century, Bryusov would attempt to turn a hysterical woman into a witch.

Incidentally, lacking any particular faith in magic, Nina also attempted to avail herself of other options. In the spring of 1905, Bely was giving a lecture in the small auditorium of the Polytechnic Museum.[13] During the intermission, Nina Petrovskaya went up to him and tried to shoot him with a Browning at point-blank range. The revolver misfired and was immediately snatched from her hands. It is worth noting that she never made a second attempt. She said to me once (much later), "The hell with him. After all, truth be told, I killed him that day in the museum."

I wasn't the least bit surprised by that "truth be told": it goes to show how muddled, how mixed-up, reality and imagination had become in their minds.

The drama that was to become the main focus of Nina's life was just another series of "moments" to Bryusov. After he had harvested all of the situation's resultant emotions, he found himself drawn to the pen. He described the entire story in the novel *The Fiery Angel*, though he took advantage of certain literary conventions, rechristening Andrei Bely as Count Heinrich, Nina Petrovskaya as Renate, and himself as Ruprecht.*

In this novel, Bryusov hacked apart all of the relationships that tied the characters together. He whipped up a denouement and wrote "the end" under Renate's story before the real-life conflict that the novel was based upon was actually resolved. Nina Petrovskaya did not die upon the death of Renate; on the contrary, her romance[14] stretched hopelessly onward. What remained real life for Nina was now just a used-up storyline to Bryusov. He found it tedious to be constantly reliving the same chapters over and over again. He started to distance himself from Nina more and more.

---

* In 1934, the Moscow publishing house Academia printed a small volume with a selection of Bryusov's poems. It contains an appendix of "Biographical Materials" compiled by his widow, who confirms that *The Fiery Angel* is based on a true "episode."

He began cultivating new love stories, less tragic ones. He began devoting more time to his literary activities and to all manner of meetings, which he greatly relished. To a certain extent, he even found himself drawn to home and hearth (he was married).

This was a fresh blow for Nina. By that time (it was already around 1906), her heartache over Bely had, to all intents and purposes, subsided, dulled. But she had already come to identify herself with the role of Renate. Now she faced a formidable danger: that she might lose Bryusov as well. Several times, she attempted to take recourse in the tried-and-true method of so many women: she endeavored to maintain her hold on Bryusov by provoking his jealousy. Her fleeting love affairs (with "passersby," as she would call them) evoked feelings of revulsion and despair within her. She despised and reviled these "passersby." However, her efforts were in vain. Bryusov cooled toward her. Occasionally, he would attempt to use her infidelities as an excuse to break things off with her altogether. Nina would pass from one extreme to another, sometimes loving Bryusov, at other times despising him. But in both extremes, she would abandon herself to despair. She would lie on her sofa for two days at a stretch, neither eating nor sleeping, her head covered with a black scarf, weeping. Her meetings with Bryusov seem to have taken place in an equally charged atmosphere. At times, she would be gripped by fits of rage. She would break furniture and smash things, hurling them "like cannonballs from a mangonel," as a similar scene is described in *The Fiery Angel*.

She vainly sought comfort in cards, then in wine. Finally, in the spring of 1908, she tried morphine. Then she made a morphine addict of Bryusov, and this was her true, albeit unacknowledged, revenge. In the autumn of 1909, she became seriously ill from the morphine; she nearly died. When she had partly recovered, it was decided that she should go abroad: "into exile," as she put it. Bryusov and I accompanied her to the train station. She was going away forever. She knew that she would never see Bryusov again. She went away when she was still not entirely well, with a doctor accompanying her. This was on November 9, 1911. She had lived in the throes of her Moscow sufferings for seven years. She was setting off for new sufferings, which were fated to last sixteen more.

I do not know the details of her peregrinations abroad. I do know that from Italy, she went on to Warsaw, and, after that, to Paris. It was here that, one day (I believe it was in 1913), she threw herself out the window of a hotel on the Boulevard Saint-Michel. She broke her leg, which healed badly, and was left with a limp.

The war found her in Rome, where she would live until the autumn of 1922 in the most appalling poverty. At times, she would be gripped by paroxysms of desperation, at times by fits of resignation, which would then give way to even more violent forms of desperation. She lived on charity, begged for alms, sewed undergarments for soldiers, wrote screenplays for a certain film actress, and periodically starved. She drank. At times, she would sink to utterly abysmal depths. She turned to Catholicism. "My new and secret name, written down somewhere in the indelible scrolls of San Pietro,[15] is Renate," she wrote to me.

She came to hate Bryusov: "I felt breathless in my wicked luck, knowing that he couldn't get at me now, that now it was others who were suffering. How was I to know who those others were; by that time, he had already finished off Lvova . . . I continued to live, taking revenge on him with every movement, every thought."

She came here, to Paris, in the spring of 1927, after leading a wretched existence in Berlin for five years. She arrived completely destitute. She found more than a few friends here. They helped her in every way that they could, and sometimes, it seems, more than they could. Sometimes they would manage to find her work, but she wasn't capable of working anymore. Perpetually intoxicated, though she never lost her reason, she was squarely on the other side of the border of life by then.

■ □ ■

In Blok's diary, there is a strange entry for November 6, 1911: *"Nina Ivanovna Petrovskaya is 'dying.'"* Blok had received this news from Moscow, but why did he put the word "dying" in quotation marks?

In those days, Nina was, in fact, dying, of the same illness she was ailing with before she left Russia, the one that I touched upon earlier. But Blok put the word "dying" in quotation marks because he approached this news with an ironic disbelief. He was well aware that Nina Petrovskaya had been vowing to die, to take her own life, on a regular basis since 1906. For twenty-two years, she lived in the ceaseless contemplation of death. Occasionally, she would make jokes at her own expense:

Ustiushka's mom
Was about to buy the farm.
But she didn't ever die—
She was only killing time.

I am looking over her letters now. February 26, 1925: "I don't think I can take it anymore." April 7, 1925: "You probably think that I have died? Not yet." June 8, 1927: "I swear to you, there can't be any other way out." September 12, 1927: "Just a little while longer, and I won't need a position, any work at all." September 14, 1927: "This time, I must certainly die soon."

This is from the letters written in her final years. I don't have anything earlier on hand. But it was always the same thing—both in letters and in conversation.

So what was holding her back? I believe I know.

Nina's life was a lyrical improvisation in which, simply by adapting to the similar improvisations of other characters, she strove to create something coherent: "an epic poem fashioned from her own personality." The end of her personality, like the end of the poem that had been written about it, lay in death. To all intents and purposes, that poem had been completed in 1906, the very year in which the narrative of *The Fiery Angel* breaks off. From that time forward, a torturous and terrible, unnecessary and motion-starved epilogue had begun to stretch relentlessly onward, both in Moscow and throughout Nina's peregrinations abroad. Nina wasn't afraid to cut it short, but she couldn't. The instinct of an artist who shaped her life as she might shape a poem hinted to her that her end should be connected with some other final event, with the rupture of some other thread connecting her to life. Finally, such an event took place.

Beginning in 1908, after the death of their mother, Nina had been charged with the care of her younger sister, Nadya, who was both mentally and physically underdeveloped (she had been scalded with boiling water in an unfortunate childhood accident). She wasn't an idiot, mind you, but she was marked by an extraordinary level of quietness and submissiveness. She was unbearably pathetic and dedicated to her older sister to the point of total self-effacement. Of course, she had no life of her own. In 1909,[16] when Nina left Russia, she took her sister with her, and, from that time on, Nadya shared in all of the miseries of her life abroad. She was the last and only creature who possessed a true connection with Nina, and she was Nina's only connection to life.

Throughout the autumn of 1927, Nadya ailed as meekly and as noiselessly as she had lived. She died just as quietly on January 13, 1928, of stomach cancer. Nina went to the morgue of the hospital where Nadya had been a patient. She pricked her sister's small corpse with a safety pin and then pricked her own hand with the same pin: she wanted to infect herself with ptomaine, to share in her sister's death. But, though her hand swelled up at first, it subsequently healed.

Nina would sometimes come to visit me during that period. Once she stayed with me for three days. She spoke to me in that strange language of the nineties, the language that had once connected us, the one that we had once shared, but which, since then, I have almost completely forgotten how to understand.

With Nadya's death, the last phrase in the drawn-out epilogue was finally committed to paper. In a little over a month, Nina Petrovskaya would punctuate it with her own death.

Versailles, 1928

BRYUSOV

When I first laid eyes on him, he was about twenty-four years old and I was eleven. I was studying in the gymnasium with his younger brother. His appearance shook my mental image of what "decadents" were supposed to be. Instead of a bare-skinned, shaggy fellow with lilac hair and a green nose (which is how "decadents" looked, according to the feuilleton *News of the Day*), I found a modest young man with short little mustaches and a closely cropped head of hair, wearing a cotton collar and a jacket of the most ordinary cut. This was the sort of young man you might see selling fancy goods on Sretenka Street. The first volume of Bryusov's works, published by Sirin, featured a photograph of him looking exactly like this[1].

Later, looking back on the young Bryusov, I realized that the acuity of his poetry from this period lay precisely in that combination of decadent exoticism with the most artless of Muscovite petty bourgeois attitudes. It was an extremely potent mixture; it represented a very sharp break, a trenchant dissonance, but that is precisely why Bryusov's early books (up to and including *Tertia Vigilia*) are, in fact, his best: they are the sharpest. They are tropical fantasies—that take place on the banks of the Yauza; they are the reevaluation of all values—in the Sretenka quarter. And, to this day, I prefer the "obscure, ridiculed, strange" author of *Chefs d'oeuvre* to the official

Bryusov. I like the fact that this bold young man, who was quite happy to casually remark, "I've come to hate my motherland"[2] was also, as it turns out, capable of picking up a mangy kitten on the street and nursing it in his own pocket with infinite solicitude during his exams.

■ □ ■

Bryusov's grandfather, Kuzma, who was of peasant stock, established a thriving business in Moscow. He ended up the owner of a rather large enterprise. His product was a foreign one: corks. He passed the family business down to his son Aviva, who, in turn, passed it down to Kuzma's grandsons, the Avivoviches.[3] The sign that hung over the firm's offices, which were located in one of the alleys connecting Ilinka and Varvarka Streets, was still intact in the autumn of 1920. Catty-corner from the business, aligned with it practically window-for-window, was P. A. Sokolov's notary office. Spiritual séances were held there on Bryusov's initiative at the beginning of the nineties. I was present for one of the last ones, held at the beginning of 1905. It was gloomy and dull. As we parted ways, Valery Yakovlevich said, "In time, someone will make a thorough examination of these spiritual forces and, perhaps, will even find a technological application for them, as they did with steam and electricity."

By that time, though, his infatuation with spiritualism had cooled, and I believe that he had already stopped collaborating with the journal *Rebus*.[4]

I don't really know why Kuzma Bryusov's cork business had been handed down to Aviva alone. What had put it into Kuzma's head to cut his second son, Yakov Kuzmich, out of his final will and testament? I think that Yakov Kuzmich must have offended his father in some way. He was a freethinker, a daydreamer; he took an interest in horses, had been to Paris, and even wrote poetry. On top of all that, he also performed zealous libations in honor of Bacchus. I first laid eyes on him when he was already a very old man with disheveled gray hair, dressed in a worn frock coat. He was married to Matryona Alexandrovna Bakulina, an extremely kind woman, a tad eccentric, and a master of needlepoint and *preferans*. The story of Yakov Kuzmich's courtship and marriage was described by his son in the short story "Dasha's Engagement." At times, Valery Yakovlevich would sign his articles using the pseudonym V. Bakulin. For the most part, these were polemical articles, and it was said that they mostly consisted of *argumenta baculina*.[5]

Having decided not to pass his business down to Yakov Kuzmich, Kuzma Bryusov also passed him over in the section of the will concerning the little house on Tsvetnoy Boulevard, across from the Solomonsky Circus. That house went directly to the testator's grandsons, Valery and Alexander Yakovlevich. And that is where the entire Bryusov family lived, right up until the autumn of 1910. And that is where Yakov Kuzmich passed away in January of 1908. Matryona Alexandrovna outlived her husband by nearly thirteen years.

The house on Tsvetnoy Boulevard was old and unwieldy, with mezzanines and additions, dimly lit rooms and creaking wooden staircases. The house contained a little hall, the middle part of which was separated from the side sections by two arches, which were flanked by semicircular stoves. The webbed shadows cast by the large patched areas and the blueness of the windows were reflected in the stove tiles. These patched spots, stoves, and windows offer a real-life explanation for one of Bryusov's early poems, which, in its own time, was proclaimed the height of nonsense:

The shadow of unformed formations
Heaves under sleep's thrall,
Palm frond blades of alterations
On my enameled wall . . .

. . . .

Selene, denuded, rises higher

Beneath the azure moon—and so forth.[6]*

In the hall, off to one side, stood a grand piano. Bentwood chairs lined the walls, which were hung with two or three discolored paintings in gold frames. The hall doubled as a dining room. A bowl would appear on the checked tablecloth covering the extendable table that stood in the center of the room; the room would smell of cabbage soup. Yakov Kuzmich would emerge from the dimly lit bedroom with his precious decanter of cognac. Holding a small glassful over the bowl with a trembling hand, he would pour the cognac into the cabbage soup. He would mix it in, dredging the cabbage up from the depths of his bowl with a spoon, and mutter guiltily, "Oh, well, it all ends up in the same place anyway."

And he would drink, having first touched glasses with his son-in-law, B. V. Kalyuzhny, who has since also passed away.

Valery Yakovlevich did not frequently appear in his parents' half of the house. He had his own apartment in the same building, where he lived with his wife, Ioanna Matveyevna, and his sister-in-law, Bronislava Matveyevna Runt, who at one time served as the secretary of *Libra* and Scorpio. The apartment's furnishings tended toward the *style moderne*.[8] Bryusov's modest study was packed with bookshelves. Exceedingly attentive to his visitors, Bryusov, who

---

* I published a detailed analysis of this poem in the journal *Sophia*[7] in 1914. When we saw each other afterward, Bryusov told me, "You gave a very interesting interpretation of my poem. From now on, I'll explain it that way myself. I didn't understand it until now."

As he pronounced these words, he laughed and gazed into my eyes with his own smiling, roguish ones: he knew that I wouldn't believe him, nor did he want me to. I smiled back and we parted ways. That very evening, he told someone, raising his voice to make sure that I would hear, "Just today, V. F. and I were discussing augurs. . . ." (We had been discussing no such thing.)

did not himself smoke in those days, kept matches on his writing desk. However, as a safeguard against the absentmindedness of his guests, the metallic matchbox was attached to his desk by a string. On the walls of the study and the dining room hung paintings by Shesterkin, one of the first Russian decadents, along with drawings by Fidus, Brunelleschi, Feofilaktov, and others. Valery Yakovlevich did not have particularly good taste in paintings, but he did have his own predilections. For some reason, he preferred Cima da Conegliano to any other Renaissance artist.

At one time, this apartment played host to the celebrated Wednesday gatherings at which the fate, if not of Russian, then certainly of Moscow modernism was decided. In my early youth, I had heard about these meetings secondhand, but I hadn't dared to dream of penetrating such a shrine. It was only in the autumn of 1904, as a newly minted university student,[9] that I received a written invitation from Bryusov. As I removed my coat in the foyer, I could hear my host's voice: "It is quite possible that every question has not one, but several true answers, maybe even eight. By maintaining that there is only *one* truth, we are recklessly ignoring fully seven more."

This idea produced considerable excitement in one of the guests, a handsome, blue-eyed university student with downy, light-colored hair. When I entered the study, the student was tearing around the room with volatile, dancer-like steps and speaking as if caught in the grips of a joyful agitation, his voice ranging from a deep bass to the most delicate alto; at times he was practically crouching, at times he stood up on his tiptoes.* This was Andrei Bely.

---

* As the years went on, these traits grew stronger within him and, toward the end, they even turned into something of a caricature. Apparently, this is how his resemblance to his father manifested itself in him. For more on this topic, see the memoirs of Professor N. I. Storozhenko.

That night was the first time I laid eyes on him. Another guest, also a student, a stout, ruddy brunet, was sitting in an armchair with his legs crossed. He turned out to be S. M. Solovyov. There were no other guests: the "Wednesdays" were already on the wane.

In the dining room, over tea, Bely read (or, more accurately, sang) some of his poems, which, in a revised edition, would later be included in his collection *Ashes*:[10] "Behind me the thundering city," "Prisoners," "The Beggar." There was something uncommonly charming about his manner of reading back then, and about his person more generally. After Bely had finished, S. M. Solovyov read out a poem that he had gotten from Blok: "I wait for death by the morning star." Bryusov harshly condemned its final line.[11] After that, he read two new poems of his own: "Adam and Eve" and "Orpheus to Eurydice." Then S. M. Solovyov read his poetry. Bryusov meticulously analyzed the poems that were read to him. His analysis was strictly formal. He didn't touch upon the meaning of the poems in the slightest, and even seemed to emphasize the fact that he viewed this as a textbook exercise and nothing more. This schoolmasterly attitude, directed toward poets as established as Bely and Blok were at that time, surprised and shocked me. Nevertheless, as far as I could tell, Bryusov maintained that same attitude for as long as he lived.

The conversation continued over tea. I noticed that Bryusov's own poems were not subjected to analysis; that simply was not done. His poems were to be accepted as biblical commandments. Finally, the moment that I had been dreading came to pass: Bryusov suggested that I, too, read "something of my own." Horrified, I declined.

■ □ ■

Bryusov was the leader of the modernists in the nineties. As a poet, many rated him lower than Balmont, Sologub, and Blok. But Balmont, Sologub, and Blok were nowhere near the man of letters

Bryusov was. By the same token, none of them was so acutely concerned with the question of his own position in literature. Bryusov wanted to create a "movement" and to take his place at its head. This is why the establishment and administration of the "phalanx," the burden of struggling against its adversaries, and the brunt of the organizational and tactical labor all fell on Bryusov's shoulders. He founded Scorpio and *Libra* and ruled over them like an autocrat: he carried on polemics, formed alliances, and declared wars; he united and divided, reconciled and estranged. In manipulating a large number of strings, both public and private, he felt himself to be the captain of a literary ship, and he dispatched his duties with the greatest circumspection. He was spurred on not only by his natural inclinations, but also by the consciousness of his responsibility for the fate of the entire vessel. Occasionally, the crew would threaten to mutiny. Bryusov would subdue them with a mighty bark—though at times he was forced to make concessions of a "constitutional" nature. Afterward, he always knew how to overthrow or paralyze his parliament via intrigue. This process only strengthened his autocracy.

The concept of equality was entirely foreign to Bryusov. Incidentally, it is altogether possible that Bryusov's petty bourgeois background played a role in this. The bourgeois has a much easier time bowing and scraping than, for example, the aristocrat or worker does. By the same token, the desire to humiliate others when given the chance overwhelms the happy bourgeois with greater force than it does the worker or the aristocrat. "Let the cobbler stick to his last," "know your place": such ideas went straight from Tsvetnoy Boulevard into our literary sphere, with Bryusov as their standard-bearer. Bryusov either knew how to give orders or how to obey them. Declaring one's independence meant making an enemy of Bryusov once and for all. A young poet who didn't come to Bryusov for evaluation and approval could be certain that Bryusov would never forgive him for it. Marina Tsvetaeva was one such example. As soon as a friendly publishing house or journal emerged outside of Bryusov's central management, an edict would immediately go out forbidding any of Scorpio's contributors to collaborate with that particular publishing house or journal. It was in this way that collaboration was forbidden first with Griffin, then with *Art* and *Passage*.[12]

Power demands a proper setting. It also breeds toadyism. Bryusov worked hard to surround himself with servility and, alas, found people who were amenable to the task. His appearances were always arranged in theatrical style. He wouldn't respond yes or no to any invitation, but would leave the inviter to wait and hope. He would not be there at the appointed hour. Soon afterward, members of his entourage would begin to filter in. I distinctly remember how once, in 1905, in a certain "literary" household, the hosts and guests speculated in whispers for about an hour and a half as to whether or not Bryusov would arrive.

They would ask each newcomer, "Do you know if Valery Yakovlevich is coming?"

"I saw him yesterday. He said he would be here."

"Well, he told me this morning that he would be busy."

"Well, he told me at four o'clock today that he would be here."

"I saw him at five. He won't be coming."

And each of them took great pains to demonstrate that he was better informed of Bryusov's intentions than the rest because he was closer to him.

Finally, Bryusov would appear. No one would initiate conversation with him: they would only speak if spoken to.

His exits would take place just as mysteriously as his arrivals: he would disappear without warning. There was one famous instance in which, before leaving the home of Andrei Bely, he unexpectedly put out the lamp, leaving the assembled company in darkness. By the time the lights had been relit, Bryusov was no longer in the apartment. The next day, Andrei Bely received the following poem:

"To Baldr, from Loki":

But creation's final ruler,
Shadows, shadows—follow me![13]

■ □ ■

He had a remarkable way of offering his hand. It was a strange operation. Bryusov would extend his hand to somebody. That person would extend his. At the very moment when their hands ought to have met, Bryusov would quickly jerk his away, gather his fingers into a fist, and press that fist into his right shoulder, while he himself, with teeth slightly bared, would eagerly gaze at his acquaintance's hand, which had been left hanging in the air. Then, Bryusov's hand would come down just as quickly as it had risen and grab the other person's outstretched one. The handshake would take place, but the interruption that had occurred, which was in itself momentary, would leave a lasting feeling of awkwardness. The person would keep thinking that he had somehow stuck his hand out at the wrong time. I noticed that Bryusov only employed this curious method in the early days of an acquaintanceship, and that he applied it particularly often when meeting fledgling poets, provincials newly arrived to the city, and novices to literature and literary circles.

In general, he somehow managed to combine an elegant (albeit formal) politeness with a love for dressings-down, discipline, and intimidation. Those who didn't like it removed themselves from his presence. Others eagerly joined his obedient entourage, which Bryusov had no scruples about using in order to shore up his influence, power, and allure. Their servility bordered on the absurd. Once, in 1909 or so, I was sitting in a café on Tverskoy Boulevard with A. I. Tinyakov, who wrote mediocre poetry under the pseudonym "Loner." My companion, who was slightly drunk, gave a lengthy speech, at the end of which he literally cried, "Vladislav Felitsianovich, here's what I think of the Lord God—tfoo!" (at this point, he spat on a green pane of the stained glass window in a manner that was far from symbolic). "If only He were Valery Yakovlevich; now *there* is someone deserving of glory, honor, and worship!"

Gumilyov informed me that this very same Tinyakov, while sitting with him on a "floating restaurant" in Petersburg and looking out over the Neva, had cried out in a burst of heavenly clairvoyance, "Look, look! Valery Yakovlevich is striding out across the water from that bank over there!"

■ □ ■

He didn't like people because, first and foremost, he did not respect them. This was certainly the case in his adult years. He seems to have loved Konevskoy in his youth. He was not badly disposed toward Z. N. Gippius. There are no other names that bear mentioning. His frequently emphasized love for Balmont was hardly what one might call love. At best, it was the wonder of a Salieri in the presence of a Mozart. He loved to call Balmont his brother. M. Voloshin once said that the roots of such brotherly feelings could be traced to deepest antiquity: all the way back to Cain himself. In his youth, perhaps, Bryusov had also loved Alexander Dobrolyubov, but later on, when he, Dobrolyubov, started down the paths of Christianity and Populism, Bryusov could no longer abide him. Dobrolyubov led a nomadic lifestyle. Sometimes he would come to Moscow and stay with the Bryusovs for several days at a time: he shared certain religious beliefs with Nadezhda Yakovlevna, Bryusov's sister. He dabbled in vegetarianism, walked with a staff, and called everybody brother and sister. Once, I stumbled upon Bryusov at a meeting of the literary-artistic circle. It was two in the morning. Bryusov was playing *chemin de fer*.[14] I was surprised.

"It can't be helped," Bryusov said. "I'm homeless now: Dobrolyubov is staying at our place."

He would not return home until Dobrolyubov had "gone away."

Boris Sadovskoy, a good and intelligent man whose dry reserve concealed an extremely tender heart, was embarrassed by Bryusov's love lyrics; he referred to them as bedroom poetry. He was wrong in saying this. There is a deep tragic vein that runs through Bryusov's erotica; not an ontological one, as the author would have liked to think, but, rather, a psychological one: because he neither loved nor respected people, not once did he fall in love with any of the women with whom he had had occasion to "fall upon the couch." The women in Bryusov's poetry are as similar as drops of water: this is because he didn't love a single one of them, didn't get to know a single one of them, didn't particularly distinguish any one of them from all the rest. Perhaps he really did respect love. But he did not notice his lovers.

We, like priests in holy orders,
Perform a rite[15]

This is a horrifying phrase because, if something is a "rite," then it makes absolutely no difference with whom it is performed. "Priestess of love" is a pet phrase of Bryusov's. But the priestess's face remains hidden; indeed, she does not possess a human face. One priestess is as good as any other: the "rite" remains the same. And, not finding, not knowing how to find the human being in all of these "priestesses," Bryusov cries out in fear:

"Trembling, I embrace a corpse!"[16]

And, for him, love always turns into torture:

> "But where are we? The seat of passion
> Or the fatal torture wheel?"[17]

■ □ ■

He loved literature, only literature. He loved himself, too, only for literature's sake. Indeed, he piously fulfilled the covenants that he had made with himself in his youth: "love no one, sympathize with no one, idolize only yourself without limit" and "worship art, art alone, wholeheartedly and without ulterior motives."[18] The idea of art without ulterior motives was his idol, and he made several human sacrifices to it—including, it must be said, himself. He saw literature as a merciless god, constantly demanding blood. To him, this god appeared in the guise of a textbook of literary history. He was capable of idolizing these academic bricks as if they were sacred rocks, manifestations of Mitra.[19] In December 1903, on the same day that he turned thirty, he actually said to me, "I want to live my life in such a way that two lines about me will appear in a general history of literature." And so they will.

Nadezhda Lvova, the late poetess, once told him that she didn't like some of his poems. Bryusov bared his teeth in the affectionately cruel smile that so many of us now remember and replied, "Ah, but they will be learned by heart in gymnasiums, and if little girls like you learn them badly, they will be punished."

He did not wish to erect a monument "not made by hands"[20] in human hearts. He wanted to force his way into "the ages" just to spite them: with those two lines in literary history (written out in black and white), with the tears of the children punished for not knowing their Bryusov, and, finally—with a bronze statue on his native Tsvetnoy Boulevard.

■ □ ■

His affair with Nina Petrovskaya was tortuous for both of them, but the one who suffered most was Nina. Upon finishing *The Fiery Angel*, he dedicated the book to Nina and, in that dedication, referred to her as "a person who loved a great deal and who perished by that love." He himself, however, had no intention of perishing. Having exhausted this plotline, both in life and in literature, he decided to distance himself from it by returning to the comforts of his hearth and home, to the lovingly prepared, plump and rosy carrot pies of which he was so fond. He indicated his desire to break things off for good with deliberate callousness.

Nina and I were bound by a great friendship. The Moscow gossips were certain it was more than friendship. We laughed a great deal over their certainty and, to tell the truth, would sometimes deliberately encourage their suspicions out of a sense of sheer mischief. I was aware of Nina's sufferings and bore witness to them personally; I discussed them with Bryusov twice. On the second occasion, I said something so insulting that he apparently didn't tell even Nina about it. We ceased to acknowledge each other. A year and a half later, however, Nina smoothed things over. We pretended as if it had never happened.

In the autumn of 1911, following a serious illness, Nina decided to leave Moscow for good. The day of her departure arrived: it was November 9. I made my way to the Alexandrovsky train station. Nina was already in her compartment, sitting next to Bryusov. On the floor stood an unstoppered bottle of cognac (which was the "national" drink of Moscow Symbolism, so to speak). They were drinking straight from the bottle, crying and embracing each another. I took a swig, too, my eyes filling with tears. It was as if we were seeing a young recruit off to war. Nina and Bryusov knew that they were parting forever. We finished off the bottle. The train began to move. Bryusov and I left the station, got into a sledge, and rode together in silence until we reached Strastnoy Monastery.

This was around five o'clock. That day also happened to be Bryusov's mother's name day. The famous house on Tsvetnoy Boulevard had been sold about a year and a half prior, and Valery Yakovlevich had rented a more comfortable apartment at 32 Pervaya Meshchanskaya Street (the very same apartment in which he eventually passed away). At the same time, his mother, Matryona Alexandrovna, along with several other family members, had moved to Prechistenka, near the Church of the Dormition on Mogiltsy. In the evening, after seeing Nina off, I went to pay my respects to Bryusov's mother.

I arrived around ten. The company had already assembled. The woman of the hour was playing *preferans* with Valery Yakovlevich, his wife, and Evgenia Yakovlevna.

Domestic, cozy, and extremely amiable, illuminated by the candles' soft blaze, Valery Yakovlevich, who had managed to get a haircut between the train station and the party and who still smelled faintly of hair tonic, said to me, eyes smiling, "See what a variety of circumstances we've met under today!"

I said nothing. Then Bryusov, hastily fanning out his cards as if to say, "So you can't take a joke?" asked sharply, "So what would you do in my position, Vladislav Felitsianovich?"

Ostensibly, this question referred to the card game, but it had another, figurative meaning. I glanced at Bryusov's cards and said, "I think you should play simple diamonds." And, after a pause, added, "And thank God if you can get away with it."

"Well, I'm going to play the seven of clubs." And he did.

■ □ ■

I've played plenty of card games in my day; I've seen plenty of gamblers, both casual and career. I believe that people reveal their true natures over card games – at least to the same extent as they do through their handwriting. It has nothing to do with the financial aspect of the game. The way in which a person plays, even the way in which he deals and picks up cards from the table, the whole style of his game—all this can reveal a great deal about one's partner, if one observes with an experienced eye. I need only point to the fact that our conception of what it takes to be a "good partner" hardly coincides with our notion of what it takes to be a "good person"; on the contrary, in some ways, these ideas are mutually exclusive. Certain qualities commonly exhibited by good people are unacceptable in the context of a card game, while, in the course of observing the most excellent of partners in a game, it might occasionally occur to you that it would be a good idea to keep your distance from them in real life.

Bryusov played games of chance in a way that was very—how shall I put it? Not timid, exactly, but thick-witted, pathetic; his style of play revealed his lack of imagination, his inability to guess, his insensitivity to that irrational element which the player of games of chance must learn how to control in order to rule over them as a mage rules over the spirits. Bryusov folded before the spirits of the game. Its mysticism, like every other form of mysticism, was inaccessible to him. His play was uninspired. He would always lose both the game and his temper—not because of his monetary losses, but precisely because he had ventured into a territory where others were able to see something that he couldn't; it was as if he had wandered into a forest. He envied successful gamblers with the same kind of envy he had once felt for the worshippers of the Beautiful Lady:

They see Her! They hear Her![21]

But he didn't hear her, didn't see her.

He did, however, play "bidding games"—like *preferans* and *vint*[22]—exceedingly well: boldly, resourcefully, and creatively.

He knew how to find inspiration in the whirlwind of calculations. The process of calculation afforded him great satisfaction. In 1916, he confessed to me that, from time to time, he enjoyed solving algebraic and trigonometric equations from his old school workbook "for the fun of it." He adored logarithm tables. He once delivered an entire "panegyric" to the chapter in his algebra textbook dedicated to permutations and combinations.

He loved the same kinds of "permutations and combinations" in poetry. For years, he worked with remarkable stubbornness and diligence on a book that was never and, in all likelihood, *could* never have been finished: he wanted to provide a series of verse imitations, stylizations that would contain little examples of "the poetry of all ages and peoples"![23] This book was to comprise several thousand poems. He wanted to strangle himself several thousand times over on the altar of his beloved Literature—in the name of "exhausting all options," out of a reverence for permutations and combinations.

Having written a cycle of poems about the various methods of committing suicide for his book *All Songs* (which had been structured according to the same principle), he assiduously asked around among his acquaintances as to whether they knew of any other strategies he had "neglected" in his catalog.[24]

He wrote an awful book according to this same system of "exhausting all possibilities": *Experiments*, a collection consisting of soulless examples of every metrical and stanzaic type.[25] Never noticing his own rhythmical poverty, he took pride in his superficial metrical riches.

How he rejoiced when he "discovered" that, in all of Russian literature, there wasn't a single poem that had been written solely in first paeons![26] And how artless was his disappointment when I told him that I had written a poem of that type, and that it had even been published, only it wasn't included in any of my collections.[27]

"But why wasn't it included?" he asked.

"It was bad," I replied.

"But it would have been the only one of its kind in the history of Russian literature!"

On another occasion, it fell to someone else's lot to disappoint him. In addition to the commonly employed rhymes of *smert'*, *zherd'*, and *tverd'*, he had discovered a fourth—*umiloserd'*—and immediately wrote a sonnet using them.[28] I offered him my congratulations, but when S. V. Shervinsky arrived, he said that Vyacheslav Ivanov already had a poem with *umiloserd'* in it. Bryusov immediately appeared dark and drawn.

■ □ ■

Perhaps all life is but a means
Of brightly singing verses . . .[29]

This couplet, written by Bryusov, has been quoted many times over. I will now relate a certain incident that, despite having no direct connection to these particular verses, is related to the idea that they convey.

In the early part of 1912, Bryusov introduced me to Nadezhda Grigoryevna Lvova, an aspiring poet. He had begun courting her soon after Nina Petrovskaya's departure. If I am not mistaken, an older lady[30] who had figured in Bryusov's poetry of the early nineties had introduced him to Lvova. This lady eagerly encouraged Bryusov's new infatuation.

Nadya Lvova wasn't beautiful, but she was also far from ugly. Her parents lived in Serpukhov; she was taking courses in Moscow. Her poetry was very green, very heavily influenced by Bryusov. It is unlikely that she possessed any significant gift for poetry. But she herself was a dear: a simple, soulful, and rather shy girl. She slouched considerably and suffered from a slight speech impediment:

she couldn't pronounce the letter *k* at the beginnings of words: she would say *ak* instead of *kak, otoryi, inzhal,* etc.[31]

She and I became friends. She made all sorts of attempts to bring me closer to Bryusov. She brought him over to my home on more than one occasion and took him along with her to my dacha.

The age difference between her and Bryusov was significant. He sheepishly put on youthful airs and sought out the company of young poets. He even wrote a little book of poems practically in the style of Igor Severyanin and dedicated it to Nadya. He couldn't bring himself to have the book published under his own name, so it was released under the ambiguous title of *Nelly's Poems. With an introductory sonnet by Valery Bryusov.* Bryusov was counting on the fact that "Nelly's Poems" would be read by the uninitiated public as "Poems Written by Nelly." And that is precisely what happened: both the general public and a number of writers fell for the trick. In reality, "Nelly" referred to the poems' dedicatee rather than to their author: they were poems *for* Nelly, dedicated to Nelly. Nelly was what Bryusov called Nadya when they were alone together.[32]

To a certain extent, Nina Petrovskaya's story was repeated in Nadya's case; she simply couldn't reconcile herself to the duality of Bryusov's desires: that he longed both for her and for his hearthside. Beginning in 1913, she became extremely melancholy. Bryusov was systematically habituating her to thoughts of death and suicide. Once she showed me a revolver—a gift from Bryusov. It was the very same Browning that Nina had used to shoot at Andrei Bely eight years prior. One evening in late November, I believe it was the twenty-third, Lvova telephoned Bryusov, begging him to come over at once. He said that he couldn't come, that he was busy. Then she called the poet Vadim Shershenevich: "I'm terribly lonesome; let's go to the movies." Shershenevich couldn't, he had guests. At around eleven o'clock, she called me—I wasn't in. Later that night, she shot herself. I was informed of this in the early hours of the morning.

An hour later, Shershenevich telephoned to say that Bryusov's wife had asked that pains be taken to ensure that nothing undesirable would be printed in the papers. I wasn't worried about Bryusov, but I didn't want reporters rooting around in Nadya's story. I agreed to go over to *The Russian Record* and *The Russian Word*.[33]

Nadya was buried in the shabby Miusskoe Cemetery on a cold, snowy day. There were a number of people in attendance. Nadya's parents, who had come in from Serpukhov, stood arm-in-arm next to the open grave. They were old, small, and stocky; he was wearing a worn greatcoat with green facing and she was dressed in an old fur coat and a pushed-in hat. No one had met them prior to that day. Once the grave had been sprinkled with earth, they went to make the rounds of the people who had gathered there, just as they had been standing, arm-in-arm. With affected cheerfulness, whispering through trembling lips, they shook hands and thanked people. For what? Many of us felt complicit in Bryusov's crime: to had seen everything and done nothing to save her. These poor old folks didn't know that. When they got closer to me, I moved off to one side, not daring to look them in the eye; I had no right to console them.

On the day after Nadya's death, Bryusov ran away to Petersburg, and from there on to Riga, to a sanatorium of some kind. After a time, he returned to Moscow, having healed his spiritual wound and written some new poems, many of which were dedicated to a fresh "meeting," which had taken place in the sanatorium. At the next Wednesday gathering of Free Aesthetics[34] in the canteen of the Literary-Artistic Circle, over a dinner at which "all of Moscow" was present—writers and their wives, young poets, artists, patrons and patronesses of the arts—he offered to audition his new verses. Everyone waited with bated breath—and not in vain, as the very first poem turned out to be a declaration. I don't remember the details; I only remember that it was some variation on the theme of:

> Lifeless, may you rest in peace,
> Use your life, o ye who live it

and that each line began with the words, "Peace to the dead!" After hearing about two lines, I stood up from the table and made my way toward the door. Bryusov paused in his reading. I was shushed: everyone knew what the poem was about and insisted that I not interfere with their enjoyment.[35]

As soon as the door shut behind me, I began to regret my trips to *The Russian Word* and *The Russian Record*.

■ □ ■

He had a passionate, unnatural love for serving on committees—and he loved being a chairman even more. In holding meetings, he performed religious rites. Resolution, amendment, vote, statute, point, paragraph: such words were music to his ears. Opening sessions, closing sessions, giving someone the floor, taking the floor back again "at the chairman's discretion," ringing his little bell, leaning intimately toward the secretary and asking him to "record that in the minutes"—all this afforded him great pleasure; it was "theater for one's own sake," a foretaste of those two lines in the literary history yet to come. In the period from 1907 to 1914, he would sit in meetings three times a day, whether or not it was necessary to do so. He sacrificed his conscience, his friends, and certain women to these meetings. At the end of the 1890s or the beginning of the 1900s, he, a decadent, infamous for shocking the bourgeoisie, who loved only that which was "depraved" and "strange," took it into his head to run for the city duma in his capacity as a property owner—the Moscow

City Duma[36] of that day and age! As managing chairman of the Literary-Artistic Circle, he would confer with the butler for hours on end on the subject of the next day's plat du jour.

In the autumn of 1914, he came up with the idea of celebrating the twentieth anniversary of his literary career.[37] The organizing committee for this event consisted of I. I. Troyanovsky and Mrs. Nemenova-Lunts, the lady musician. Bryusov's place was decorated with flowers at a dinner held after a regular meeting of Free Aesthetics. The jubilee organizers took turns entreating various people to give speeches. No one said a word—it wasn't an appropriate time. Bryusov left for Warsaw as a war correspondent for *The Russian Record*. He did not abandon his dreams of a jubilee.

He was an anti-Semite. When one of his sisters married S. V. Kissin, a Jew, not only did he categorically refuse to attend their wedding, but he didn't even congratulate the newlyweds, and he didn't once darken their doorstep in the years that followed. This began in 1909.[38]

In the period leading up to 1914, relations between them warmed slightly. Samuil Viktorovich, who had been mobilized, ended up working as a bureaucrat in a hospital office in Warsaw—the very same city where Bryusov was living as a war correspondent. They would see each other from time to time.

After the disappointment of his Moscow jubilee, Bryusov decided that he could at least have a celebration in Warsaw. Some Polish writers deigned to honor him. Afterward, he told me:

> The Poles are much stricter anti-Semites than I am. They wanted to hold a dinner in my honor, and I would have invited Samuil Viktorovich, but they crossed him off the list, saying that they wouldn't sit down at the same table as a Jew. I was forced to deny myself the pleasure of seeing Samuil Viktorovich at my jubilee, even though I pointed out that he was, after all, both my relative and a poet.

But he could not deny himself the pleasure of celebrating his jubilee.

He did eventually manage to celebrate the ill-fated jubilee in Moscow in December of 1924. The festivities took place at the Bolshoy Theater. Posters were hung up all over the city, inviting all and sundry. In larger letters than Bryusov's own name appeared the words, "Featuring Maxim Gorky." This was despite the fact that the organizers and, of course, Bryusov himself knew perfectly well that Gorky was in Marienbad and had no intention of returning to Russia at that time.[39]

■ □ ■

How and why did he become a Communist?

At one point, he shared the views of the most vulgar of Black Hundredists. During the Russo-Japanese War, he would talk about Masonic plots and Japanese money.[40]

In 1905, he denounced the socialists up and down, demonstrating an absurd level of ignorance. He once said, "I know what Marxism is: steal what you can and share your husbands and wives."

He was given the Erfurt Program[41] to read. When he reached the end, he said brusquely, "Nonsense."

I am writing memoirs, not criticism. For that reason, I will only briefly point out that his "leftist" poems, including the celebrated "Dagger," do not, in fact, contain any actual leftism. "The poet's with the crowd whenever thunder rolls" is a literary program, an aesthetic program, but not a political program. In *Letters of a Russian Traveler*, Karamzin describes an aristocrat who has cozied up to the Jacobins. In response to the bewildered questions posed to him, he answers, "*Que faire? J'aime les t-t-troubles.*" (The aristocrat was a stutterer).[42]

These words could serve as the epigraph to all of Bryusov's radical poetry from the era of 1905. The celebrated poem "The Stonemason" doesn't reflect its author's views either. It is a stylization, precisely the same kind of imitation, the same kind of poetic exercise, as the children's song that was printed along with it (the one about the helper-outer), the collectors' song ("Contribute alms, good citizens, to buy us a new bell"), and other poems in that style. Bryusov's own views are not reflected in "The Stonemason" just as they are not reflected in his "Australian Song," which he wrote in the spirit of "exhausting all themes and possibilities":

> Swiftly ran the kangaroos–
> Swifter still was I.
> The kangaroo was very fat,
> And I ate him up.[43]

The true origins of "The Stonemason" are purely literary. It was an edited version of a poem that had been written before Bryusov was born—nothing more, nothing less. It was published under the same title in *The Lute*, an old foreign collection of banned Russian poems. I do not know the author.

While the feuilletonists were writing articles about the "aesthete" Bryusov's appeals to the "community," Bryusov was in the attic of his house, learning how to shoot a revolver "in case the strikers come to rob us." Sergei Krechetov composed some verses about certain discussions that had taken place in the offices of Scorpio, and, though the poems are not particularly brilliant, they certainly make their point:

> They would meet as a group of a Tuesday,
> Voicing lofty goals,
> Plan pogroms with the cleaner on duty

At the Metropol.*

How touching it was of a Tuesday,

To see shared tastes made use of;

How well-matched were the cleaner on duty

And Valery Bryusov.

Around the same time, his younger brother wrote him a poem in Latin addressed to "*Falsas Valerius, duplex lingua!*"[44]

In 1913, he was invited to edit the literary section of *Russian Thought*.[45] In this capacity, he once said, "As one of the editors of *Russian Thought*, I am in agreement with Pyotr Berngardovich (Struve) on all political matters."

Later on, in Tbilisi, on the eve of the February Revolution, at a banquet given by a group of Armenians in honor of Bryusov, who had edited a collection called *Poetry of Armenia*, he stood up, and, to the great confusion of those present, raised his glass "to the health of His Majesty the Emperor, the sovereign leader of our army."[46] I was informed of this by one of the banquet's organizers, P. N. Makintsian, who later edited the celebrated *Cheka Red Book* (he was shot in 1937).

■ □ ■

Bryusov despised democracy. The cultural history that he idolized was, to him, a history of "creators," demigods who stood apart from the crowd, who despised it, who were hated by it. In his view, any sort of democratic power smacked either of utopianism or ochlocracy, mob rule.

He considered absolutism to be a demiurgical force, culture's protector and creator. Accordingly, the poet must always side with

---

* The Scorpio publishing house was located in the Metropol building

the powers that be, no matter what those powers represent—so long as they hold themselves apart from the people. Like the "trireme's rower," to him it was

all the same,
to carry Caesar or a pirate.[47]

All true poets have been court poets: during the reigns of Augustus and Maecenas, of all the Louis, of Friedrich, of Catherine, of Nicholas I, and so on. This was one of his most cherished beliefs.

This is why he was a monarchist in the time of Nicholas II. This is why, while he still cherished hopes that the Provisional Government might yet "rein in the masses" and prove itself to be a "solid power," he was so keen to serve on various committees, and why he wrote and published a small, pink brochure titled "How Do We End the War?" accompanied by the epigraph "*Si vis pacem, para bellum*"[48] in an attempt to support the principles of defensism. The gist of this brochure was "war to a victorious end."

After October,[49] he fell into despair. At the beginning of November, while visiting the home of the poet K. A. Lipskerov, I ran into a certain lady who prefaced everything she said with the phrase "Valery Yakovlevich says . . ." When our host left the room to see about the tea, the lady glanced after him warily and, leaning over to me, whispered, "Valery Yakovlevich says that the yids will rule over us now."

I did not see Bryusov myself that winter, but I was told that he was in a depressed state, mourning the imminent death of culture. It was only in the summer of 1918, after the dissolution of the Constituent Assembly and the beginning of the Terror, that he perked up a bit and declared himself a Communist.[50]

But this made perfect sense: he saw before him a "strong power," absolutism in one of its many forms—and he bowed down before it; he felt that it would constitute a sufficient shield against *demos*, the lower strata, the rabble. It didn't cost him anything to declare himself a Marxist—for so long as there was power, what difference did it make what it stood for?

He bowed before the new autocracy of Communism, which, in his view, was even better than the old autocracy had been: after all, the Kremlin was more personally accessible to him than Tsarskoe Selo. And the old autocracy hadn't exercised any sort of official, protectionist aesthetic policies, whereas the new one wanted to be active on that front. It seemed as if it would be possible for Bryusov to have a direct influence over literature; he cherished hopes that the Bolsheviks would offer him his long-awaited opportunity to "govern" literature through firm administrative measures. If this came to pass, he would be able to issue commands without getting involved in any writers' intrigues, without being forced into alliances with them—he could accomplish everything with a single shout. And just think of the meetings, the statutes, the resolutions! And there was always the hope that literary history would one day declare that "in such-and-such a year, he turned Russian literature around by however many degrees." In that moment, his personal interests aligned with his beliefs.

■ □ ■

This dream did not come true. Inasmuch as it had proven possible to force literature into submission, the Communists preferred to reserve the dictatorship for themselves rather than handing it over to Bryusov, whom they still considered to be an outsider and whom, in spite of everything, they still didn't trust. He was furnished with several more or less prominent posts, though not particularly important ones. He served with the same strong-willed punctiliousness that had always been the hallmark of his work, no matter what sort. He "served" and "oversaw" with all his might.

He distanced himself from the literary scene even more sharply than the literary scene distanced itself from him. When a writers' union formed in Moscow, Bryusov took a considerably more forceful and hard-nosed position toward it than the actual Bolsheviks did. I remember one story on this subject in particular. When the Literary-Artistic Circle was abolished, its library was requisitioned and, as often happened in such cases, plundered. The books were under the jurisdiction of the Moscow Council, and the Writers' Union requested that the library be transferred over to them. Kamenev, who was chairman of the council at the time, agreed. As soon as Bryusov got wind of this, he immediately lodged a complaint and began demanding that the library be given to Lito, an utterly lifeless establishment that happened to be under his control.[51] I was a member of the Union administration and was charged with trying to convince Bryusov to abandon his claims on the books. I immediately picked up the telephone to call Bryusov. After hearing me out, he responded, "I don't understand you, Vladislav Felitsianovich. You are appealing to a civil servant, attempting to persuade him to act against the interests of an organization that has been put into his trust."

Upon hearing the words "civil servant" and "organization put into his trust," I made no further attempts to continue our conversation. The library was transferred over to Lito.

Unfortunately, Bryusov's zeal for service ran even deeper than that. In March of 1920, I fell ill from malnutrition and from living in an unheated cellar. After spending two months in bed and ailing the entire summer, at the end of November I decided to move to Petersburg, where I had been promised a dry room. In Petersburg, I spent another month in bed, but since I didn't have anything to eat there either, I also set about petitioning to have my writer's rations transferred from Moscow to Petersburg. I was forced to expend about three months' worth of extraordinary effort toward this end; moreover, I constantly found myself running up against an invisible, but clearly perceivable obstacle. It was only two years later that I learned from Gorky that this obstacle had come in the form of a certain document located in the Petersburg Academic Center. In this document, Bryusov had confidentially reported that I was an untrustworthy individual. It is worth noting that, even in his "professional capacity," this sort of thing was not one of his responsibilities.*

■ □ ■

The Bolsheviks did not appreciate him in spite of all his zeal. He was reproached for his erstwhile affiliation with "bourgeois" literature at every opportunity. His verses, which were written in full accordance with the authorities' views, were nevertheless irrelevant, for they were ill suited to straightforward agitation. The problem was that, even when Bryusov was writing on commissioned topics or churning out his umpteenth slogan, he remained independent in regard to form. It is my belief that a painstaking formal study of Bryusov's communist poems would reveal their strained inner workings, which were aimed at destroying old harmonies, "creating new sounds." Bryusov went about achieving his goal by orchestrating a conscious cacophony. Whether or not he was right and whether or not he actually achieved something are two separate matters. But it was precisely this type of work that rendered his poems hyperrefined to the point of woodenness, that made them difficult to assimilate,

---

* The late critic Yu. I. Aikhenvald, who was exiled from Russia in 1922, later wrote to me, saying: "As for Bryusov . . . I myself would be the last person ever to idealize him. He did me more than a few bad turns and, when he joined the ranks of the powers that be, he took his revenge on me in an unseemly, which is to say, monetary, fashion for a negative review that I gave him in one of my old articles. Even my exile took place at his incitement—I know this for certain, having heard it from a reliable source" (from a letter dated August 5, 1926).

inaccessible to the primitive mind. They were unfit to be used as agitational materials—and so Bryusov proved to be essentially useless as a poet. All that remained was Bryusov the old campaigner, whom they drove from "post" to "post," occasionally crossing over the line into witting or unwitting mockery. And so, for instance, in 1921, Bryusov occupied both a high-ranking position in the People's Commissariat for Education and an equally important one in Gukon—or, as it was better known, Horsebreeding Headquarters.[52] *

And so? He did an honest job there, too, and, in order to keep in step with the New Economic Policy,[53] he even led a print campaign for the restoration of games of chance and betting.

Bryusov was, of course, aware of his utter isolation. In the beginning of 1922, a certain person close to Bryusov told me that he was very lonely, very gloomy and dejected.

Apparently, he had become addicted to morphine as early as 1908. He tried to kick the habit, but he couldn't. In the summer of 1911, Dr. G. A. Koiransky managed to wean him from the morphine for a time, but in the end, his efforts came to nothing. Morphine had become indispensible to Bryusov. I remember how, during one conversation in 1917, I noticed Bryusov gradually sinking into a sort of stupor, practically falling asleep. Finally, he got up, went into an adjoining room for a short period of time—and came back rejuvenated.

At the end of 1919, I had occasion to fill in for him at one of his posts. Glancing into the otherwise empty desk drawer, I found a syringe needle and a piece of newspaper with spots of blood on it. In his final years, he often took to his bed—apparently, due to intoxication.

---

* Strange as it might seem, there was a certain logic to this: the very first work that Bryusov published consisted of two articles about horses printed in one of the specialty journals: either *Trotter and Prancer* or *Horsebreeding and Sport*. As I mentioned earlier, Bryusov's father had been an amateur horse dealer. Once I saw Bryusov's childhood letters to his mother, which were chock-full of racing affairs and his own impressions of them.

Lonely and tortured, he nevertheless found joy in unexpected places. Toward the end of his life, he took his wife's young nephew under his wing and looked after him with the same tenderness that he had once shown that kitten. He would come home laden with sweets and toys. He would spread out a rug and play with the little boy right there on the floor.

When I read reports of Bryusov's death, I assumed that he had killed himself. Perhaps that's how he would have ended up if death itself hadn't forestalled him.

Sorrento, 1924

ANDREI BELY

I n 1922 in Berlin, Andrei Bely presented me with a new edition of *Petersburg*,[1] inscribed: "With feelings of concrete love and lifelong connection."

In ideology, in literature, and in life, fate pushed us along in opposite directions—if not for our entire lives, then for nineteen years at least.[2] I did not share the greater part of Bely's views, but he exercised a greater influence over me than any other person I have known. I didn't belong to the same generation as Bely, but I first came into contact with his generation when it was still young and active. Many people and circumstances that played a conspicuous role in Bely's life turned out to do the same in mine.

For various reasons, I cannot relate everything that I know and believe to be true about Bely at this time. But even in the context of this short narrative, I would rather preserve a few truthful sketches for the benefit of literary history than satisfy the curiosity of the contemporary reader. After all, literary history has already begun to demonstrate an interest in the era of Symbolism in general and in Andrei Bely in particular—with time, this interest will only grow more acute. I feel compelled to be exceptionally fussy with the truth. I consider it my (far from easy) obligation to omit any hypocritical thoughts or euphemistic language from this account. You mustn't expect me to offer up an iconic or canonical image of my subject. Such images are harmful to history. I am certain that they are immoral as well, since only a complete and truthful image is capable of revealing the finest attributes of a truly remarkable person. By its very nature, the truth cannot be low because there is nothing higher than the truth. It seems appropriate to counter Pushkin's "uplifting deception"[3] with an equally uplifting truth: we must learn to respect and love a remarkable person together with all of his weaknesses, and occasionally even because of them. Such people require no embellishment. They require something far more difficult from us: our total understanding.

■ □ ■

Before I was even born, an unusually good-looking little boy began appearing with his governess and little dog on Moscow's Prechistensky Boulevard. This was Borya Bugaev,[4] the son of a mathematics professor known throughout Europe for his scholarly works, among Moscow students for his phenomenal absentmindedness and preposterous vagaries, and among first-year gymnasium students for the arithmetic textbook that he had authored, which I myself would later study from.[5] The little boy had golden curls that reached down to his shoulders and his eyes were deep blue. He rolled a golden hoop along a golden path with a golden stick. Eternity, "that child at play," pushes the golden circle of the sun along in precisely the same fashion. The image of Bely as a young child is closely linked with the image of the sun.

In those days, Professor Bugaev would say, "I hope that Borya will inherit his mother's face and my brain." These lighthearted words masked a family drama that was no laughing matter. The professor wasn't just an eccentric; he also possessed a truly freakish face. One time, at a concert (this was in the beginning of the nineties), N. Ya. Bryusova, the poet's sister, nudged Andrei Bely with her elbow and said, "Just look at that man! You don't happen to know who that gorilla is, do you?" "That's my dad," Andrei Bely replied with the broadest, most obliging of smiles. It was a smile of utter satisfaction, almost happiness—precisely the kind of smile he loved to employ when answering unpleasant questions.

His mother was very attractive. At a certain event held in Turgenev's honor, the organizers felt it necessary to seat the leading Moscow beauties on either side of the famous author. These beauties were Ekaterina Pavlovna Letkova (later Sultanova), a contributor to *Russian Wealth* with whom Boborykin was hopelessly in love for many years, and Alexandra Dmitrievna Bugaeva. These two women also sit side by side in K. E. Makovsky's famous painting *A Boyar Wedding Feast*: the bride herself was modeled on Alexandra Dmitrievna, while Ekaterina Pavlovna provided the inspiration for one of the bride's friends.[6] I never set eyes on Bely's father, and I first saw his mother when she was already a plumpish, elderly woman who still bore the traces of an undeniable beauty and the habits of a dyed-in-the-wool coquette. Once, I came upon Alexandra Dmitrievna while I was accompanying a female relative to the seamstress. Lifting her wide taffeta skirt up ever-so-slightly with her fingertips, she was twirling in front of the mirror, repeating over and over again, "But really, I've still got it!" In 1912, I had occasion to observe that her heart was not yet a stranger to agitation.

The physical discrepancy between the two spouses was a reflection of their inner dissimilarity. They weren't suited to each other, either in terms of intelligence or interests. Their situation was an extremely typical one: an ugly, unkempt husband with his head stuck in the clouds paired with a beautiful, coquettish wife caught up in the grips of the most earthly desires. This was also the source of the discord that is equally typical of such situations. This discord manifested itself day after day in violent quarrels that took place at the slightest provocation. Borya bore witness to them.

Bely talked openly about the autobiographical nature of *Kotik Letaev* more than once. However, if you read Bely's late prose carefully, and even if you don't take particular pains to do so, you will find that this same family conflict furnishes the plotlines not just for *Petersburg* and *Kotik Letaev*, but for *Nikolai Letaev's Crime, The Baptized Chinaman, The Moscow Eccentric,* and *Moscow Under Fire* as well.[7] These are all variations on the drama that once played itself out in the Bugaev household. Not just the configuration of the characters, but the specific images of the father, the mother, and the son are repeated down to the very last detail. The least realistic depiction of these characters appears in *Petersburg*. In the later novels, though, their portrayal approaches near-photographic precision. The older Bely became, the more stubbornly he returned to these childhood memories, the more meaning they took on in his eyes. Starting in *Petersburg*, all of the political, philosophical, and everyday tasks that Bely's novels set for themselves fade into the background, superseded by autobiographical ones. In reality, though, these autobiographical tasks were merely an excuse for Bely to mentally resurrect and relive his own childhood impressions.* Not only had Andrei Bely's nerves been shaken by the "earthly storms" (his words) that took place in the Bugaev household; his very imagination had been affected. These storms had an incredibly deep impact on Andrei Bely's character and on his life in general.

He felt like a leaf or a grain of sand swept up in these family storms: between his father, a freakish thunder god, shrouded in clouds of black soot from the kerosene lamp that had been hurled down onto the floor, and his dear mama, frivolous and charming, calling wrath and ruin down on herself like the sinful inhabitants of

---

* The real-life counterparts to the characters and situations found in Andrei Bely's novels are discussed an article I wrote, entitled "Ableukhovs—Letaevs—Korobkins." See *Contemporary Annals*, 1926, issue 31.

Sodom and Gomorrah. His feeling was essentially this: he was afraid of his father, and secretly hated him with a very strong passion; it is no coincidence that real or imagined crimes against fathers (up to and including attempted patricide) make up the narrative bulk of the aforementioned novels. He pitied his dear mama and would go into practically carnal ecstasies over her. But over the years, though his feelings retained all of their original acuity, they became complicated by feelings of a completely different nature. Bely's hatred for his father, combined with a respect for his intelligence and a reverent wonder for the cosmic expanses and mathematical abstractions that unexpectedly revealed themselves through him, turned into love. His infatuation with his dear mama coexisted alongside an unflattering impression of her intellect and an instinctive revulsion for her distinctive, piquant fleshliness.

Every event that occurred in the Bugaev household was interpreted by Bely's father and mother in completely different ways. What his father accepted and approved of, his mother rejected and condemned—and vice versa. "Torn" (as he put it) between his two parents, Bely experienced each of their relative truths and untruths in a variety of contexts. Each event proved itself to be ambiguous, revealed itself to have two different sides, two different meanings. At first, this frightened and bewildered him. Over the years, he got used to it, and this became his way of relating to people, events, and ideas. He came to love the reconciliation of the irreconcilable, the tragedy and complexity of internal contradiction, the truth in untruth, and, perhaps, the good in evil and the evil in good. First, he became accustomed to hiding his love for his mother (and for all things "motherly") from his father and his love for his father (and for all things "fatherly") from his mother—and taught himself to believe that there was no inherent lie in such deceit. Later on, he began to transfer this same ambivalence onto other people—which earned him a reputation for being two-faced. I will be entirely frank:

it is true that he often behaved in a two-faced manner, and he did derive from that two-facedness the advantages that two-facedness sometimes provides. But there was no guile or opportunism at the base of his two-facedness; there was nothing like that in its nature. He genuinely hated both of those things. But he sought, and, naturally, found, reasons not to love the people that he loved. He wasn't afraid to see the good in those he didn't like or even those whom he despised, and at times he found himself disarmed by them to the point of tenderness. Having entered a situation with every intention of behaving in a conciliatory manner, he would suddenly explode and burst into wild diatribes; having set out to thunder and denounce, he would unexpectedly find himself agreeing with his adversary. At times, he would change his mind when it was already too late, when a person who had once been dear to him had already become his enemy, while someone he despised was sidling up for an embrace. At times, he would lie to those close to him and bare his soul to passersby. But, even when telling a lie, he would often express only what appeared to him to be "the truth turned inside out," while in his moments of frankness he would keep mum "about the latter."

For all intents and purposes, it was also to this fact of "being torn" between his parents that he owed his future worldview. His father wanted to mold him into his pupil and successor, while his mother fought this plan with music and poetry: not because she loved music or poetry, but because she truly hated mathematics. As time went by, it became progressively clearer to Bely that everything "positive" and dear to his father was dear to him as well, while art and philosophy must be reconciled with hard knowledge—"otherwise, it would be impossible to live." He came to mysticism and then to Symbolism via the difficult path of reconciling the nineteenth century's positivistic tendencies with the philosophy of Vladimir Solovyov. It is no coincidence that, before entering the department of philology, he received a degree from the department of mathematics. He tells this story best himself. I wish only to point out the early biographical sources for his later opinions and literary destiny.[8]

■ □ ■

I met him during the period of his love affair with Nina Petrovskaya, or rather, I should say, at the very moment of their break.

Andrei Bely was much more flustered by women than is generally thought to be the case. Nevertheless, Bely's ambivalence manifested itself with a particular clarity in this sphere. His tactics were always the same: he would charm a woman with his near-magical charisma, appearing to her surrounded by his mystical halo, as if to nip any thoughts of sensual pursuit in the bud. Later on, he would start to force his attentions on her, and if she, struck (and sometimes offended) by the unexpectedness of these attentions, did not respond in kind, he would fly into a rage. On the other hand, every time he did manage to achieve his desired result, he would feel besmirched and defiled, and would likewise fly into a rage. It also sometimes happened that, at the very last moment before the "fall," he would manage to escape, like Joseph the all-comely[9]—but in that case, he would be twice as indignant: both because a woman had almost seduced him and because she hadn't quite managed it.

Nina Petrovskaya suffered for having become his beloved. He broke with her in the most degrading manner. She cultivated her relationship with Bryusov in order to take revenge on Bely—and with the secret hope of winning him back by arousing his jealousy.

Once, in the beginning of 1906, when *The Golden Fleece*[10] was just getting started, I had some guests over. Nina and Bryusov arrived long before anybody else. Bryusov asked if he could retire to my bedroom to finish a poem that he had started. After a time, he emerged and asked for some wine. Nina took him a bottle of cognac. An hour or more later, when the other guests had already assembled, I glanced into the bedroom and found Nina and Bryusov sitting on the floor and crying, the bottle empty and the poem finished. Nina requested in a whisper that I ask Bryusov to read out his new poem over dinner. Not suspecting that anything was amiss (I had a very murky understanding of what was going on between Nina, Bely, and Bryusov at the time), I did. Addressing himself to Bely, Bryusov said, "Boris Nikolaevich, I shall read a poem in imitation of you."

And he did. Bely had a poem called "A Fable," in which he depicted the story of his break with Nina through allegory and euphemism.[11] It was this "Fable" that Bryusov imitated in his poem, preserving Bely's original form and style, but changing the story's ending and presenting Bely's role in the most pathetic terms imaginable. Bely listened, staring at his plate. When Bryusov finished reading, everyone was embarrassed and silent. Finally, with his arms crossed, as was his habit, Bryusov looked Bely straight in the eye and said in his most guttural, squawking voice, "Does that sound like you, Boris Nikolaevich?"

The question was ambiguous: it could simultaneously refer both to the style of Bely's poem and to his behavior. Utterly embarrassed, Bely pretended that Bryusov had had only the poetic aspect of the question in mind and that he hadn't guessed the poem's backstory. He replied with his broadest smile, "It's terribly similar, Valery Yakovlevich!" And he would have set about showering him with compliments, but Bryusov interrupted him sharply: "So much the worse for you!"

Because he was aware of my friendship with Nina, Bely believed that I had purposefully conspired with Bryusov to arrange the reading. Bely and I saw one another after that, but he always gave me a wide berth. By that time, I knew why, but I didn't attempt to justify myself: partly because I didn't know how to broach the subject, partly out of vanity. We only managed to have it out with each other after nearly two years had passed—under circumstances just as strange as everything else about the life that we were leading at the time.

■ □ ■

In 1904, Bely met a young writer who was fated to become one of our most cherished Russian poets.[12] Their personal and literary destinies were to be forever intertwined. In his memoirs, Bely presented two different versions of the bond between them: each version was mutually exclusive of the other and each one was equally untrue. The future biographers of both poets will be obliged to take great pains to establish the truth of the matter.

The poet arrived in Moscow with his young wife, who was already known to several Moscow mystics, friends of Bely's. She was already encircled by their ecstatic adoration; a repressed eroticism seethed under their seductive, if somewhat hypocritical, pretense of mystical service to the Beautiful Lady. Bely immediately succumbed to this general atmosphere and his new friend's wife became the object of his undivided attention. The mystics nurtured and encouraged these attentions. Later on, these attentions didn't even need to be encouraged: they metamorphosed into a love that, in effect, served as the final push toward his break with Nina Petrovskaya. I won't take it upon myself to provide a detailed account of this affair, which ran its course at times in Moscow, at times in Petersburg, and at times in the countryside. It was complicated in the extreme by the complicated characters of its protagonists, the peculiar structure of the Symbolist lifestyle, and, finally, by the diverse literary, philosophical, and even societal events that acted as its backdrop. Sometimes, their love affair would become deeply intertwined with this backdrop, and sometimes the former would even influence the latter. In summary, I will say that this love played an important role in the literary relationships of its era, in the fate of a number of individuals who weren't involved in it directly—and in the history of Symbolism itself. Much about this affair remains unclear even to this day. Bely described it to me more than once, but his stories were full of contradictions, omissions, variations, and the figments of a nervous mind. I would like to highlight the fact that the stories he told verbally differed significantly from the versions printed in his memoirs.

All things considered, this love affair seems to have proceeded in the following manner. Apparently, the young lady received the brotherly feelings that Bely initially extended to her favorably. But when Bely, as was his wont, progressed from such brotherly feelings to feelings of a different nature, his task became immeasurably more complicated. Perhaps it would have been entirely insoluble if it hadn't been for his dazzling charm, which, it seemed, was genuinely irresistible. But every time his romantic pursuit was nearing the point of success, Bely's unavoidable ambivalence would bubble up to the surface, just as it always did. He was mad enough to convince himself that his actions had been taken the wrong way, "sinfully"— and he said as much to the lady in question, who, in all likelihood, had undergone significant sufferings before offering up her consent. The consequences of Bely's backpedaling aren't difficult to imagine. The woman he loved was seized with wrath and contempt. And she got her own back in a way that was a hundred times more painful and humiliating than what Nina Petrovskaya had attempted, for she herself was a hundred times tougher and stronger than Nina Petrovskaya had been. And as for Bely? I can say with great certainty that, from that moment onward, he actually began to love her genuinely, with all his soul, and, I am deeply convinced, forevermore. He experienced both other loves and fleeting infatuations later in his life, but this love remained throughout it and above it all. She was the only woman he ever truly loved, she and she alone. As the years passed, his pain dulled, as is typically the case, but its sting stayed with him for a long time. Bely's sufferings were unspeakable; he would swing from mortified submission to rage and pride: he would shout that rejecting his love was a sacrilege. Sometimes, his sufferings would lift him up to great spiritual heights; at other times, writhing with jealousy, he would stoop to exacting literary revenge upon his rivals, real or imagined. He spent several months abroad—and returned with his suffering unassuaged and with a draft of *The Blizzard Cup*, which is the weakest of his symphonies for having been written in anguish.[13]

■ □ ■

In August of 1907, personal misfortunes brought me to Petersburg for several days and I ended up staying there for a long time: I lacked the strength to return to Moscow. I rarely associated with men of letters; I was surviving only with great difficulty. At night, I would loaf around in restaurants, gambling dens, or simply on the streets, and during the day, I would sleep. Nina Petrovskaya arrived unexpectedly, driven from Moscow both by the tensions that had risen up between her and Bryusov and by a fleeting, whirlwind passion for a certain young Petersburg writer whose "stylized" short stories were in fashion at the time. Bryusov had followed her and was trying to bring her back to Moscow, but she wouldn't go immediately. Now and again, we would while away the evenings together— with our own neuroses, I'll admit. She was living in the very same English hotel where Esenin later killed himself.[14]

On September 28 of that year, Blok wrote to his mother from Petersburg: "Mama, I haven't written for a long time, and am writing very little now owing to a great number of worries, great and small. The big ones are about Lyuba,* Natalya Nikolaevna,† and

---

* Lyubov Dmitrievna, Blok's wife.
† The actress N. N. Volokhova, to whom "The Snowy Mask" is dedicated.

Borya. Borya is coming to see me soon. He is growing increasingly dearer to me and is terribly unhappy." Finally, Bely arrived on the scene, only to be spurned once more. We ran into each other by chance. One evening, after a literary gathering at which Bunin had read aloud a manuscript of the ailing Kuprin's new short story ("The Emerald"), I went out onto Nevsky Prospect. A street woman accosted me next to the public library. Looking to kill some time, I offered to treat her to dinner. We went into a small restaurant. When I asked her what her name was, she answered in a very strange fashion: "Everyone calls me poor Nina. You should, too."

The conversation didn't come together. Poor Nina, a scrawny brunette with a snub nose, made eyes at me wearily and talked about how dreadfully she loved men, while I contemplated how tedious it would be to get rid of her. Suddenly, Bely burst in, agitated and not entirely sober. He sat down with us, and, over a bottle of cognac, we forgot about our companion. We began to talk about Moscow. Softened by the wine, Bely admitted his suspicions regarding my "provocations" on the evening when Bryusov had read his poem in my home. We had it out, and the ice that had crept in between us was broken. By that time, the restaurant was closing, so Bely took me to a certain, in his words, "completely Petersburgian place." We arrived at a spot somewhere near the end of Izmailovsky Prospect. It was the lowest sort of club. We were greeted by an extraordinarily venerable-looking man with gray muttonchops whom everybody called the colonel. Bely furnished me with a recommendation and, having paid a three-ruble note apiece (the surest recommendation of them all), we went into the hall. Clerks and petty bureaucrats in little jackets were dancing quadrilles with young women dressed (or, rather, undressed) as gypsies and naiads. Later in the evening, prizes were awarded for the best costumes; there was a minor scandal, someone was offended, someone cursed. We asked for wine and sat in that "completely Petersburgian place" until the redheaded Petersburg dawn.

As we parted ways, we made plans to have lunch at Vienna[15] with Nina Petrovskaya.

The lunch was gloomy and silent. I said, "Nina, it seems as if your bowl has more tears in it than soup."

She lifted her head and replied, "They should call me poor Nina."

Bely and I exchanged glances—she knew nothing of the woman on Nevsky Prospect. In those days, that sort of coincidence meant a lot to us.

And so our lunch drew to a close in oppressive silence. Several days later, I dropped in on Bely (he was living on Vasilyevsky Island, practically on top of Nikolaevsky Bridge) and spotted a round bandbox. Inside it were a red satin domino and a black mask. I realized that Bely must have appeared in that "completely Petersburgian place" in this getup. Later on, the domino and the mask would appear in his poetry,[16] and, later still, they would become one of the central images of *Petersburg*.

Several days after our lunch together, Nina set off for Moscow, and, at the very end of October (if memory serves), Bely and I left as well. He drank vodka at the station stops and stayed in Moscow for two days before rushing back to Petersburg. He couldn't live with her or without her.

■ □ ■

I look back on the four years that followed with gratitude: as the years, dare I say, of our friendship. At that time, Bely was in full bloom, both romantically and artistically speaking. He was finishing *Ashes* at the same time as he was writing *Urn*, *The Silver Dove*, and his seminal articles on Symbolism. This same period witnessed the publication of his most cutting polemical articles. Though later he often regretted their tone, he never regretted their contents. It was also at that time that he staged his most fantastic public scandals:

once, they had to lower the curtain on the stage of the Literary-Artistic Circle to prevent Bely's words from reaching the audience. He showed a different side of himself in our meetings, though. He would usually arrive in the morning, and on some occasions we would spend the entire day together, either remaining in my apartment or going out for walks: on the square near the Church of Christ the Savior, through Novodevichy Convent; one time we went to Petrovsko-Razumovskoe, to the grotto associated with the murder of the student Ivanov. Bely knew how to be both artless and inviting: *gemütlich*, to use his favorite word. His conversations would cross over into sparkling improvisations and were always extraordinarily inspiring in one way or another. He also loved just telling stories: about the Solovyov family, about the fateful dawning of the year 1900, and about professorial Moscow, which he imitated with both fury and humor. Sometimes, he would read something he had recently written and listen eagerly to my critiques, though he usually stood by what he had done. Only once did I succeed in convincing him to change something: at my advice, he scrapped the first page and a half of *The Silver Dove*. It was an imitation of Gogol that had obviously been written simply to warm up his pen.[17]

We often had discussions that were dedicated to poetry. The following question tormented us: apart from their instrumentation, what makes two lines in the same meter sound different? In the summer of 1908, when I was living outside of Moscow, he telephoned me, shouting with laughter: "Come up to the city, straightaway if you can. I only arrived here this morning myself. I've made a discovery! A real, honest-to-God discovery, just like Archimedes!"

Naturally, I went. It was a sweltering evening. Bely, tanned and triumphant, greeted me clad in a Russian shirt with an open collar. On the table stood an enormous stack of papers ruled into vertical columns. The columns were filled with dots, which had been whimsically connected using straight lines. Bely slapped the stack with a heavy palm.

"Here you have iambic tetrameter. It's all right here, spread out before your eyes. Verses of a single meter differ in rhythm. Rhythm and meter do not always correspond, and rhythm is determined by the omission of metrical stresses. 'My uncle, man of honest habits' has four stresses, while 'And unembarrassedly bowed low'[18] has two: the rhythms are different, but the meter remains the same, iambic tetrameter."

Now all of this seems as simple as *ABC*. On that day, though, it was a discovery, a genuinely simple and unexpected one, as Archimedes's had been. Andrei Bely's name should be synonymous with the noncoincidence of meter and rhythm in poetics. In its further elaborations, this discovery would be found to have its imperfections, which have since been written about extensively. Back then, in those early days, they were harder to work out. However, Bely and I immediately began to clash over one issue in particular. At the time, he was preparing *Ashes* and *Urn* for publication— and suddenly, he set about fundamentally reworking many of his poems, twisting the rhythms to fit his recently discovered formulae. Naturally, their rhythmic design was rendered highly remarkable when considered in abstraction. But, in the broader sense, his poems were being ruined left and right. No matter how much I argued with Bely, it was all to no avail. These poems went into his collections in their new editions, which were painful for me to listen to. And this was when I began to insist on the absolute necessity of studying rhythmic form together with semantic content. We quarreled over this issue both tête-à-tête and in the circle of rhythmicists that used to gather at the Musagetes Publishing House.[19] I felt that rhythmics divorced from semantic comment was a false and harmful subject of study. Finally, I stopped going to the meetings.

Bely was all the rage back then. The madames and mademoiselles would lay siege to him. He was happy to turn their heads, but he would also make them study Kant—and that wasn't at all what these ladies were after.

"She starts in with her flowery speeches and I say to her, 'My dear lady, if you are so interested in Symbolism, then you should spend some time with the *Critique of Pure Reason* first!' " Or: "Ah, what a delightful creature that dear mademoiselle Shtanevich[20] is! I'm simply in raptures over her!"

"Boris Nikolaevich, her surname is Stanevich, not Shtanevich!"

"No, really? But I've been calling her Shtanevich all this time. Do you think I've offended her?"

A week later, again: "Ah, mademoiselle Shtanevich!"

"Boris Nikolaevich! Stanevich!"

"My God! Really? How unfortunate!"

But his eyes were merry and deceitful.

Sometimes a note would appear on his door: "B. N. Bugaev is busy and asks not to be disturbed." "That's for the young ladies," he explained, but he wasn't always honest on that front. He would complain to me, "I'm sick of Pasternak." I assume that he would also complain to Pasternak, "I'm sick of Khodasevich."

One day he said, practically in a rage, "Really, just think: last night, during a snowstorm, I came home to find Marietta Shaginyan sitting by the entrance on a stool, like a porter. I'm sick of it!" But, at the same time, he was writing her extremely long philosophical letters, which poor Marietta was so grateful to receive that she was even willing to freeze for them.

In 1911, I took up residence in the countryside and we began to see each other less often. Then Bely got married, went away to Africa, returned to Moscow for a little while, and went away again, this time to Switzerland, to be closer to Rudolf Steiner. Immediately before the war, I received a letter from him, a cheerful, comparatively calm letter that described the muscles he had earned while working as a carver in the construction of the Goetheanum. I thought that he was finally happy.

■ □ ■

On the evening when we received the telephone call with the news that Rasputin had been murdered in Moscow, Gershenzon took me to see N. A. Berdyaev. The assembled company was discussing the events, and it was there that I saw Bely for the first time after our long separation. He was there without his wife, whom he had left behind in Dornach. From the very first glance, I realized that there had been no "calming down" to speak of. Physically coarsened, with calloused hands, he seemed to be in a state of extreme agitation. He spoke little, but his eyes, which had changed from deep to pale blue, would dart about, then freeze as if in horror. His balding pate with its tufts of graying hair resembled a copper ball that had been charged with millions of volts of electricity. Then he came up to me to tell me about the spies, provocateurs, and shadowy figures who had followed him, both in Dornach and on his trip back to Russia. They were watching him, following him; they wanted to ruin him, both in the literal sense of the word and in a few other senses as well.

This idea, which practically bordered on a persecution mania, had always been close to his heart. It is my deeply held conviction that this obsession began in his childhood, when he believed that some sort of dark forces were plotting to destroy him by provoking him into committing a crime against his father. In fact, these monsters, which were both the instigators and the Erinyes[21] of his potential patricide, dwelled within Bely himself. However, his instinct for self-preservation forced him to seek these monsters outside of himself so that he would be able to shift the blame for his own darkest thoughts, longings, and impulses onto them.

Andrei Bely \ 65

All of the aforementioned autobiographical novels, starting with *Petersburg* and ending with *Moscow Under Fire*, are chock-full of such repulsive monsters, partly invented, partly recreated from real life in fantastical style. Bely's struggle with these monsters, which is to say, with the embryo of betrayal and patricide that he harbored within his soul, became the primary, fundamental, and central theme of all of Bely's novels for the remainder of his life, *The Silver Dove* excluded. This theme was not, for all intents and purposes, connected either with the revolution or with the war, nor is any sort of historical framework required in order to understand it. Bely managed to do without one in *Kotik Letaev*, *Nikolai Letaev's Crime*, and *The Baptized Chinaman*. Only *Petersburg*, *The Moscow Eccentric*, and *Moscow Under Fire* bear any connection to the events of 1905 and 1914. But it should be entirely obvious to anyone who has read these last two novels that this connection is tenuous in the extreme. Bely wrote *The Moscow Eccentric* and *Moscow Under Fire* in the mid-twenties, in Soviet Russia. Both in the texts themselves and in the forewords he wrote to them, he took great pains to underscore the fact that the main character of both of these novels, the mathematician Korobkin, was intended as an embodiment of that "science, free in essence" against which the capitalist world was carrying on such a terrible intrigue, using Mitya, Korobkin's son, as its instrument. In reality, Bely had no interest whatsoever in this completely unrealistic "construct." His real aim was to provide yet another variation on his pet theme: crimes against the father. The dark forces that urge Mitya toward his crime take on the guise of capitalist demons because that is what the "social mandate" dictated. It is worth noting that, according to Bely himself, *The Moscow Eccentric* and *Moscow Under Fire* were meant to be the beginning of a vast cycle of novels. This cycle, however, was not to be completed, just like his cycle about Nikolai Letaev. Why? Because, in both cases, Bely lost interest in his idea immediately after he had finished the only part that mattered to him: the son's crime against the father.

It was only in *Petersburg*, the earliest of the novels in this "oedipal" series, that the theme of the 1905 Revolution actually interested Bely. According to the writer himself, however, the idea of linking the private with the political in *Petersburg* first came about because the motifs of incitement and provocation, familiar to Bely from his childhood, resonated with the political events of the era. With his unfailing predilection for sketches, he depicted *Petersburg*'s structure as two circles of equal size, describing the private and the political, respectively. The distance separating the centers of the two circles was rather insignificant (much shorter than their radii), and so most of their area was shared; this shared area represented the theme of provocation, which united the two halves of this construction and occupied the most central place within it.

Petersburg was conceived in precisely those years when the police department's instigative activities were first coming to light and becoming the object of general unease and revulsion.[22] In Bely's case, such feelings were mixed with, and even dominated by, horror of an entirely mystical character. The police would provoke a criminal, then track him and punish him for the fruits of their own provocations: in other words, they acted in exactly the same fashion as the dark forces that Bely had projected his patricidal thoughts onto. The similarity of their methods led his mind—or, more accurately, his feelings—to seek a single source for both. In his eyes, political provocation took on characteristics that were demonic in the most literal sense of the word. He imagined supernatural provocateurs lurking behind every member of the police force, from the department head to the custodian. His narrow-minded fear of policemen, which had been instilled in him as a child, gradually grew to monstrous forms and proportions. Policemen of all kinds, all descriptions, and all nations plunged him into a maniacal horror.

In the grips of this horror, he would be reduced to terrible and at times pathetic escapades. One miserable, rainy spring evening, we were making our way back from Gorky's to our hotel in the deserted German town of Bad Saarow. I was lighting our way with a flashlight. Saarow's only night watchman, an elderly veteran worn down by darkness, rain, and boredom, was shuffling along the road at a distance of ten paces or so behind us—the light must have attracted him, like a moth. Suddenly, Bely caught sight of him: "Who's that?"

"The night watchman."

"Oho, so it's the police, then? Are we being followed?"

"Of course not, Boris Nikolaevich, he's just tired of walking around by himself."

Bely quickened his step—the watchman lagged behind. Unfortunately, having rushed to the hotel practically at a trot, we were forced to stand there ringing the doorbell for some time. Meanwhile, the watchman drew closer. He stopped at some distance away from us in his rubber raincoat with its sharply pointed cowl. Finally, he took several steps toward us and asked what was the matter. Instead of answering, Bely fell to banging his staff against the door with all his might. They let us in. Bely stood in the lobby, drenched in sweat and breathing shallowly.

■ □ ■

He lived through War Communism the way all of us did, in sickness and in want. He took shelter in the apartment of acquaintances, feeding the tiny stove with his manuscripts, going hungry, and standing in lines. He traveled the length and breadth of Moscow to feed himself and his mother, who was by that time ailing and old. He gave lectures at the Proletkult and in various other locations, sat for days on end in the Rumyantsev Museum, his ink freezing over, fulfilling some pointless commission from the Theatrical Department (something about theaters during the era of the French Revolution) and filling up heaps of paper, which he would eventually misplace. At the same time, he was teaching classes at the Anthroposophical Society and writing *Notes of an Eccentric*, a book on the philosophy of culture, a book about Lev Tolstoy, and some other texts besides.[23]

I began living in Petersburg at the end of 1920. In the spring of 1921, he moved there, too—it was easier for writers there. He was given a room in a hotel on Gogol Street, practically across the road from where Vienna used to be (that was the restaurant where we had had lunch with Nina Petrovskaya nearly fourteen years prior). He distanced himself from poetic Petersburg, taking long trips to visit Ivanov-Razumnik in Tsarskoe Selo. We began to see each other and take walks again, this time along Saint Petersburg's embankments. During White Nights, in the indescribably beautiful Petersburg of that time, we would make quiet pilgrimages to the Bronze Horseman. Once, I took Bely to the house where Pushkin died.[24]

On one occasion, he burst into my home, more cheerful and radiant than I had seen him in some time. He had brought me his long poem, *The First Meeting*: it was the best thing he had ever written in verse. I was the first person to hear this poem: may I be forgiven for this prideful recollection. May I be forgiven for another one as well: around that same time, he also wrote his first article about me. It was for the fifth and final issue of *Dreamers' Notes*, which would be edited by Blok, but published only after his death.[25]

Bely had long dreamed of going abroad. He said that he wanted a rest, but he had other reasons, too, reasons he did not share with me at the time and that I could only guess at. The Bolsheviks wouldn't allow him to go. He became so anxious that he was obliged to see a doctor. He considered making a break for it—nothing came of that, either, and, in fact, nothing could have come of it: he had "confided" in all of Petersburg that he was planning to run. People started asking him: will you be making a run for it soon? Naturally, this led him

to believe that he was being watched by the Cheka,[26] which, naturally, reduced him to fits of wild terror. Finally, after Blok's death and
Gumilyov's execution, the Bolsheviks felt ashamed enough to issue
him a passport.

■ □ ■

At the beginning of 1919, he received word that, from then on, his
personal ties with several dear friends residing in Dornach[27] were
to be severed.

He had been anticipating this particular blow, but, nevertheless, he felt a desire to have it out with them, to clarify something
about their relations. And this is what finally pushed him to venture
abroad.

The second aim of his trip, also related to Dornach, was more
important. One must bear in mind that Bely colossally overesti-
mated the weight and meaning of anthroposophy.[28] He believed
that the anthroposophists in general, and Rudolf Steiner in particular, possessed some influence in the world. And so he raced to tell
his brother anthroposophists and their chief ("on whose shoulder
he had once reclined") about the difficult spiritual birth pangs that
Russia was experiencing and the sufferings of its many millions
of people. He considered it his mission to open their eyes to the
situation that was unfolding in Russia, and he considered himself
Russia's ambassador to anthroposophy (those were his words). As
I mentioned before, this mission might not, in itself, seem particularly worthwhile. But Bely felt differently, and the subject at hand is
his psyche.

So what happened? As far as his personal affairs were concerned,
people were distinctly uninterested in "having it out with him":
in fact, they demonstrated their contempt for him in ways that
were provocative, public, and unbearably insulting. The status of

his "embassy" proved to be even worse. As it turned out, neither Dr. Steiner nor his entourage had any intention whatsoever of getting involved with anything as transient and trivial as Russia. Perhaps Steiner had other reasons as well: he might have (rightly) anticipated that Bely did not in the least equate Russia with the Bolsheviks, while, in the meantime, the Treaty of Rapallo[29] was just around the corner. . . . In any case, Dornach decided to ignore Bely's mission, and Steiner himself was clearly avoiding him (for which, again, there might have been reasons beyond the political). Finally, at a gathering in Berlin, Bely managed to catch sight of Steiner. He rushed up to him—and was greeted with a pointedly conventional question uttered in a tone of fatherly condescension: "*Na, wie geht's?*"[30]

Bely realized that there was no point in talking to him, and answered with contemptuous rage: "*Schwierigkeiten mit dem Wohnungsamt!*"[31]

Perhaps it was that very day he took to drink.

He was living in Zossen, a town near Berlin, not far from a graveyard, in the home of some sort of coffin-maker.* We saw each other in the summer of 1922, when I had just arrived from Russia. By that time, his hair was entirely gray. His eyes had faded even further: they were now nearly white.

He moved to the city that autumn—and all of Russian Berlin bore cruel and curious witness to his hysteria. They saw it, they delighted in it, and far too many of them mocked him for it. I will describe this hysteria in a few brief words. It manifested itself primarily in the drunken dances he gave himself over to on various Berlin *Dielen*.[32] It wasn't that his dancing was bad; it was that he was terrifying when he did it. He brought his own "variations" to the monotonous

---

* To read more about his life in Zossen, see Marina Tsvetaeva's remarkable reminiscences, which were published in *Contemporary Annals*, 1934, issue 55. I published three of his letters in the same issue.

crush of foxtrots: it was a funhouse mirror image of the unswerving originality he displayed in everything else he set his hand to. When he danced, his performances would turn into monstrous mimed dramas—sometimes even obscene ones. He would ask ladies he did not know to dance. The bolder women would accept him to amuse themselves and their companions. Others would decline—in Berlin, this was almost an insult. Still others were forbidden by their husbands and fathers. Bely's performances were not just the stumblings of some drunk: they were, in the end, a symbolic violation of that which was best in himself; they were a blasphemy against himself, a diabolical grimace he made at himself for the sake of making one at Dornach. Dornach never left his mind. His thoughts would return to Steiner on all manner of occasions. Once, we were riding together in the *Untergrund*, where he was inadvertently conducting himself entirely à la Prutkov: whispering the Russian words, which were incomprehensible to the people around us, into my ear and shouting out the German ones for the whole wagon to hear. He told me, "I just feel like going to Dornach and shouting at Dr. Steiner like a street urchin: '*Herr Doktor, Sie sind ein alter Affe!*' "[33]

It was as if he were purposefully trying to stoop ever lower. Who knows, maybe he was hoping that someone would hear him and respond. . . . But Dornach did not descend from its heights and Bely continued living on tenterhooks. He "shouted his troubles out the window"[34]—at times in poor poetry (which nevertheless displayed rare flashes of genius), at times through his innumerable confessions. He made these confessions, positively spilling his guts, to anyone who would listen, at times to near or even complete strangers: his companions at the table d'hôte, the people he met out late at night, well-beseen boardinghouse maids, and even foreign journalists. He half fell in love with a certain Mariechen,[35] a sickly, timid girl, the daughter of the proprietor of a modest bar. She would look embarrassed nearly to the point of tears when Herr Professor would dance his furious dances with her, crushing her fingers in his own great paws. Meanwhile, in between dances, knocking back glass after glass, he would tell her, snarling, hissing, and squealing, the same old tangled-up story, which she could make neither heads nor tails of. It is remarkable that so many people would listen to him, spellbound, sensing that the tipsy Herr Professor was no ordinary man, even though they didn't understand a word of what he said. Returning home, he would strip naked and dance again, dance away his misfortune. This kind of behavior went on for months. It sometimes seemed a pity that he enjoyed such inexhaustible good health: it would have been better for him to have taken ill and dropped out of sight.

He was protected, he was cared for: some helped him out of curiosity, others out of a feeling of genuine love. I would like to mention by name two of the people who watched over him so selflessly and lovingly: S. G. Kaplun (Sumsky), his then-publisher, and the poetess Vera Lourié. Unfortunately, he was more strong-willed and stubborn than all of his guardians put together.

We would see each other almost every day, sometimes from morning until late into the night. In the autumn, Nina Petrovskaya arrived in Berlin, half-mad and wretched, old, emaciated, and lame. On November 8, on the eve of the eleventh anniversary of her departure from Russia, they met in my home, departed together, and then whiled away the evening together. Both of them complained about it afterward. There had been no desperate scenes. Instead, what had happened was the bitterest thing imaginable: they had simply been bored in each other's company. This was the last earthly meeting Renate and the Fiery Angel were to have. They would never meet again.

In the middle of November, I took up residence in a place two hours' drive from Berlin.[36] Bely would come to visit for three or four days at a time, and sometimes for a whole week. He worked as if by some sort of miracle: his very capacity for work was miraculous. Sometimes he would write nearly a quire's worth in a single day.

He would bring his manuscripts along with him, write during the day, and read to us what he had written in the evening. These were his recollections of Blok, which had ballooned into recollections of the Symbolist era as a whole. We brainstormed titles for these texts together. Finally, we settled on one suggested by N. N. Berberova: *The Beginning of the Century*.

Sometimes his work would be interrupted: he would drink and then start making his erratic confessions. I will, for the most part, refrain from referring to these confessions in this article because Bely mixed truth with imagination in such moments. It was so exhausting to listen to him in these situations that I often didn't understand what he was talking about and would only pretend to be listening. Then again, he himself didn't seem to take much notice of his interlocutor. His confessions were, to all intents and purposes, monologues. It is also important to note that, sometimes, when he had finished telling a story, he would immediately forget that he had done so and would launch into telling it all over again. One night, he repeated the same story to me five times. After the fifth telling (each repetition of which had lasted about forty minutes), I went into my room and passed out. While I was being revived, Bely was there, too, banging on the door: "Let me in, I want to tell you . . ."

Still, I did learn one thing from all of his hysterics in those days: that his new pain, the one he was experiencing at that time, had woken up his old pain, and his old pain turned out to be even more painful than the new one was. An idea occurred to me then that, later, taking into account a number of different factors, turned out to be correct: everything that occurred in Bely's love life after 1906 was simply an attempt to heal the wound he had incurred in Petersburg.

Nevertheless, as spring approached, he began to tire. Smiling bitterly, he would say, "I need to get married, or else who's going to put me to bed when I'm drunk?" K. N. Vasilyeva, an anthroposophist, came from Moscow to ask him to return to Russia with her, to devote himself to the anthroposophical movement there. Bely, closing the door against her, hissed, "She's trying to get me to marry her."

"Don't you want to get married?"

"Not to her!" he wheezed furiously, "the hell with that! The anthroposophy lady!"

He still wouldn't leave; it was as if he wanted to drain his cup to the very dregs. Toward the autumn of 1923, it seems, he did drain it—and, at the very last moment before madness would have set in, he decided to leave. First and foremost, of course, so that he would have someone to take care of him, to "put him to bed" when he was drunk. Secondly, because he realized that he did not and would never have an audience in emigration, while in Russia he still did. He went back to the anthroposophists, to the youths who had given him such an affectionate send-off when he left the country two years prior. In those days, after a lecture, the audience had shouted out to him, "Remember that we love you here!"

■ □ ■

It is an undeniable fact that he cannot be held completely responsible for his behavior in the time leading up to his departure. But, as is often true in such cases, there was an element of cunning in his near-madness. Fearing that his proximity to emigrants and semi-emigrants (many people found themselves in this position at that time) might make him seem suspicious, he began severing his ties with individuals living abroad. He slammed the door on a girl to whom he owed a great deal. He slandered his publisher in an entirely senseless manner. In short—he sought out quarrels and he knew how to find them. Unfortunately, his last one was with me. I will only touch upon this incident, omitting several curious but overly complicated details.

In order to obtain a visa, he was obliged to make several trips to the Soviet authorities in Berlin. There, he abused his foreign friends so roundly that even the Communists were put off by it. One of them, a certain G., informed M. O. Gershenzon, who was abroad taking a medical cure. Gershenzon also happened to be trying to return to Russia at the time, and was also going to great lengths to secure a visa. Gershenzon, who loved Bely dearly, was extremely depressed by the information he received from G. And it was impossible not to believe it, seeing as he repeated word-for-word several phrases that we had also heard from Bely's own lips. Gershenzon left the country long before Bely did, but, in the days leading up to his departure, he couldn't hold back any longer: he told me everything. Knowing Boris Nikolaevich's current state of mind, I decided to bite the bullet and keep my mouth shut. In the end, though, I did not withstand this trial.

In those days, Russian writers were leaving Berlin left and right. Some were planning to go to Paris, while others (including myself) were headed to Italy. Approximately a week and a half before Bely's departure, we decided to organize a general farewell party. At the dinner, a certain lady who knew Bely well suddenly said, "Boris Nikolaevich, don't abuse us too badly when you arrive in Moscow."[37] In response, Bely gave a speech in which he literally declared that he would be our friend and intercessor in Moscow and that he was ready to "go to the cross" for us. I believe that, in the moment, he almost believed this himself. Nevertheless, I snapped, replying that we had no right to send him to the cross; that we could not give him such a "mandate." Bely flew into a rage and declared that, from that day on, he would be ceasing all relations with me. As it turned out, "all his life" I had been poisoning his finest moments with my skepticism, thwarting his noblest acts. Of course, these were all empty words. In fact, he had lost his temper because he had guessed my true thoughts. He knew that I knew that he would not "intercede" on our behalf. On the contrary . . .

To all intents and purposes, he was in the wrong—even extravagantly so. But I was no less guilty: I had taken it into my head to demand that he be held responsible for his words and actions when this was already beyond him. Truly, my actions were motivated by my great love for him: I didn't wish to insult him with my condescension. But it would have been better for me to understand that I needed only to love him—in spite of everything, above it all. I only came to this realization when it was already too late.

I don't know much about how he lived in Soviet Russia. He did end up marrying K. N. Vasilyeva, and he did busy himself with anthroposophical work for some time. He made his peace with Bryusov in the summer of 1923, in Crimea, where he was staying with Maximilian Voloshin.[38] He was rarely printed in Soviet publications. He devoted a great deal of time to writing his autobiography.

The story behind that work is a singular one. Even before Bely went abroad, he gave a lecture in Petersburg—his recollections of Blok. He reworked these recollections twice after that, expanding them considerably each time. The second of these adaptations, which was published in the Berlin journal *Épopée*,[39] inspired him to transform his memoirs about Blok into memoirs encompassing the entire Symbolist era. He only managed to complete the first volume while he was living in Berlin. The manuscript of this work remained abroad and was not published. In Russia, Bely set about writing a fourth edition of his work. This time, he began with an even earlier era, with the story of his days as a child and as a young man. This volume was released under the title *On the Border of Two Centuries*. The first volume of his literary memoirs followed closely on its heels and was called *The Beginning of the Century*. At this point, Bely underwent a psychological shift of the kind that was characteristic of him. Already in Berlin he had complained that the work emerging from his memoirs of Blok had taken on an overly apologetic tone: Blok was being whitewashed, "scrubbed clean like a samovar."

In Moscow, Bely resolved to remedy this shortcoming. However, at around the same time, some of Blok's letters were published, and they became a source of great unpleasantness for Bely. He had a breakdown: rather than writing an apologia for Blok, he set about making a mockery of his memory.

He did, however, manage to write yet another volume, *Between Two Revolutions*, which appeared only toward the end of 1937,[40] which is to say, nearly three years after his death. In this book, which left a permanent stain on Blok's reputation, Bely dealt even more mercilessly with nearly all of his other lifelong companions. It is possible that he was somehow extrapolating from the position that, if Blok was to be presented in such a negative light, then everyone else was all the more deserving of such treatment. But, knowing Bely as intimately as I did, I am certain that there was another idiosyncratic motive at work.

With his involvement in religion, mysticism, and anthroposophy, it stands to reason that he should appear guilty in the eyes of the people who surrounded him, the people on whom he was, in all senses of the word, dependent. In his autobiography, these themes needed to be either obscured or presented in a different light. Already in the previous volume, Bely had obviously been groping around for some sort of conceptual spin, the kind that would allow him to present his spiritual journey as the search for a revolutionary worldview. Now, when he talked about the era "between two revolutions," he began painting himself as a stubborn, conscientious, dyed-in-the-wool rebel, and not just any rebel, but a Marxist (or near-Marxist), a zealous champion fighting against the "hydra of capitalism." He did this not only for the Bolsheviks' sake, but also for his own (this, of course, was extremely typical of him). At the same time, however, the objective and widely known facts of his personal and literary biography did not align with such notions. Any Bolshevik could reproach him for not having served as an active revolutionary and claim this as his cardinal sin against the proletariat. And just as he had fobbed off his hidden guilt about his father onto the mysterious demonic provocateurs of his autobiographical novels, he now took to portraying his entire life as an endless battle with the people around him, as if they had been the ones seducing him away from the revolutionary path. The closer a person had been to him, the more essential it was to depict that person as a secret agent, a traitor, a provocateur, a mercenary, and an agent of capitalism. He only spared a few individuals who were still living in Soviet Russia. Had they been living abroad, they would not have been so lucky. And, just as he had demonized and caricatured the characters surrounding the heroes of his novels, he now caricatured his former friends, presenting them in diabolic guises. Here, too, his remarkable gifts shone through: everyone came out looking very like themselves, but even more like characters from *Petersburg* or *Moscow Under Fire*. I don't doubt that Bely worked with a true artistic ardor—and that, in some corner of his soul, he himself believed in the words issuing forth from his pen. However, if the Bolsheviks had possessed a higher degree of artistic sensibility, they would have been able to tell him that, insofar as his autobiography consisted of unreal characters acting against an unreal backdrop, it was just as much of a fantasy as his quasi-historical novels had been. What's more, they might have told him that he had definitively outed himself as an incorrigible mystic: he had not only concocted lies, distorted truths, and turned facts inside out together with his characters, but, in general, he had presented his entire life as an otherworldly battle against demons rather than a real-life struggle with capitalist stooges. Bely's autobiography is just as much a "series of fictional events" as his autobiographical novels are.*

---

* To learn more about Bely's memoirs, see my articles in the newspaper *Renaissance* from June 28 and July 5, 1934 and May 27, 1938.

I do not wish to suggest that the idea of revolution was entirely alien to Bely. But, like Blok and Esenin, he understood revolution differently than the Bolsheviks did and embraced it in a way that did not involve Bolshevism. However, this is a particular and complicated topic, and not one that is appropriate for memoir.

He died, as is well known, on January 8, 1934, as a consequence of sunstroke. And that is why, before his death, he asked to hear a poem that he had written long ago:

> He trusted in the golden brilliance,
> But perished in the sunlight's rays.
> He measured eras in ideas,
> But couldn't live out all his days.[41]

As he listened to these prescient verses for the final time, he probably didn't remember that they had, at one time, been dedicated to Nina Petrovskaya.

Paris, 1934–1938

MUNI

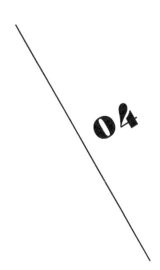

I WAS HERE, AFTER ALL

Samuil Viktorovich Kissin, whom I'd like to talk about now, did not, to all intents and purposes, accomplish anything in literature. But it is necessary and worthwhile to discuss him because, although he was a man "in a league of his own," his essence reflected something deeply characteristic of the age during which his short life took place. All of literary Moscow at the end of the 1900s and the beginning of the 1910s knew him. He didn't play a conspicuous role there; rather, he was one of the people who made up the "background" to the day's events. However, his personal qualities guaranteed that he wouldn't be "just one of the crowd"—far from it. He was too complicated and too original to fit into any "type." He was a symptom, not a stereotype.

We first met at the end of 1905. At the time, Samuil Viktorovich was living in Moscow as a "poor student" on the twenty-five rubles a month that his relatives in Rybinsk would send him. He wrote poems and had them printed in an insignificant little journal called *Daybreak*[1] under the pseudonym Muni. And he would be known as Muni to all of Moscow until the end of his days (though toward the end he did begin signing his works S. Kissin). And Muni is how I shall refer to him here.

At first, we took a strong dislike to each other, but then, beginning in the autumn of 1906, we somehow suddenly "discovered" each other and became fast friends. After that, for the nine years leading up to Muni's death, we lived in such a state of steadfast brotherhood, in such intimate love, that now, looking back on that time, it seems like a miracle to me.

On the surface, Muni's life story seems quite simple. He was born in October of 1885 to a Jewish family of modest fortune in Rybinsk. Upon graduating from the Rybinsk gymnasium, he enrolled in the law faculty of Moscow University. In the summer of 1909, he married Lidia Yakovlevna Bryusova, the poet's sister. He was mobilized in the very first days of the war and made a noncommissioned officer, and he passed away in Minsk on March 28, 1916.[2] The trace he left on life, like the one he left on literature, was not deep. But, shortly before his death, with the sense of irony that rarely left him, he said to me, "Mark down that I was here, after all."

THE OMENS ARE EMPTYING OUT

We muddled through the years that came after 1905, years of spiritual exhaustion and mass aestheticism. In literature, the modernist school unexpectedly gained recognition from the public for precisely those qualities that were trivial or even bad about it; countless low-grade imitations followed along in its wake. In society circles, frail, barefooted maidens were resurrecting Hellenism. The bourgeoisie, suddenly feeling the urge "to dare," plunged itself into the gender question. Somewhere further down the ladder, the Saninists and candle-end clubs were fruitful and multiplied. Decadent homes lined the streets. And over all this, electricity was imperceptibly gathering. The storm broke in 1914.[3]

Muni and I were living in a complex and difficult world, one that is no longer easy for me to describe in the way we understood it then. It was hard to breathe in the hot, pre-storm air of those years. Everything appeared ambiguous and equivocal; the outlines of objects seemed unsteady. Reality, bleeding over into consciousness, became permeable. We were living in the real world—and, at the same time, in some special, hazy, and complex reflection of it, where everything was "the same, but different." It was as if every object, every step, and every gesture were being tentatively reflected, projected onto an alternative surface, onto a screen that was close, but untouchable. Everyday happenings were transformed into visions. In addition to its obvious, primary meaning, each event took on a secondary meaning that had to be deciphered. This meaning wouldn't yield itself to us without a fight, but we knew that it was the true one.

And so we lived in two worlds at once. But, as we didn't know how to uncover the laws governing the events taking place within that second world (which seemed much more real to us than the real one was), we could only wallow in our dark and troubled premonitions. We perceived everything that happened then as an omen. But of what?

Like many others in those days, we believed that, before long, "certain events must come to pass." But unlike most others, our premonitions came in rather gloomy tones. We didn't have a clear picture of exactly what we thought was going to happen. We tried not to discuss it with outsiders. But the remarks that did manage to slip through the cracks were not pleasant. People disliked us for our "skepticism" and "cawing." Muni wrote to me on precisely this topic in a verse letter in 1909:

Russia won't be saved with verse,
And might not manage the reverse.

We were only inexperienced boys, just twenty years old, or twenty and a bit. We had accidentally scooped up a ladleful of the otherworldly element a certain poet once described. But there were others, too, individuals more experienced and responsible than we, who were stumbling around in that very same darkness. We, as the insignificant apprentices of bad sorcerers (and sometimes downright charlatans), had learned how to conjure up petty and disobedient spirits that we didn't know how to control. And this upset us. We got lost in the "forest of symbols," we tottered on the "seesaw of correspondences." Symbolism became more than just a method to us; it simply became a way of life, though it itself was far from simple. This Symbolist way of life that we created for ourselves would sometimes play nasty tricks on us. Here are a few examples.[4]

Once, Muni and I were sitting in the Prague Restaurant,[5] the main hall of which was divided by a broad archway. Curtains hung along either side of the arch. At one end, a waiter in a white shirt and white trousers was standing with his back to us, gripping the lintel with his right hand and tucking his left hand behind his waist. A little while later, another waiter of similar height appeared from behind the arch and stood facing both us and the first waiter. He had accidentally duplicated the first waiter's pose exactly, only in reverse: this waiter was gripping the lintel with his left hand while holding his right hand tucked behind his waist, and so forth. It was as if it were one person standing in front of a mirror. Muni said with an ironic smile, "And here's his reflection now."

We began to observe them. The waiter standing with his back to us dropped his right hand. At the very same moment, the other waiter dropped his left. The first one made some other movement— and again, the second one mirrored him exactly. This went on and on. It became uncanny. Muni watched in silence, tapping his foot. Suddenly, the second waiter made a quick about-face and disappeared behind the projecting portion of the arch. Someone must have called for him. Muni jumped to his feet, white as chalk. Then he recovered himself and said, "If our waiter had left and the reflection had remained, I wouldn't have been able to bear it. Just feel what my heart is doing."

Another time, we were walking along Tverskaya Street. Muni was saying that there were moments in which he was able to predict the future with complete accuracy. But this talent only applied to trivial events.

"Right, so, over there! See that carriage? Its back axle is about to break."

We were overtaken by an old carriage drawn by a pair of sorry-looking nags. A little old gray-haired man was sitting in it, accompanied by a little old lady to match.

"Well?" I said. "It doesn't seem to be breaking."

The carriage rolled on for ten or so more *sazhens*:[6] it was already starting to be obscured by other vehicles. Suddenly, all at once, it stopped in the middle of the pavement across the street from Yeliseyev's store. We ran up to it. The back axle had split down the middle. The old folks clambered out. They had escaped with only a fright. Muni wanted to go up to them and beg their forgiveness. It was only with great difficulty that I was able to dissuade him.

On the very same day, late in the evening, we were walking along Neglinny Drive. We were with V. F. Akhramovich, who went on to become a zealous Communist. At the time, he was a zealous Catholic. I was telling him about the incident that had occurred earlier that day. Akhramovich asked Muni jokingly, "Couldn't put in an order for something like that, could I?"

"Give it a try."

"Well then, could we run into Antik?" (V. M. Antik published the yellow booklets for Universal Library. All three of us had worked on them.)

"Sure, why not?" Muni said.

We were nearing the intersection where the Petrovsky Lines converge. A coachman pulled out right in front of us, heading our way. As he drew even with us, a gray-haired man tipped his hat and bowed. It was Antik.

Muni said to Akhramovich reproachfully, "Oh, you! Couldn't have wished for the Messiah, could you?"

This style of life was exhausting. Muni used to say that it was all degenerating into filth and neurasthenia, like a spiritual runny nose. And from time to time he would announce, "The omens are emptying out."

He donned his blue glasses "so as not to see more than was necessary" and carried around a spoon and a big bottle of bromine with ever-changing contents . . .

FROM THE UNFINISHED WORKS (*D'INACHEVÉ*)

Muni wasn't lazy. But he didn't know how to work. A man of remarkable talents and at times extraordinary intuition, he also commanded an enormous body of knowledge. But he could not concentrate, could not keep himself on track. Work of any description was bound to frighten him off before long: insurmountable difficulties and complications would inevitably arise. Regardless of the matter at hand, an image of unachievable perfection would loom up over Muni—and he would throw up his hands in defeat. It seemed as though, no matter what he set his hand to, everything should have been started when he was practically in diapers, and so the time for it had already passed.

He wrote poetry, short stories, and dramatic works. To all practical purposes, he never saw anything through: either he would simply stop working on a text or, having written something, would fail to polish it. Everything he wrote was worse than what he was capable of writing. Needless to say, he was always full of projects, ideas, and plans. He would poke fun at himself, saying that he, like Kozma Prutkov, kept his major works in a leather briefcase marked "From the unfinished works (*d'inachevé*)."

He was infinitely severe in his literary reviews and almost openly despised anything that wasn't a work of utter genius. His views were uncompromising, but he also had the misfortune of being entirely honest, at least as far as literature was concerned. Kind and soft-hearted by nature, he would attempt to conceal his opinions entirely, but, if the occasion called for it, he would present them in all their unvarnished glory. He made an unpleasant and inconvenient addition to the literary world. At friendly private readings, where one wishes to hear nothing but compliments (either honest or otherwise), he would occasionally contrive to spoil the entire evening, which had started out so nicely. Everyone, from literary novices to celebrated men, feared and disliked him, and so great pains were taken not to invite him anywhere. Apparently, apart from me, only B. K. Zaitsev and the late S. S. Goloushev (Sergei Glagol) were able to approach him with love in their hearts. And he needed that greatly.

The more favorably disposed he was toward a person, the more pitilessly he would act in relation to him—and this was especially true in my case. I went to him with all of my new poetry. After listening, he would say, "Give them here, I'll look them over. The voice allows you to gloss things over, tart things up."

In the best cases, having read them, he would declare that "they weren't all that bad." But, far more often, he would pull a bored, weary face and moan: "Lord, what drivel!" Or, "What have I ever done to you? Why would you read me something like that?"

And then he would start in on his analysis, which would be detailed, extensive, and decimating. If I remained too unyielding in the defense of my own work, Muni would eventually say, "Fine, have it your way. Publish it and sign it Nikolai Poyarkov." (Poyarkov, it must be said, was a deeply untalented poet. He was wretched, pathetic. He is no longer with us today.)

I must admit that I felt more or less the same about his writing. And we each felt that way about our own writing, too. Year in and year out, we would dig into each other and ourselves with all our might. Truly, no one could say that we flattered each other. True to our own consciences, we preferred "biting judgments" to "intoxicating praise."[7] It was only after the war began, when Muni had already left, that I gradually began to liberate myself from his tyranny. I knew that, no matter how constructive Muni's severity had been for my work, nevertheless, it would end up by suffocating me. When he would occasionally come back on leave, Muni would notice this change and become visibly angry, as if jealous of someone or something. Toward the end of his final visit to Moscow, immediately before his departure, I was slated to read my poetry at an evening gathering at the Polytechnic Museum. Muni had said that he would come to hear me read, but, an hour before the gathering was scheduled to begin, he telephoned me.

"No, I'm sorry, I won't be there."

"Why?"

"I just don't see the point in it. It's all superfluous. Take care."

And he hung up. That was our final conversation. The next day he left without saying goodbye, and, two days later, he was no more.

SMOKE'S SHADOW

In earlier years, we had been practically inseparable. We spent all of our free time (and we had plenty of that) together, sometimes at Muni's place, more frequently at mine, but, more often than not, either out and about or in restaurants. Our endless discussions, which touched upon an endless number of topics, gave rise to our own peculiar language consisting of quotations, allusions, and terms that were established gradually over time. We could understand each other from the slightest allusions; other people couldn't understand us at all—and were offended by it. But at times it felt as though we had lost our ability to speak in a generally accepted language. I must admit that other people probably found our company rather insufferable.

Usually, our evenings would start out in a café on Tverskoy Boulevard and finish up nearby, in the International Restaurant on the corner of Malaya Bronnaya. We would sit in its large, misshapen hall until closing time, under the shelter of its dusty laurels, amidst the shorthaired public, listening to the sounds of the rowdy, hysterical orchestra, accompanied first by a decanter of vodka, and then by a quarter-liter bottle of Martell. Afterward, we would go out onto the streets and, no matter the weather (for what did we care about rain or snow?), we would roam the city, wandering through Petrovsky Park and the Zamoskvorechye District. We were like lovers who couldn't bear to part: we would walk each other home several times over, standing for hours on end under one streetlamp or another—only to set out on the same walk all over again. We kept the following agreement:

> Wherever you might chance to rush, /
> Romantic rendezvous included, /
> Whatever secret daydream's flush /
> Your heart might foster in seclusion[8]

The end of every evening, or at least the end of every night, must find the two of us together. We would plan our meetings for three, four, five in the morning. In spring and summer, when the weather wasn't cloudy, we would conduct our meetings "by the star": we would meet on Tverskoy Boulevard at daybreak, when the morning star was only just appearing over Strastnoy Monastery.

Muni saw everything that lay beyond the limits of our lives and their Symbolist practices as a tiresome succession of coarse and monotonous dreams. Because reality was merely a dream, it grew to be a burden. To him, life was a "light burden": in fact, he wanted to use this phrase as the title for a book of poetry that was never fated to appear. His family and certain close friends prepared this book for publication in 1917. During the years of revolution, it managed to get all the way to the typographer's twice, and once it was even set, but the finished product never saw the light of day.[9]

None of the projects Muni undertook ever amounted to anything, which caused him great pain. This is probably the reason why he set about his projects with a secret fear and loathing. He found anything that was "merely real" to be unbearable. He felt oppressed by everything that happened in life, as the "other end" would invariably come down to strike him.[10] All of life's phenomena eventually turned into what he liked to call "unpleasantnesses." His life was an unbroken chain of such unpleasantnesses. If he wanted to avoid them, he had to make contact with reality as infrequently as possible. There were times when, no matter what you might say to him, no matter what you might suggest, he would wince and answer: "Now what would you say that for?" He said that he considered "pouring water into the mill of reality" to be a terrible and repulsive thing. But he envied anyone capable of living a life free from such terror and revulsion. One autumn night, we were passing by Iverskaya Chapel, which was closed at the time. Cripples, invalids, beggars, paralytics, and hysterics were splayed across the steps, sitting, standing up, and lying down. Muni said, "They know what they want. But I—not my poetry, but I myself, the way that I am— should bear the following epigraph:

The rest are smoke, while I'm smoke's shadow
I envy those who live as smoke.[11]

The actual moment of his death passed unnoticed amidst the din of war. Even now, people sometimes ask me: "Where is Muni these days, anyway? Do you know anything about him?"

THE SEVEN-POOD[12] MERCHANT'S WIFE

Muni was composed of a broad skeleton with skin stretched tightly over it. But he dressed in baggy clothing, walked with a heavy tread, and disguised his sunken cheeks with a large beard. He had extravagantly long arms that he swung like a gorilla or a wrestler.

"You see," he would say, "I don't really exist, as you know. But other people can't know that, or else you can see for yourself what kinds of unpleasantness would ensue."

And he would always finish up by saying, "My dream is to be reincarnated—but irreversibly, for good—into some fat, seven-pood merchant's wife."[13]

In one of his short stories,[14] the luckless protagonist, Bolshakov, tormented by various passions and unpleasantnesses, decides to be "fully reincarnated" as the calm and carefree Pereyeslavtsev. Everything goes smoothly at first, but then he begins to rebel, and, finally, Pereyeslavtsev kills him.

After a difficult love affair in the early part of 1908, Muni took it into his head to be "fully reincarnated" as a certain Alexander Alexandrovich Beklemishev (the story about Bolshakov was written later and was actually based on his experience with Beklemishev). For approximately three months, Muni acted entirely unlike himself: he walked differently, talked differently, dressed differently; he changed his voice and even his thoughts. Muni kept the existence of Beklemishev a secret, but knew in his heart that, really, it was Muni who was no more. Beklemishev, on the other hand, did exist, and was only forced to bear the name Muni "for police and passport purposes."

Alexander Beklemishev turned his back on everything that was in any way connected with the memory of Muni; in this rejection, he saw his opportunity to go on living. To shore up the reality of his own existence, Beklemishev wrote poetry and stories; he sent them around to journals under the strictest secrecy. But the very same editors who had just printed something of Muni's would return the unknown Beklemishev's manuscripts without so much as reading them. Only Yu. I. Aikhenvald, who was the editor of *Russian Thought*'s literary section at the time, accepted several poems from the unknown writer.

Of course, Muni's double life didn't make things any easier for him; in fact, it made things exponentially more complicated. A host of entirely improbable situations arose. "Meanings" for us were no longer double, but quadruple, octuple, and so on. We were unable to see anyone or do anything. Hence our impecuniousness and our inaction. It would happen that, for a day, two days, and once even three days at a stretch, we would consume just a bottle of milk and a single bun between us. On top of all that, Muni was in the process of rebelling against Beklemishev: "getting out from under his skin," as we called it. The whole affair might have ended up the way things did for Bolshakov and Pereyeslavtsev. And so one day I put a rather rude end to it all. After leaving for the dacha, I wrote a poem and had it printed in a newspaper under the name of Elisa-veta Maksheyeva (a girl of that name had lived in Tambov in the eighteenth century; the only remarkable thing about her was that she had once participated in a production of one or another of Der-zhavin's plays). The poem was dedicated to Alexander Beklemishev and revealed his secret in a rather transparent and sarcastic manner. Afterward, this poem was included in my book *The Happy Little House*[15] under the title "To the Poet." Muni read it in the newspaper, but did not immediately guess the author. I came upon him in Moscow, sitting on a bench along the boulevard, looking bewildered and depressed. We cleared the air between us. At any rate, now that Beklemishev had been exposed and turned into a laughingstock, there was only one thing left for him to do: disappear. And that is how the whole affair came to an end. Muni "recovered himself," though not all at once. Unfortunately, the "Beklemishev incident" and his attempts to "be reincarnated as a seven-pood merchant's wife" resulted in other, more earthbound events, which I will not attempt to discuss here. However, we lived in such extreme intimacy and I had such a hand in all of Muni's mistakes that I cannot help blaming myself, at least in part, for his demise.

A BLACK MAN POSSESSED

Muni wrote two little "tragedies" with rather wild contents. One was called *A Black Man Possessed*.[16] The protagonist, a black man dressed in a starched shirt and suspenders, simply shows up in various Petersburg locales: on the Winter Canal, in a fashionable atelier, and in the window of a restaurant where a party of lawyers and ladies are dancing a cakewalk. Each time he appears, the black man beats a drum and, each time, he utters approximately one and the same phrase: "Things cannot go on like this. Rat-a-tat-tat. I am torn apart." And also: "There wi-ill be no-o mo-ore of thi-is."

In the final act, a cross section of a tram appears on stage. Humming and swaying, it appears to be moving away from the audience. The tram driver can be seen in the depths of the tram through the glass. It is late evening. The passengers are dozing, swaying back and forth. Suddenly, there is a crash and the wagon comes to a halt. There is a commotion backstage. Afterward, a stage technician comes out and says, "There has been an accident. In the play, the black man gets run over by a tram. But in our theater, the sets are constructed so conscientiously and realistically that our hero has actually been crushed. The performance is canceled. We will issue a refund to any audience members who feel dissatisfied."

In this "tragedy," Muni predicted his own fate. When the "events" he had been waiting for began to come to pass, he perished under their "overly realistic" scenery. The final and most crushing "unpleasantness" that the real world ever dealt him was the war. Muni was mobilized on the very day war was declared. I visited him the day before he was required to report to the barracks. As I was leaving, he escorted me out of the entryway and said, "It's all over. I won't come back from this war. Either I'll be killed or I simply won't be able to bear it."

It turned out that he, as a Jew, would not be made an ensign; rather, he was unexpectedly assigned to a desk job in a hospital office. He was sent in the exact opposite direction from the front, to Khabarovsk. From there, he was transferred to Warsaw, and, when Warsaw was taken over by the Germans, he was transferred again, this time to Minsk. But life in the infirmary proved just as challenging for him as life in the trenches would have been. He tried not to complain too much when he came back here on leave. But his letters "from the field" were full of despair. "Reality" had descended on him in its most terrible form. All of our attempts to liberate him, or at least to get him transferred to Moscow, were in vain. The authorities would say, "But he's in the rear. What more do you want?"— and, in their own way, they were right.

Toward the end, even his visits became difficult. As he was leaving Moscow for the last time, on March 25, 1916, he sent a postcard from the road asking to be informed of the outcome of one of my affairs. Not only did he not live to see my reply, but his own postcard arrived when he was already no longer among the living. At daybreak on March 28, upon his arrival in Minsk, Muni took his own life. He left behind the draft of a little ditty he had composed, probably while on the train. It is called "Automatic."[17]

Once, in the autumn of 1911, when I was going through a rough patch in my life, I stopped by my brother's place. There was no one at home. As I went to retrieve the little box that held his pens, I opened a desk drawer and the first thing that caught my eye was a revolver. The temptation was great. Without stepping away from the desk, I telephoned Muni, "Come here immediately. I'll wait twenty minutes, I can't wait any longer."

Muni came.

In one of the letters he sent me from the war, he wrote: "Far too often I feel the way that you did that time in Mikhail's empty apartment—do you remember?"

Naturally, he recalled that incident even as he was dying: "the things we shared" were not forgotten. Muni was visiting the home of one of his comrades, who was subsequently called away on some errand. Left on his own, Muni took a revolver out of someone else's desk drawer and shot himself through the right temple. Forty minutes later, he died.

Robinson, September 1926

GUMILYOV AND BLOK

Blok died on the seventh of August, 1921 and Gumilyov passed away on the twenty-seventh. But as far as I was concerned, they both died on August 3. Why? I shall explain below.

I dare say it would be difficult to imagine two people more different from each other than Blok and Gumilyov were. It seems that age was the only category in which they weren't so far apart: Blok was only six years older than Gumilyov was.

Though they belonged to the same literary epoch, they were from different poetic generations. Blok, who would periodically rebel against Symbolism, was, in fact, one of the purest Symbolists who ever wrote. Gumilyov, who remained under Briusov's influence until the end of his days, made himself out to be a staunch and profound enemy of Symbolism. Blok was a mystic, an admirer of the Beautiful Lady—but he wrote blasphemous poetry, and not just on that topic. Gumilyov never forgot to cross himself in front of any church, but I have rarely met an individual so unaware of what religion truly is. For Blok, poetry was the truest, most important spiritual achievement; it was inseparable from life itself. For Gumilyov, poetry was a form of literary activity. Blok was always a poet, every moment of his life. Gumilyov was only a poet while he was writing verses. All of these differences (along with many others besides) meant that they couldn't stand each other—and they didn't hide that fact. However, they often appear together in my memory. The final year of their lives, which was, in fact, the only year I knew them, ended in their near-simultaneous deaths. And there was something that connected these two men, both in their deaths and in the shockwaves that those deaths sent crashing through Petersburg.

Gumilyov and I were born in the same year and began publishing in the same year, but for a long time we didn't meet: I rarely visited Petersburg and he seems never to have gone to Moscow. We met in the autumn of 1918 in Petersburg, at a board meeting of World Literature. The solemnity with which Gumilyov "presided" over the meeting immediately reminded me of Bryusov.[1]

He invited me to his home and greeted me there as if the visit were the meeting of two monarchs. There was something so unnatural about his ceremonious courtesy that at first I wondered if he might be joking. However, I was obliged to adopt a similar tone: anything less would have smacked of familiarity. In starving, deserted Saint Petersburg, surrounded by the stench of roach-fish, we sat in the middle of his unheated, untidy study; both of us were hungry, even emaciated, dressed in threadbare jackets and half boots riddled with holes, but we conversed with extravagant solemnity. Recalling that I was a Muscovite, Gumilyov felt obliged to offer me tea, but he did so in such an uncertain voice (there probably wasn't any sugar) that I refused; I seemed to help him out of his difficulty by doing so. Meanwhile, my attention was increasingly drawn to the room's decoration. The writing desk, the triple bookcase, the tall pier glasses, the armchairs, and so on: it all seemed extremely familiar to me. Finally, I ventured to ask whether he had been living in the apartment long.

"Actually, this isn't my apartment," Gumilyov replied. "It's M's."[2] And, in that moment, I understood everything: Gumilyov and I were sitting in my old study! About ten years earlier, this furniture had partly belonged to me. It had its own life story. Admiral Fyodor Fyodorovich Matyushkin, a friend of Pushkin's from the lycée, had taken it off of some ship and used it to furnish the house on his lakeside estate near Bologoe. The estate was called "Hunters' Lodge." Of course, according to local legend, Pushkin had visited "Hunters' Lodge" more than once; the residents would show off an armchair upholstered in green morocco: "Pushkin's favorite armchair." As tends to be true in such cases, this was no more than a legend: Pushkin hadn't visited the area at all, and, besides, Matyushkin had purchased the estate some thirty-odd years after Pushkin's death. After Matyushkin's demise, "Hunters' Lodge" had passed from hand to hand and was rechristened "Lidino," but the old house's furnishings remained intact. Even the special adjustments that had been made to the sideboard in order to protect the dishes from the rolling of the ship hadn't been replaced with ordinary shelves. In 1905, I happened to become joint owner of this furniture and took it back to Moscow with me. Later on, it was fated to resurface in Saint Petersburg, and, now that the Revolution had uprooted decidedly everyone and everything from their original places, I found Gumilyov sitting in its midst. Its true owner was in Crimea.

Having sat under such strained circumstances for as long as good manners dictated, I finally rose. As Gumilyov was escorting me out, a pale, scrawny boy with a face as long as Gumilyov's own, dressed in a grimy Russian shirt and felt boots, jumped out through a side door and into the foyer.[3] He had a lancers' helmet on his head and was waving a little toy saber in the air, shouting something. Gumilyov sent him off immediately, in the tone of a king sending the dauphin off to his tutors. However, there was clearly no one in the damp and dank apartment apart from himself and his son.

Two years later, I moved to Petersburg. We began to see each other more frequently. There was a great deal that was good in Gumilyov. His taste in literature was excellent: somewhat superficial, but, in its own way, unerring. His approach to poetry was formal, but he was both sharp-sighted and subtle in his judgments. He was capable of penetrating the mechanics of verse as very few people can. I believe that his analyses were deeper and more sharp-sighted even than Bryusov's. He adored poetry and strove to be impartial in his judgments.

In spite of all this, his conversation, like his poetry, rarely felt "substantial." He was surprisingly young at heart, and perhaps he was young in mind as well. He always seemed like a child to me. There was something childlike in his buzz cut and in his bearing, which was more like a student's than a soldier's. This same childishness showed through in his infatuations with Africa and with war and, finally, in the kind of affected solemnity that had taken me so much by surprise upon our first meeting. This solemnity would suddenly fall away, fly off somewhere, until the moment would arrive when he suddenly thought the better of it and drew it over himself once more. He, like all children, enjoyed impersonating grown-ups. He loved playing "maestro" in the literary administration of his "gumilyovlets," which is to say, the little poets and poetesses who flocked around him. The kiddies loved him dearly. Sometimes, after giving a lecture on poetics, he would play blindman's bluff with them—in the literal rather than figurative sense. I saw this happen twice. In such moments, Gumilyov resembled a happy-go-lucky fifth-grader running wild with a gang of kindergarteners. It was funny to watch him playing at grown-ups half an hour later, conversing gravely with A. F. Koni—and to see how greatly Koni deferred to him in the solemnity of his address.

During the 1920 Christmas season, a ball was held at the Institute of Art History. I remember it well: the meager lighting and the frosty steam in the enormous, frozen halls of Count Zubov's mansion on Saint Isaac's Square. Damp logs smoking and smoldering in the fireplaces. All of literary and artistic Petersburg is there.

The music roars. People are moving around in the semidarkness, sticking close to the fireplaces. My God, how the crowd is dressed! Felt boots, sweaters, threadbare fur coats that they cannot part with, even in the ballroom. And then, after an appropriate delay, Gumilyov appears. On his arm is a lady shivering with cold, clad in a black dress with a plunging neckline.[4] Upright and arrogant in his tailcoat, Gumilyov makes the rounds of the rooms. He is shivering with cold, but bows courteously and majestically right and left. He is chatting urbanely with his acquaintances. He is playing at "ball." His entire appearance says, "Nothing has happened. Revolution? Never heard of it."

■ □ ■

Blok was avoiding people that winter. Naturally, he didn't attend this ball either. But another night sticks out in my memory. The House of Writers, one of the final havens for our people, came up with the idea of organizing annual, pan-Russian celebrations on the anniversary of Pushkin's death (later on, they would be moved to Pushkin's birthday; this is where the Days of Russian Culture celebrated in Russian émigré communities come from, too). The first gathering took place on the evening of February 11, 1921. A. F. Koni, N. A. Kotlyarevsky, Blok, and I had been invited to give speeches. Kuzmin was slated to read his poetry. I was ill and didn't have time to prepare a speech before the deadline; I declined the invitation to speak, but I did attend the gathering. Representatives from the House of Writers, N. M. Volkovysky, B. O. Khariton, and V. Ya. Iretsky, were seated onstage. Kotlyarevsky (the chairman) was sitting at the center of the head table; Akhmatova, Shchegolyov, and I were seated to his right, while Koni, Kuzmin, and Blok were on his left. Blok, who occupied the end of the table, sat with his head bowed low for the entire evening.

The speeches were preceded by a series of short announcements from various organizations detailing how they intended to celebrate Pushkin Days in the future. The delegates included an official representative of the government, a man called Kristi, who was in charge of the so-called Academic Center. Writers and academics were constantly obliged to have dealings with him. He was an elderly man, tenderhearted and good-natured. He became visibly embarrassed in the face of the unsympathetic gazes emanating from the packed hall. When it was his turn to speak, he stood up, turned red, and, being a quiet man by nature, immediately faltered: he lost track of his negative particles and ended up making the following pronouncement:

"Where the immortalization of Pushkin's memory is concerned, Russian society should not assume that it will not be met with impediments from the Workers' and Peasants' Government."

Ripples of laughter spread throughout the hall. Someone said loudly, "We don't assume any such thing." Blok lifted his head and shot Kristi a crooked grin.

Blok went on last with his inspired Pushkin speech. He wore a black jacket over a white turtleneck sweater. Wiry and desiccated, with his weather-beaten, reddish face, he looked like a fisherman. He spoke in clipped tones and in a slightly muffled voice; his hands were stuffed into his pockets. He would periodically turn his head in Kristi's direction and say distinctly: "Bureaucrats are the rabble, they were the rabble of yesterday and they are the rabble of today . . . May those bureaucrats who seek to turn poetry to their own ends, to encroach upon its secret freedom and to prevent it from fulfilling its inscrutable purpose, guard against this vilest of appellations . . ." Poor Kristi was noticeably suffering, squirming in his seat. Someone told me that, as he was putting his coat on in the foyer before he left, he said loudly, "I hadn't expected such tactlessness from Blok."

However, under the circumstances, and coming from Blok's lips, this speech had not sounded like tactlessness. Rather, it had been endowed with a deep sense of tragedy and perhaps even an element of repentance. The author of *The Twelve*[5] was entrusting Russian literature and Russian society with the preservation of Pushkin's final legacy: freedom, if only of a "secret" kind. As he spoke, you could feel the barrier between him and his audience gradually breaking down. In the ovations that accompanied him off the stage, there was a whiff of that peculiar brand of enlightened joy that attends a reconciliation with a loved one.

Gumilyov arrived in the middle of Blok's speech. He walked grandly down the aisle, across the entire length of the hall, arm in arm with the same lady who had accompanied him to the ball. This time, however, there was something unpleasant in his late arrival, in his tailcoat (perhaps in contrast with Blok's sweater), and in the low-cut dress of his companion. There was a place waiting for him on the stage.

He had already brought his foot up to the creaking stair, but Kotlyarevsky waved a hand at him sharply. Gumilyov sat down somewhere in the audience, and, several minutes later, he left.

There were three more gatherings of this kind. I finally finished writing my own speech (called "The Shaken Tripod") and began delivering it along with the rest. Backstage, Blok and I would chat as we waited for our turns. In fact, those evenings were the only opportunity we had to speak together more or less privately. At the final gathering, which took place at the university, we wound up sitting together at a cold, oilcloth-covered table in a deserted room for an hour and a half or so. We began by talking about Pushkin, then moved on to discussing early Symbolism. When Blok talked about that era, about its mystical obsessions, about Andrei Bely and S. M. Solovyov, he did so with a loving grin, the way people reminisce about their childhoods. Blok admitted that he no longer understood many of the poems he had written in those days: "I've forgotten what a number of words meant back then. And they seemed to be so sacred at the time. But when I read those poems now, it's as if they were written by someone else. What's more, I don't always understand exactly what the author was trying to say."

On that evening, the twenty-sixth of February, he was more melancholy than ever. He spoke about himself at great length. It was as if he were talking to himself; he became deeply introspective. He spoke very restrainedly, sometimes in allusions, sometimes vaguely and confusedly, but one could sense a stern, sharp honesty behind his words. It seemed as if he were seeing himself and the world around him with a tragic rawness and simplicity. And this honesty and simplicity forever remained connected in my mind with memories of Blok.

■ □ ■

Gumilyov was too great a connoisseur of poetic mastery to not appreciate Blok at all. But that didn't stop him from disliking Blok on a personal level. I don't know what their relationship had been like earlier, but when I arrived in Petersburg, I found only mutual hostility between them. I don't believe that the reasons behind this hostility were trivial ones, though Gumilyov, who placed a great deal of stock in knowing who stood where in the poetic hierarchy, might have been envious of Blok. There were probably more serious issues at work. Their worldviews were entirely at odds, their literary missions completely antithetical. The most important aspects of Blok's poetry, its "subtle engine" and its spiritual-religious meaning, must have been quite alien to Gumilyov. Gumilyov must have felt that Blok's poetry was a particularly clear example of those aspects of Symbolism that were hostile and not entirely comprehensible to him. It is no coincidence that the Acmeist manifesto was written primarily as a reaction to Blok and Bely. And Blok must have been annoyed by the "petty triviality," "irrelevance," and "superficiality" that he found in Gumilyov. Incidentally, if the problem had only been with Gumilyov's poetry, Blok probably could have hidden his distaste; in any case, he would have been able to view Gumilyov's poetry with greater tolerance. But there were two complicating factors at play. The student—Gumilyov—was being crushed under the hostility that had accumulated over the years against his teacher—Bryusov. This hostility was all the keener for having emerged from the ruins of an erstwhile love. Blok viewed Acmeism and everything that would later be referred to as "Gumilyovism" as a degraded version of "Bryusovism." Secondly, Gumilyov was not alone. His influence over the literary youth was growing year by year, and Blok believed that this influence was both spiritually and poetically pernicious.[6]

At the beginning of 1921, this hostility broke through to the surface. I will begin my story from a bit of a distance so that I can touch on several other points in the process of its telling. About four years before the war broke out, a poetic society called The Poets' Guild appeared in Petersburg. Blok, along with Sergei Gorodetsky, Georgy Chulkov, Yury Verkhovsky, Nikolai Klyuev, Gumilyov, and even Alexei Tolstoy, who was still writing poetry at the time, were all members. From the younger generation, there were O. Mandelshtam, Georgy Narbut, and Anna Akhmatova, who was married to Gumilyov at the time.[7] The group initially remained nonpartisan so far as literary matters were concerned. Later on, the Acmeists took control; members who were not sympathetic to Acmeism, including Blok, gradually broke away from the group. In the era of war and War Communism, Acmeism came to an end and the society died out. At the beginning of 1921, Gumilyov took it into his head to resurrect the organization and invited me to participate. I asked whether it would be like the first Guild—which is to say, its nonpartisan incarnation—or the second, Acmeist one. Gumilyov replied that it would be like the first, so I agreed. There happened to be a gathering scheduled for that very evening; it was to be the organization's second meeting. I was living in the House of Arts at the time; I was frequently ill and saw practically no one. Before the meeting, I dropped in on my neighbor, Mandelshtam, and asked him why he hadn't said anything to me about the Guild's revival. Mandelshtam burst out laughing: "Because there isn't any Guild! Blok, Sologub, and Akhmatova have refused to participate. Gumilyov just wants something to preside over. You know how he loves playing toy soldiers. And you fell for it. There's no one in it apart from the gumilyovlets."

"Beg your pardon, but if that's the case, what are you doing in such an organization?" I asked, vexed.

Mandelshtam pulled a very serious face: "I drink the tea and eat the sweets."

Apart from Gumilyov and Mandelshtam, there were five other people at the meeting. They read poetry and analyzed it. It seemed to me that the Guild was pointless, but also harmless. But an unpleasant surprise lay in store for me at the third meeting. A new member was to perform: Neldikhen, the young versifier. The neophyte read his verses, which were essentially prose poetry. In their own way, they could even be called ravishing: ravishing in the playful stupidity that they exuded from beginning to end. The "I" Neldikhen used to express himself with seemed the epitome of first-rate, utter stupidity, but nevertheless, he was a happy fool, triumphant and infinitely self-satisfied. Neldikhen recited:

Women, dolls two-and-a-half *arshins*[8] high,
Giggling, hillocky-bodied,
Soft-lipped, clear-eyed, chestnut-haired.
Clad in all variety of vests and lusterless pendants and earrings,
Enamored of my alto-voiced homilies, miserable housewives—

O, how such women thrill me!
Couples stroll down every street,
Everyone has mistresses and wives,
While I can't find a woman who will do:
I'm certainly not some freak,
When I gain a little weight, my face sometimes even looks a bit
like Byron's . . .[9]

What followed was the story of how some Zhenka or Sonka did turn up after all, how he gave her a flashlight as a gift, but she started deceiving him with an accountant and how, to get some of his own back, he stole the flashlight from her while she was out. All of this was recited in a singsong voice, in utter seriousness. The listeners smiled. The only reason they weren't falling off their chairs with laughter was because they already knew the story of the flashlight practically by heart: Neldikhen's outpourings had become infamous by this time. His reading at the Guild was a mere formality—Gumilyov was a great one for formalities. When Neldikhen had finished his reading, Gumilyov, in his capacity as "syndic," offered some words of welcome. First and foremost, he noted that, up until that point, stupidity had been given a bad reputation; poets had unfairly shunned it. The time had come for stupidity to have its own voice in literature. Stupidity is a natural quality, just like intelligence is. It can be developed, cultivated. Gumilyov invoked Balmont's couplet:

But vile is the idiot's appearance;
Stupidity I cannot comprehend,[10]

and declared it to be cruel. Finally, he welcomed the introduction of blatant stupidity into the Poets' Guild in the person of Neldikhen.

After the meeting, I asked Gumilyov whether it was such a good idea to mock Neldikhen and whether the Guild really needed him in the first place. To my surprise, Gumilyov declared that he hadn't been mocking him at all.

"It is not my job," he said, "to puzzle out what every poet thinks. I make my judgments based solely on the ways in which they develop their thoughts or their stupidity. I wouldn't care to be a fool myself, but I don't have any right to demand intelligence from Neldikhen. He expresses his stupidity with a talent that lies beyond the reach of many intelligent people. And, after all, poetry is a skill. Therefore, Neldikhen is a poet and it is my duty to admit him to the Guild."

Some time later, there was to be a public meeting of the Guild featuring Neldikhen. I sent Gumilyov a letter informing him of my withdrawal from the club. This was not, however, only on account of Neldikhen. I had another reason, too, a far weightier one.

Even before I had moved to Petersburg, a section of the Pan-Russian Poets' Union had formed there.[11] The Union's administration was based in Moscow and practically headed by Lunacharsky himself. I don't remember who constituted the administration, but Blok was chairman. One night, Mandelshtam came over to inform me that the "Blokian" Union administration had been toppled an hour earlier. It had been replaced by another administrative group consisting solely of Guild members—including me. Gumilyov had been appointed chairman. This coup had occurred in a rather strange manner: notices had been sent around barely an hour before the meeting was scheduled to take place and not everyone had received them. I didn't like any of this, and said that it had been pointless to elect me without consulting me about it first. Mandelshtam set about persuading me "not to kick up a fuss" so as to avoid insulting Gumilyov. From what he said, I gathered that certain members of the Guild had cooked up these "reelections" in order to take control of the Union's printing capacities, which they wanted to use in order to conduct affairs of a dishonest and commercial character. To achieve this end, they had sought protection in Gumilyov's name and position. They had tempted Gumilyov, like a child, with the title of chairman. In the end, I promised not to officially abandon the administration, but, in practice, I participated neither in the Union's meetings, nor in the running of its general affairs. This was the event that prompted me to leave the Guild.

Of course, Blok had not cared too much about his position as the Union chairman. But he was unhappy about the elections, which had clearly been rigged, and he was displeased that, from that time on, Gumilyov's literary influence would be shored up by pressure from the Union administration. And so Blok decided to bestir himself from his inactivity.

At just around that time, he had managed to obtain permission to publish a weekly periodical called *The Literary Gazette*. Its editors were to include A. N. Tikhonov, E. I. Zamyatin, and K. I. Chukovsky. For the first issue, Blok submitted an article directed against Gumilyov and the Guild. It was titled "Without divinity, without inspiration." *The Literary Gazette* perished before it was ever published: a short story of Zamyatin's and an editorial of mine caused the issue to be confiscated by order of Zinovyev while it was still at the printer's. I read Blok's article only many years later, in his collected works. I will admit, it felt rather torpid and hazy, like many of Blok's articles. But, at the time, there were rumors that it was quite cutting. Blok himself told me as much during one of our meetings. He expressed his annoyance at the fact that Gumilyov was making poets "out of thin air."

That was the final conversation that I had with Blok. But I saw him again from a distance. A performance of his poetry had been scheduled for the evening of March 1 at the Maly Theater.[12] In Soviet time, it was already nearly eight o'clock; in reality, it was only five.[13] I was strolling along Teatralnaya Street at a leisurely pace because I love that time of day. The streets were bright and deserted. When I reached

Chernyshev Square, I heard light, hurried steps coming up behind me, and, immediately afterward, a hasty but weak voice saying:

"Faster, faster, or you'll be late!"

It was Blok's mother.[14] Small and shriveled, with burning roses on her wrinkled little cheeks, she practically ran along beside me. Gasping for air, she prattled on to me without pause: about how worried she was for her Sasha, about how we were going to be late, about how she was afraid that Chukovsky (who was slated to give the opening remarks) would utter all sorts of banalities. Then she started saying how I must, simply must, drop in backstage to see Sasha, how Sasha's leg aches now and again, but, most important, most important of all—oh, if only we wouldn't be late! Finally, we arrived. We happened to be seated next to each other, but, after having a fuss and a flap, she leapt up and ran away—probably to go onstage.

Blok went on during the second act, after intermission. Calm and pale, he stopped in the middle of the stage and started to read, tucking first one hand and then the other into his pocket, as was his habit. He read only a few poems, but he did so with a poignant simplicity and profound gravity that are best described using Pushkin's phrase: "with solemnity." He pronounced his words very slowly, joining them together into a barely distinguishable melody, which was perhaps only intelligible to those capable of discerning poetry's internal movement. He read clearly and distinctly, articulating every letter, but, at the same time, he moved only his lips, without ever unclenching his teeth. When he was met with applause, he neither expressed gratitude nor affected disregard. His face remained motionless; he would lower his eyes, stare at the ground, and wait patiently for silence. The last thing he read was "On the Stand,"[15] one of his most hopeless poems:

Why do you cast down your eyes, embarrassed?
Look upon me in your former way.

So this is who you are today—made humble
In the uncorrupted light of day!
Nor do I shine with my former glory:
Out of reach, proud-hearted, perfect, mean.
I now observe more kindly and forlornly
Our simple and insipid life routine.

Every so often, someone in the crowd would shout out: "*The Twelve! The Twelve!*"—but he didn't seem to hear them. His gaze would only turn gloomier and he would clench his teeth. And though he read splendidly (I have never heard a better reading in my life), it became increasingly noticeable that he was reading mechanically, simply repeating habitual, long-memorized intonations. The audience demanded that he appear before them as the former Blok, the way they had known him or imagined him to be—and he, like an actor, agonizingly played that Blok for them, that Blok who no longer existed. Perhaps I did not see all this so clearly written on his face at the time, but only later on, in my memory, when death had furnished an end and explanation to the final chapter of his life. But I do distinctly and definitively remember how suffering and alienation filled his entire being on that night. It was so striking, so obvious to me, that when the curtain fell and the final shouts and applause had died out, the idea of going to see him backstage seemed to me awkward and coarse.

A few days later, already ailing, he left for Moscow. Upon his return, he took to his bed and never got up again.

In his Pushkin speech, delivered exactly six months before his death, he said: "Peace and free will. The poet needs both of these things in order to liberate his harmonies. But his peace and free will are being taken away. Not his peace in the superficial sense, but his artistic peace. Not his childish will, not the freedom to play at being a liberal, but his artistic will, that secret freedom. And the poet is dying because there is nothing left for him to breathe: his life has lost its meaning."

In all likelihood, the first person to say that Blok had suffocated got the idea from this speech. And that person was right. Isn't it peculiar? Blok was dying for several months before everybody's eyes, he was being treated by doctors—but no one ever named, or was capable of naming, his disease. It started with a pain in his leg. Then there was talk of his having a weak heart. He suffered greatly before his death. But what did he actually die of? No one knows. He somehow died "in general": because he was sick all over, because he could no longer go on living. He died of death.

■ □ ■

Leaving the Poets' Guild did not affect my personal relationship with Gumilyov. He, too, moved in to the House of Arts around that time, and we began to see one another more frequently. He led an active and cheerful life. His death began around the same time as Blok's did.

One of our mutual friends, a person of great talent and frivolity, returned from Moscow to Petersburg around Easter time.[16] He lived as if he didn't have a care in the world, just said whatever came into his head. Provocateurs and spies cozied up to him for precisely that reason: one could use him to find out anything one needed to know about writers. He brought a new acquaintance along with him from Moscow. This acquaintance was young, pleasant, and generous with small gifts: cigarettes, sweets, and so on. He called himself an aspiring poet, was in a hurry to make everyone's acquaintance. They brought him round to me as well, but I soon sent him packing. Gumilyov was very fond of him.

This new acquaintance became a frequent guest at Gumilyov's. He helped to organize the House of Poets (a branch of the Writers'

Union), and flaunted his highly placed connections in Soviet society. I wasn't the only one who found him suspicious. We tried to put Gumilyov on his guard, but nothing came of it. In short, though I cannot say with complete certainty that this man was the principal or even sole culprit behind Gumilyov's ruin, after Gumilyov was arrested, he immediately disappeared without a trace. After I had gone abroad, I learned from Maxim Gorky that this person's testimony had figured in Gumilyov's trial and that he had been a plant.

At the end of the summer, I began making preparations for a holiday in the countryside. I was supposed to leave on Wednesday, August 3. On the evening before my intended departure, I went to say goodbye to some of my neighbors in the House of Arts. When I knocked on Gumilyov's door it was already around ten o'clock. He was at home, relaxing after a lecture.

We were on good, but not intimate, terms. And, just as I had been surprised by the overly formal reception that Gumilyov had given me two-and-a-half years prior, I didn't know how to explain the unusual liveliness with which he greeted my arrival then. He even exhibited a certain special warmth that seemed entirely alien to his character. I also needed to drop in on the Baroness V. I. Ikskul, who lived on the floor below. But every time I rose to leave, Gumilyov began imploring me to "stay a while longer." And so I didn't manage to see Varvara Ivanovna: I remained sitting with Gumilyov until about two in the morning. He was uncommonly merry. He spoke at great length on various topics. For some reason, only one of his stories sticks in my mind—it was about his sojourn in the Tsarskoe Selo infirmary, the Empress Alexandra Fyodorovna and the grand duchesses. Later on, Gumilyov fell to assuring me that he was destined to live for a very long time: "to the age of ninety, at the very least." He kept on repeating, "Most certainly, to the age of ninety and not a day less."

Even then, he was still planning to write a whole pile of books. He reproached me: "Here we are, the same age, but look at us: I swear, I'm ten years younger than you are. It's all because I love the youth. I play blindman's bluff with the girls at the studio—just today I played with them. And that's why I'm certain to live to the age of ninety, while you'll go sour in five years' time."

And, chuckling, he demonstrated how I would be hunched over, shuffling along in five years' time, and how he would still be acting the "gallant young man."

As I was taking my leave, I asked permission to bring a few things over the next day for safekeeping. When I arrived at Gumilyov's door with my things in the morning at the agreed-upon time, no one answered my knock. In the dining room, the servant Efim informed me that Gumilyov had been arrested and taken away during the night. This meant that I had been the last person to see him as a free man. In his exaggerated delight at my arrival, there must have been some premonition that, after me, he would never see anyone again.

I went home to find the poetess Nadezhda Pavlovich, Blok's and my mutual friend, waiting there for me. She had just run over from Blok's. She was flushed from the heat and her face was swollen with tears. She told me that Blok was now in agony. I set about comforting her, offering her hope, as one does in such situations. In deepest desperation, she ran up to me and said, choking with tears, "You have no idea . . . don't tell anyone . . . it's been several days now . . . he's lost his mind!"

A few days later, when I had already arrived in the countryside, Andrei Bely informed me of Blok's demise. On the fourteenth, a Sunday, we held a memorial service for him at the village church. In the evenings, the local youth would gather around campfires and sing songs. I felt the urge to pay Blok a secret tribute. I suggested singing "The Peddlers," which he had loved a great deal. Strangely, no one knew it.[17]

At the beginning of September, we learned that Gumilyov had been killed. Cheerless letters arrived from Petersburg, thick with allusions and omissions. When I returned to the city, the people there still hadn't recovered from these deaths.

At the beginning of 1922, a theater that Gumilyov had gone to great lengths to help in the days before his arrest staged a production of his play *Gondla*. Both at the dress rehearsal and later on, at the first performance, the audience began calling for the "Author!"

It was ordered that the play be withdrawn from the repertoire.

Paris, 1931

GERSHENZON

One winter night in Moscow, in the early days of our acquaintance, Gershenzon was walking me across his little garden so he could lock the gate behind me. He joked, "That's just the sort of people you are, you poets: we write about you, but you'll never catch anybody writing poetry about us historians."

"Just you wait, Mikhail Osipovich, you'll see. I'll write about you."

He grinned into his mustaches, "No, you won't. Well, g'night."

"G'night."

Later on, I would always remember my promise, and more than once I even sat down to write a poem—but I just couldn't do it: everything I wrote seemed feeble and unworthy of him.

Nevertheless, I am happy to say that our meetings did leave a certain mark on my poetry. In my book *Grain's Way*, there is a poem called "November 2nd"[1] It is about the day after the October coup, when the people of Moscow first

Began crawling out from their stone cellars
Onto the streets.

Later on in it, I briefly recount the story of my visit to Mikhail Osipovich:

> I also went to see my friends that day.
> I learned they were alive and well, their children home—
> What more was there to ask? I shuffled home.

The book came out in 1920 and Gershenzon read it at the time, but we never talked about that particular poem. It was only in 1922 that I sent him a second, updated edition from Petersburg, jotting down a note in the margins across from the lines quoted above: "This is about you." I relied upon the fact that, having read the book so recently, he wouldn't immediately sit down to reread it. He would see my note, perhaps, in several years' time, when I would, in all likelihood, be far away from him. And that is exactly what happened. On October 23, 1924, he wrote to me: "I don't know where you are now . . . I sit at home, pace back and forth in my room, and read— today, I read your *Grain's Way.*"

In all likelihood, he had picked up that second edition, read it, saw my note—and felt the urge to write to me. That was his final letter. Addressed to Ireland, it did not reach me in Italy until the final days of 1924. I sent off an answer within a few days, but I never received a reply: Gershenzon was dying.

■ □ ■

In the summer of 1915, I had sent Gershenzon an offprint of my article on Pushkin's Petersburg tales. The letter I received in reply surprised me with its simplicity and sincerity. I was not personally acquainted with Mikhail Osipovich at the time, and, though I thought highly of him, I still hadn't imagined him as being separate from that flash of self-satisfied grandeur that allows one to spot an "established academic" from a mile away. It hadn't even occurred to me that such an important figure would condescend to write to the author of a single article on Pushkin.

However, B. A. Sadovskoy, who arrived in town shortly afterward, came to me one evening and said, "Let's go to Gershenzon's tomorrow. He's invited you."

The Arbat, 13 Nikolsky Alley. A wooden fence, a courtyard overgrown with grass. A gatehouse stands on the right side of the courtyard and another old building stands on the left. A stone path leads into the depths of the courtyard, up to a newly constructed two-story building. Behind the house is a garden with a modest vegetable patch. The second floor is occupied by Gershenzon—or, more accurately, by his family. The modest dining room doubles as a "receiving room." But Gershenzon himself lives higher up, in a mezzanine hidden from the courtyard.

Though the letter and the invitation (delivered via Sadovskoy) had been encouraging, nevertheless I must admit to feeling some trepidation when I first arrived. But my trepidation fell away on that very same evening, and, for fully seven years afterward, up until the very last day before I left Russia, I would go there certain of a warm reception. I went there to share my everyday cares, new poems, the projects I was planning, and, it seems, all my disappointments and my joys—though I dare say there weren't so very many of the latter.

■ □ ■

He would throw his head back frequently. He was small, with thick eyebrows and a little black beard that had grown terribly gray over the last few years. A mustache of the same sort hung over his plump mouth. He had ever-so-slightly bulging eyes, a meaty, slightly hooked nose squeezed tight by a pince-nez, hairy arms, and knobby knees: as far as his appearance was concerned, he was a stereotypical

Jew. He gesticulated a great deal. He spoke quickly and was nearly always in a state of agitation. His speech, though in itself extremely clear, gave the false impression of his being tongue-tied. This was a result of his muffled voice, bad diction, and extremely strange accent, in which the distinctly Jewish tones of a Kishinyov[2] native mingled with the overstressed *o*'s of a son of the Volga region (though who knows where those had come from).

His room was large and square. It had three windows and very little furniture. There were two short (waist-high) bookshelves, two tables (one was a sort of dining room table, though not a very large one, while the other was a writing desk, quite small), and a low, flat bed with a gray baize blanket and a single pillow by the wall. That was all, I think, apart from two bentwood chairs and an antique high-backed leather armchair. Gershenzon would have his guests sit in this chair (whose left arm had come unglued and was constantly falling off). It was a historical artifact, having once stood in Chaadaev's study.

The walls were white, smooth, and practically empty. All that hung on them was a phototype of Tropinin's famous portrait of Pushkin and a plaster mask, also of Pushkin. I believe someone else's portrait was hung there, too—perhaps Ogaryov's, I don't remember. Gershenzon's study was bright, spacious, and very clean. It looked a bit like a sanatorium. There was nothing deliberate about its design, but everything in it had somehow naturally oriented itself to the simplest objects and lines. This principle even extended to his books: he left out only those books that were most indispensible to his current work; the rest were kept in another room. This was the home of a man who did not care for excess.

■ □ ■

At the end of his school days, Gershenzon dreamed of enrolling in the philological faculty, but his father wouldn't hear of it. In the

eighties, and even later on, there were only two paths open to phi-
lologists: they could either become schoolteachers or, in the best-
case scenario, professors. This meant that they would serve in the
Ministry of Education. For a Jew, this represented an inevitable road
to baptism. Old man Gershenzon was horrified. Mikhail Osipovich
was sent away to Germany, where he enrolled in an engineering or
technical program at some specialized institute of higher learning.
I believe he lasted for about two years there before he couldn't take
it anymore: he sent a petition to the minister of education asking
to be admitted to the philological faculty of Moscow University as
an auditor. He asked to be admitted as an auditor because he didn't
dare to dream of becoming a student: ethnic quotas dictated that
only Jews who had finished gymnasium with a gold medal would
be considered, and Gershenzon hadn't. But then, something happened that bordered on the miraculous: a reply came back from
the ministry stating that Gershenzon had been enrolled not as an
auditor, but as a fully fledged student. The reason was simple: Jews
didn't tend to enroll in the philological faculty and Mikhail Osipovich's petition had been the only one they had received from a Jewish
person that year: thus, he automatically fulfilled the demographic
requirements. However, this stroke of good luck turned out to be
a catastrophe for Gershenzon: his father, who was generally dissatisfied with Mikhail Osipovich's stubbornness, refused to believe
that this was a "miracle" and decided that Mikhail Osipovich must
have already been baptized. The whole affair ended, if not in a
parental curse, then, at any rate, in a complete financial cutoff. His
mother scraped together the money for his trip from Kishinyov to
Moscow on her own. Gershenzon sallied forth onto the squares of
Moscow practically penniless. However, acquaintances arranged
some teaching jobs for him. But this gave rise to a fresh catastrophe: in those days, discipline was no laughing matter and students
were obliged to have a uniform and at times to wear a sword. Once

again, kind people came to the rescue: Gershenzon was given an old student's frock coat that hung on him like a sack, and a sword, and even . . . for lack of a uniform greatcoat, he was given a Nikolai overcoat![3] A Nikolai overcoat, light gray, with a beaver-skin collar and a fur cape that fell almost to his knees! It was so extravagantly big on him that: "Can you imagine? I had to carry the tails around in my hands at all times!"

Thus began Gershenzon's scholarly career and his poverty.

■ □ ■

Jabbing himself with three fingers somewhere near "the pit of his stomach," where a watch chain ran through the buttonhole of his threadbare vest, Gershenzon would say, "To this day, I only get flustered and upset on the inside: on the surface, I am always calm and serene."

Everyday anxieties often "drove him to smoke." But he knew how to keep these anxieties fenced off from his mind and his heart; they did not embitter him, they did not cast a shadow over him, and they did not muddy his spirit's marvelous purity.

However, his attitude never crossed over into carelessness or that barbaric contempt for creature comforts that certain ill-kempt "thinking men" are pleased to flaunt. Nor did he pretend to be completely unmercenary. On the contrary, he knew how to be economical, thrifty, and careful; he enjoyed discussing honoraria in exhaustive detail. He even knew himself to be "a maximalist in that regard." The Writers' Bookstore moaned a little moan when, in 1919, he took it into his head to sell them the unwanted books from his library.

During the difficult years of the Revolution, he occupied himself by coming up with "useful inventions." It got to the point where, after smoking a cigarette, he wouldn't throw away the butt. Rather, he would carefully fish the little cylinder of cigarette paper out of its holder, refill it with tobacco, and thus make one cylinder serve double duty. With practice, he honed his technique to perfection. Later on, he invented a box lined with newspaper that could be shut very tightly: if you put boiling porridge inside, the steam would allow it to finish cooking all by itself, without any firewood. You could do the same thing with soup.

This is all ancient history, but I know for a fact that sometimes, behind their children's backs, Gershenzon and his wife, Maria Borisovna,[4] wouldn't eat for days on end, subsisting on plain tea and saving everything in the house for the children. And so, going hungry, standing in lines for hours on end in the frost, chopping firewood and dragging it up the stairs – he didn't pretend that any of this was easy for him, but he didn't play the martyr, either. He was simple and serious, yet serene. He would cast the bundle down from his shoulders, dust himself off, recover his breath, and then, suddenly, he would take on a merry look and immediately start talking about something important, necessary, big: how he, trudging along somewhere in the Kremlin, had taken it into his head to petition on behalf of an arrested author.

■ □ ■

Somehow it came to pass that we would frequently walk around the city together. These walks were absolute torture for me. I do a reasonable job of taking stock of my surroundings on the street— but I become stupid in the process. It seems that, over the course of my entire life, not a single useful thought has ever entered my head while walking. With Gershenzon, it was just the opposite. We would barely reach the street before he began either philosophizing or comparing variants of Pushkin poems. Meanwhile, I wouldn't understand a word of it and so my replies would be completely off the mark. On top of all that, Gershenzon was constantly rushing off either to cross the street for no apparent reason, going out of his way to land himself under a draft horse's hooves—with a quotation from Plato on his lips—or to turn down an alleyway that would take us in the exact opposite direction from where we were headed.

He was nearsighted, suffered from something akin to night blindness, and had absolutely no sense of direction; his ignorance of Moscow's geography was absurd. One day, in the spring of '17, he and I set off for a writers' meeting at the Moscow Art Theater. I took him up to Strastnoy Monastery by tram. Then we started down toward Kamergersky Alley on foot. The sun had hardly begun to set. The stores were glowing. A solid wall of people lined the sidewalks—for the most part, officers on leave, soldiers tasting the delights of commerce and of prostitutes for the very first time. Gershenzon was practically swept off his feet, but he was dumbstruck. Suddenly, he even stopped: "Listen, what street is this?"

"Mikhail Osipovich, what's the matter with you? It's Tverskaya."

"Tverskaya? Ah, yes! Phoo—what opulence!"

His idea of "opulence" was unique. He fully understood the value of the necessary and he knew how to appreciate it, but he was childishly artless with regard to anything that appeared in the least bit extravagant. In 1920, we were staying at the same sanatorium. Each day, I wore a brown silk tie, which my brother had long since discarded and which I had burned holes in while smoking my cheap tobacco. But it had swirls on it. Gershenzon never failed to touch my tie each day, repeating, "Phoo, what a dandy he is!"

One day he took it into his head to describe the "opulent" dress of a certain lady philanthropist to Maria Borisovna and me. We couldn't contain ourselves; we rocked with laughter upon hearing Mikhail Osipovich's observations on fashion: it turned out that the lady had somehow managed to dress herself in nothing but "galloons" and "plunging necklines."

In the summer of 1923, on a very hot morning in Berlin, he was obliged to run back and forth between a number of different police agencies. He returned home, gasping for air and dripping with sweat: "Do you know what matters have come to? It got to the point where I took it into my head to stop in at one of their cafes to drink a cup of coffee. But then I thought the better of it: after all, I'm a family man!"

This was said in utter seriousness, without the slightest trace of irony.

Without resorting to anecdotes to illustrate my point, I will say that I believe that a genuine asceticism underlay his self-restraint.

■ □ ■

Those of us who lived through the most difficult years in Moscow—'18, '19, and '20—will never forget what a fine comrade Gershenzon proved himself to be. It was he who first came up with the idea of forming a writers' union, which made our lives so much easier back then and without which, I believe, many writers would simply have perished. He was the most active of the union's organizers and the first of its chairmen. But, after getting the union up and running and sacrificing a tremendous amount of time, effort, and nerves to the project, he resigned his chairmanship and stayed on as a rank-and-file union member. And, nevertheless, in its darkest moments, the union still turned to him for advice and help.

Gershenzon knew how to help in personal situations as well as in public affairs, and he enjoyed doing both. Many people are indebted to him for many different reasons. He knew how to divine other people's misfortunes and would always rush to help them, not just in word, but in deed. For my part, I can say that if it hadn't been for Gershenzon, I would have had a bad time of it in the years 1916–1918, when I was seriously ill. Gershenzon found me work and money; it was Gershenzon who looked after my affairs when I left for Crimea. And that's to say nothing of his moral support. But he did it all with an astonishing simplicity, devoid of any posing or sentimentality. His attentiveness and sensitivity were practically miraculous. Unfortunately, at the moment I cannot provide the details of a certain instance in which Gershenzon demonstrated his sly and merry acumen, which bordered on clairvoyance.

Kindness rendered him neither insipid nor feeble. He was ebullient and impetuous, and he loved the truth, the whole truth, in all of its parts, whatever it might be. He said everything that he thought and he looked you right in the eye as he was saying it. He was never coarse or offensive, but he didn't smooth down rough edges, didn't sugarcoat things.

"Frankly!" he would cry. "Frankly!"

That was one of his favorite words. And this frankness, this purity of truth, was present in all of Gershenzon's actions, as well as in his home, and in his attitude toward children.

■ □ ■

For all his kindness, he wasn't blind. He was an excellent judge of character, and, being nonconfrontational by nature, simply avoided those people whom he didn't like. He tried to find the good in everyone, but, if he didn't find it, he would cross that person off his list.

He knew how to speak cruelly and pointedly when the situation called for it. Referring to a certain multitalented and multifaceted man of letters, he said, "He's like a store with a sign outside saying: 'everything is fifty kopecks' ".

Once I expressed my surprise at the fact that X[5] always mentioned his Siberian exile in his writing, no matter what the subject was at hand.

"How can you not understand it?" Gershenzon said. "It's his medal. The medal is sewn onto his uniform, so when he dons the uniform, the medal goes on, too."

At times, he even exhibited a distinct intolerance. Once, we were taking the tram from Devichye Polye to the Arbatsky Gates. Around Smolensky Market, a venerable gentleman entered the car, greeted Gershenzon, and struck up a conversation. Gershenzon made his replies while glancing out the window. Suddenly, at the end of the Arbat, he dashed toward the exit. I went to hold him back: "Where are you going? We have two more stops to go."

"No, it's time for us to get off!"

And, ignoring me, he leapt out of the car. When we reached the sidewalk, he laid into me:

"Why did you hold me back? What, did you want me to talk to him any more than I already had? No, it's better that we finish our journey on foot."

"Who was that?"

"Professor R.,[6] the most puffed-up idiot I know."

Though he could not abide stupidity, hypocrisy, and doctrinarism—and would even take offense at them—he was forgiving where personal insults were concerned. One day, a certain Bobrov sent him his book, *A New Work on the Versification of Pushkin*. However, the book came wrapped in an issue either of *Zemshchina* or of *Russian Land* featuring a rabble-rousing, anti-Semitic article also written by Bobrov. The article had been meticulously outlined in red pencil. Gershenzon laughed as he told this story, but, when referring to Bobrov, he would always add, "Nevertheless, he is an intelligent person."[7]

■ □ ■

In the early days of our acquaintanceship, he suddenly asked, "Do you have a good temper?"

"Not especially."

"Well, then, we'll soon have a falling-out: I have a terrible temper. You'll see."

We did not have a falling-out, thank God. It turned out that there was only one thing about his disposition that was "terrible," and that was his stubbornness. For the most part, he was capable of listening to other people's arguments and occasionally he was even capable of agreeing with them. But often things would happen otherwise: he would suddenly wave his hand forlornly and, with a cry of "God knows what you're saying!" abruptly change the subject.

He was one of the most profound and subtle judges of poetry I have ever met. But here, too, he had a couple of "little quirks" that it was no use arguing with him over. First of all, he insisted that the quality of the first line invariably determined the quality of the entire poem. Secondly, for whatever reason, he believed that, if the first line in a quatrain rhymed with the fourth and the second line rhymed with the third, then the poem was vulgar. I was willing to go against my own better judgment and make peace with him via compromise: such poems might be considered tasteless. But Gershenzon insisted on "vulgar." And so we never came to terms with each other.

He and I had the occasion to work together twice; in that context, too, I was occasionally forced to yield not only to his experience and expertise, but to his stubbornness as well. However, I must give him credit where credit is due: in those instances when he was obliged to concede to me, he didn't scowl or sulk. There was a lofty honesty to his thinking: each time he admitted to being wrong, he actually seemed glad that a truer path had been found.

Incidentally, his stubbornness was partly a result of the approach that he took in his work. He applied not only artistic, but even intuitive principles to his historical-literary research. It seems to me that he viewed factual analysis as a way of testing out his own conjectures rather than as the collection of materials to be used to draw conclusions from. This method frequently led him astray. His *Pushkin's Wisdom*[8] became, to a certain extent, *Gershenzon's Wisdom*. But, firstly, it remained "wisdom" nonetheless, and, secondly, those things that Gershenzon divined could have been divined only by him and only by using his method. In a sense, Gershenzon's mistakes were more valuable and more profound than many truths. He divined a great deal about Pushkin that "our wise men haven't dreamt of." Then again, we would also have conversations that went something like this:

> *Me:* Mikhail Osipovich, I believe you are mistaken. That isn't so.
> *Gershenzon:* But I know that it is!
> *Me:* But Pushkin himself . . .
> *Gershenzon:* Who cares what 'Pushkin himself . . .'? Perhaps
> I know more about Pushkin than he knew about himself.
> I know what he wanted to say and what he wanted to hide—
> and what he said without understanding it himself, like
> the Pythia.[9]

He had an extremely peculiar relationship with the figures whom he studied. It was strange and fascinating to hear his stories about Ogaryov, Pecherin, and Herzen. It was as if he were talking about his own personal acquaintances. He had the same feel for the dead as he did for the living. Once, in response to my interpretation of a Delvig poem, he objected: "No, in Delvig those words mean something else; after all, he was fat, bloated . . ."

■ □ ■

He couldn't bear it when people called him a critic. He would correct them, saying, "I am a historian, not a critic." However, though he avoided expressing his opinions on new literature in print, he followed its development quite closely. Of the contemporary Russian writers, he particularly admired Andrei Bely; his favorite poets were Vyacheslav Ivanov, Sologub, and Blok; he held A. M. Remizov in high esteem and loved him as a person; he spoke of Alexei Tolstoy's talent with affection. Though he didn't care for Bryusov's poetry, he respected him as a literary historian. All in all, Gershenzon was an expansive person who tried to find the good even in those authors whose work was inherently foreign to him.

Over the nine years of our acquaintance, it became customary for me to read or to send to him nearly all of my poems. His criticism was always well meant—and merciless. He would state his opinions harshly, "frankly." I didn't always agree with them, but I am indebted to him for many of the keenest words ever said about my writings. No one abused me more severely than he did, but then again, I didn't value anyone else's praise as highly as I did Gershenzon's. After all, I knew that both the praise and the abuse came from what was perhaps the purest heart that I ever chanced to meet.

He ailed for a long time, but he died as the result of an unanticipated bad turn.* He suffered greatly. He knew that he was dying, but the end came on so suddenly that he didn't have time to say goodbye to his loved ones. He was buried in the unassuming Vagankovsky Cemetery. One might have inscribed the words from Pushkin's "Message to Chaadaev"[10] on his grave:

Always a wise man and sometimes a dreamer.

Sorrento, April 12, 1925

---

* On August 31, 1926, the All-Russian Central Executive Committee *Izvestia* published a letter from S. Mitskevich, the deputy chairman of the housing section of the CCAELA (the Central Commission for the Advancement of the Everyday Lives of Academics). Mitskevich wrote, "The housing section of the CCAELA has already borne witness to several difficult instances in which the agitation, suffering, and affliction provoked by housing-related issues have led to the premature deaths of academic researchers (the well-known professor Dr. Tezyakov, the celebrated man of letters Gershenzon, and others)."

SOLOGUB

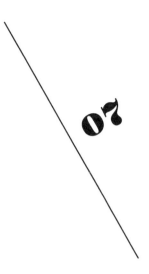

And still I keep, my Demon father,
The oath I took, nearly destroyed,
When on the stormy seas I faltered
And You redeemed me from the void.
You, my father, I shall praise and,
Scorning the unrighteous day,
Incite above earth desecration
And through betrayal, I'll betray.[1]

Fyodor Sologub

You, o benignant Creator,
Have great glory, and power, and light.
Grant me life here on earth, as you're able,
That I might find some new songs to write.[2]

Fyodor Sologub

He was the son of a tailor and a cook. He was born in 1863. In those days, it wasn't easy for a person of such origins to "rise in the world"; it couldn't have been easy for him, either. But he worked his way up, got an education, and became a teacher. We know almost nothing about the years of his childhood and youth. Neither do we see the teacher, Fyodor Kuzmich

Teternikov,[3] author of the geometry textbook. He enters our field of vision fully formed as the writer Fyodor Sologub, already over thirty years old and in looks a great deal older. No one had seen him as a young man, no one had seen him age. It was as if he had suddenly appeared from out of nowhere, already ancient and taciturn. "This being neither the first time I have been born nor the first cycle of outer incarnations I am bringing to a close . . ."—thus begins the foreword to his finest book of poetry, the one that has proved most central to his artistic career. Someone used to talk about how Sologub would occasionally abandon a crowded gathering of his own guests, silently withdraw into his study, and remain there for a long time. He was a cordial host, but his thirst for solitude was stronger than his sense of hospitality. Similarly, there were times when he would be sitting in company and it was as if he wasn't there. He would listen—but not hear. Be silent. Close his eyes. Fall asleep. Hover somewhere inaccessible to us. They called him a wizard, a witch doctor, a sorcerer.

I first laid eyes on him in the beginning of 1908, in Moscow, at the home of a certain man of letters. What I saw was the very same Sologub whose likeness was captured so precisely by Kustodiev in his famous portrait. He is slouching in an armchair, legs crossed, rubbing his small and very white hands together lightly. He is bald, with a slightly pointed crown; a canopy of gray hair surrounds his bald spot. His face is somewhat floury, somewhat puffy. There is a great white mole on his left cheek, next to his slightly hooked nose. His small, reddish-gray beard hangs down in a wedge and his reddish-gray mustache is droopy. His pince-nez hangs from a delicate cord; there is a crease above the bridge of his nose and his eyes are half-closed. When he opens them, their expression can best be conveyed by the question: "Oh, do you still exist?"

This was the same expression with which Sologub met me when I was first introduced to him. I was twenty-two and Sologub frightened me. And that fear never left me.

I saw Sologub for the last time fourteen years later, in Petersburg, also in the spring, after the terrible death of his wife. Had he aged? No, not a bit, he was exactly the same. He had never been young, and neither did he age.

■ □ ■

It is usually easy to trace changes in technical skill across a poet's artistic career. The rate at which such changes occur varies from case to case: in some poets, it is slower, in others, faster; changes occur in one and the same poet at different speeds in different periods of his life. The ways in which this evolution of form takes place also vary: one poet will move from complexity to simplicity, another from simplicity to complexity; some broaden their vocabulary, others narrow it; some modernize their approaches, others make them more arcane; some poets find their independence after churning out a series of imitations, while others (and this happens far less rarely than is generally thought to be the case) do the opposite: they squander their store of independence and turn into imitators. I am only outlining the most basic trajectories that artistic paths tend to take as examples. In reality, of course, there are incomparably more of them, and, more importantly, they are incomparably more complicated. Each poetic destiny represents a unique and inimitable instance of poetic development. Of course, it goes without saying that all this is a commonplace, and I wouldn't bother bringing it up if it weren't for the fact that I believe Sologub's poetry to be virtually the only instance in which it is nearly impossible to trace any evolution in form whatsoever. It seems almost not to exist.

We have known Sologub's poetry for forty years now. He wrote a great deal, perhaps too much. In any case, the number of poems he produced could be expressed in the quadruple digits. Sologub always had at his disposal a large store of unpublished pieces that had been written at various points in his life. When he compiled them into collections, he was guided not by chronology, but by other, frequently thematic, characteristics (though sometimes by purely prosodic ones: his book consisting entirely of triolets,[4] for example). He would arrange books in approximately the same manner as people arrange bouquets; the aforementioned stores served him as a rich hothouse. And the remarkable thing is that his bouquets would always turn out to be extremely well composed, light, devoid of any garishness or stylistic dissonance. Poems from the most varying eras and bygone years not only went together perfectly, but seemed to have been written at the very same time. Doubtless, Sologub himself was aware of this quality in his poetry. At times, when he needed to, he would take poems from one book and transfer them into another. Once again, they would find their own place and weave themselves into new combinations that were just as well composed as the ones that they had been plucked from.

Such is the case, for example, with his book *Pearly Stars*.[5] It contained poetry from the years 1884 to 1911. This represented only a small portion of what he had written over that period. But Sologub had taken it into his head to offer up a certain range of styles, to compile poems of a particular complexion—and was entirely capable of doing so simply by choosing the appropriate pieces from what he had written over a span of twenty-eight years. And again, not only did this book not contain a single technical or stylistic leap, rush, or dissonance, but, on the contrary, it was as if all of the pieces in it had been written at once. Doubtless, one might discern a greater confidence, firmness, and completeness, more taste and mastery in the later items—but that is only in comparison with the very earliest. To all intents and purposes, Sologub appeared at the beginning of the nineties in full armor. He immediately "found himself," immediately defined himself—and he never once strayed from that definition. As the years went on, he only became better and more comfortable in executing the methods that had constituted the essence of his style from the very start. The mortar hardened and became denser, but its chemical composition remained unchanged.

Sologub appeared on the literary scene as one of the pioneers of the youngest poetic group then in existence. But he joined it when he himself was no longer young in the poetic sense. He immediately proved himself to be the most mature, established, and polished of his literary peers. As his life had been without youth, so his poetry was without juvenilia. And just as he had entered life as an old man and never subsequently aged, his prowess was not fated to experience decline. Having outlived some of his literary peers physically, he outlived others poetically: he died at the height of his artistic powers, a master of diligence who held himself to extremely high standards.

■ □ ■

More than once, I have had occasion to read claims that, during his final years, he renounced his "satanic" predilections, rid himself of the poisons contaminating his soul, ceased to linger in the world of specters and of sin, came to terms with the simple life that he once cursed, turned his benevolent gaze toward the soil, and came to love his motherland. Furthermore, it was claimed that Sologub's enlightenment had been heavily influenced by the grievous fate of Russia, which the decadent poet had seemed not to notice up until that point. After finally seeing it, he came to love it in its years of suffering.

I won't dispute that this theory contains a very great deal that is appealing. We love to watch poets turn over a new leaf and achieve enlightenment right before their deaths. Deathbed evolution is our hobbyhorse. As soon as we uncover such "evolution," we can praise the deceased with a clear conscience: even if it was right before his death, he became just as good as we are, the way he ought to have done a long time ago.

Unfortunately, I shall nevertheless be forced to refrain from offering any thoughts on Sologub's evolution—because there wasn't any. I have no intention of denying that Sologub's works do feature the motifs of "enlightenment" and "reconciliation"—and in particular, of his love for Russia. But I am incapable of seeing any "evolution" in them. It would have been evolution if those motifs had been characteristic of and exclusive to the final period of Sologub's poetry, if it were possible to observe their first appearance, then their growth, and, finally, how they squeezed out those earlier attributes with which they were inconsistent. But the specific phenomena that would be necessary for talking about evolution are not present. The motifs that should have disappeared from Sologub's poetry if an evolution had, indeed, occurred actually remained there to the end. Those motifs that should have appeared in his poetry for the first time had, in fact, always been present, or had been present for so long that it would be impossible to link their appearance to Russian life in recent years or to Sologub's personal deathbed "enlightenment."

I am not writing a case study, but neither do I wish to make unfounded assertions. In his final years, Sologub allegedly turned his benevolent gaze to the facts of everyday life, began to love the soil, blessed his motherland, and came to terms with God. But the fact is that his final years had nothing to do with this process. Weren't the simple little verses addressed to the brook that "chased away sorrowful thoughts" written in 1884? And wasn't his clear, entirely unclouded admiration for the creek and its bathing children marked as having been written in 1888?[6] Are there really so few poems like this in Sologub's œuvre? For example:

No, we won't forget the roads
To God's exuberant abodes,
Dwelling place of all His blessèd;

We, an army of God's slaves,
Will go to shelter in his shade,
Uncomplaining and submissive.[7]

Was it really Russia's sufferings or the nearness of his own death that
led Sologub to write this poem—in 1898? And here is one about
the earth:

You know not how to kiss my earth,
To listen to Moist Mother Earth,
The way I hearken unto her,
The way I press my lips to her.

Oh, I'll cling with my entire body
To my mother's holy body,
In inspiration white and holy
Inclining toward the final border—

Whence the grasses and the flowers,
Whence you, my sisters and my brothers.
My kiss alone is pure and righteous.
My embrace alone is holy.[8]

I don't know when this poem was written, but, as of 1907, it had
already been published in *Fiery Circle*.[9]

It would also be incorrect to say that the "decadent" Sologub
only truly saw and fell in love with Russia after the Revolution.
A book of his poetry with the brief and expressive title *To the Motherland* came out in 1906. That was also the year in which his *Political
Fairy Tales* appeared, bearing witness to the fact that the "singer of
sin and murky mysticism" had not held himself entirely aloof from
the most pressing questions of the age.[10]

And in 1911, he wrote:

They're excellent, exotic,
They put me in a trance
But you, my Russia, are the
Most excellent of lands.[11]

No, Sologub did not owe his love for Russia to some sort of deathbed epiphany. It was not he who did not see Russia, but we who had overlooked his love for her.

On the other hand: was his enlightenment really so complete, did he really run so determinedly from his past, did he really turn to God in such a clear and simple fashion?

Adonai
Has ascended the thrones,
Adonai
Demands our adulation—
And our weakness,
Earthly weakness
Has raised monuments to him.
But Lucifer, all-merciful, is with us,
The fiery breath of total freedom,
The righteous light of knowledge,
Lucifer is with us,
And Adonai,
The dark and vengeful God,
Will be toppled
And dethroned
By your angels, Lucifer,
By Moloch and Beelzebub.[12]

That was written in Bolshevik Russia, several years before his
death. It is true that, several pages later, we read something very
different:

> I know with my last knowledge
> That the darkness is confined
> And I don't believe the nonsense
> Of the superstitious mind.
> To encroach on Godly wisdom
> Is like crucifying Christ,
> Fencing off a mouth unsullied
> With a pack of earthly lies.[13]

Or:

> In the clear heavens sits radiant God the Father,
> Here with me is Earth, the holy Mother . . .[14]

But after several pages, we see again:

> Why love? The earth's unworthy
> Of your precious love.
> Pass over it, an asteroid,
> Pass high above.[15]

However, for the time being, exalting the "cunning path of the
merry sinner" that he has traveled on this earth, Sologub invites us:
"Sin with me."[16]

Honestly, all this is quite far from repentance and reform. No, we
will not find any sort of spiritual "progress" in Sologub's work—and
we won't find any "regress" in it, either. And, as it happens, this is

what makes his poetry so remarkable: the fact that it contains no evolution whatsoever. Sologub never renounced his past and he never discovered anything that he didn't already know. Of course, he didn't immediately hit upon those notions that would come to constitute his poetry's guiding motifs. But just how and when Sologub came to be "composed" we do not know. We immediately come across him as an already established entity—and that is how he would remain until the very end. His "composition" was complex; judging solely by his poetry, it appeared to be full of internal contradictions. It burst forth in many different floods, but, in its essence, in its constitution, it remained unchanged. As Sologub's life had been without youth, as his poetry had been without juvenilia, his spiritual life was without evolution.

Sologub blasphemed and exalted, cursed and blessed, sang the praises of sinfulness and saintliness alike, was both cruel and kind, invoked death and reveled in life. All this and a great deal more can be proven using an enormous number of quotations. Only one thing will never be proven: that Sologub "departed" from one thing and "arrived" at something else, from blasphemy to exaltation or from exaltation to blasphemy, from blessings to curses or from curses to blessings. Nothing in him was ever excluded by anything else; contradictions coexisted peacefully within him because their very existence was a part of his worldview. I will now say a few words regarding that worldview, without criticizing it and or pointing to its sources. The issue is not whether this worldview was original or correct, or what contradictions might have existed within it. This worldview is the key to understanding Sologub and it is only in this capacity that it is of interest to us at the moment.

"This not being the first time I have been born or the first cycle of outer incarnations I am bringing to a close, I am quietly and simply uncovering my soul," Sologub says in the foreword to *Fiery Circle*—and he does not tire of repeating it in his poetry and his prose.

Sologub considered his life, which came to an end on December 5, 1927, to be neither his first one, nor his last. He believed that it was one link in an endless chain of incarnations. His physical appearance might change, but an unchanging "I" would remain constant underneath it: "For all and in everything is I, and I alone, and nothing else, is, was, or ever shall be . . . A person's dark, earthly soul blazes in sweet and bitter ecstasies, grows thin, and ascends the endless ladder of perfection to the dwelling place of the ever-unattainable and eternally longed-for."[17] Over the course of it's endless ascension, this "I" creates worlds both visible and invisible: things, phenomena, and ideas, both good and evil, God and the devil. Both good and evil and God and the devil are merely equivalent forms of the sweet and bitter ecstasies that blaze within the soul. This temporary life, this cycle of experiences, ends in death, which is itself equally temporary. With death comes the transition into a new cycle:

And all that here has lived and breathed
And left our sight,
Another land will once again conceive,
Afresh, alight.[18]

That one link in this chain, the one life that the poet Fyodor Sologub lived out before our very eyes, provided him with a great multitude of experiences, "ecstasies," to use his word (and Pushkin's). He felt surges of passionate love toward women, beauty, life, the motherland, and God. The charms of evil, malice, vice, ugliness, the devil, and death also filled his soul with ecstasies, albeit of a different color and taste (they were "bitter").

However, insofar as his entire life was only one rung on the "endless ladder leading to perfection," it could not help seeming all too incomplete to Sologub. I dare say that the even less perfect lives that he had lived out prior to that point must have given that impression, too.

But the commonly held opinion that Sologub deemed life to be utterly loathsome, coarse, and dirty was wrong. Life was only loathsome, coarse, and vulgar in comparison with the rungs on the ladder yet to come. Sologub knew how to love life and find joy in it, but only to the extent that he could contemplate life outside of the framework of the "ladder leading to perfection." In comparison with the missing and perpetually sought-after Lilith, this life is Eve, a "great peasant woman, plump and rosy." It is the dirty maiden Aldonza, worlds away from the beautiful Dulcinea who appears in the dreams of mankind, that eternal Adam and eternal Don Quixote. But even in his future incarnations, on the rungs of the ladder yet to come, he is not destined to meet his true Dulcinea, who lives in "the dwelling place of the ever unattainable and the eternally longed-for."

But where is that dwelling place? Sologub knew that it was not our Earth, not Mars, not Venus, and not a single one of the planets currently known to exist. This dwelling place is unattainable; it bears the provisional and sacred name "the land of Oylé." Over that land shines the unparalleled star Maïr and it is watered by an unparalleled stream:

The star Maïr shines high and bright above me,
   The star Maïr,
And in the light of that fair star emerges
   A distant sphere.

The land Oylé floats by on waves of ether,
   The land Oylé,
And clearly shines the flickering Maïr
   Upon this lay.

The stream Ligoy flows through its love and quiet,
   The stream Ligoy

Maïr's distinctive countenance sways silent
Along its coil.

The lyres' cheer, the fragrant smell of flowers,
The lyres' cheer
Has merged with women's singing, growing louder
To praise Maïr.[19]

Did he himself find comfort in his "ladder"? I don't know.
I believe that the very question of whether or not it was possible to
find comfort in anything did not exist as far as he was concerned.
He bravely faced up to the truth that he had, at one time, created
for himself; and, in any case, it would not have been in his character to attempt to whitewash or sugarcoat it. Apparently, he sometimes found his "ladder" to be a bit boring. That it was tiresome and
severe—there was no question:

Who gets to laugh? The godheads,
The children and buffoons.
People, walk a straight tread,
Let wisdom be your boon.
And let them laugh, the godheads,
The children and buffoons.[20]

Incidentally, he himself was quite the joker. But his jokes were
invariably bitter and almost always boiled down to a pun, a smile
rendered in words: "If it's a bread knife, then how does it cut?"
"I just can't seem to wrap my head around it: am I Mimi or is Mimi
you?" "He's called Asimov—he's cold as a moth."[21] Funny circumstances were essentially alien to him; he did not see the smiles in
life's phenomena. And if he did see them, he found them to be either
fearsome or evil.

■ □ ■

In Sologub's eyes, life seemed imperfect, all too imperfect. Too often, he found "the earthly grind, space and time" to be difficult. People held no appeal for him, either: he could see the "petty demons" lurking over their shoulders. Once Russian society had been introduced to Peredonov, it felt a keen desire to discern Sologub's self-portrait within him. "He's talking about himself here," the criticism hinted. In the foreword to the second edition of his novel, Sologub replied calmly and clearly: "No, my dear contemporaries, I am talking about you."[22]

People generally refer to him as being spiteful. However, I never considered Sologub to be actively spiteful. It was more that he didn't like to forgive. After his marriage to Anastasia Nikolaevna Chebotarevskaya, who, they say, came armed with a cantankerous character (though I never had reason to complain of it myself), it seems that Sologub was frequently forced to quarrel with other people in order to stand up for Anastasia Nikolaevna—whether she deserved it or not. Incidentally, he had a long memory for insults himself. In 1906 or 1907, Andrei Bely published an article in *Libra*[23] about Sologub that Sologub found to be unpleasant. In 1924, which is to say, about seventeen years later, Bely appeared at a public gathering in Petersburg that was being held to honor Sologub on the occasion of his sixtieth birthday. In Bely's usual fashion, he gave an extraordinarily rapturous, violently ecstatic speech (I base this characterization on the report of someone who was present). When he had finished, Bely beamed with a smile that was as rapturous and insincere as his speech had been and fell to shaking Sologub's hand with all his might. Sologub screwed up his face with loathing and said distinctly, through his teeth, "You're hurting me." And not another word. The effect of the rapturous speech had been ruined. Sologub had taken his revenge.*

In general, I think that people exhausted Sologub. He often tried to avoid seeing them or hearing them:

Life with others is a trial!
  Why must I live within their midst?
  Why can't I make my time worthwhile,
    Tell fortunes, use my magic gifts?[24]

For me, this note always resonated very clearly in Sologub's words, in his lazy, peevish gestures, in his dozing, in his silence, in the way he closed his eyes; in short, in all his habits. While I was living in Petersburg, we would see each other fairly frequently and would go to visit each other's homes, but in general, in spite of Sologub's admirable mind, in spite of the wonderful poetry he would read when we were together, in spite of his courteous if slightly dry manner of address—for whatever reason, I tried to catch his eye less often. I realized that, when all was said and done, Sologub had decidedly no need for people and that I was no exception. I am sure that he had a very large supply of love within him, but he was incapable of using it on people.

---

* Andrei Bely himself (in *The Beginning of the Century*) portrays this scene in a slightly different manner: "While the address was being read to him, the courtly old man remained silent, standing there in his tailcoats, with his mummy-like head thrown back, white as death; suddenly, showing his teeth (and lack thereof) in an enchanting manner, he shook my hand eagerly and—kissed me. Backstage, after shaking his hand, I nearly fell over along with him as he gasped like a sturgeon: "Ow, you've hurt me." He shook out his fingers, wincing, "oh, how can you squash someone's fingers that way?" And, wagging his finger in front of my nose, he leaned back, shook out his coattails, and gave me a good dressing-down."
    I must note, however, that the person who reported this episode to me had been in the audience and could only have seen what happened onstage and not what happened in the wings.

On Oylé, the faraway and lovely,
The only dream and only love I know . . .

On this earth, he knew only the imperfect reflection of Oylé's light.

■ □ ■

Incidentally, he did love two people, two women—and he lost both
of them. The first was his sister, Olga Kuzminishna,[25] a quiet girl
no longer in her first youth, sickly, barely audible, who always went
about in black. She died of consumption, I believe, in 1907. Many of
Sologub's poems bear the traces of this love. He never forgot her. In
1920, he wrote:

. . . To tell him what the heart had lived for,
What it yearned for, what it burned for,
And the people that it worshipped
And the things that it was drawn toward.

So you dream, a moment only,
Of the distant, disregarded.
That delicious name, the Volga,
Like the name of the departed.[26]

The second woman was Anastasia Nikolaevna Chebotarevskaya, whom he married shortly after his sister's death. The Sologubs
spent the years of War Communism partly in Kostroma, partly in
Petersburg. It was their dream to leave Soviet Russia, where, in his
words, "human beasts" held sway. Sologub wrote:

Once again, they've put their shrouds on,
Meadows, fields of wheat, and groves.

Oh, how irksome, oh, how irksome
Are these white, unsullied snows,

Is this buried, lifeless wasteland,
And this drowsy, dozing hush!
Why, my soul, you fettered bondsman,
Don't you fly free from this crush,

To the ocean's stormy surges,
To the city's noisy squares,
To the airplane's sweeping wingspan,
To the thunder-like train's blare,

Or, to quench our thirst fraternal
With a bitter, poison bane,
To the flawless, ever-vernal,
To the broad Champs-Élysées?[27]

Anastasia Nikolaevna happened to be related to Lunacharsky (I believe she was his first cousin). In the spring of 1921, Lunacharsky issued a statement to the Politburo regarding the necessity of allowing certain ailing writers—in this case, Sologub and Blok—to go abroad. Gorky supported this petition. For some reason, the Politburo decided to allow Sologub to leave, but prevented Blok from doing so. Upon receiving word of this, Lunacharsky sent the Politburo a letter bordering on the hysterical that scuppered Sologub for no apparent reason. His argument went something like this: comrades, what in the world are you doing? I interceded on behalf of Blok *and* Sologub, but here you are allowing only Sologub to leave. Blok is a poet of the revolution, a source of pride for us; there was even an article written about him in *The Times*! Meanwhile, Sologub despises the proletariat, writes counterrevolutionary pamphlets, and so on.

A copy of this letter, which was dated, I believe, June 22, was sent to Gorky, who immediately showed it to me. The Politburo reversed its decision: Blok was granted a foreign passport, which he never had the opportunity to use, while Sologub was denied. In the autumn, after a great deal of effort on Gorky's part, Sologub was eventually issued a foreign passport; then it was taken away from him again, then it was given back to him again. The whole affair shook Anastasia Nikolaevna's mental balance: when everything had already been arranged and the departure date had practically been set, she threw herself into the Neva from Tuchkov Bridge in a fit of melancholy.*

Her body was recovered from the water seven-and-a-half months later. For that entire time, Sologub had held out hope that perhaps the woman who had thrown herself into the Neva had not been Anastasia Nikolaevna. He allowed for the possibility that she might be hiding out somewhere. He would set an extra place at the dinner table—just in case she returned. This gave rise to a vulgar story about how Sologub "would dine in the invisible presence of the deceased." I saw him twice during that period: once shortly after Anastasia Nikolaevna's disappearance, in the home of P. E. Shchyogolev, where he did not utter a single word the entire evening, and

---

* Her sister, Alexandra Nikolaevna Chebotarevskaya, who was also a translator and writer, lived in Moscow. It had been decided that there would be no speeches on the day of Gershenzon's burial (which took place in February of 1925). However, some Communist pushed everyone aside, went up to the grave, and started going on about how, though Gershenzon "hadn't been one of ours," the proletariat nevertheless respected the memory of this holdover from bourgeois culture. Alexandra Nikolaevna couldn't contain herself and said everything that was bubbling up inside her at the moment. After they went their separate ways from the cemetery, she couldn't calm down for the rest of the day. In the evening, after experiencing a fit of nerves, she went to the Bolshoy Kamenny Bridge, crossed herself, made the sign of the cross over Moscow in all four directions, and threw herself off of the bridge and through a hole in the ice. She was dragged out by some passersby, but died of heart failure in the hospital waiting room an hour later. I am reporting this incident as it was described to me by a Soviet writer who was in Moscow at the time and later came to Paris for a while. Andrei Bely (in *The Beginning of the Century*) writes that both sisters killed themselves "as the result of mental disorders."

once in the spring of 1922, in my home. He arrived unexpectedly, sat down, read a few poems, and left just as abruptly as he had arrived, as if he hadn't noticed I was there.

Once he had become convinced of his wife's demise, he never again felt the desire to leave Russia. His works almost never appeared in print (in the final three years of his life, they weren't published anywhere at all), but he wrote a great deal. This was not the first time that he had used a dream to overcome reality, to spiritually triumph over it. It is no coincidence that, over a span of twelve days in the spring of 1921, unyielding, unvanquished, in cold and in hunger, he wrote a merry, boisterous cycle of poems that should have been unthinkable under the circumstances: twenty-seven pieces in the style of the French bergerette.[28] Having gritted his teeth, the stubborn dreamer, the confident, firm, and unflinching master, came out with this work in the era of "proletarian art." He did so with an ironical smile for his enemies, for himself, and for this "cruel life":

Thyrsis in the willow's shade,
Dreams of his Nanette
And, head on shoulder laid,
Sings a sweet musette:
In my love I—tra-ta-tam-ta—repine,
Towards the grave I—tra-ta-tam-ta—incline.

The echo in the hedge,
Heeding mountains' keening,
Won't change a single pledge,
Worn melodies repeating:
In my love I—tra-ta-tam-ta—repine,
Towards the grave I—tra-ta-tam-ta—incline.[29]

Paris, January 1928

ESENIN

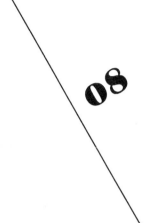

08

In the summer of 1925, I read a short book by Esenin that bore an unusually simple title: *Poems. 1920–24.*[1] It was a collection of his poems, new and not entirely new, which is to say, works that had already been included in his earlier collections. Evidently, the author had wished to consolidate the poems of what might be termed his penitential cycle, which so affected and moved even those who had previously disliked or simply overlooked Esenin's poetry.

I liked this little book. I wanted to write about it. And I would have gone about doing so, but I quickly realized that this collection represented the sum total of an entire life and that it would be impossible to discuss it outside the context of Esenin's past as a whole. Then I reread his *Collection of Verses and Epic Poems*—the first and only volume he published with Grzhebin.[2] And, after rereading that, I realized that it would be impossible to talk about Esenin at that time. This book, which had so touched me (along with many others), was evidence of a sharp and painful break, a difficult and torturous drama that was playing itself out within Esenin's art. I realized beyond a shadow of a doubt that the attitudes reflected in this little collection were transitional ones; they had been building for some time, but by then they had come to such a head that they could hardly prove to be stable or enduring; it seemed to me that, in one way or another, Esenin's fate must soon be decided, and that this decision was to determine the position that these new poems were to occupy, the meaning that they were to acquire. In that moment, writing about such poetry would either have meant leaving certain things unsaid or attempting to tell fortunes. I couldn't muster the courage to tell fortunes. I decided to wait and see what happened. Unfortunately, it turned out that I hadn't long to wait: on the night of December 27, at the Hotel Angleterre in Petersburg, "Sergei Esenin wrapped a rope (from a suitcase he had brought back from Europe) twice around his neck, kicked the stool out from under his legs, and dangled with his face turned toward the deep blue night, looking out over Saint Isaac's Square."

■ □ ■

He was born on September 21, 1895 into a peasant family in the Kozminskaya District of Ryazan Governorate and County. Owing to his family's poverty and size, he was given up at the age of two to be raised by his maternal grandfather, a more prosperous *muzhik*.[3] Esenin began writing poetry around the age of nine, but his more or less self-conscious compositions began when he reached the age of sixteen, after he had graduated from his private, church-run teacher-training school.

In his autobiography, he writes: "At 18, I was surprised that the poems I had sent out to various editorial offices weren't being published, and so, without warning, I rumbled into Petersburg. I was received quite cordially there. The first person that I saw there was Blok, the second was Gorodetsky. . . . Gorodetsky put me in touch with Klyuev, whom I hadn't heard a word about before."[4]

He "rumbled into" Petersburg a rather simple fellow. Later on, he himself said that, upon first catching sight of Blok, he began to sweat in agitation. If we read his first collection, *Radunitsa*,[5] carefully, we see that he didn't bring any clearly expressed ideas, abstractions, or schemae along with him from his native Kozmin-skaia District to Petersburg. He arrived with a store of familiar observations and feelings. But, though Esenin may have already sensed and experienced certain "ideas" (if, indeed, there had been any ideas to be sensed and experienced), he was not, as yet, consciously aware of them.

At the foundation of Esenin's early poetry is a love for his native land—a love specifically for his native, peasant land, and not for Russia, with its cities, plants, and factories, with its universities and theaters, with its political and public life. Practically speaking, he did not know Russia as we understand it today. For him, the motherland was made up of its villages and the fields and forests into which they disappeared. The best possible world would comprise a set of such villages: a Rus' of huts, a native corner rather than a country: a social and popular entity rather than a national or even geographic one. For Esenin, the borderlands were not, of course, Russia. Russia was Rus', and Rus' was the village.

The entire life's work of the inhabitants of this Rus' consisted of peasant labor. The peasant was downtrodden, impoverished, and naked. His land was as miserable as he was:

The willows listen calmly
To the whistling of the wind . . .
You, my cast-off country,
You, my native land.[6]

Merging with the land as he walked across it, the *muzhik* God was just as wretched:

The Lord went out to test the people's love,
He went forth as a poor man in the forest.

An old man on a dry stump in the oak grove
Was gumming a stale doughnut with great purpose.

The old man saw the poor man on his journey,
On the footpath, with his stick of iron,
Staggering with hunger, feeling poorly
And he thought: "Just look how god-forsaken . . ."

The Lord approached him, hiding grief and torment:
It's clear, he thought, their hearts can't be awakened . . .
The old man, he reached out his arm before him:
"You'll feel a little stronger, brother—take it."[7]

We can reconstruct Esenin's early "peasant" religious tendencies based on his poetry. Briefly put, according to these views, the peasant's mission is divine, for the peasant is, so to speak, complicit in God's creation. God is the father. Earth is the mother. The Son is the harvest. As we can see, the origins of Esenin's cult are ancient. A number of steps are required to bridge the gap between these origins and Christianity. Did Esenin pass through them all? Probably not. The early Esenin was a demi-pagan. But in no way did this prevent his faith from coming clothed in the traditional imagery of the Christian world. His religious experiences were expressed using ready-made Christian terminology. And this is the only thing that can be said about them with any certainty. To talk about Esenin's *Christianity* would be risky. For Esenin, Christianity consisted not in its content, but in its form, and his use of Christian terminology is more or less a literary device. Alongside the imagery that he borrows from Christianity, Esenin exposes his very same peasant faith in completely pagan forms:

I came to love this world, the ages
Like my parents' hearth and home.

All in them is soft and sacred,
All is restless and ablaze.
The sunset's crimson poppy dances
On the blown-glass lakes.

My tongue lets slip an image,
Unbidden, to the sea of bread:
The heavens, fresh from labor,
Lick a calf of copper-red.[8]

There we have it: the heavens are a cow; bread, the harvest, is a calf; the heavens give birth to the harvest and a higher truth manifests itself therein. But, for the time being, Esenin himself treats this formula as a simple image, a poetic metaphor that has accidentally slipped from his lips. He himself remains unaware of the fact that it encapsulates his fundamental religious and social worldview. But later on, we shall see how and under what kinds of influences this image came to develop within him and what it came to mean.

■ □ ■

At the end of 1912, a certain X began to visit me in Moscow. He called himself a peasant poet; he was handsome, black-browed, and stately; he diligently retained his overstressed *o*'s and enjoyed conversing on various topics, both vernal and hibernal. He styled himself a young hero, a Bova Korolevich. Unsurprisingly, he assured us that he hadn't studied anywhere. I learned from my late friend S. V. Kissin (Muni) that X had been enrolled in the law faculty either as a student or an auditor at the same time as Muni had. He wrote poetry reasonably well and fluently, but in that pseudo-Russian style that I do not particularly care for.[9]

His speech contained a mixture of self-effacement and insolence. At the time, this irritated me; later on, I would get my fill of it in the proletarian poets. X didn't go anywhere, didn't look at anything, and yet he somehow still managed to get around and to pry into other people's affairs, sometimes pretending to be timid, at other times brimming with spite. He never laughed, he only smirked. Sometimes he would burst in making apologies left and right: was it all right for him to be there? and he wasn't interrupting, was he? and perhaps he had come at a bad time? and he hadn't made a nuisance of himself, had he? and wasn't it time for him to be going? But he himself would occasionally let drop a barb. When he read his own poetry, he would ask in the most deferential manner for others to let him know if something wasn't right: to teach him, to offer him counsel. Because—of course it's not our place, we're unenlightened folk, only look, it stands to reason that the academics—though they've left it all behind, but it's completely pointless the way they, and ... He loved talking politics. Yes, the landowners must certainly be set fire to one day (it was unclear who would be doing the lighting: us or someone else). So that the tsar and the *muzhik* would be left and no one else besides. We're up to our necks in capitalists because the kikes (pardon me, you aren't a Jew yourself, are you?) want to topple the tsar and then take control of all of Christian Rus'. We should bow down before the intelligentsia for bringing enlightenment down to us ignorant folks. But we won't let them sponge off us, either: as soon as we've sorted out the rich folks, we'll give it to them good, too. And don't forget the factory workers: they're all hooligans, riffraff, loafers. Rus' is a Christian land, yes, she is. As for the *muzhik*? Phoo, in the end, in a word—he's a bondsman. But the first place must belong to him alone because he is like the salt of the earth ...

And then, after a silence: "Yes. But what is salt worth, really? A half-kopeck a pound."

Muni once said of him: "Your Bova is like the sun: he sets on the left and rises on the right. And we'll be lucky if he doesn't pop up again in the secret police."

Meanwhile, X was languishing in jealousy: he was haunted by the laurels of another *muzhik*, Nikolai Klyuev, who had appeared on the scene not long before he did and had already had two books published: one with a foreword by Bryusov, the other with an introduction by V. Sventsitsky, who, without mincing words, hailed Klyuev as a prophet.

Klyuev, who was, in fact, far more gifted than X was, went on to Petersburg and managed to cause quite a stir there: Gorodetsky shouted his praises from the rooftops. Naturally, X did not take this lying down: he, too, made a dash for Petersburg. Things didn't go particularly well for him there: he didn't cut it as a prophet and, before long, he came back—though not without a trophy: he returned with a photograph of himself posing with Gorodetsky and Klyuev: all three of them were wearing traditional Russian shirts and greased boots and were holding balalaikas.

G. Ivanov did an excellent job of describing this moment in one of his sketches of Petersburg literary life:

> Upon his arrival in Petersburg, Klyuev immediately fell under Gorodetsky's influence and completely internalized the devices of *muzhik travesty*.
>
> "So, Nikolai Alexeyevich, how are you settling in Petersburg?"
>
> "Glory to God, the Intercessor doesn't forsake us sinners. I found myself a little box of a room—do we need much? Drop in sometime, my boy, and brighten up my day. I live on Morskaya, just around the corner from here."
>
> This "little box" was a room at the Hotel de France with fitted carpeting and a broad Turkish divan. Klyuev was sitting on the divan, wearing a shirt collar and tie and reading Heine in the original.

"I'm tossing off a little trifle in the infidel's tongue," he said, noting my surprised look. "I'm tossing off a little trifle. Only my heart's not in it. Our nightingales are fuller-voiced, yes, fuller-voiced. But how is it that I,"—here he became agitated—"can be receiving a cherished guest in such a manner? Sit down, my boy, sit down, my dove. What can I offer you? I don't drink tea, I don't smoke tobacco, and I haven't laid in any stores of honey cakes. But apart from that," he winked, "if you aren't in a rush, perhaps we can spend the afternoon together? There's a little inn nearby. The innkeeper is a good person, though a Frenchman. It's right here, just around the corner. His name is Albert."

I wasn't in any rush.

"Well, that's just fine, that's just fantastic—I'll get changed . . ."

"Why should you change?"

"What do you mean, what do you mean—it simply wouldn't do! The fellows would laugh. Wait just a moment—I'll be quick as a wink."

He emerged from behind a screen in a long, tight-fitting coat, greased boots, and a raspberry-colored shirt: "There, now—that's better!"

"Well, they certainly won't let you into a restaurant looking like *that*."

"But we're not asking to go into the main hall. What business could we *muzhiks* possibly have among the masters? The cobbler must stick to his last. But we aren't going into the main room, we are going to the little shoebox room; that's something separate. Even we can go *there*.[10]

And it was precisely in the little shoebox rooms of such French restaurants that the Gorodetsky-Klyuev *style russe* was being developed at that time—not quite Russian Orthodoxy, not quite Khlysticism, not quite Revolution, not quite Black Hundredism.

Of course, for Gorodetsky, it was all just another round of brou-haha and blabber: by that time, he had already put in his time as a Symbolist and a mystical anarchist and a mystical realist and an Acmeist. He adored masquerades and guises. Dressing up as a *muzhik* was amusing and it was also good advertising. But, though Klyuev would "toss off trifles in the infidel's tongue," he was nevertheless a man of the village. Of course he knew that the kind of *muzhiks* Gorodetsky dressed him up as did not, in fact, exist—but he did not contradict the master: let 'im have 'is fun. But in the meantime, he, not so as completely mum and dumb, but subtle-like, with nudges and with ditties, nodding his head and winking to the right and left, to the Black Hundredist Gorodetsky and to the SRs and to the members of the Religious-Philosophical Society and to some of the Khlystic youth—was biding his time. But for what?[11]

■ □ ■

The harebrained, fragmented, and scattered ideas that my X let slip might be organized into to a certain system, which boils down to something like this:

Russia is a *muzhik* country. Anything in her that is not by and for the *muzhik* is scum that must be scraped away. The *muzhik* is the sole champion of the genuinely Russian social and religious idea. Currently, he is oppressed and exploited by people of every other class and profession. The landowner, the manufacturer, the bureaucrat, the intellectual, the worker, and the priest—all of them are different varieties of parasites that suck the *muzhik*'s blood. They must be swept away, along with everything that they have created, and then the *muzhik* will build a new Rus' and imbue her with a new truth and a new authority, for he is the only source of either of these things. He will reverse the laws that were cooked up by the Petersburg bureaucrats in favor of his own, unwritten ones. And the *muzhik* will cure Rus' of the faith that has been taught to her by the priests trained in the seminaries and academies, and, in place of the synodic church, he will erect a new one—one that is "earthen, sylvan, and green." And that is the moment when he will make his transformation from downtrodden Ivan the Fool to Ivan Tsarevich.[12]

Such was his program. But how was it to be carried out? X adopted a wait-and-see approach. The *muzhik* is surrounded by enemies: everyone is exerting pressure on him and everyone is stronger than he is. But if his enemies should fall into dissension, if the claws should come out, that is the moment when the *muzhik* will stand up tall and utter his final and decisive word. Thus, for the moment, he shares his path with no one. He has to wait a little longer: the first one to "light the blaze" will be the one to cozy up to. And as to the questions of which side will be the first to catch flame and which will be the one to set the blaze—for the time being, that is irrelevant. Whether a blue-collar rabble-rouser will go after the tsar or whether the tsar will call upon the oprichnina to silence the restless zemshchina[13]—it will make no difference. Whether the spark comes from the bottom, the top, the right, or the left—it's all tinder. All it needs to do is catch fire.

Such was Klyuev's perspective in the days leading up to 1913, when Esenin first appeared in Petersburg. He immediately made friends with Klyuev and fell under his influence. Esenin was young, inexperienced in many ways, and, though he wasn't exactly simple, he definitely wore his heart on his sleeve. Those things that had been vaguely and unconsciously fermenting within him developed considerably under the influence of Klyuev's worldview. Esenin had come to Petersburg knowing one thing: that things were bad for the *muzhik* and bad for the *muzhik* God. In Petersburg, he became enlightened: if things were bad, that means that they must get better.

And they would get better: give things a little time and the village Rus' would rise. And a new motif rang out in Esenin's poetry:

> O, Rus', spread wide your wingspan,
> Erect a new support.
> . . . .
> Away with rot and cowards,
> And flights that praise abuse—
> The tar's been washed and scoured
> From our empowered Rus'[14]

He already sees himself as one of the prophets and psalmists of this Rus'—along with Alexei Koltsov, "Humble Mikolai" Klyuev, and the writer Chapygin:

> Begone, decamp, you nation
> Of fetid thoughts and dreams!
> For on our stony pates can
> We carry astral din.

The imminent annihilation of such "fetid dreams" and the establishment of "a new support" are as yet only dimly visible to Esenin. The "astral din" borne by the *muzhik* prophets can also be interpreted in different ways. But Esenin was certain of one thing: that

> . . . we'll not avoid the darkening storm
> We'll gladly pay our dues
> So that the ring of unseen doors
> Might echo in the blue.[15]

The liberated Rus' is an azure, invisible city. It is something amorphously bright. Esenin does not endow it with any concrete features.

But he knows concretely that the path to that liberated Rus' lies through the "storm," during which the *muzhik's* daring will emerge. In other words—through revolution. The emergence of this idea is the most important stage in Esenin's spiritual biography.

The year seventeen knocked us senseless. It is as if we had forgotten that revolution does not always come from below, but that it can come from the very top as well. Klyuev's worldview had taken this into account. He did not forswear his connections with the lower stratum, but—and this is important to note—in those years, he was more inclined to anticipate a revolution from above. A year after Esenin's appearance in Petersburg, war broke out. And, for as long as it lasted, Gorodetsky and Klyuev clearly oriented themselves toward the right. Many still remember *The Year Fourteen*,[16] a book of Gorodetsky's vehemently patriotic poetry. In this book, not just the word "Tsar," but even the words "Palace" and "Square" were printed with capital letters. Gorodetsky received the loftiest possible reward for his book: a golden quill.[17] He even brought Klyuev to Tsarskoe Selo, to the same place where Grigory Rasputin, a *muzhik* just like him, had vainly attempted to set a fire from above. Klyuev's worldview heavily echoed Rasputin's.

In those years, the unfledged Esenin remained an obedient fellow traveler to Klyuev and Gorodetsky. He strutted around with them like a gilded *muzhik*, wore dandified little morocco boots and a light blue silk shirt belted with a golden cord; from this cord hung a comb with which he would brush his dashing curls. It was in precisely such getups that I ran into Klyuev and Esenin one day on a Moscow tram; they had come to read poetry at the Society for Free Aesthetics.[18] Indeed, Esenin's trusty instincts had hinted to him that adding Lord Gorodetsky to the catalog of peasant prophets would be ridiculous, but, nevertheless, he did not eschew his company. Or his fondness for Tsarskoe Selo, either.

■ □ ■

This last fact has been confirmed by a curious document. The truth is that, in addition to the autobiography I mentioned earlier, which was written in Berlin in the summer of 1922, Esenin composed a second autobiography after returning to Soviet Russia. It was published in the journal *Red Wheat Field*[19] after Esenin's death.

It appears that this second, Moscow autobiography was written with an ulterior motive. I don't know the specific circumstances and influences that brought it into being and where it was first introduced, but there is one critical difference between this autobiography and the Berlin version: this time, in a special, supplemental fragment, Esenin discusses what he had always kept silent about before then: specifically, his relations with the upper echelons and the period 1915–1917 more broadly. The Moscow biography is written in the same easy tone as the Berlin one, but in the Moscow biography, one can sense the author constantly casting a wary eye toward the Soviet authorities. This makes itself apparent even on the level of trivial details. For instance, this time, Esenin does not give his date of birth in the old style, but in the new one: it is now presented as October 3 rather than September 21; this time, he prudently refers to the *church-run* teacher-training school that he had trained in simply as a teacher-training school—and so on. So far as the unpleasant topic of his relations with Tsarskoe Selo is concerned—it is unlikely that we will be mistaken if we state that this is the main reason why the second autobiography was written in the first place. Rumors of these relations had been circulating for some time. Apparently, the moment had finally arrived for Esenin to justify himself on this count before the Soviet powers and put the rumors to rest (perhaps this was around the same time as Esenin's anti-Soviet debauches were taking place). Regardless of whether or not this was the case, this time around, Esenin was obliged to be more frank. And though he was far from entirely frank, we nevertheless find ourselves with a substantial confession on our hands.

"In 1916, I was called up for military service," Esenin writes. "Since I enjoyed a certain degree of protection from Colonel Loman, the empress's personal aide, I had access to a number of different advantages. I was living in Tsarskoe, not far from Razumnik-Ivanov. I once read poetry to the empress at Loman's request. After the reading, she said that my poetry was beautiful, but very sad. I replied that this was true about all of Russia. I cited poverty, the climate, and so forth."

Doubtless, a great deal is being said here—and a great deal is being papered over, starting with the fact that it wasn't so easy, either for a simple lad from the village or for a Russian poet, to come under the protection of the empress's aide. Esenin hadn't just wandered in off the street to Colonel Loman. Doubtless, there were various connections between them, but the most crucial one lay in whatever circumstances had led Loman to deem it necessary to involve himself in Esenin's fate in the first place. It is also unlikely that poetry would have been read to the empress simply "at Loman's request." Judging by the letters that were sent from the empress to the sovereign at that time, we know what a painfully nervous state she found herself in in the year 1916 and how sincerely she was trying to distance herself from everything that didn't bear the stamp of approval of her "Friend"[20] or his circles. In any case, she didn't have the time or inclination to listen to poetry—much less that of the entirely unknown Esenin. And, in general, it was difficult to secure an audience with her in those days—but here it suddenly happens that she invited Esenin herself. In reality, of course, events had transpired differently: the reading had been organized on Esenin's behalf by some connections of his who happened to be close to the empress . . . By employing his rather naïve device, Esenin is attempting to lead the reader's thoughts away from those particular circles in Tsarskoe Selo: he casually drops in a phrase about how he was living in Tsarskoe "not far from Razumnik-Ivanov." He might not have lived far from Razumnik-Ivanov, but by no stretch of the imagination did he socialize with him alone.

Farther down, Esenin writes: "The Revolution found me at the front, in one of the disciplinary battalions, where I had been assigned for refusing to write poetry in honor of the tsar."[21] Now that is like nothing else I've ever heard of. First of all, it is highly improbable that it would have been possible to land in a disciplinary battalion for refusing to write poetry in honor of the tsar: for better or for worse, whether or not one wrote poetry in honor of Nicholas II was not a matter that was assigned that sort of weight. Secondly (and this is the most important point), it is difficult to understand why Esenin would have considered it impossible to write poetry in honor of the tsar, but would not only have read his poetry to the tsarina, but would also have dedicated poetry to her. He kept mum about this last fact as well. At around the same time, in the summer of 1918, a certain Moscow publisher, bibliophile, and fancier of literary rarities, offered me the opportunity to buy or trade something for a galley proof of Esenin's second book, *Azure*,[22] which the publisher had acquired through dubious channels. This book came out after the February Revolution, but in a heavily edited form. Esenin had actually started compiling it as early as 1916 and the full galley contained an entire cycle of poems dedicated to the empress. I don't know whether or not Esenin was at the front at the end of 1916 and beginning of 1917, but it definitely would have been extremely difficult to obtain permission to dedicate poetry to the empress at that time—and, in any event, such permission could not possibly have been granted to a soldier serving in a disciplinary battalion.

One of Esenin's Soviet biographers, a certain Georgy Ustinov, who appears to have known Esenin quite well, tells another version of this story. His report, though rather vague and apparently not overly concerned with facts, nevertheless seems closer to the truth. After remarking that Esenin's literary birth had taken place "amid the storm and gale of patriotism" and that it had come "at just the right time" for the "Rasputin set," Ustinov recounts the story of how Esenin had been forced to write a poem at the order of some carousing officers during the war. Ustinov glosses over the fact that the poem in question was to be dedicated to the tsar, but later adds that, when "the poet-youth rebelled, he was shown a straight path to the disciplinary battalion." Naturally, reading between the lines, we can understand that, for some act of "mutiny," perhaps while under the influence, some officers had threatened Esenin with the disciplinary battalion, which he, according to Ustinov's testimony, "managed to avoid." We must conclude that, later, when compelled to inform the Bolsheviks of his court readings, Esenin had remembered this threat and, in order to create a more balanced impression, had tried to pass it off as an actual dispatch to the disciplinary battalion. In this way, he could even make himself out to be a "revolutionary."

In his account of Esenin's later life, Ustinov tells the story of how Esenin grew closer to the SRs under the Provisional Government and how, after the October Revolution, he "swung round toward the Bolshevik Soviets." In reality, Esenin was no turncoat. He was already more or less close to the SRs when he was still writing patriotic poems and reading them in Tsarskoe Selo. It is no coincidence that, while insisting that he had refused to glorify the emperor, Esenin said that he "sought support in Ivanov-Razumnik." But the fact of the matter is that Esenin was not engaged in any double-dealing, was not merely covering his bases in order to protect his personal career; he was simply applying Klyuev's tactics in a completely logical manner. He simply didn't care whether the revolution came from above or below. He knew that, at the last possible second, he would join forces with whomever was poised to set

Russia ablaze first; he expected *muzhik Rus'* to rise from the flames like a phoenix, a firebird. After the February Revolution, he found himself in the ranks of the SRs. After the SRs split into right and left factions, he found himself siding with the left, with the "extremists," with the ones who, in his view, had more flammable material at their disposal. Their programmatic differences weren't important to him; in all likelihood, he didn't know very much about them. To him, the Revolution was simply a prologue to far more significant events. To him, the SRs (right or left, it made no difference), like the Bolsheviks after them, were the ones clearing a path for the *muzhik* and the ones who would be swept aside by the *muzhik* in their turn. In 1918, he attended a Bolshevik gathering and "smiled affably at positively everyone—regardless of who was speaking or what was being said. Then the fair-haired boy took it into his head to speak his piece . . . and said: 'Revolution . . . is a raven . . . a raven that we send forth from our minds . . . on a reconnaissance mission . . . The future is greater . . .' "

In his 1922 autobiography, he writes: "I have never belonged to the CPSU[23] because I consider myself to be far more left-wing."

To him, "left-wing" meant further, later, *beyond* the Bolsheviks, *above* the Bolsheviks. The more "left-wing," the better.

■ □ ■

If we recall the set of impressions with which Esenin had, at one time, arrived in Petersburg (and which, as I have already noted, he probably sensed rather than consciously recognized), then we can see how they evolved quite consistently after the Revolution, even if they didn't gain much in terms of clarity.

The heavens are a cow. The harvest is a calf. Truth on earth is a manifestation of truth in heaven. The earthly is every bit as sacred as the heavenly, but only insofar as it represents the pure, unalloyed continuation of the primordial cosmogonical moment. The earth must remain exactly as it was when it was created: it must continue to exist as a great sprouting. The introduction of anything else beyond that, no matter what that something might be, is a perversion of the earth's pure image, a hindrance to the ever-developing manifestation of heaven on earth. Earth is the mother, giving birth from the heavens. From a religious standpoint, the only correct thing to do is to assist in that birth, to till the earth, to toil close to it.

Esenin himself observed that the image of the calf as harvest had once "slipped from his lips." When he came back to this image after the Revolution, Esenin introduced a substantial correction to it. After all, the calf is born of the cow as the harvest is born of the earth. Consequently, if we place an equals sign between the harvest and the calf, we must put one between the earth and the cow as well. We are left with a new image: the cow as earth. This is a very ancient image, not one that Esenin invented. But somehow, Esenin stumbled upon it all by himself, while going along his own path; having stumbled upon it, he sensed that it was fully compatible with the foundations of his worldview. Of course, under such circumstances, his original formula, which equated the heavens with a cow, was obliged, if not to fall away entirely, then to undergo a temporary change. (This, as we would subsequently learn, was exactly what would happen: Esenin came back to this image again later on.)

For Esenin, Russia is Rus', the fruit-bearing earth, the motherland where his forebears once labored and where his father and grandfather still labor now. Hence this very basic identification: if the earth is a cow, then all of the attributes associated with that idea can be transferred onto the concept of the motherland; similarly, one's love for the motherland can be manifested in one's love for the cow. And Esenin comes to that cow bearing the good tidings of Revolution, just as he would come heralding something "greater than revolution":

> Oh, motherland, what hour
> Unending and divine!
> No eyes are better, finer,
> Than yours, ideal, bovine.[24]

Esenin sees the process of revolution as a merging of the heavens and the earth, enacted amidst storm and gale:

> Our shoulders shake the heavens,
> Our hands upset the dark,
> Amidst the meager wheat shafts
> We breathe the grassy stars.

> O Rus', o steppe and cyclone,
> O you, my fathers' land.
> In the golden storeroom
> The thunder makes its den.

> With oats we feed the turmoil,
> With prayers we quench the lochs,
> And this our sky-blue soil
> Is tilled by reason's ox.

That looming something "greater than revolution" was heaven on earth, and that heaven would give shelter to the *muzhik*:

> Hosanna in excelsis!
> The hills sing of the sky.

And in that sky I see you,
My fatherland, abide.

Beneath Mauritian oak trees
My red-haired grandpa rests
And his fur coat shines brightly
With star-spots on his breast.

The hat made out of catskin
That he thought was so gay
Appraises, chilly, lunar,
The snow of native graves.

■ □ ■

Everything that looked like "counterrevolution" to the left SRs and the Bolsheviks in 1917–1918 was, of course, anathema to Esenin. The Provisional Government and Kornilov, the Constituent Assembly and the monarchists, the Mensheviks and the bankers, the right-wing SRs and the landowners, the Germans and the French—all of them constituted, in equal measure, the "hydra" poised to swallow up the kindled "Eastern Star."[25] Though Esenin proclaimed that

In the *muzhik's* mangers
A fire has been born, with
Peace for friends and strangers,[26]

Esenin genuinely believed that England, for example, harbored particularly malicious intentions against his Rus':

Get gone, you English monster,
Splash away to sea!

Our cherished northern wonder
Your sons shall never reach!

He believed that Russia was suffering because dark forces had
laid siege to it:

Lord, I do believe in you!
But use your rainy darts
To lead into your heaven
My piercèd native parts.[27]

Thus begins his epic poem "Advent." It is unique among Esenin's
works. In the lines that follow, Rus' reveals itself to him as the future
source of the ultimate truth on earth:

Beyond the mountain still untrod,
Amidst the azure dales,
Before my eyes I see, o God,
Your son come down a trail.

I pine for you with all my might,
Here from my *muzhik* house;
Here from a Rus' that's seen the light
He's carrying his cross.

Later on, Esenin introduces the forces and events that, in his
opinion, are hindering the advent of truth. He employs images of
soldiers scourging Christ, of Simon Peter denying Him, of Judas
betraying Him, and, finally, of Golgotha. It seems as if the whole
thing was clearly written about Christ, but in reality, this isn't the
case. If we carefully reread Esenin's revolutionary poems leading up
to "Inonia,"[28] we see that all of the Christian images are presented

in altered (or distorted) forms, including the image of Christ himself. Here, as in his early poetry, this stems from the fact that Esenin takes names from the Gospel and arbitrarily imbues them with content of his own. As it is, acting in perfect accordance with the fundamental principles of Esenin's faith, we can decode his pseudo-Christian terminology to arrive at the following:

> The Virgin Mary = the earth = a cow = *muzhik* Rus'.
> God the Father = the heavens = truth.
> Christ = the son of heaven and earth = the harvest = a calf = the manifestation of heavenly truth = the Rus' that is to come.

For Esenin's Christ, the crucifixion is no more than an incidental, tragic episode that it would have been better to avoid. And, in fact, it *could* have been avoided, had it not been for "counterrevolutionary" forces. It is worth noting that, in "Advent," the scourging of Christ, the denial of Peter, and the betrayal of Judas are described in great detail, while the crucifixion itself, which is to say, the complete, albeit temporary, triumph of Christ's enemies, is only mentioned vaguely and in passing. This is because counterrevolution, which Esenin uses as a sort of life model for depicting the torments of *his* Christ, never actually triumphs for an instant. So, to all intents and purposes, *Esenin's* Christ isn't really crucified: the crucifixion is invoked for the sake of completing the analogy, for the benefit of artistic integrity, but in contradiction of historic and religious truths (which is to say, those of Esenin's religion).

And that is why "Advent" ends in what appears to be a paradox; however, as far as Esenin is concerned, this "paradox" is entirely logical.

> The hills sing of this wonder,
> The sands ring to the skies.

I trust, I doubt no longer:
The Eastern calf is nigh!

In seas of oats and buckwheat,
He'll cast to us this calf . . .
But it is long before we meet
And ruin stalks our path!

In other words, I trust that there will be life "post-revolution,"
but I am afraid of counterrevolution.

And this is how we are to understand Esenin's exclamation at the
beginning of the following poem:

Storm clouds are barking,
The golden-toothed heights roar their wrath . . .
Singing out, I am calling:
Lord above, bear your calf![29]

In its own time, this last line provoked an explosion of bewil-
derment and unease. Both kinds of reaction were futile. There was
nothing to be bewildered by; Esenin had expressed his main idea
not affectedly, but with the utmost simplicity, with the kind of
precision attainable only by great artists. Feelings of unease were
futile, too, or, at any rate, they had come about too late, because
Esenin was already addressing his pagan god with great faith and
piety. He would say: "My God, manifest Your truth in the Rus'
that is to come." And as for the fact that he was usurping the
images and names of the Christian faith, people should have taken
exception to that much earlier, upon the first appearance not of
Esenin, but of Klyuev.

Unpleasant as it is to admit, there can be no doubt that Esenin's
calf is a parody of the Lamb. The Lamb is bred for sacrifice; the calf

is prosperous, rust-colored, and well-fed, full of the promise of prosperity and satiety.

From the morning through the noontime,
To the heavens' thundersong,
Our days, like pails, are fast lined
With the milk he's freshly drawn.

And from evening on through midnight,
Praising lands that know no grief,
He'll divine with stars the first light
Of the harvest's silver wheat.

Such will be the kingdom of the calf. And it will be a new Rus', transfigured, other: not Rus', but *Inonia*.

■ □ ■

Esenin's poetry hadn't contained any direct manifestations of hostility toward Christianity up until "Inonia" because there hadn't been any real reason for them to appear. Apparently, Esenin even considered himself to be a Christian. The thing that was most precious to him, his faith in a higher calling for *muzhik* Rus', was capable of coexisting not just with his demi-paganism, but with genuine Christianity as well. Even if Esenin himself recognized some of the discrepancies in his beliefs, then it was only in relation to historical Christianity. At the same time, he was certain that he had identified historical Christianity's fallacies, and that he and Klyuev and someone else besides were quite capable of taking Christianity down the path it needed to go. He did not take into account the fact that, in order to perform such a task, it would be necessary to know a bit more both about history and about Christianity; talented Russians generally do not care to take such matters into consideration. He relied more on his connection with "the people" and "the earth," on the firm conviction that "the people" and "the earth" were, in fact, the originators of truth; he also relied on his own intuition, which was incredibly keen. But his intuition was also unformed, incoherent, and contradictory. Vaguely aware of this fact, Esenin went to others in search of coherence and molding. In his search for the one idea that would give his instincts structure, he fell under the influence of others.

In 1917, Klyuev's influence, which essentially resonated with Esenin's own worldview, gave way to the influence of the left-wing SRs. It was at that time that the SRs explained to Esenin that the Rus' that was to come, the one he had been dreaming of, was, in fact, the new state. This new state would also be built on a religious foundation: not on a pagan or a Christian foundation, but, rather, on a socialist one; not on a faith in redeeming gods, but on faith in the self-organized human being. They explained to him that "there is socialism and then there is Socialism"—that socialism with a lowercase letter is merely a social and political program, but that there is Socialism with a capital letter, too: a "religious idea, a new faith and a new knowledge to which the knowledge and old faith of Christianity are giving way ... The best even of professional Christian theologians see this, know this." "The new universal idea (Socialism) will act as dynamite; it will break the chains that Christianity has fastened even more securely over the human body than ever before." "In Christianity, the whole world was saved by the sufferings of one Person: in the Socialism that is to come, each person will be saved by the sufferings of the whole world."

These quotations are drawn from Ivanov-Razumnik's foreword to Esenin's poem. Chronologically speaking, this article was written after "Inonia" was, but the internal order of the two works is, of course, reversed. It was not "Inonia" that led Ivanov-Razumnik to the ideas, new or otherwise, that are expressed in his article, but "Inonia" that emerged as a vivid poetic manifestation of all the ideas that Ivanov-Razumnik had inculcated in Esenin.

> I fear not spears, nor arrows' rain,
> Nor for my own survival,
> Says Esenin, the Prophet Sergei,
> In keeping with the Bible.[30]

Here, Esenin is mistaken. He only wrote "Inonia" "in keeping with the Bible" in the sense that he borrowed several of its literary devices. Of course, it would have been more accurate to say not "in keeping with the Bible," but rather "in keeping with Ivanov-Razumnik."

Esenin, in all his artlessness, went too far. His epic turned out openly anti-Christian and coarsely sacrilegious. For various reasons, Ivanov-Razumnik would later attempt to gloss over both of these facts, to lay the blame at someone else's door. He assures us that Esenin is "wrestling" not with Christ, but with that false likeness of Him, that "Anti-Christ under whose powerful hand the historical church has grown and spread for twenty (?) centuries." According to Ivanov-Razumnik's version of events, it appears as if it is he and Esenin who have the Christian faith's best interests at heart. True, he also immediately lets slip that this faith is dear to him only insofar as it is the precursor of a greater truth, the Socialism that is to come, which will correct the faith once and for all and, in doing so, destroy it, so that, from that moment on, the world will no longer be saved by the "sufferings of one Person" . . . but no, the honest anti-Christianity that Esenin expresses in "Inonia" is a phenomenon unto itself; it does not fully fit Ivanov's interpretation.

I won't mince words. In "Inonia," Esenin rejects Christianity as a whole, not just Christianity as a historical entity. From the

Christian standpoint, the Christianity whose truth he continued to refer to as Christ, only "without the cross and torments," was the greatest sacrilege of all. He might have rejected Christianity with the same naïve levity as he had formerly considered himself to be a Christian—but that does not change the facts.

The literary merits of "Inonia" are a different matter. This poem exhibits a great deal of talent. But in order to bask in its merits, one must immerse oneself in it, must have in one's possession something like a sturdy diving costume. Only a reader equipped with such a costume can look with spiritual impunity upon the seductive beauties of "Inonia."

■ □ ■

"Inonia" was Esenin's swan song as a poet of revolution and the sought-after new truth. Whether or not he had erred, whether or not the logic of his writings was sound, whether they were bad or good—no matter how you look at it, Esenin undeniably gave voice to and indeed "sang out" much of what was floating around in the catastrophic air of that time. In that sense, he was truly a "prophet," if you will. A prophet of his own errors and of the errors of others, a prophet of failed expectations and of mistakes—but a prophet nonetheless. In "Inonia," he expressed himself completely, to the last. After that, he didn't really have anything left to say. His Word was inextricably connected with events. The real Inonia must come—or it must not. At any rate, Russia must move toward it—or must not.

I met Esenin for the first time in Moscow in the spring of 1918. I found him to be physically pleasing; I liked his slenderness, his soft, yet sure movements, his face, not handsome, but good-looking. But the most appealing thing about him was his cheerfulness, which was brisk and easy without being noisy or shrill. He was extremely rhythmical. He would look you right in the eye and immediately give you the impression that he was a person of true heart, someone who would probably make for the most excellent of comrades.

We didn't meet often and we almost always met in the company of others. Only once did we roam around Moscow all night, just the two of us. We talked about the Revolution, of course, but only inconsequential fragments of that conversation have lodged in my memory. I remember that we parted ways by the building where Esenin lived, on Tverskaya, by Postnikovsky Passage, when the sun was already rising. We parted quite pleased with each other. Each of us earnestly invited the other one to visit—and neither of us followed through. I believe that this was because Esenin didn't particularly care for my circle of friends, just as I didn't care for his.

At the time, he was moving with a nasty crowd. For the most part, it was made up of young people who had joined the ranks of the left-wing SRs and the Bolsheviks: fairly ignorant folks, but people who were prepared to remake the world without hesitation. They philosophized constantly, and always in extremist tones. They were expansive people. They ate little, but drank a great deal. They went through periods of fervent belief and periods of fervent blasphemy. They visited prostitutes to preach the Revolution—and beat them after they were done. They mostly consisted of two types. The first type was the gloomy brunet with the bushy beard. The second was the golden-haired youth with long tresses, a seraphic gaze, and a physiognomy vaguely reminiscent of the paintings of Nesterov. Both types were ready to give the shirts off their backs and send their souls straight to ruin for the sake of their neighbor. They were also prepared to shoot that same neighbor on the spot if "the Revolution demanded it." All of them wrote poetry and all of them were in direct contact with the Cheka. In fact, later on, one of the seraphic blonds would rise to fame in connection with an execution. I believe that Esenin fraternized with them out of a sense of unflinching curiosity and a love of extremes, regardless of what those extremes actually were.

I remember one story in particular. Around that same time, in the spring of 1918, Alexei Tolstoy took it into his head to celebrate his name day. He invited all of literary Moscow: "Come yourselves and bring a crowd along with you." There were some forty people in attendance, if not more. Esenin was there, too. He had brought along a bearded brunet in a leather jacket. The brunet stood there, listening to the conversations. Occasionally, he would let drop a phrase—and not a stupid one, either. This was Blyumkin, who, three months later, would kill Count Mirbach, the German ambassador. Esenin appeared to be friends with him. The poetess K. was among the guests. Esenin took a shine to her. He grew very attentive toward her. He decided to make a spectacle of himself—and artlessly made the poetess the following offer: "Would you like to see how people are executed? I can arrange the whole thing for you with Blyumkin in a matter of minutes."[31]

It seemed as if he was living in a fairly irrational manner. That was also around the time he was drawing closer to the Bolshevik "spheres."

Even before "Inonia," he had written a poem called "Comrade,"[32] a very weak piece, but a curious one nonetheless. It was in this poem that he first broadened his "social base" to include the working class. His workers came out looking rather far-fetched, but the important thing was that, now, the very same proletariat who had formerly been represented by the peasant poets as "hooligans" and "riffraff" now numbered among the builders of the new truth. This change took place with striking speed and abruptness, which, again, can be explained by looking at the influences that Esenin had fallen under.

At the beginning of 1919, he took it into his head to apply for membership in the Bolshevik party. He wasn't accepted, but his intention was significant. Did Esenin understand that, for a prophet of something "greater than revolution," joining the CPSU would have come as an enormous "demotion," that, from being one of the creators of Inonia, he would have been downgraded to a rank-and-file builder of the RSFSR? I believe that he didn't. During that period, he exclaimed with pride: "My mother, my homeland! I am a Bolshevik."[33]

His "prophetic" period came to an end. Esenin began to look toward the present rather than the future.

■ □ ■

If he had been accepted into the CPSU, no good would have come of it. His infatuation with the proletariat and the proletarian revolution proved to be insubstantial. Before many others who had been seduced by the intoxication of War Communism,[34] he realized that the current situation was not only not leading to Socialism with a capital letter, but that it was not even leading to socialism with the most lowercase of letters. He understood that the Bolsheviks were not fellow travelers on the road to Inonia. And so he hurled a bitter and venomous reproach in their direction:

> With oars made out of severed arms
> You row to the land of the future![35]

He still didn't have the courage to admit that Inonia had not come to pass and never would. He still wanted to hope, and so once again he pinned all of his hopes on the village. He wrote "Pugachyov"[36] and immediately set off for someplace in the countryside so that he could touch the earth and draw fresh strength from it.

The village did not live up to his expectations. Esenin saw that it wasn't at all like the songs he had sung about it. But, in his human weakness, he did not wish to acknowledge the organic, inherent reasons why, even in the wake of the "storm and gale," it had not gone down the road to Inonia. He heaped the blame upon the "city," upon the "city culture" with which, in his opinion, the Bolsheviks were poisoning village Rus'. He believed that it was the automobile, newly arrived from the city, blowing its "fateful horn," that was to blame. By some twist of fate, it was only at that time, when the plants and factories had virtually ground to a halt, that he suddenly took notice of them. He fancied that they had gotten too close to the country—and were poisoning it:

> O, electrical ascent,
> The dead-eyed grasp of pipes, conveyors;
> The timber bellies of our tents
> Are shaken by a steely fever.[37]

He also curses the train whizzing past, chased by a foal in a foolish, ridiculous manner:

> The devil take you, nasty guest!
> Our song won't mix with yours, you rotter.
> Too bad in childhood, we weren't blessed
> To see you drowned in deep well water.
> It's fine for them to look and lean,
> To deck their mouths with tinny kisses,
> Only I, the psalmist, sing,
> An alleluia for my province.
> That's why, in autumn's liquid glut,
> On loam that stood by—frigid, arid—
> Its thatched head like the roofs of huts,
> Ash berries bled out, bright and lurid.
> And so accordions were able
> To usher in our tragic pining;

The *muzhik*, smelling like a hay bale,
Has drowned in heady, hearty moonshine.

The city's looming power evokes a hopelessness and animosity within him:

O secret world, my world primeval,
You quieted, died down, like wind,
And so the country's throat was strangled
In the highway's stony grip.[38]

He compares himself, "the last village poet," to the cornered wolf that throws itself upon the hunter:

I, like you, am always ready,
And though I hear the hunter's blast,
I hold my fatal last jump steady,
To taste my foe's blood-spattered flesh.

He came back to Moscow in a state of depression. "I have no love, neither for the city, nor for the country."[39] Huts and houses were now unpleasant to him in equal measure. He wanted to become a tramp:

Because the winds sing out more loudly
To the wino than the rest.

He is eager to mask his grief with holy foolishness and freakish whims:

Because without these foolish fancies
I cannot live upon this earth.

And so the prophet of failed miracles became a holy fool—but this was not yet his final fall. Esenin's final fall would come about while he was off on a spree, a bender. He imagined that all of Russia was drowning its sorrows for the same reasons that he was: because its hopes for something "greater than revolution," "more left-wing than the Bolsheviks" had been dashed; because it had destroyed everything that had been and had not yet come any closer to the things it had been dreaming of:

> They drink again, fight here and cry here,
> To the squeezebox's yellow-tinged blues.
> They curse their ill fortune with hot tears;
> They remember old Muscovite Rus'.

> And I, with my head not quite lifted,
> Let my eyes get glazed over with wine
> To not see that disastrous visage,
> To let my mind rest for a time.
> . . . .
> Something cruel in the gaze of the crazy,
> Something bold in their thundering speech.
> They feel bad for those fools, young and hasty,
> Who have snuffed out their lives in the breach.

> Oh, where are the men who've pushed limits?
> Are your pathways lit up by our flames?
> The accordion man uses spirits
> To treat syphilis caught on the plains.

> No, you can't crush such men, you can't budge them.
> Their dare-devilry passes for blight.
> You are my Rasha . . . my Rasha . . .
> The pure Asiatic side![40]

Surrounded by this blight, by urban hooligans, Esenin nevertheless felt more at home than he did amongst the well-heeled bourgeoisie of Soviet Russia. By that time, the Bolsheviks and those who
stood alongside them had become loathsome in his eyes. He was
sick and tired of his erstwhile friends, who occupied more or less
bloody, but cushy positions:

> I won't fool myself that I've no foibles,
> In the haze of my heart lurks disorder.
> Why do they think I sell snake oil?
> Why do they think I'm a brawler?
>
> I'm no villain, I don't lurk in forests,
> I'm no other man's paid assassin.
> I'm just a back alley Lothario
> Who smiles at people in passing.
> . . . .
> The citizens here aren't my allies,
> My allegiance is to different kingdoms.
> I'm ready to give my best neckties
> To whichever young tomcats might need them.[41]

He did not join the disgraced revolutionaries, but he did distance himself from his native villages.

> Yes! Now it's decided! Forever
> I'll leave behind these native fields.
> . . . .
> I read out my verses to hookers,
> And brew homemade spirits with hoods.[42]
> . . . .
> I'm ready now. I'm humble.

Take a look at this bottle patrol!
I'm gathering up all the wine corks
To stop up the neck of my soul.[43]

In literature, he attached himself to the same kinds of circles, began associating with people who had nothing to lose, poetic vagabonds. Esenin was dragged into imaginism[44] just as he might have been dragged to the tavern. His talent was used to spruce up the performances of the talentless imaginists; they lived off his name like a tavern rat lives off a rich man gone on a spree.

He sunk lower and lower, as if actively striving to hit rock bottom, to come into contact with the worst filth contemporary Moscow had to offer. It was in this same spirit that he married. I will not dwell on this period of his life for too long. It is too widely known. Esenin and Isadora Duncan's honeymoon morphed into a wild road trip across Europe and America and ended in divorce. Esenin returned to Russia. Thus began the final period of his life, which was characterized by sudden mood swings.

At first, it seemed as if Esenin had decided to settle down and wash himself clean of the filth that had caked onto him. He began to display a sorrowful indifference, a resignation to his fate—and his thoughts, of course, immediately turned to the village:

I've never before felt so tired.
In this leaden gray hoarfrost and slime
I dreamed of Ryazan's broad horizons
And my own reprehensible life.
. . . .
Inside, by the very same strictures,
The furious dust settles down.
But I nevertheless feel respect for
Those fields that once made me so proud.

To the land where I grew under maples,
Where I frolicked on yellow-tinged grass,
I send my regards to the ravens,
To the sparrows and owls flying past.

I cry to them in the spring distance:
"Sweet birds, in your blue trepidation,
Tell them all that I'm through with my mischief..."[45]

. . . .

He writes his profoundly heartfelt "Letter to Mother":[46]

They write me that you, in your worry,
In your grief over me are consumed,
That you rush to the road in a hurry
In your old-fashioned, threadbare *shushun*.[47]

And that, in the evening's blue darkness
You're haunted by one single dream:
In a tavern somewhere lies my carcass,
With a Finnish knife stuck in my spleen.

. . . .

Don't awaken those things that lie dreaming,
Don't disturb those that haven't come true,
In my life, I've been forced into feeling
Loss and weariness far, far too soon.

In the end, he did go to his native village, which he hadn't laid eyes on for many years. A final disappointment lay in store for him there—the most crushing one of all, in comparison with which all of his previous disappointments had been nothing.

■ □ ■

Immediately before the Revolution, in December of 1916, the peasant poet Alexander Shiryaevets, who has since passed away, sent me a copy of his poetry collection *Song Introductions* along with a request for my opinion on it. I read the book and replied to Shiryaevets, clearly indicating that I didn't understand how "writers of the people," who know the *muzhik* better than we, the intelligentsia, do, could portray the peasant as some sort of fairy tale hero in the style of Churilo Plyonkovich, in silken peasant shoes.[48] After all, the type of *muzhik* that the peasant poets were depicting probably never existed—and, in any case, no longer exists and never will exist in the future. On January 7, 1917, Shiryaevets replied to me in the following manner:

> *My dear Vladislav Felitsianovich! I am very grateful to you for your letter. You needn't have thought I would be "angry" at what you said—on the contrary, I am glad to hear such candid thoughts.*
>
> *I will say a few words in my own defense. I am perfectly aware that the sort of people that Klyuev, Klychkov, Esenin and I write about won't exist any time soon, but is that not the very reason why we hold them so dear—the fact that they will not exist any time soon? . . . and what is better: the Churilo of yesteryear, dressed in silken peasant shoes, with all of his choruses and flourishes, or today's Churilo, dressed in American half-boots, with a copy of Karl Marx or Chronicles in his hand, gasping at the truths revealed to him therein? . . . By God, the former is sweeter to me! . . . I know that the rusalkas' whirlpools will soon be replaced with bathhouses, bathhouses for people of both sexes, furnished with every possible convenience; nevertheless, whirlpools are sweeter to me than bathhouses. . . For it is not so easy to part with the things that we have lived with for centuries! And how are we expected not to retreat back into the olden days, away from the confusion of the modern world, away from all the hysterical howling that has been triumphantly labeled as "slogans" . . . Let Bryusov write*

*about the charms of modernity; I will go off in search of the Firebird,
I will make my way toward Turgenev's estates, even though my ances-
tors were thrashed within an inch of their lives there. Indeed, how is
it possible not to be enchanted by scenes like this one? . . . (At this
point he quotes S. Klychkov's poem "The Windmill in the Wood" in
its entirety, which I have chosen to omit.—V. Kh.).*[49]

*Nothing like that will ever exist either! Some enterprising person
will come along and (after tearing down the mill) erect some "Grand
Hotel," and then a city with smokestacks will grow up around it . . .
And even now, a bob-haired lady student is sitting by a sky-blue river
reach, with a copy of either Weininger or* The Keys to Happiness *in
her hands.*[50]

*Pardon my digression, Vladislav Felitsianovich. Perhaps I am
talking dreadful nonsense. It is all because I hate this accursed modernity that has ruined our fairy tale; and without fairy tales, how are
we to live upon this earth? . . .*

*There is a great deal of merit in your ideas, and I agree with them,
but, for the time being, I will tread familiar grounds, with the miller's
daughter rather than the bob-haired lady student. Let voices stronger
than mine sing of modernity, of the future; my voice is too weak for
that . . . (I omit the end of this letter, as it is unrelated to the current
topic.—V. Kh.)*

When Shiryaevets wrote to me, "I am perfectly aware that the
sort of people that Klyuev, Klychkov, Esenin and I write about
won't exist any time soon," did he know that, in reality, it wasn't simply that they wouldn't exist any time soon or that they no longer
existed, but, more accurately, that the "people" he knew from the
bylinas[51] and songs had, in fact, never existed? I believe that he did,
but that he took great pains to drive that thought from his head: he
lived by his faith in the ideal peasant, by the "fairy tale"—and "without fairy tales, how are we to live upon this earth?"

It is no coincidence that Shiryaevets invokes Esenin's name: the whole thrust of Esenin's poetry was based on his faith in such an imaginary "people." And Esenin lived in a "fairy tale," the finest page of which was Inonia, the shining city erected by *muzhiks*.

The first blow to this dream had been inflicted even before Esenin's marriage. But, as we have already seen, Esenin did not dare admit the truth just then: he laid the blame for all of the discrepancies he found between his dream and reality on the encroachment of the city into village life. At the same time, though, he continued to believe that this encroachment was purely mechanical and that it didn't change anything about the essence of the village. He even thought a time would come when the village would feel the urge to stand up for itself—and when it would be capable of doing so. Now, having returned to the village again after a prolonged absence, Esenin saw the real truth. "Visiting his native parts once more,"[52] he notes with horror:

> What a bounty of discoveries
> Followed closely on my heels!

At first, he doesn't recognize his surroundings. Then he can't immediately find his mother's house. Then he meets a passerby and doesn't recognize him as his own grandfather, the very one he had so vividly imagined sitting in heaven "beneath Mauritian oak trees." Later on, he finds out that his sisters have joined the Komsomol and that "the commissar has taken down the cross." They arrive home and he sees "the wall hung with a paper Lenin." And so,

> The more depressed granddad and mother,
> The cheerier my sister's smile.

And his sister, "having opened, like the Bible, barrel-bellied *Kapital*," "waters down" "Engels and Marx":

Regardless of the weather,
Such books, of course, I've never read.

And, listening to his sister's words, he remembers how, even as he was approaching the house:

Our tiny pup, just like in Byron,
Barking, meets me at the gates.

As we can see, Esenin's grandfather and mother, who cast hopeless glances at his sisters, appear to Esenin as the final bearers of the *muzhik* truth: Esenin comforts himself with the idea that such a truth did exist once—even if it was only in the past. But in the poem "Soviet Rus'," which has been the object of so much attention, Esenin takes things even further: he plainly states that he cannot find safe haven in anybody's eyes—regardless of whether they are old or young. The timbered Rus' from which Inonia was meant to emerge does not exist. What does exist is a coarse, cruel, vulgar "Soviet Rus' " caroling the "agitprop of Demyan Bedny." And, for the first time, Esenin realizes that not only does the Rus' he had sung about not exist, but that perhaps it never had, and that his faith in his own divine ministry, for which he had been anointed by the "people," had been mistaken:

What a land! why did I cheer
And cry in verse, "I'm with the people"?
My poetry's not needed here;
I dare say I'm not needed either.[53]

He bids the village farewell, pledging to humbly come to terms with reality as it is. Now not only were his dreams of Inonia dashed (that had happened even earlier)—now it turns out that there had been nothing for Inonia to emerge from in the first place: Esenin's ideal, peasant-hut Rus' had itself turned out to be a dream.

But Esenin's humility only extended so far. Upon returning to Moscow, he immersed himself in the swamplands of NEP[54] (he had gone abroad at the very beginning of that period) and, having felt the enormous, shameful gap between Bolshevik slogans and Soviet realities even in the city—Esenin spiraled into spite. He started drinking again. In the beginning, his drunken scandals manifested themselves in anti-Semitic pranks. This was partly his old-school mindset rearing its ugly head. Esenin's hostility poured forth in its coarsest and most primitive forms. He (and Klychkov, who also took part in these scandals), were summoned to the civil court, which was located in the so-called Press House. It is still too early to discuss the tactlessness and humiliation that accompanied their trial. In any case, Esenin and Klychkov were "forgiven." It was around that time that Esenin's anti-Soviet tavern performances began. One of his judges, Andrei Sobol, who also went on to take his own life, told me in Italy at the beginning of 1925 that to "drub" the Bolsheviks the way Esenin was doing in public couldn't possibly have occurred to anyone living in Soviet Russia at that time; any person who had said a tenth of what Esenin was saying would have been executed long ago. As for Esenin, it was only in 1924 that the *militsia* issued an order to have him escorted to the station, left there to sober up, and released without letting the matter go any further. Soon, all of the policemen in the central stations knew Esenin by sight. Of course, this order had not been given out of love for Esenin or concern about the fate of Russian writers: it was given in an attempt at public relations. The powers that be did not want to officially admit or call attention to the rift between the "Workers' and Peasants' " regime and a writer known as a peasant poet.[55]

However, these scandals gave way to different moods. Esenin attempted to travel. He spent some time in the Caucasus and wrote a cycle of poems about his experiences there, but this gave him no relief. He was once again gripped by the desire to "turn to his native land."[56] Once more, he attempted to come to terms with his situation: having rejected both Inonia and Rus', he attempted to accept and love the Union of Soviet Socialist Republics as it was. He even diligently sat down to read the USSR's version of the Bible, Marx's *Capital*—but couldn't stomach it, and so he tossed it aside. He attempted to retreat into his personal life—but couldn't seem to find safe haven there, either. At a certain point, virtually every one of his poems began to end with predictions of imminent death. At last, he drew the final, operative conclusion from the poetry he had written long ago, when the truth about the unfulfilled Inonia had only just begun to dawn on him:

> My friend, my friend! Eyes that now see
> Can only be shuttered by death.[57]

Esenin's eyes had been opened at last, but he did not wish to see what was happening around him. There was only one thing left for him to do: he had to die.

■ □ ■

Esenin's story is a story of misguided thinking. The ideal *muzhik* Rus' that he believed in did not exist. The Inonia that was to come, the Inonia that was supposed to descend from heaven onto that Rus' did not and could not in fact do so. He believed that the Bolshevik Revolution was the path to something "greater than revolution," but it turned out to be the path to the worst abomination possible: NEP. He thought that he believed in Christ, but he didn't really believe. And in turning his back on Christ and blaspheming against Him, Esenin experienced all of the torture and pain that he might have felt if he had actually been a believer. He turned his back on God for the sake of his love of Man, but all Man did was take the cross down from the church, hang Lenin up in place of the icons, and open Marx up like the Bible.

But, nevertheless, in spite of all of the errors and lapses that occurred throughout his life, there is still something deeply attractive about Esenin. It is as if there is some enormous, precious truth that binds together all these errors. So what is it about Esenin that makes him so attractive, and what is that truth? I beleive that the answer is clear. What makes Esenin so wonderful and noble is that he was endlessly truthful in his art and in his conscience; that he saw everything in his life through to the end; that he was not afraid to admit his mistakes; that he took responsibility even for those mistakes that others had seduced him into making—and that he felt the desire to pay a terrible price for everything he did. And his truth manifested itself in his love for the motherland. His was a great love, albeit a blind one. He professed it even in his hooligan persona:

I love my motherland,
I love my motherland a lot![58]

His grief lay in the fact that he didn't know what to call her: he sang of timbered Rus' and *muzhik* Rusia[59] and socialist Inonia and Asiatic Rasha, and he even tried to accept the USSR—but his motherland's one true name never passed his lips: *Russia*. This was what constituted his principal error, not ill will, but a bitter mistake. Therein lay both the entanglement of his tragedy and its denouement.

Chaville, February 1926

GORKY[1]

09

I remember Gorky's first books distinctly; I also remember the narrow-minded comments that were made at the time about the newly minted writer-vagabond. I attended one of the first performances of *The Lower Depths* and once wrote a bombastic prose poem inspired by the "Song of the Falcon." But that was in my early youth. In the spring of 1908, my friend Nina Petrovskaya was in Capri and spotted a copy of my first book of poetry lying on Gorky's table. Gorky asked her about me because he read absolutely everything and took an interest in absolutely everyone. For many years, though, we had no contact at all. My literary life ran its course among people who were entirely alien to Gorky, and to whom Gorky seemed equally alien.[2]

Kornei Chukovsky arrived in Moscow in 1916. He informed me that the Sail publishing house, which had just emerged on the Petersburg scene, was planning to publish some children's books. He asked if I knew of any young artists from whom he could commission illustrations. I named two or three options in Moscow and gave him the address of my niece, who was living in Petersburg at the time. She was issued an invitation to work at Sail; she met Gorky there and soon became an intimate member of his noisy, perpetually crowded household.[3]

In the autumn of 1918, at the time when Gorky was assembling his famous Literature publishing house,[4] I was summoned to Saint Petersburg and offered the management of its Moscow branch. Having accepted this offer, I felt that I should meet Gorky in person. He came out to see me looking like an erudite Chinese man: he was dressed in a red silk robe and a garish little hat, had prominent cheekbones, wore large glasses perched on the tip of his nose, and was holding a book in his hands. To my surprise, he had no interest whatsoever in discussing the publishing house. I realized that the enterprise was merely borrowing his name.

I stayed on in Petersburg for about ten days after that. The city was dead and sinister. The odd tram would creep lazily past the boarded-up shops. The unheated buildings smelled of fish. There was no electricity. Gorky used kerosene. A great lamp burned in his dining room on Kronverksky Prospect and, every evening, a crowd would gather around it. A. N. Tikhonov and Z. I. Grzhebin, who ran the show over at World Literature, would visit. Shalyapin, who had loudly denounced the Bolsheviks, would be there, too. One day, Krasin showed up—wearing tailcoats, since he had come straight from some "diplomatic" dinner, though I can't imagine what kind of diplomacy would have been possible in those days. Maria Fyodorovna Andreyeva would emerge to greet her guests accompanied by her secretary, P. P. Kryuchkov. The wife of one of the members of the imperial family would make appearances there—the man himself lay ailing in the depths of Gorky's apartment. A large portrait of Gorky—my niece's work—stood in the sick man's room. It was asked that I be allowed to enter. The sick man extended a hot hand in my direction. A bulldog was growling and flopping around next to the bed—it had been wrapped up in a blanket to prevent it from attacking me.[5]

In the dining room, conversations took place about hunger, about the civil war. Drumming his fingers against the table and glancing up over his interlocutor's head, Gorky would say: "Yes, affairs are in a very bad state, very bad"—but it was impossible to tell exactly whose affairs he considered to be in a bad state and where his sympathies lay. Incidentally, he always tried to cut such conversations short. Afterward, the guests would sit down to play lotto; they would play for long periods of time. My niece and I would return to our home on Bolshaya Monetnaya in the miserable Petersburg night, escorted by the pop of distant gunshots.

Soon after that time, Gorky came to Moscow. The administration of the newly formed Pan-Russian Writers' Union charged me with inviting Gorky to join its ranks. He immediately agreed and signed an application, which, according to our statutes, had to be accompanied by the recommendation of two members of the administration. These recommendations came from J. K. Baltrušaitis and myself. This amusing little document can probably be found in the union's archive, if it has been preserved.[6]

In the summer of 1920, I suffered a great misfortune. It came to light that one of the medical commissions that was reviewing individuals who had been called up to serve in the war had been taking bribes. Several doctors were shot and all of the people whom they had cleared from military service were subject to reexamination. I found myself among the many unfit, unfortunate souls whom the new commission, blinded by its fear, declared fit for duty. I was given two days, after which time I was to travel straight from the sanatorium to Pskov, and from there on to the front. By chance, Gorky happened to be in Moscow at the time. He told me to write a letter to Lenin, which he then took to the Kremlin himself. I was examined once more, and, of course, released from service. As we parted, Gorky said, "Why don't you move to Petersburg? Here, you have to serve; there, you can still write."

I took his advice and moved to Petersburg in the middle of November. By that time, Gorky's apartment had become quite densely populated. A number of people were living there: Gorky's new secretary, Maria Ignatyevna Benkendorf (later the Baroness Budberg), a tiny female medical student nicknamed Molecule (a lovely girl, an orphan, the daughter of some of Gorky's long-held acquaintances), the artist Ivan Nikolaevich Rakitsky, and, finally, my niece and her husband. It was this last circumstance that ultimately defined the character of my relationship with Gorky: our connection was not dependent on business or literature, but was entirely intimate and earthbound in its nature. Of course, we would occasionally collaborate on literary affairs, both at that time and later on, but such matters remained more or less in the background. Given the difference in our ages and literary tastes, matters could not have been otherwise.

A crowd would gather in his apartment from early morning until late at night. People would stop by to visit each of its inhabitants. Gorky himself was constantly besieged by visitors who had come on business from the House of Arts, the House of Writers, the House of Academics, and World Literature. Academics and men of letters, natives of Petersburg and out-of-town visitors: everyone would come to pay him a call. Workers and sailors would come to ask for his protection against Zinovyev, the all-powerful commissar of the Northern Oblast'. Actors, artists, profiteers, former dignitaries, and high-society ladies would all come to see him. He was asked to intercede on behalf of those who had been arrested; he helped connect people with rations, apartments, clothing, medicine, oils, train tickets, travel orders, tobacco, writing paper and ink, false teeth for old men and milk for newborns—in a word, all of those things that were impossible to come by without somebody's patronage. Gorky listened attentively to everyone's stories and penned countless letters of recommendation. Only once did I ever see him deny a request: Delvari the clown had had his heart set on having Gorky stand godfather to his soon-to-be-born child. Gorky came out to see him, completely red, pumped his hand for a long while, cleared his throat, and finally said: "I have thought it over. I am most sincerely flattered, you understand, but, to my deepest regret, you understand, I couldn't possibly. It wouldn't be right somehow, you understand, and so I humbly beg your forgiveness."

And, suddenly, with a wave of his hand, he fled the room, forgetting to say goodbye in his confusion.

I lived a good distance away from Gorky. Walking the streets at night was exhausting and not without its dangers: a person could get robbed. For this reason, it was not uncommon for me to stay the night; a bed would be made up for me on the divan that stood in the dining room. Late in the evening, the hustle and bustle would die down. The hour would arrive for the family to take their tea. I served as an audience for Gorky's much-loved reminiscences, the ones that he always trotted out when he wished to "charm" his new acquaintances. Later on, I would learn that these stories were rather limited in number and that, though they retained the appearance of improvisations, they would repeat themselves verbatim, year after year. More than once, I came across character sketches written by people who had happened to visit Gorky's at one time or another and each time I would laugh when I arrived at the stereotypical phrase: "Alexei Maximovich's thoughts unexpectedly turn toward the past, and he involuntarily gives himself over to his reminiscences." In any case, these false improvisations were magnificently rendered. I would listen to them with great pleasure, without understanding why the rest of his audience would be winking at one another and disappearing off to their own rooms one by one. Later on—though now I repent of it—I would do the exact same thing myself, but, in those days, I relished the nocturnal hours when Gorky and I would remain alone together beside the long-cold samovar. We gradually grew closer to each other in those hours.

Gorky's relations with Zinovyev were bad and growing worse with each passing day. It got to the point that Zinovyev arranged to have Gorky's home searched and threatened to arrest certain people who were close to him. But then again, sometimes Communists hostile to Zinovyev would assemble in Gorky's home. Such meetings would be camouflaged as mild carouses that included outsiders. I accidently found myself at one of these meetings in the spring of 1921. Lashevich, Ionov, and Zorin were in attendance. As dinner drew to a close, a tallish, slender, blue-eyed young man dressed in a cunningly fitted soldier's blouse came to sit down next to me. He showered me with all sorts of compliments and quoted my verses by heart. We parted friends. The next day, I learned that the man had been Bakaev.

The animosity between Gorky and Zinovyev (which went on to play an important role in my life as well) came to a head in the autumn of 1921, when Gorky was forced to leave not just Petersburg, but Soviet Russia altogether. He went to Germany. In July of 1922, circumstances in my personal life took me there as well. I lived in Berlin for some time, but then, in October, Gorky convinced me to relocate to the little town of Saarow, near Fürstenwald. He was staying at a sanatorium there, while I was living in a modest hotel next to the train station. We would see each other every day, sometimes two or three times a day. In the spring of 1923, I moved into the very same sanatorium. Our life together in Saarow came to an abrupt halt that summer, when Gorky and his family moved to somewhere near Freiburg. I believe that there were political reasons behind the move, but officially, everything was explained using Gorky's illness.

We went our separate ways. That autumn, I went to Freiburg for several days and after that, in November, I left for Prague. Some time later, Gorky arrived there himself. He took up residence at the Hotel Beranek, which was where I was living, too. We both, however, heard the call of the backwaters, and, at the beginning of December, we moved to empty, snowbound Marienbad. At the time, both of us were in the process of applying for Italian visas.

My visa arrived in March of 1924, and, since I was running low on funds, I left in a hurry, without waiting for Gorky. After spending a week in Venice and about three weeks in Rome, I left on April 13— the very day on which Gorky was scheduled to arrive in the evening. Financial matters forced me to remain in Paris until August and, later on, to spend some time in Ireland. Finally, at the beginning of October, Gorky and I met up in Sorrento, where we lived together until April 18, 1925. After that day, I never saw Gorky again.

And so my acquaintance with him stretched on over seven years. If you put together all of the months that we spent living under the same roof, it would work out to about a year and a half, so I have grounds to believe that I knew him well and know a good deal about him. I will not attempt to set forth here every detail that has lodged itself in my mind, both because it would take up too much space and because I would be forced to go into too much detail about the lives of people who are still alive and well. Incidentally, it is the latter circumstance that compels me to pass over an important aspect of Gorky's life almost entirely. I am referring to the subject of his political views, relationships, and actions. At this time, I cannot say everything that I think and know, and it would be useless for me to speak in allusions. I offer up a rough sketch for the reader's consideration, with but a few observations and thoughts that I believe to be not entirely useless to gaining an understanding of Gorky's personality. I will even make so bold as to suggest that such observations might also come in handy in understanding that aspect of his life and activities that I do not intend to address at the present moment.

■ □ ■

The greater part of my interactions with Gorky took place in a practically village-like atmosphere, one in which a person's inherent character was not eclipsed by the practicalities of city life. Thus, to begin with, I will briefly address the most superficial features of his life: his everyday habits.

His day would begin early: he would get up around eight and, having drunk his coffee and gulped down two raw eggs, would work without pause until one in the afternoon. Lunch was served faithfully at one, and, including post-lunch conversation, would go on for about an hour and a half. After that, people would begin coaxing Gorky to go out for a walk, which he would avoid using any means possible. After his walk, he would once again rush to his desk and remain there until about seven in the evening. His desk was always large and spacious and his writing implements were always laid out on it in perfect order. Alexei Maximovich was a lover of good paper, colored pencils, and new pens and quills—he never used a stylus. His supply of cigarettes and motley array of cigarette holders—yellow, red, and green—were always kept in the same place. He smoked a great deal.

The hours between his walk and his dinner were largely dedicated to correspondence and the reading of manuscripts, which were sent to him in overwhelming quantities. He replied promptly to all letters, apart from the most absurd ones. He read all of the manuscripts and books (sometimes in many volumes) that were sent to him with a striking level of attention and set forth his opinions in highly detailed letters to their authors. He not only made notes on the manuscripts, but he painstakingly corrected their errata and inserted missing punctuation marks in red pencil, too. He did the same thing with books: he corrected all of their typos with the futile stubbornness of the most zealous of proofreaders. Sometimes he would do the same thing with newspapers—and then promptly throw them away.

Dinner was served around seven, and afterward there would be tea and general conversation, which usually ended in a game of cards: either 501 (to quote Derzhavin: "a groat on trust, no hope of its return"[7]) or bridge. In the case of the latter, what actually took place would be a sort of card-slapping: Gorky did not, and could not, have the faintest notion of what this game entailed; he was absolutely devoid of combinatorial abilities and didn't have the memory for cards. Taking (or, more frequently, giving away) his thirteenth trick, he would sometimes ask, glumly and timidly: "Excuse me, but which ones were the trumps?"

Laughter would ring out, which would make him resentful and angry. He would also get angry at the fact that he always lost, but perhaps it was precisely for this reason that he loved bridge best of all. His partners were another matter: they would make up absolutely any excuse not to play with him. Finally, we had to institute "bridge duty": people were obliged to play with him in turns.

Around midnight, he would retire to his room and either write, clad in his red dressing gown, or read in his bed, which was always kept simple and tidy in hospital fashion. He slept little and spent around ten hours a day working, sometimes more than that. He did not care for lazy people and had earned the right to that opinion.

He read a colossal number of books in his day and remembered everything that was written in them. His memory was astonishing. Sometimes, conversing on one topic or another, he would begin peppering his argument with quotations and statistics. When asked "how he knew that," he would shrug his shoulders and appear surprised: "Pardon me, but how could I not know it? There was an article on the subject in the October 1887 issue of *Messenger of Europe*."[8]

He took all academic articles as gospel, though he viewed fiction with mistrust and suspected all fiction writers of distorting reality. To a certain extent, he regarded literature as something akin to a reference text on everyday topics. As a result, he would go into genuine rages when he stumbled upon errors in quotidian facts. When he received Nazhivin's three-volume novel on Rasputin, he armed himself with a pencil and sat down to read. I teased him, but he toiled away at it earnestly for a good three days. At the end of that time, he declared the book repulsive. What was wrong with it? Apparently, the heroes of Nazhivin's novel, who live in Nizhny Novgorod, go off to dine on a steamer that has recently arrived from Astrakhan. At first, I didn't understand what he had found so scandalous and said that I myself had had occasion to dine on the Volga steamers docked at the pier. "But that's before a run, not after!" he cried. "The buffet isn't open after a run! One needs to know that sort of thing!"

He died of pneumonia. Doubtless, his final illness was connected in some way to the tuberculosis he had contracted in his youth. But that had been cured forty years earlier, and, even if it did make itself felt in his bouts of coughing, bronchitis, and pleurisy, then not to the extent that was constantly being written about and how it was regarded by the public. Overall, he was a cheerful and hardy person—it was not for nothing that he lived to the age of sixty-eight. He had long since grown accustomed to turning the myth of his serious illness to his benefit whenever there was somewhere that he didn't want to go or, conversely, somewhere that he needed to get to. He would cite a sudden ailment when declining to participate in various meetings or receive unwanted guests. But at home, among his own set, he didn't like to talk about his illness even when it really was rearing its head. He bore physical pain with remarkable courage. When he had some teeth pulled in Marienbad, he refused any sort of anesthetic and didn't complain a single time. Once, when he was still in Petersburg, he was riding in an overcrowded tram, standing on the lower step. A soldier who had jumped onto the tram as it was traveling along at top speed favored him with a full-force steel heel to the foot, fracturing his little toe. Gorky didn't even go to see a doctor at the time, but for nearly three years afterward, he would occasionally give himself over to an unusual evening project: picking splinters of bone out of the wound with his bare hands.

■ □ ■

For more than thirty years, rumors of Gorky's luxurious lifestyle circulated through Russian society. I can't vouch for the period when I didn't know him, but I can definitively state that, in all the years of our intimacy, there was absolutely no luxury to speak of. All of the cock-and-bull stories about the villas Gorky owned and the near-orgies that occurred within them are lies that I find simply ridiculous, lies born of literary jealousy and entangled in political hostility. The philistines were not only eager to believe such gossip; they were loath to part with it at any price. The persistence of such rumors was striking. One could say that they were cherished and reopened like spiritual wounds—for many people found the idea of Gorky's opulent lifestyle offensive. The satirists returned to this topic every time Gorky gave them an excuse to talk about him. Several times during the years 1927–1928, I pointed out to the now-deceased A. A. Yablonovsky that he shouldn't write about the fabled villa on Capri, at the very least because Gorky was living in Sorrento and hadn't set foot on Capri for the past fifteen years: in fact, his Italian visa had been issued on the condition that he would not live in Capri. Yablonovsky would listen, nod his head, and soon fall back into his old ways: he didn't like to disappoint the philistines.

As a matter of fact, in later years, the villa in Capri *would* occasionally be replaced by a villa in Sorrento, but the imaginary life that went on inside it was even more opulent and evoked even greater indignation than the old one had. Thus, I must repent before all mankind: this unlucky villa was rented not only with my encouragement, but even at my insistence. Upon his arrival in Sorrento in the spring of 1924, Gorky took up residence in a large, comfortless, neglected villa that had only been rented to him through December because it needed to be completely overhauled. And it was in this villa that I caught up with Gorky once more. As the day of his departure drew near, we began searching for a new haven. As Sorrento gets fairly cold in the winter, we had planned to move to the southern slope of the peninsula, close to Amalfi. We found a villa there that we were totally prepared to rent. Maxim,[9] Gorky's son from his first marriage, went to look at it again. For lack of anything better to do, I went along with him. The villa turned out to be situated on a minuscule rock ledge; a precipice of approximately fifty *sazhens* dropped straight into the sea from its southern façade. Only a thin strip of road separated the northern façade from an enormous cliff face, which was not only sheer, but also jutted out over the road. This cliff face was constantly crumbling, like the rest of the Amalfi coast. Just seven months earlier, the villa that we were planning to move into had stood on the western edge of a small settlement, which had literally been crushed and swept out to the sea by the latest in a series of landslides. I remembered this well because I happened to be in Rome at the time. About a hundred people had perished in the catastrophe. Field engineers dug out the people who had been buried alive; the king came to visit. Through some sort of miracle, this villa had remained intact, hanging out over the newly formed precipice, such that its eastern façade was now also looking out over an abyss, the bottom of which was still awash with bits of wood, brick, and iron. I announced to Maxim that I valued my life and was not about to live there. Maxim scowled—there were no other villas available. We went to Amalfi, and, when we returned about two hours later, we were forced to stop a kilometer away from "our" villa and wait for the road to be cleared: yet another landslide had taken place while we had been having lunch.

We had no other choice: we rented that villa, "Il Sorito," which was to be Gorky's final haven in Italy. It was located not in Sorrento proper, but a kilometer and a half outside the city, on the Sorrento Cape, the Capo di Sorrento. Smart-looking and handsomely situated, with a fantastic view over the entire gulf, including Naples,

Vesuvius, and Castellammare, the interior nevertheless suffered from some crucial drawbacks: there was very little furniture inside and it was cold. We moved in on November 16 and suffered terribly from the cold throughout the entire winter, feeding the small number of fireplaces with damp olive branches. The villa's chief merit lay in its cheapness: we rented it for six thousand lira a year, which, at the time, was the equivalent of five thousand francs. The upper level housed the dining room, Gorky's room (a bedroom and study combined), his secretary's room, Baroness M. I. Budberg's room, N. N. Berberova's room, my room, and one more, a small room for visitors. Below, flanking the modest vestibule, were two additional rooms: one of them was occupied by Maxim and his wife, the other by I. N. Rakitsky, the artist, who was a sickly and unusually agreeable person: in 1918 in Petersburg, during his soldiering days, he had stopped in at Gorky's to warm up when he was sick. Somehow, he managed to remain in the household for a number of years. To the ranks of this core population I must also add my niece, who lived at Il Sorito all through January and sometimes later on when she would come to visit from Rome, and also E. P. Peshkova, Gorky's first wife, who would visit from Moscow for a couple of weeks at a time. Sometimes guests would come to visit from the neighboring Minerva Hotel: the writer Andrei Sobol, who had come from Moscow to recover after a suicide attempt, Professor Starkov and his family (from Prague), and P. P. Muratov. Sometimes, two young ladies would drop by to take tea in the evenings; they were the villa's owners, who had set aside a portion of the ground floor for themselves.

Life on each of these two floors worked very differently. On the top floor, people worked; on the lower floor, which Alexei Maximovich had dubbed the nursery, they played. Maxim was almost thirty then, but, judging by his character, it would have been difficult to believe that he was older than thirteen. At times, he engaged in entirely innocent tiffs with his wife, an extremely beautiful and kind woman whom we affectionately referred to as Timosha.[10] Timosha had a talent for painting. Maxim also liked to do a bit of drawing. Sometimes it would happen that they both needed a certain pencil or eraser at the same time: "That's my pencil!" "No, it's mine!" "No, it's mine!"

Upon hearing this racket, Rakitsky would emerge from his room. Clouds of tobacco smoke would roll forth from the open door behind him (his room was always kept shut because the fresh air made his head hurt. "Fresh air is poison to the organism," he said). Standing amidst the smoke, he would shout: "Maxim, hand that pencil over to Timosha right this instant!"

"But I need it!"

"Would you be so kind as to hand it over immediately? You're the older one, you should be nice to her!"

Maxim would surrender the pencil and slink off with a pout. But, just wait—in five minutes he would already have forgotten all about it and be whistling and dancing about.

He was a lovely boy, easygoing and merry. He truly loved the Bolsheviks: not out of any sort of conviction, but because he had grown up among them and they had always spoiled him. He would refer to "Vladimir Ilych" and "Felix Edmundovich," but it would have been more appropriate for him to call them "uncle Volodya" and "uncle Felix."[11] He dreamed of traveling to the USSR because they had promised him a car there: this was the object of his most passionate reveries, and sometimes even of his dreams. For the time being, he looked after his motorcycle, collected postage stamps, read detective novels, and went to the nickelodeon; afterward, he would retell the movies scene by scene, doing imitations of his favorite actors, especially the comic ones. He had a remarkable talent for clowning, and, if he had ever needed to work, he would have made a first-rate comic actor. But he never lifted a finger in his life. Viktor Shklovsky dubbed him the "Soviet prince." He was the apple of Gorky's eye, but his was a bestial sort of love, mainly consisting of concerns that Maxim be alive and well and happy.

Sometimes Maxim would take one or two passengers in the sidecar of his motorcycle and we would ride around the neighborhood or pop over to Sorrento for coffee. One time, we all went to the nickelodeon together. On Christmas Eve, there was a Christmas tree and presents on "the kids' side." I received a deck of cards for playing patience and Alexei Maximovich got a set of warm long underwear. When things got very dull indeed (which would happen around once a month) Maxim would buy two bottles of Asti, a bottle of mandarin orange liqueur, and some candy and invite everyone over in the evening. We would dance to the gramophone, Maxim would clown around, we would play charades, and then we would all sing together. If Alexei Maximovich was being stubborn and refused to go to bed, we would croon "The sun rises and sets."[12] At first, he would plead with us ("Knock it off, you ragdoll devils"), but then he would get up, and, hunching his shoulders, disappear upstairs.

However, our peaceful way of life would be shaken up each Saturday. In the morning, we would send over to the Hotel Minerva to order seven baths and, from around three o'clock till dinnertime, we would take turns crossing the road—there and back again—with our dressing gowns, towels, and sponges. Over dinner, we would all congratulate one another on a good steam, eat soup with pelmeni that had been prepared by the women, and praise the Minerva's capable proprietress, Signora Cacace. Alexei Maximovich insisted that her surname was a comparative. And so, when discussing the hopeless romance of one of his acquaintances, he once said: "The situation couldn't be cacachier."[13]

Then, upon my arrival in Paris, I was informed that Gorky was living on Capri and spending his days in what essentially amounted to orgies.

■ □ ■

One could only gain a true sense of just how internationally famous Gorky was by living with him. Not a single Russian writer I have met could compare with him in terms of fame. He received an enormous number of letters in every possible language. No matter where he went, strangers would come up to him asking for his autograph. He was besieged by interviewers. Newspaper correspondents would take rooms in the hotels he was staying at for two or three days at a time just to catch a glimpse of him in the garden or at the table d'hôte. Fame brought him a great deal of money; he was earning about ten thousand dollars a year, a negligible portion of which he spent on himself. He was uncommonly easy to please as far as food, drink, and clothing were concerned. Cigarettes, the odd glass of vermouth at the corner café on Sorrento's only square, a cab ride home from the city—I can't recall him having any other expenses in terms of his personal needs. But his circle of permanent dependents was very large; I would say that it comprised no fewer than fifteen or so people, both in Russia and abroad. They included people from absolutely every walk of life, up to and including titled émigrés, and people with all different kinds of connections to him: from blood relatives and relations by marriage to people he had never laid eyes on in his life. Whole families lived much more liberally at his expense than he did himself. Apart from his long-term beneficiaries, there were a number of incidental ones as well; among the other supplicants, certain émigré writers would occasionally come to ask him for his help. He never refused anyone. Gorky handed out money regardless of the petitioner's actual needs and without concerning himself with how his money would be spent. Occasionally the money would get stuck in its transfer channels: Gorky would pretend he didn't notice. And that's not all. Certain members of his circle who had taken refuge in his name and position would get mixed up in all sorts of despicable affairs—up to and including extortion. The same people who fought one another tooth and nail over Gorky's money would keep a sharp eye out to make sure that Gorky's public behavior was lucrative enough and guide his actions through coordinated efforts and friendly pressure. On some rare occasions, Gorky attempted to rebel, but in the end he always knuckled under. This was, in part, due to the most basic psychological motivations: habit, attachment, and the desire to be left to do one's work in peace. But the primary reason, the most important one (albeit one that he probably didn't recognize himself) lay in one peculiar and very important circumstance: his extremely complicated attitude toward truth and lies. This attitude was formed quite early on and bore a decisive influence both on his work and his entire life.

He grew up surrounded by all sorts of worldly filth and lived in that way for a very long time. The people he saw were occasionally the perpetrators of such filth and occasionally its victims, but, more often than not, they were both victims and perpetrators at once. It was completely natural that a dream of other, better people should take shape within his mind—though to a certain extent he also discredited this dream. Later on, he learned to distinguish the undeveloped germs of other, better people in certain individuals who surrounded him. By mentally cleansing these seeds of the savagery, coarseness, spite, and filth that had caked on to them, he was able to unearth a half-real, half-imaginary breed of noble tramp, who, in his essence, could pass for a cousin of the noble robber of Romantic literature.

He received his first literary education among people for whom literature's significance was limited to its social and everyday content. In Gorky's eyes, a hero could gain social significance and, thus, literary justification, only against the backdrop of reality and only as an authentic part of it. Gorky began to set his vaguely realistic heroes against backgrounds of profoundly realistic scenery. He was forced to pretend, both to the public and to himself, that he was portraying everyday life. He himself half-accepted this half-truth for his entire life.

By philosophizing and moralizing through his characters, Gorky endowed them to the greatest possible extent with his dream of a better life, which is to say, with his dream of a sought-after moral and social truth that was to shine out over everything and arrange everything to the benefit of all mankind. In the beginning, Gorky's heroes did not yet know precisely what this truth consisted of, just as Gorky didn't know himself. At a certain point, Gorky went searching for, and didn't find it in religion. At the beginning of the nineties, he saw (or was trained to see) the promise of it in Marxian social progress. If he never, then or afterward, managed to turn himself into a genuine, systematic Marxist, he nevertheless embraced Marxism as his official faith and the working hypothesis on which he attempted to base his artistic efforts.

I am writing memoirs about Gorky, not an article on his work. I will return to my intended topic further down, but first I must take a moment to consider one of his works, perhaps the best thing he ever wrote, and, without a doubt, the text that has proven most central to his literary career: I am referring to the play *The Lower Depths*.

Its primary theme is truth and lies. Its main character is the wanderer Luka, the "cunning elder." Luka arrives on the scene in order to seduce the denizens of the "lower depths" with his comforting lie about a kingdom of good that exists somewhere out there in the distance. Believing in this kingdom, they find it easier not only to live, but also to die. After Luka's mysterious disappearance, their lives become mean and terrifying once more.

Luka caused a great commotion among the Marxist critics, who tried with all their might to explain to readers that Luka is a pernicious character who further weakens the downtrodden by feeding them dreams that distract them from reality and the class struggle, which is the only chance they have at securing a better future. In their own way, the Marxists were right: Luka, who believes that the enlightenment of society is achieved through the enlightenment of the individual, was, in fact, harmful to their cause. Gorky anticipated this and thus, by way of a corrective, provided a counterbalance to Luka in the character of Satine, who personifies the awakening of the proletarian consciousness. Indeed, Satine is, so to speak, the play's official philosophizer. "Lies are the religion of slaves and landlords. Truth is the god of the free man," he proclaims. But if only we read the play carefully, we immediately notice that, compared to the figure of Luka, the figure of Satine is depicted insipidly and—more importantly—without any particular love for the character. Gorky's positive hero has turned out far less successfully than his negative one has. This is because he endowed his positive hero with his official ideology, while he imbued his negative hero with his living feelings of love and pity for human beings. It is remarkable that, anticipating the accusations that would be leveled against Luka, Gorky chose to make Satine his defender. When the other characters in the play abuse Luka, Satine shouts at them: "Silence! You're all beasts! Blockheads . . . Not one word about the old man! . . . The old man is no charlatan . . . I understand the old man . . . yes! He lied . . . but—he did it out of pity for you, the devil take you! There are plenty of people who lie out of a sense of pity for their neighbors . . . There is such a thing as a comforting lie, a healing lie." It is even more remarkable that Satine should attribute his own enlightenment to Luka's influence: "The old man? He's a fine fellow! He's acted on me like acid on a dirty old coin . . . Let's drink to his health!"

Satine also delivers the famous line, "A person is a marvelous thing! The word has a proud ring to it!" But the author knew, in the back of his mind, that it also had a bitter ring to it. His entire life was tinged with a keen feeling of pity for humankind, whose fate seemed to him to be hopeless. He saw that humankind's only path to salvation lay in the sort of artistic energy that would be inconceivable outside the context of the perpetual defeat of reality at the hands of hope. He didn't have high expectations for humankind's ability to put such hopes into practice, but the ability to dream, the gift of dreaming—such talents sent him into ecstasies and palpitations. In his view, the successful weaving of any dream capable of captivating the human imagination was an indication of true genius and the preservation of such a dream was an act of great charity.

> Gentlemen! If truth supreme
> Can't be found in earthly mire
> Glory be to cranks who inspire
> The people with a golden dream.

In these rather feeble, but highly expressive verses, which are delivered by one of the characters in *The Lower Depths*, we find Gorky's motto, if you will: the motto that defined his entire life on a literary, social, and personal level. Gorky happened to live in a time when the "golden dream" manifested itself in the dream of social revolution as a panacea for all human sufferings. He cherished this dream and became its apostle—not because his belief in the Revolution was particularly strong, but because he believed in the inherent redemptive qualities of the dream itself. In a different era he would have championed other faiths, other hopes just as passionately. During the time of the Russian liberation movement, and then, later on, during the Revolution, he acted as an advocate and defender of that dream, was a Luka, a cunning wanderer. Starting with his early short story (dated 1893) about the lofty siskin "who lied" and the woodpecker who basely "loved the truth," his entire literary oeuvre, like his life, became permeated with a sentimental love for lies of all sorts and a stubborn, enduring distaste for truth.[14] "I despise the truth in a most sincere and unshakeable manner," he wrote to E. D. Kuskova in 1929. And I can still picture him painstakingly writing out those words, his face filled with spite, his hackles raised, a swollen vein throbbing on his neck.

■ □ ■

On July 13, 1924, he wrote to me from Sorrento: "It is the holiday season here, you know—there are fireworks, parades, music, and 'people's jubilees' practically every day. 'And what have we got?' I think. And—forgive me! I become envious to the point of tears, to the point of rage, and it's painful and it makes me sick, and so on."

He adored Italian festivities, with their music and their flags, all accompanied by the crackling of fireworks. In the evenings, he would go out onto the balcony and gather everyone together to watch as the rockets and roman candles shot up into the air, scattered along the edges of the gulf. He would get excited, rub his hands together, and shout: "That one's in Torre Annunziata! And that one's by Herculaneum! And that one's in Naples! Ooh, ooh, ooh, look how they sizzle!"

This "great realist" truly enjoyed only those things that embellished upon reality or diverted one's attention away from it—things that didn't quite match up with reality, or that simply added something to reality that it did not already possess. I have seen quite a few writers take pride in the fact that Gorky cried while listening to their works. This was really nothing to be proud of: I can't recall a work that didn't make him cry—complete and utter trash being the sole exception. Not infrequently, once he had worked out what it was that had made him cry, he himself would criticize it, but his initial reaction was almost always tears. What struck him was not the quality of what he read, but the fact that he found himself in the presence of art, the fact that here was something that had been written, created, invented. It was a low blow for Mayakovsky to declare in print that he was willing to sell a vest that Maxim Gorky had cried on for cheap.[15] He took the liberty of making light of the best and purest stirrings in that man's soul. Gorky was not ashamed to cry over his own works, either: the second half of every short story he ever read to me was invariably inundated with weeping, sobbing, and the wiping of fogged-up glasses.

He held a particular affection for young and aspiring writers: he liked their faith in the future, their dreams of fame. He didn't discourage even the genuinely bad ones, the notoriously hopeless cases: to him, destroying any sort of illusion whatsoever was a sacrilege. And most importantly, he cherished his own dreams for these aspiring writers (again, even those showed very little promise), and was happy to deceive himself along with them. It is important to note that he had a different attitude toward already-established writers. As far as the truly outstanding ones were concerned, he either already loved them—as was the case with Bunin, whom he understood,—or else he forced himself to love them—as was the case with Blok, whom he did not fully understand, but whose significance he could not help but sense. By contrast, he tended not to like those authors who had already graduated from their diapers, who had managed to attain a certain status, but who had not become entirely worthy of note. It was as if he was angry with them for the fact that he could no longer dream of their ascent to fame, of their elevation to prominence and greatness. What especially irritated him about such mediocre writers was their solemnity, their olympianism, their consciousness of their own significance, which was, in fact, more typical of this kind of writer than it was of the truly outstanding ones.

He loved anybody with a creative bent, anybody who brought, or even dreamed of bringing, something new into the world. What that novelty might be, and the quality with which it ought to be expressed, were of secondary importance in his eyes. His imagination was excited in equal measure by poets and by academics, by daydreamers and by innovators of all stripes—up to and including the inventors of perpetual motion. This excitement merged with his lively, exceptionally fervent and brightly hued love for people who disturbed—or endeavored to disturb—the established social order. The spectrum of this love perhaps ran even broader: it ranged from self-proclaimed violators of the natural order, which is to say, from conmen and sharpers, to the most profound social reformers. I am not at all trying to say that the carnival jester and the great revolutionary were of equal value in his eyes. But there isn't any doubt in my mind that, though he might have held different attitudes toward them in his head, he loved both with the same region of his soul. It is no coincidence that he didn't have any scruples about making Satine from *The Lower Depths*, his positive hero and the herald of a new social truth, a sharper by trade.

He liked absolutely any person who introduced an element of rebellion or, at the very least, mischief, into the world—up to and including maniacs and arsonists, whom he wrote about extensively and was happy to talk about for hours on end. He was a bit of an arsonist himself. Not once did I ever see him put out a match after lighting a cigarette: he would invariably throw the match away unextinguished. After lunch or during his evening tea, when the ashtray would be filled with a sufficient quantity of cigarette butts, matches, and papers, he made it his cherished habit to furtively shove a lit match inside the pile. After doing so, he would attempt to distract the attention of those around him—while he himself cast cunning glances over his shoulder at the blazing bonfire. It seemed that these "little family fires," as I once suggested calling them, took on a certain wicked and joyful symbolic meaning in his eyes. He felt great respect for the experiments being done in atomic fission; he would often talk about how, for example, if the scientists were to succeed, a stone picked up from the street could produce enough energy to facilitate interplanetary communication. But he said this in a weary, hackneyed tone of voice. It was as if he was only doing it so that he could put in at the very end, in a fervent and merry fashion, that "one fine day, these experiments, hm, yes, you understand, could lead to the destruction of our universe. Now *that* will be a fire!" And then he would cluck his tongue.

From the arsonists down through those magnificent Corsican bandits whom he never had the opportunity to meet, his love continued downward to the numerous counterfeiters who were working in Italy at that time. Gorky would talk about them at great length and occasionally visited one of their ringleaders, who was living in Alessio. After the counterfeiters came opportunists, swindlers, and thieves of all descriptions. Some of them remained in his circle until the very end of his life. Though their escapades cast suspicions on him, he bore it with a patience that bordered on incitement. Not once can I recall him condemning a single one of them, nor did he ever once express the slightest displeasure with them. There was a man called Rode, the ex-owner of a celebrated café chantant, who had invented an entire revolutionary biography for himself. Once I personally heard him speaking in solemn tones about his "many years of revolutionary work." He was the apple of Gorky's eye, and had been appointed by Gorky to head up the House of Academics, which was the primary channel through which the rations for Petersburg academics, writers, artists, and actors flowed. When I accidentally took the liberty of referring to the House of Academics as Rode's syndicate, Gorky remained angry with me for days.

He tended to be overrun by petty thieves and beggars each time that he went out on the street. He liked how truth and lies would merge together in their trade, as if they were magicians. He succumbed to their tricks with a visible pleasure and beamed whenever a waiter or a merchant would overcharge him for some bit of rubbish. What he particularly appreciated about it was their brazenness in the act—he must have seen a glimmer of rebelliousness and mischief in it. And, in his home life, he himself was not above testing out his skills in that arena. For want of anything better to do, we took it into our heads to publish our own *Sorrento Pravda*. It was a manuscript newspaper, a parody of certain Soviet and émigré journals; we put out three or four issues. Gorky, Berberova, and I were the contributors, Rakitsky was the illustrator, and Maxim was the copyist. We elected Maxim to serve as editor as well—in light of his extreme literary incompetence. And so, Gorky would endeavor to trick him in all sorts of ways, attempting to pass off excerpts from old works of his as unpublished texts. And he derived his greatest pleasure from the obsession Maxim had with uncovering his pranks. Because of Gorky's penchant for senseless expenditures, the other members of the household had stripped him of all his cash, leaving him a pittance for pocket money. One day, he ran into my room beaming, practically waltzing, and rubbing his hands together with the air of a workman on a bender. He announced: "Here! Just look—I swiped ten lira from Maria Ignatyevna! Let's go to Sorrento!"

We went to Sorrento, drank some vermouth, and got a ride home with a cabbie we both knew. Having received the infamous tenner from Alexei Maximovich's hands, instead of giving back seven lira in change, the cabbie lashed his horse and galloped off, cracking his whip, casting glances back at us, and laughing at the top of his voice. Gorky went bug-eyed in ecstasy: he set his eyebrows on end, doubled over, slapped his sides, and was unspeakably happy until evening.

■ □ ■

He never denied anyone help in the form of money or personal effort. But his philanthropy was of a peculiar sort: the more bitterly his petitioner complained to him, the more deeply the person despaired, the more indifferent Gorky would feel toward him— but not because he demanded perseverance or restraint from others. His demands went much further than that: he couldn't bear dejection, and so he demanded that people have hope—hope in anything at all. This was where his singular, stubborn egoism lay: in return for his involvement in someone's case, he demanded that he be given the right to dream of a better future for the person he was helping. So if the petitioner interrupted those dreams with his despair, Gorky would get angry and help him grudgingly, making no effort to conceal his annoyance.

As a stubborn inventor and admirer of uplifting deceptions, he treated every disappointment, each base truth as a manifestation of metaphysically evil origins. Any ruined dream would evoke his disgust and fear, as if it were a dead body, as if he sensed something unclean within it. This fear, which was accompanied by a certain animosity, was evoked in him by anyone guilty of destroying illusions, any disturbers of the spiritual complacency predicated upon dreams, and any violators of festive, elevated moods. In the autumn of 1920, Wells came to Petersburg. At a luncheon that had been organized in his honor, Gorky, along with some other speakers, talked about the horizons that the young proletarian dictatorship was opening up in the fields of science and art. Suddenly, A. V. Amfiteatrov, whom Gorky held in extremely high regard, got up and said something that contradicted the earlier speeches. From that day forward, Gorky despised him—not because he had come out against Soviet power, but because he had shown himself to be a destroyer of the festive, a *trouble-fête*.[16] At the very end of the final act of *The Lower Depths*, everyone is singing together. Suddenly, the door bursts open and the Baron shouts from the threshold: "Hey ... you! Come ... come here! In the vacant lot ... over there ... The Actor ... has hanged himself!" In the silence that follows, Satine answers him quietly: "Ah . . . he's spoiled the song . . . the fool!" And, with that, the curtain falls. It is not clear whom Satine is reproaching: the Actor, for hanging himself at such an inopportune time, or the Baron, for bringing the news. In all likelihood, the answer is both, because both are guilty of spoiling the song.

That is Gorky in a nutshell. In life, too, he had no scruples about becoming openly angry with the bearers of bad news. I once said to him, "You, Alexei Maximovich, are like Tsar Saltan:

In his rage, he started ranting,
Sent the courier for hanging.[17]

He answered with a scowl: "That tsar had a head on his shoulders. Such nasty couriers ought to be put to death."

Perhaps he recalled this conversation when he responded to Kuskova's "base truths" with the ferocious wish that she might drop dead as quickly as possible.

■ □ ■

He himself never took the liberty of announcing any mishap or misfortune. When it was impossible for him to remain silent, he preferred to lie, and was completely certain that he was acting in a humane manner.

Baroness Varvara Ivanovna Ikskul belonged to that category of charming women who know just how to captivate both young and old, rich and poor, nobleman and commoner alike. Foreign crowned heads and Russian revolutionaries both numbered among her admirers. In her salon, which was, at one point, known throughout all of Petersburg, she brought together people of the most diverse parties and positions. It is said that she once received the ferocious minister of the interior while a man wanted by the police was hiding in the depths of her apartment. She maintained friendly relations with the Empress Alexandra Fyodorovna up to the very last days of the monarchy. Rasputin's admirers and his enemies both considered her their ally. Needless to say, the Revolution completely beggared her. They managed to secure her a place in the House of Arts, where I became her frequent guest. At the age of seventy, she was just as charming as ever. Gorky, like the numerous others who were indebted to her for something that had happened in the past, asked me about her on multiple occasions. I told her about it. One day, she said, "Ask Alexei Maximovich if he could arrange for me to be allowed to go abroad." Gorky replied that this would be simple. He instructed Varvara Ivanovna to fill out a form, write a petition, and enclose some photographs. Soon afterward, he set out for Moscow. This was in the spring of 1921. It is easy to imagine the impatience with which Varvara Ivanovna awaited his return. Finally, he returned and I went over to see him on the very same day. He informed me that permission had been granted, but that the passport would only be ready "today, toward evening," and so it would be delivered by A. N. Tikhonov in a couple of days or so. Varvara Ivanovna thanked me with tears in her eyes, which it shames me to recall. She set about selling some of her belongings; the rest she gave away. Every day, I telephoned Tikhonov. He hadn't yet arrived before I went to visit him myself, and I found, to my consternation, that Alexei Maximovich hadn't asked him to do anything at all; this was the first Tikhonov was hearing of the whole affair. It would be of little interest to describe the ways in which I tried to get an explanation out of Gorky, and, at any rate, I don't remember the details. The short version is that, at first, he referred to the matter as a "misunderstanding" and promised to set everything straight, then he declined to speak about it, and then he went abroad himself. Varvara Ivanovna did not wait around to receive her passport and she made a run for it: in the winter, with a little boy as her guide, she made her way into Finland over the ice that was covering the Gulf, and from there she went on to Paris, where she died in February of 1928. A few months later, I was in Moscow and learned from the Narkomindel[18] that Gorky had, in fact, presented her petition, but that he had immediately received a categorical denial.

It is impossible to explain away this incident as a reluctance to admit his helplessness before the powers that be: at the time, Gorky actually enjoyed talking about that sort of helplessness. Insofar as I know Gorky, there isn't a doubt in my mind that he simply wanted to keep the petitioner's hopes alive for as long as possible and—who knows?—perhaps he was able to deceive himself along with her. This sort of "theater for one's own sake" was entirely his style; I can think of several plays he staged in that same theater. I'll describe only one of them now, but it is the most striking one, the one in which the invention of a happy illusion was pushed to the point of utter cruelty.

In the early years of the Soviet regime, while he was living in Petersburg, Gorky maintained relationships with many members of the imperial family. One day he invited Princess Palei, the widow of Grand Duke Pavel Alexandrovich, over to his home and informed her that her son, the young poet Prince Palei, had not been executed, but was alive and well and living in Ekaterinoslav, whence he had just sent Gorky a letter and some poems. It is not difficult to imagine his mother's astonishment and joy.[19] To her own misfortune, a certain coincidence that Gorky himself could not have been aware of had made her even more inclined to believe him: the Paleis had close friends in Ekaterinoslav, and so, having avoided execution, it would have been entirely logical for the young man to take refuge with them. After a while, of course, Princess Palei learned that he had, in fact, been killed, and, in this way, Gorky's consolatory deception became a source of fresh suffering to her: Gorky forced her to relive the news of her son's death.

I don't remember what led him to confess this to me in the year 1923; he did so not without a certain regret (which I nevertheless found to be insufficient). I asked him: "But there really was a letter with some poems?" "There was." "But why didn't she ask you to show it to her?" "She did ask, but I had tucked it away somewhere and couldn't find it."

I did not conceal my strong distaste for this story from Gorky, but I couldn't get him to tell me what had actually happened. He simply threw up his hands and seemed to regret having started the conversation in the first place.

A few months later, he gave himself away. After he had left for Freiburg, he wrote to me in one of his letters: "It turns out that the poet Palei *is* alive and that I had something of a right to mislead the Countess (sic!) Palei (sic!). I am sending along some of the poet's poems, which I have just received; they seem rather bad."

Having read these poems, which were extremely clumsy, I made certain inquiries, from which I grasped the situation: both then, in Petersburg, and later on, abroad, Gorky had received letters and poems from the proletarian poet A. R. Palei, who was of working-class origins. It is possible that Gorky didn't know him or didn't remember him personally. But neither in the content, nor in the form, nor in the orthography, nor even in the handwriting could the poetry of this Palei have possibly been taken for the work of a Grand Duke's son. I didn't see the letters, but, doubtless, they were even less capable of giving Gorky the opportunity to make this error in good faith. Gorky had purposefully deceived himself and he had misplaced the letter and the poems in order to hide them not just from Princess Palei, but, first and foremost, from himself, because he had already taken it into his head to play out the diabolical tragicomedy of consoling the unfortunate mother.

Apart from the fact that it would be difficult to provide another explanation for this story, I can also insist upon my own version because I bore witness to other incidents of precisely the same character.

■ □ ■

His attitude toward lies and liars was, one might say, solicitous, protective even. I never knew him to unmask anyone or expose a lie—even the feeblest or most brazen attempts at one. He was a genuinely trusting person, but, on top of that, he also pretended he was trusting. This was partly because he would have felt bad about embarrassing the liars, but mostly because he saw it as his duty to respect the artistic impulses, or dreams, or illusions of others, even on those occasions when they manifested themselves in the most pathetic or disgusting of their forms. More than once, I even saw him glad to be deceived. For this reason, it was incredibly easy to deceive him, or even to make him complicit in a deception.

He himself not infrequently told untruths. He did this with a surprising cheerfulness, as if he were certain that no one would be able to catch him in a lie—or, for that matter, would even want to. Here is one such instance that is typical both in this regard and for the fact that his lie had been elicited by a desire to show off—not even to me, but to himself. Generally speaking, I believe that the main object of most of his deceptions was himself.

On November 8, 1923, he wrote to me:

> In the category of news that defies all reason, I can report that *On the Eve* has printed the phrase "Michelangelo's painting La Gioconda." Meanwhile, in Russia, Nadezhda Krupskaya and someone called M. Speransky have forbidden the reading of Plato, Kant, Schopenhauer, V. S. Solovyov, Taine, Ruskin, Nietzsche, L. Tolstoy, Leskov, Yasinsky (!) and many other heretics of that sort. And they are saying that "the religious office should contain only antireligious books." All of these things are supposedly (the word "supposedly" has been written in above the rest of the line.—V. Kh.) not just some anecdote, but are written down in a book called *A Guide to the Removal of*

Anti-Artistic and Counterrevolutionary Literature from Libraries Servicing the Mass Reader.[20]

We must trust in that "supposedly" which I have written in above the line, for I still cannot bring myself to believe in such spiritual vampirism and will not believe it until I see this *Guide* with my own eyes.

My first impression was such that I have begun writing a letter to Moscow renouncing my Russian citizenship. What else can I do if such an atrocity turns out to be true?

If you only knew, my dear V. F., how desperately difficult and distressing this is for me!

The only true statement contained within this letter is the fact that the situation was, indeed, "difficult and distressing" for him. Having learned of the confiscation of these books, he felt that it was his duty to strongly protest against such "spiritual vampirism." He even consoled himself by dreaming that he would manifest his protest by sending in notice that he was renouncing his Soviet citizenship. Maybe he even started writing such a notice, but, of course, he knew that he would never send it. He knew that all of this was, once again, just "theater for one's own sake." And so he took refuge in the most naïve lie imaginable: first, he wrote me a letter describing the release of the *Guide* as a fait accompli, then he added in the "supposedly" and pretended that the affair needed further looking into—and, moreover, that he "could not bring himself to believe" in the existence of this *Guide*. Meanwhile, there could have been no doubt in his mind on the subject: he had had this *Guide*, a little white pocket-sized volume, in his possession for quite some time already. On September 14, 1923, two months before this letter was written, I had gone into the publishing offices of Epoch in Berlin and met Baroness M. I. Budberg there. I personally witnessed as the head of the publishing house, S. G. Sumsky, handed her that very *Guide*, which was to be passed along to Alexei Maximovich. On that same day, Maria Ignatyevna and I set off for Freiburg together. The *Guide* was given to Gorky immediately upon our arrival, and it was the subject of many conversations over the course of my three-day stay in Freiburg. But Gorky had forgotten these conversations and about the fact that I had seen him with the *Guide* in his hands—and so he assured me in the most carefree tone that he hadn't yet seen the book and that he even doubted its existence. It is also remarkable in all of this that he should recount the story of his intention to give notice to Moscow for no other reason apart from his desire to act out a scene for me, but more particularly—I'll say it again—for himself.

If he was caught in his deviations from the truth, he would offer his excuses helplessly and shamefacedly, much like the Baron in *The Lower Depths* does when the Tatar shouts at him: "Ah! He shoved card up sleeve!"—and the Baron embarrassedly replies: "What was I supposed to do, shove it up your nose?" Sometimes, in such circumstances, Gorky would assume the manner of a person who was intolerably bored living among people who did not know how to appreciate him. The exposure of a petty lie evoked in him the same peevish boredom as the destruction of a lofty fantasy. He saw the restoration of the truth as the gray and vulgar victory of prose over poetry. It is not without reason that, once again, in *The Lower Depths*, the champion of the truth is Bubnov, a talentless, coarse, and tedious character whose surname appears to come from the verb *bubnit'*—"to drone on."

■ □ ■

"Sometimes, people, but sometimes, persons," the elder Luka says, no doubt employing this somewhat unclear formula to express the well-defined thoughts of the author himself. Really, "persons" should have been written with a capital letter. Gorky held "persons," which is to say, the heroes, creators, and catalysts of his beloved progress, in high regard. People, on the other hand, mere people, with their dingy faces and modest biographies, he held in contempt; he called them "philistines." He did, however, admit that even people sometimes have the desire, if not to be, then at least to appear to be better than they truly are: "All people have gray little souls; they all wish to make themselves up." He regarded this making-up with an earnest, active sympathy and considered it his duty not only to support such people in maintaining their elevated opinions of themselves, but also to instill such ideas in them, insofar as this was possible. He appeared to believe that this sort of self-deception could serve as a jumping-off point or initial push toward an inner triumph over philistinism. And so he loved acting as a kind of mirror in which any person could see himself as being loftier, nobler, more intelligent, and more talented than he was in real life. Naturally, the greater the disparity between reflection and reality, the more grateful people would be to him: therein lay one of the devices of his undeniable, much remarked-upon *charme*.

And he himself was no exception to the rule that he had written. There was somewhat of a difference between his real self and the make-believe version of him—the ideal version, as it were. However, it is extremely curious and significant that, in this particular case, what he was pursuing was not so much his own fantasy as it was a certain external, yet collective imagining. More than once he would recall how, at the beginning of the nineties, in the period of his first and unexpected fame, some minor publisher of what were euphemistically referred to as "books for the people" (which is to say, fairy tales, dream dictionaries, and songbooks) in Nizhny Novgorod had exhorted him to write his own pulp autobiography. The publisher predicted tremendous sales for the book and serious profits for the author. "Your life, Alexei Maximovich, is pure gold," he said. Gorky would relate this story with a laugh. Nevertheless, such a biography gradually took shape and hold within the consciousness of certain social classes—if not at that time, then later, and if not pulp, then something like it: the biography of Gorky the natural talent, Gorky the stormy petrel,[21] Gorky the martyr and the frontline fighter for the proletariat. It is impossible to deny that his life (which was, in fact, remarkable) did indeed exhibit such heroic traits—but fate did not test them nearly so severely, so completely, and so dramatically as his biography, idealized or official, might lead one to believe. Now, I would not, by any means, suggest that Gorky came to believe in this biography, or that he necessarily wanted to believe it. However, compelled by circumstances, fame, and outside pressure, he did finally accept it and integrate it into his official worldview once and for all. Having done so, he became, to a significant extent, its slave. He considered it his duty to stand before humanity, before "the masses," in the exact guise and pose that those masses expected from him: the image that they demanded in exchange for their love. Often, all too often, he was made to feel that he himself was a sort of mass illusion, a part of the "golden dream" that he had once inspired and that he now had no right to destroy. He probably even liked the enormous shadow that it cast, liked it for its size and its harsh outlines. But I'm not certain that he loved it. In any case, I can vouch for the fact that he was often exhausted by it. A great many times, when he was doing something that wasn't to his liking or something that went against his conscience, or, on the contrary, during those times when he was holding himself back from doing something that he felt like doing or that his conscience prompted him to do, he would say, with melancholy, with a grimace, with a vexed shrug of his shoulders: "You can't, you'd spoil the biography." Or, "What can you do? You have to, or else you'll spoil the biography."

■ □ ■

There was an enormous gap seperating Alexei Peshkov[22] of the Nizhny Novgorod workshop, who completed his studies on a shoestring budget, and Maxim Gorky, the world-famous writer. This gap speaks for itself, whatever one might think of Gorky's talent. One would think that the combination of an awareness of what he had achieved and this constant recollection of his "biography" would have had a negative effect on his character. This wasn't the case. Unlike many other people, he didn't chase after fame or wallow in concerns over how he would maintain it; he was not afraid of criticism, just as he did not experience joy upon receiving praise from any idiot or ignoramus; he didn't seek out opportunities to consolidate his fame, perhaps because it was genuine rather than inflated. He did not suffer from conceit and did not, like many other celebrities, play the spoiled child. I have never seen a person who wore his fame with greater grace and nobility than Gorky did.

He was exceptionally modest—even when he happened to be pleased with himself. This modesty was unfeigned. It stemmed primarily from his reverent worship of literature, and also from his lack of self-confidence. Having permanently internalized some fairly elementary aesthetic notions (ones that had been popular in the seventies and eighties or thereabouts), he drew a sharp line between the form and content of his work. He viewed his content as beyond reproach because it was based upon deeply ingrained social attitudes. However, he felt himself poorly equipped in the area of form. When he compared himself to his favorite—and even to his least favorite—masters (for example, Dostoevsky and Gogol), he found in them a flexibility, complexity, elegance, and refinement that were not at his disposal—and he admitted to this more than once. I have already stated that he would, on occasion, read his own short stories aloud through tears. But once his tender agitation had waned, he would demand criticism, listen to it gratefully, and only pay attention to the reproaches, allowing the praise go in one ear and out the other. Not infrequently, he would argue and defend himself, but just as often he would cede the argument, and, having ceded it, would, without fail, set about making modifications and corrections. It was in this manner that I convinced him to rework part of "A Story about Cockroaches" and rewrite the last section of *The Artamonov Affair*.[23] Ultimately, there was only one area in which he admitted himself to be helpless—and he suffered from it in a very real way.

"But tell me, please—about my poetry, is it very bad?"

"It's bad, Alexei Maximovich."

"That's a pity. A terrible pity. All my life, I've dreamed of writing just one good poem."

He cast his sad, dull eyes toward the heavens and was obliged to take out his handkerchief to give them a wipe.

I was always surprised and almost touched by the uncommonly human inconsistency with which this constant execrator of the truth would suddenly become a truth-lover, if only so far as his writing was concerned. In this area, not only did he not want to hear flattery, but, on the contrary, he manfully sought out the truth. He once declared that Yu. I. Aikhenvald, who was still alive at the time, was unfairly abusing his new stories in order to settle political and personal scores. I replied that this couldn't be the case because, although I frequently disagreed with Aikhenvald, I knew him to be an extremely impartial critic. This was at the end of 1923, in Marienbad. Gorky and I were coeditors of *Discourse* at the time. Our argument reached the point where I, almost as a bet, suggested printing two of Gorky's stories in our forthcoming issue—one under his real name, the other under a pseudonym—in order to see what would happen. And so we did. In the fourth issue of *Discourse*, we printed "A Story about a Hero" under Gorky's byline and, next to it, another story, called "About a Certain Novel," under the pseudonym "Vasily Sizov." A few days later, an issue of the Berlin *Rudder* arrived in which Sizov caught it almost worse than Gorky did—and Gorky said to me with a genuine, unfeigned delight: "You're obviously right. This is very good, you see. That is, it's not good that he gave me such a dressing-down, but it's good that I was obviously wrong about him."[24]

Nearly a year later, in Sorrento, a curious incident occurred in relation to that very same story. Andrei Sobol, who had recently arrived from Moscow, had asked to be given all the back issues of *Discourse* so that he could familiarize himself with them (they were not permitted in Soviet Russia). About three days later, he brought the volumes back. Dinner was drawing to a close, but everyone was still sitting around the table. Sobol began setting forth his opinions. He praised various items that had been printed in *Discourse*, including Gorky's stories—and then suddenly blurted out: "But you shouldn't have published that what's-his-name, Sizov. He's absolute rubbish."

I don't remember how Gorky replied, or whether or not he even did, and I don't know what sort of look was on his face because I averted my gaze. Before going to sleep, I went into Gorky's room for one reason or another. He was already in bed, and he said to me from behind the screen: "Don't even think about telling Sobol what the matter is, or else we'll be as embarrassed around each another as two naked nuns."

■ □ ■

Before sending my reminiscences about Valery Bryusov to the editors of *Contemporary Annals*,[25] I read them aloud to Gorky. When I had finished reading, he said, after a pause: "What you've written is harsh, but—magnificent. When I die, please write something about me."

"All right, Alexei Maximovich."

"You won't forget?"

"I won't forget."

Paris, 1936

TRANSLATOR'S NOTES

INTRODUCTION

1. Vladimir Nabokov, *Speak Memory: An Autobiography Revisited* (New York: Putnam, 1966), 285.
2. Marina Tsvetaeva, "Plennyi dukh (Moia vstrecha s Andreem Belym)," in *Izbrannaia proza v dvukh tomakh* (New York: Russica, 1979), II:98.
3. Simon Karlinsky, ed., *The Nabokov-Wilson Letters, 1940–1971* (New York: Harper and Row, 1979), 94.
4. O. Nemerovskaia and Ts. Volpe, eds., *Sud'ba Bloka* (Leningrad: Izdatel'stvo pisatelei v Leningrade, 1928), 65.
5. Andrei Belyi (Boris Bugaev), "Apokalipsis v russkoi poezii," *Vesy* 4 (April 1905): 11–28.
6. Vladislav Khodasevich, "Viktor Gofman," *Poslednie novosti* (14 October 1926).
7. David M. Bethea, *Khodasevich: His Life and Art* (Princeton, N.J.: Princeton University Press, 1983), 262–272.

1. THE DEATH OF RENATE

1. For more information on the Symbolist idea of "life creation," see the introduction to this volume.
2. Excerpt from the poem "Gold" ("Zoloto"), written by Valery Bryusov in 1899. Khodasevich misquotes Bryusov slightly, replacing the original *blednoi* (pale) with *bednoi* (poor).
3. Most accounts state that she was born in 1884, but her correspondence with Bryusov suggests that she was actually born in 1879. See the commentary of N.A. Bogomolov in *Vladislav Khodasevich, Vladislav Khodasevich: Sobranie sochinenii v chetyrekh tomakh*, eds. I.P. Andreeva, S.G. Bocharov, I.A. Bocharova, and I.P. Khabarova, vol. 4 (Moscow: Soglasie, 1997), 537.
4. In this context, a gymnasium is a rigorous type of secondary school.

5. **Scorpio** (*Skorpion*) and **Griffin** (*Grif*) were major Symbolist publishing houses. Scorpio, the first and more significant of the two, was founded in 1899 by S. A. Polyakov, Valery Bryusov, and Jurgis Baltrušaitis. Griffin was founded by in 1903 S. A. Sokolov (pseudonym Sergei Krechetov). Griffin attracted a more mystical breed of Symbolists, including the younger generation and the so-called Argonauts (*argonavty*).

6. This quotation is taken from a letter dated January 14–15, 1904. Khodasevich appears to have omitted the end of this sentence ("smarter than her husband") out of consideration for the man in question, S. A. Sokolov, who was still alive at the time of publication (Bogomolov, 537-8).

7. Excerpt from the poem "Habet ilia in alvo," written by Valery Bryusov in 1902.

8. Reference to Alexander Pushkin's play, *The Miserly Knight* (Skupoi rytsar'), written in 1830.

9. A line from Alexander Blok's 1906 play in verse, *The Fairground Booth* (Balaganchik).

10. Probably a reference to Balmont's poem "Praise" ("Khvalite"), whose first two lines are "Praise, praise, praise, praise, / Madly love, praise love . . ."

11. Balmont.

12. The other woman Khodasevich refers to is **Lyubov Dmitrievna Blok**, née Mendeleyeva (1881–1939), who was an actress, dancer, and wife of Alexander Blok. Her mother's name was Anna, like the mother of the Virgin Mary. The **"Woman clothed with the Sun"** is a reference to Revelation 12:1: "And there appeared a great wonder in heaven; a woman clothed with the sun, and the moon under her feet, and upon her head a crown of twelve stars. . . ." This image would play a large role in Russian Symbolist mythology, particularly through the works of poet and philosopher Vladimir Sergeyevich Solovyov. The **mystics** are a reference to Alexander Blok's 1906 play in verse, *The Fairground Booth* (Balaganchik), which prominently features a group of pompous, hapless mystics. The **"Beast that ascendeth out of the bottomless pit"** is a reference to Revelation 11:7: "And when they shall have finished their testimony, the beast that ascendeth out of the bottomless pit shall make war against them, and shall overcome them, and kill them."

13. This incident actually took place on April 14, 1907. It was described in a letter from Bryusov to the poet Zinaida Gippius dated April 16–21, 1917, as well as in Bely's memoir *Between Two Revolutions* (Mezhdu dvukh revoliutsii), published in 1934 (Bogomolov, 538).

14. Here, Khodasevich is punning on the word *roman*, which is the Russian for both "novel" and "romantic affair."

15. Saint Peter's Basilica in Rome.

16. This is a mistake on Khodasevich's part: Petrovskaya left Russia in 1911 (Bogomolov, 539).

2. BRYUSOV

Khodasevich believed that the publication of this memoir was one of the reasons his Soviet passport for travel abroad was not renewed. As a result of this experience, he became an émigré (Bogomolov, 539).

1. For information about the **gymnasium**, see note 4 in "The Death of Renate." Valery Bryusov's **younger brother**, Alexander Yakovlevich Bryusov (1885–1966), was an archaeologist. *News of the Day* (Novosti Dnia) was a Moscow-based tabloid published 1883–1906. It printed numerous unflattering portrayals of the Symbolists in the 1890s. **Sirin**, named after the half-woman, half-bird of Russian myth, was a Saint Petersburg-based Symbolist publishing house active from 1912 to 1915.

2. *Tertia Vergilia* (Latin: Third Watch) was Bryusov's third collection of poems. It was published in 1900 and brought Bryusov his first positive recognition as a poet. The mention of the **Yauza** River is a reference to Bryusov's 1895 poem "Nighttime" ("Noch'iu"): "Moscow slumbers, like a sleeping ostrich's mate . . . Its neck outstretched—the noiseless, black Yauza." **"Obscure, ridiculed, strange"** is a phrase taken from Bryusov's poem "It was the madness of a reverie" ("Eto bylo bezumie grezy"), dated August 27, 1896. *Chefs d'oeuvre* was Bryusov's first poetry collection, published in 1895. **"I've come to hate my motherland"** is a line from Bryusov's 1896 poem "I do not see the world at hand" ("Ia deistvitel'nosti nashei ne vizhu").

3. Russian names are usually made up of first names, last names, and patronymics: middle names based on the first name of one's father. Male sons of someone named "Aviva" would bear the patronymic "Avivovich."

4. *Rebus* (Rebus) was a weekly journal published in Saint Petersburg in the years 1881–1918. It began as a collection of riddles and rebuses and then became a forum for spiritists and mediumists.

5. *Preferans* is a bidding card game that became popular in Russia in the mid-1800s and is still played to this day. **"Dasha's Engagement"** (Obruchenie Dashi) was first published in 1913 and bears the subtitle "Scenes from life in the 60s." An *argumentum ad baculum* (Latin: "appeal to the stick") is a fallacious logical argument in which the arguer uses force (or the threat of force) to persuade the listener.

6. Excerpt from Bryusov's poem, "The shadow of unformed formations . . ." ("Ten' nesozdannykh sozdanii"), first published in 1895.

7. *Sofia* (Sofiia) was a literary-artistic journal published by Pavel Pavlovich Muratov (1881–1950) and Konstantin Fyodorovich Nekrasov (1873–1940) in 1914. It was dedicated to the study and comparison of medieval Russian with European art.

8. *Libra* (Vesy) was the leading Symbolist literary journal, published in the years 1904–1909 by the Scorpio publishing house. It was edited by Bryusov. For information on **Scorpio**, see note 5 in "The Death of Renate." The *style moderne* refers to the French art deco.

9. Khodasevich was a student at Moscow University, first in the law faculty, then in the historical and philological faculty.

10. Pepel, 1908.

11. Written in January of 1904, "I wait for death by the morning star . . ." ("Zhdu ia smerti bliz dennitsy . . .") ends with the lines: "The tsar-like stony smile / I won't disturb on earth."

12. For information on **Griffin**, see note 5 in "The Death of Renate." *Art* (Iskusstvo) and *Passage* (Pereval) were Symbolist journals active in the years 1905 and 1906–1907, respectively. S. A. Sokolov, the founder of Griffin, was active in both of these publications; Bryusov also published in them.

13. Excerpt from Bryusov's 1904 poem "To Baldr, from Loki" ("Bal'deru Loki"). This was one of a series of poems mythologizing the love triangle between Bryusov, Bely, and Nina Petrovskaya.

14. *Chemin de fer* is a version of the card game baccarat.

15. "**Fall upon the couch**" is a line from Bryusov's 1901 poem "Woman" ("Zhenshchina"). "**We, like priests in holy orders,** / **perform a rite**" is an excerpt from Bryusov's 1903 poem "To Damascus" ("V Damask").

16. Excerpt from Bryusov's poem "To Baldr, From Loki."

17. Excerpt from Bryusov's 1904 poem "In the torture chamber" ("V zastenke").

18. A misquotation of Bryusov's 1896 poem "To the Young Poet" ("Iunomu poetu"). The first quotation should read, "Sympathize with no one, / But learn to love yourself without limit." The second should read, "without thinking" ("*bezrazdumno*") rather than "wholeheartedly" ("*bezrazdel'no*").

19. Ancient Persian sun god.

20. Reference to Pushkin's 1836 poem "I have built myself a monument not made by hands" ("Ia pamiatnik sebe vozdvig nerukotvornyi"), which was itself a recasting of Horace's "Exegi monumentum," which has a long history of reference and reinterpretation in Russian poetry.

21. Excerpt from Bryusov's 1903 poem "To Those Younger than Myself" ("Mladshim"). **The Beautiful Lady** (*Prekrasnaia Dama*) is a reference to Blok's first poetry collection, *Verses on the Beautiful Lady* (Stikhi o prekrasnoi dame), released in 1904, which was inspired by Blok's wife, Lyubov.

22. *Vint* is a Russian card game sometimes referred to as Russian whist.

23. Reference to Bryusov's book *The Dreams of Mankind* (Sny chelovechestva), which he worked on between 1911 and 1917 (though some of the materials included had been written earlier).

24. The 1909 collection *All Songs* (Vse napevy) does not actually contain such a cycle, though it does contain a poem titled "The Suicide" ("Samoubiitsa"). Khodasevich might have been thinking of Bryusov's poem "Suicide Demon" ("Demon samoubiistva") or his epic "Underground dwelling" ("Podzemnoe zhilishche"), which are included in the collection *Shadow Mirror* (Zerkalo tenei), published in 1912 (Bogomolov, 542).

25. *Experiments in meter and rhythm, euphony and consonance, stanzaic and other kinds of form* (Opyty po metrike i ritmike, po evfonii i sozvuchiiam, po strofike i formam) was published in 1918.

26. A first paeon is a metrical foot consisting of four syllables, the first of which is long and the last three of which are short.

27. The poem was called "Mouse" ("Mysh' ") and was first published in 1908.

28. *smert', zherd', tverd',* and *umiloserd'* translate to "death," "pole," "firmament," and the imperative form of the archaic verb "take mercy on," respectively.

29. Excerpt from Bryusov's 1907 poem "To the Poet" ("Poetu").

30. A. A. Shesterkina (Bogomolov, 543).

31. Actually, Lvova's parents lived in Podolsk, not **Serpukhov** (Bogomolov, 543). *'kak,' 'kotoryi,'* and *'kinzhal''* translate to "how," "that/which," and "dagger," respectively.

32. *Nelly's Poems* (Stikhi Nelli) was published in 1913. In Russian, the foreign name "Nelli" does not decline, which causes the ambiguity over whether these poems were written by or for Nelly. Igor Severyanin wrote a poem entitled "Nelly" ("Nelli") in 1911.

33. *The Russian Record* (Russkie Vedomosti) was a liberal broadsheet newspaper published in Moscow from 1863 to 1918. *The Russian Word* (Russkoe Slovo) was a cheap daily newspaper published in Moscow from 1895 to 1918.

34. Free Aesthetics (*Svobodnaia Estetika*) was a Moscow artistic society cofounded by Bryusov and modeled on the Belgian group Libre Esthetique. It was active in the years 1907 to 1917.

35. "**Lifeless, may you rest in peace,** / **Use your life, o ye who live it**" is a reference to Vassily Andreyevich Zhukovsky's 1828 poem "The Triumph of the Victors" ("Torzhestvo pobeditelei"), itself a translation of Schiller's 1803 poem "Das Siegesfest." The Bryusov poem referenced here is his 1914 "**Peace to the dead!**" ("Umershim mir!").

36. The Moscow city council.

37. The timeline that Khodasevich gives here is incorrect. On July 24, 1914, a farewell dinner was held for Bryusov, who was setting off to become a war correspondent. Polish writers did host an event in honor of Bryusov's arrival in August of 1914, but it was not considered to be a jubilee. The twentieth anniversary of Bryusov's literary career was celebrated in Moscow in January of 1915 (Bogomolov, 543).

38. Other accounts, including that of L. S. Kissina, dispute Bryusov's anti-Semitism (Bogomolov, 543).

39. This event took place on December 17, 1923 (Bogomolov, 543).

40. The **Black Hundredists** were a group of Russian ultranationalists active in the early twentieth century. They were known for their violence, monarchism, xenophobia, anti-Semitism, and anti-Communism. The **Russo-Japanese War** was an imperial war fought between Russia and Japan in the years 1904–1905. Russia suffered a humiliating defeat, dealing a serious blow to the monarchy.

41. The Erfurt Program was the program adopted by the Social Democratic Party of Germany during their congress in Erfurt in 1891. It stated that, since the collapse of capitalism was inevitable in any case, socialists should focus their efforts on the improvement of workers' lives rather than on bringing about a revolution.

42. Bryusov's **"Dagger"** ("Kinzhal' ") first appeared in 1903. Karamzin's *Letters of a Russian Traveler* (Pis'ma russkogo puteshestvennika), based on his impressions of a journey to Europe undertaken in the years 1789–1791 and inspired by the sentimental works of Rousseau and Sterne, earned him instant literary fame. **"Que faire? J'aime les t-t-troubles"** is French for "What can I do? I love unrest."

43. **"The Stonemason," "the one about the helper-outer," "The Collectors' Song,"** and **"The Australian Song"** refer to "Kamenshchik" (1901), "Detskaia" (1901), "Pesnia Sborshchikov" (1898), and "Iz pesen avstraliiskikh dikarei" (1907), respectively.

44. Latin: "False Valery, double tongue!" The phrase "duplex lingua" does not appear in the actual letter (Bogomolov, 543).

45. *Russian Thought* (Russkaia mysl') was a monthly Moscow literary-political journal active in the years 1880–1918. Bryusov was actually the editor of the journal's literary criticism section in the years 1910–1912 (Bogomolov, 543).

46. The first of two Russian revolutions in 1917, the **February Revolution** resulted in the abdication of Tsar Nicholas II and the end of the Russian Empire. *Poetry of Armenia* (Poeziia Armenii) was published in 1916.

47. From Bryusov's 1904 poem "The Trireme Rowers" ("Grebtsy triremy").

48. Latin: "If you want peace, prepare for war."

49. Here, **October** refers to the October Revolution of 1917.

50. The Russian **Constituent Assembly** was a constitutional body convened after the October Revolution; it was almost immediately dissolved. Bryusov became a member of the **Russian Communist Party** (Bolsheviks) in 1920.

51. **Lito** is an abbreviation for the Literature Section of the People's Commissariat for Education. Bryusov became vice chair of Lito in February 1920 and chairman in November of the same year.

52. Gukon is a portmanteau from *Glavnoe Upravlenie Konevodstva i Konnozavodstva* (Central Office of Horsebreeding and Husbandry).

53. New Economic Policy (NEP) was a looser, more market-oriented Soviet economic policy instituted in the years following the Russian Civil War (1918–1922) in order to aid in the country's recovery.

3. ANDREI BELY

1. *Petersburg* (Peterburg) was a Symbolist novel written by Andrei Bely and first published in 1913. Vladimir Nabokov declared it one of the four greatest masterpieces of the twentieth century (along with *Ulysses*, *The Metamorphosis*, and *In Search of Lost Time*).

2. 1904–1923.

3. This phrase is a reference to Alexander Pushkin's 1830 poem "The Hero" ("Geroi"), which contains the lines: "Dearer to me than a multitude of low truths / is a deception that uplifts us."

4. This child is Andrei Bely. Borya is a nickname for Boris, which was Andrei Bely's real first name. His real last name was Bugaev.

5. Andrei Bely's father, **Nikolai Vasilyevich Bugaev** (1837–1903), was a prominent professor of mathematics at Moscow University. For more about the **gymnasium**, see note 4 in "The Death of Renate."

6. Bely's **mother** was Alexandra Dmitrievna Bugaeva, née Egorova (1858–1922). Public celebrations were held in honor of world-renowned writer Ivan Sergeyevich **Turgenev** (1818–1883) in February and March of 1879. *A Boyar Wedding Feast* (Boiarskii svadebnyi pir), 1883, was painted by Konstantin Egorovich Makovsky (1839–1915), a painter of the Slavophilic school known as the Wanderers (*Peredvizhniki*).

7. *Kotik Letaev*, *Nikolai Letaev's Crime*, *The Baptized Chinaman*, *The Moscow Eccentric*, and *Moscow Under Fire* are Kotik Letaev (1922), Prestuplenie Nikolaia Letaeva (1921), Kreshchenyi kitaets (1922), Moskovskii chudak (1926), and Moskva pod udarom (1926), respectively.

8. Bely studied in the faculty of physics and **mathematics** 1899–1903, and in the faculty of history and **philology** 1904–1906. Bely "**tells this story best himself**" in his 1930 memoir *On the Border of Two Centuries* (Na rubezhe dvukh stoletii).

9. Joseph the all-comely is an Old Testament Biblical figure known for his coat of many colors, his interpretation of the pharaoh's dreams, and his narrow (but costly) escape from committing adultery with Potiphar's wife.

10. *Golden Fleece* (Zolotoe runo) was a monthly literary-artistic journal associated with the Argonaut (*argonavt*) circle of Symbolists. It was active in the years 1906–1909.

11. First published in 1904, this poem ("Predanie") was written before his break with Nina Petrovskaya (Bogomolov, 546).

12. This section refers to Alexander Blok and his wife, Lyubov Dmitrievna. Their names are not mentioned here out of consideration for Lyubov Dmitrievna, who was still alive at the time of publication (Bogomolov, 546).

13. Bely spent the period from September 1906 to February 1907 living in Munich and Paris. *The Blizzard Cup* (Kubok metelei) was started there, but finished in Russia in 1907.

14. In all likelihood, the "**personal misfortune**" that Khodasevich refers to here is the worsening relations between Khodasevich and his first wife, Marina Erastovna Ryndina (1886–1973), with whom he parted ways at the end of 1907. The "**certain young Petersburg writer**" is a reference to Sergei Abramovich Auslender (1886–1937), who based one of his protagonists on Nina Petrovskaya; Petrovskaya also dedicated a book of short stories to him (Bogomolov, 546).

15. Vienna was a famous Petersburg restaurant and meeting place for literary bohemians.

16. Specifically, a number of poems in his collection *Ashes* (Bogomolov, 546).

17. *Urn* and *The Silver Dove* are the poetry collection Urna (1909) and the novel Serebrianyi golub' (1909), respectively. The **murder** referenced here was committed in 1869 by members of a revolutionary terrorist group. Its leader, Sergei Nechaev, orchestrated the killing in order to solidify his control over the other members. This incident formed the basis of Dostoevsky's 1872 novel *Demons*. *Gemütlich* is German for "cozy." The **Solovyovs** refer to the family of Mikhail Sergeyevich Solovyov (1862–1903) and Olga Mikhailovna Solovyova (1855–1903), whose son was a very close friend of Bely's. The **dawning of the year 1900** is a reference to Bely's 1921 long poem, *The First Meeting* (Pervoe svidanie), which contains the line, "The year—nineteen hundred: dawn, dawn!" (*"God—deviat'sotyi: zori, zori!"*).

18. Lines from Pushkin's famous novel in verse, *Eugene Onegin* (Evgenii Onegin) (1825–1832).

19. Musagetes (*Musaget*) was a Symbolist publishing house active in the years 1909–1917.

20. Vera Oskarovna Stanevich (1890–1967) was a poet and translator known for her masculine habits, which included walking around in short pants in her home. Thus, Bely, with whom she was in love, would tease her by calling her "Shtanevich"—a combination of her last name and the Russian word for "trousers" (*shtany*).

21. Greek deities of vengeance (also known as the Furies).

22. It had recently been discovered that Yevno Fishelevich Azef (1869–1918) was an agent provocateur serving simultaneously as a spy for the Imperial secret police (*Okhrana*) and as the leader of the terrorist branch of the Socialist-Revolutionary Party. Similarly, Dmitry Grigoryevich Bogrov (1887–1911), a double agent working for the Okhrana, had assassinated Pyotr Arkadyevich Stolypin (1862–1911), Russian minister of the interior.

23. **War Communism** was a Soviet political and economic system (1918–1921) put into effect during the Russian Civil War (1917–1922). Its strict controls and nationalization were designed to keep the Red Army supplied with food and weapons during wartime. The **Proletkult** was a Soviet artistic organization for the promotion of a new, revolutionary, proletarian aesthetic (portmanteau from "*proletarskaia kultura*"—"proletarian culture"). *Notes of an Eccentric* (Zapiski chudaka) was published in 1922.

24. Thanks to Petersburg's proximity to the Arctic Circle, it enjoys unusually long periods of daylight during the summer months; this phenomenon is called **White Nights**. It pays for this largesse in the winter, when the days are short and dark. **The Bronze Horseman** is an equestrian monument to Peter the Great created by the French sculptor Étienne Falconet. Completed in 1782, it was commissioned by Catherine the Great and has become one of the most famous symbols of Saint Petersburg. It takes its name from Pushkin's 1833 poem

The Bronze Horseman (Mednyi vsadnik), which describes the struggle of the individual against the cruel forces of nature and the state.

25. *The First Meeting* (Pervoe svidanie) was written in 1921. The article that Khodasevich refers to is "Rembrandt's truth in the poetry of our time" ("Rembrandtova pravda v poezii nashikh dnei"). *Dreamers' Notes* (Zapiski mechtatelei) was a Symbolist literary-artistic journal published in Petersburg in the years 1919–1922.

26. Soviet secret police organization.

27. This is primarily a reference to Anna (Asya) Alexeyevna Turgeneva (1890–1966), who was the writer Ivan Turgenev's niece and, along with Bely, a disciple of Rudolf Steiner (Bogomolov, 550).

28. Anthroposophy is a philosophical movement founded by Rudolf Steiner (1861–1925). Rooted in German idealist philosophy and mysticism, the anthroposophical worldview is centered on the idea that the spiritual world can be reached through personal development.

29. The Treaty of Rapallo was a 1922 agreement between Germany and Russia in which the countries renounced all territorial and financial claims against each other after World War I.

30. German: "So, how are you?"

31. German: "Difficulties with the housing office!"

32. German: "floorboards." In this context, dance floors.

33. German: "Doctor, you are an old monkey!"

34. Reference to Bely's 1922 poem "A little buffoonery on a little planet called Earth" ("Malen'kii balagan na malen'koi planete 'zemlia' "), which opens with the stage direction, "Shouted out a Berlin window without pause."

35. Mariechen was the daughter of the proprietor of a bar on the corner of Lutherstrasse and Augsburgerstrasse. She was somewhat reminiscent of Nadya Lvova in appearance (Bogomolov, 550).

36. In the resort town of Saarow (Bogomolov, 551).

37. According to A. B. Bakhrakh, this was Vera Alexeyevna Zaitseva, née Oreshnikova (1878–1965), the wife of writer Boris Konstantinovich Zaitsev (1881–1972) (Bogomolov, 551).

38. This actually happened in 1924 (Bogomolov, 551).

39. *Epopée* (Epopeia) was a monthly Russian-language literary journal published in Berlin in the years 1922–1923.

40. 1935 (Bogomolov, 551).

41. Excerpt from Bely's 1907 poem "To my friends" ("Druz'iam").

4. MUNI

1. Zori.

2. March 22, 1916 (Bogomolov, 552). For more about the **gymnasium**, see note 4 in "The Death of Renate."

3. **The barefooted maidens** are a reference to the many women who were imitating famed American dancer Isadora Duncan (1877–1927), who had recently toured Russia and was incredibly popular there. *Sanin* was a novel written in 1904 by Mikhail Petrovich Artsybashev (1878–1927) and published in 1907. It deals frankly with sex, was thought to promote "free love," and was later banned as a work of pornography. **Candle-end clubs** were secret "free love" youth meetings. A candle would be lit and attendees would read erotic poetry and hold discussions on erotic themes until the candle had burned down to its end. Once the candle had gone out, theory would turn into practice.

4. The **certain poet** who described this otherworldly element was the lyric poet Afanasy Afanasyevich Fet (1820–1892), whose 1884 poem "Swallows" ("Lastochki") contains the lines: "And do not I, the weaker vessel, / Venture on the forbidden path, / Trying to scoop at least a drop / Of that alien, otherworldly element?" The **bad sorcerers** are a reference to Goethe's 1797 poem "The Sorcerer's Apprentice" ("Der Zauberlehrling"), but also to Bryusov, who had a reputation as a "sorcerer," especially after Bely's 1903 poem "The Sorcerer" ("Mag"), which was dedicated to him. The **forest of symbols** is a reference to Baudelaire's poem "Correspondences." The **seesaw of correspondences** is a corrupted reference both to that work and to Fyodor Sologub's 1907 poem "The Devil's Seesaw" ("Chertovy kacheli").

5. The double mirrors of this restaurant encouraged the Symbolists' already active mystical imaginations.

6. A *sazhen* is an obsolete unit of measurement equal to seven feet.

7. Reference to elegiac poet Evgeny Abramovich Baratynsky (1800–1844) and his 1827 poem "Do not fear biting judgments" ("Ne boisia edkikh osuzhdenii").

8. Excerpt from Pushkin's 1832 poem "The Beauty" ("Krasavitsa").

9. A version of Muni's *Light Burden* (Legkoe bremia), edited by Inna Andreyeva, was published by the Avgust publishing house in 1999; along with poetry and prose, it includes Muni's correspondence with Khodasevich.

10. Reference to Nikolai Alexeyevich Nekrasov's epic poem *Who Lives Well in Russia?* (Komu na Rusi zhit' khorosho?), which was released serially starting in 1869 and remained unfinished at the time of the author's death in 1878. The poem contains the lines: "The great chain has broken, / It has broken, flown apart: / One end hit the master, / The other struck the *muzhik!*"

11. Excerpt from Balmont's poem "Smoke's shadow" ("Ten' ot dyma"), first published in 1905.

12. A pood is an obsolete Russian unit for measuring weight; seven poods is equal to about 250 pounds.

13. Reference to Dostoevsky's *The Brothers Karamazov*, in which the Devil expresses the same wish to Ivan Karamazov. He wants to become the fat merchant's wife in order to enjoy her uncomplicated religious faith and peace of mind.

14. "In the Summer of 190*" ("Letom 190* goda"), 1907.

15. *A Happy Little House* (Schastlivyi domik) was published in 1914.
16. This play was actually called *The Black Man's Revenge* (Mest' negra).
17. "Samostrel'naia."

5. GUMILYOV AND BLOK

1. It is not entirely true that Gumilyov and Khodasevich **began publishing in the same year**: though Gumilyov's first poetry collection was released in 1905 (the year when Khodasevich began publishing), his first poem was published in 1902. **World Literature** (*Vsemirnaia literatura*) was a publishing house founded by Gorky in 1919. Its mission was to bring the best works of world literature to Soviet audiences. Gumilyov was a member of the board, while Khodasevich was at this meeting to pitch some of his translations (Bogomolov, 554).

2. This is a reference to Sergei Konstantinovich Makovsky (1877–1962), who was a poet and art scholar, as well as the second husband of Khodasevich's first wife (Bogomolov, 554). He was also the son of the artist Konstantin Makovsky (see note 6 in "Bely").

3. This is Lev Nikolaevich Gumilyov (1912–1992), the son of Nikolai Gumilyov and the great poet Anna Akhmatova (1889-1966). He went on to become a famous historian and ethnologist.

4. This is a reference to Iraida Gustavovna Heinike (1895–1990), an Acmeist writer who wrote under the pseudonym Irina Vladimirovna Odoevtseva. She was a great disciple of Gumilyov. In 1921, she married writer and memoirist Georgy Ivanov (1894-1958) (Bogomolov, 555).

5. *The Twelve* (Dvenadtsat') was a long poem written in 1918 as a response to the October Revolution of 1917. This poem and, in particular, its biblical imagery, has been interpreted in various ways and ultimately remains ambiguous in its depiction of Bolshevism. Blok himself declined to clarify the poem's meaning and refused to recite the poem in public, recruiting his wife, who was an actress, to do it for him.

6. The **"subtle engine"** is a reference to Blok's 1914 poem "O, I madly want to live . . ." ("O, ia khochu bezumno zhit' . . ."). **Acmeism** was a literary movement cofounded in the early 1910s by Nikolai Gumilyov and Sergei Gorodetsky as a direct response against the mysticism and obscurity of Symbolist literature.

7. Khodasevich was in Moscow at the time of the Guild's formation and makes several mistakes in its initial roster. Chulkov and Verkhovsky were never members of the Guild, and the Narbut in question was not Vladimir, but his brother, the artist Egor Narbut (1886–1920) (Bogomolov, 556).

8. An *arshin* is an obsolete Russian unit of length equal to 28 inches.

9. Excerpt from Neldikhen's 1922 poem "Women" ("Zhenshchiny").

10. Excerpt from Balmont's 1899 poem "Accursed stupidity" ("Prokliatye gluposti").

11. This event took place in 1918 (Bogomolov, 556).

12. This event took place on April 25, 1921 in the Bolshoy Dramatichesky Theater, which was formerly known as the Maly, or Suvorinsky, Theater (Bogomolov, 557).

13. In the years following the Revolution, policies on time changes varied widely from year to year. Prior to the Revolution, Moscow had been on GMT+2:30; on April 25, 1921, it was on GMT+5.

14. Alexandra Andreyevna Kublitskaya-Piottukh (née Beketova, Blok during her first marriage, lived 1860–1923).

15. "Pered sudom," 1915.

16. Possibly a reference to Andrei Bely, who returned to Petrograd on March 31, 1921 (Bogomolov, 557-8).

17. Bely delivered this news in a letter dated August 9, 1921 (Bogomolov, 558). "The Peddlers" ("Korobeiniki") is a Russian folk song better known in the West as the theme song of the iconic video game Tetris.

6. GERSHENZON

1. Khodasevich's 1918 poem "November 2nd" ("2-ogo noiabria") appeared in his 1920 collection *Grain's Way* (Putyom zerna).

2. Now Chişinău, Moldova.

3. A European-style overcoat with cape that was common in the first half of the nineteenth century.

4. née Goldenveizer (1873–1940).

5. This is a reference to Georgy Ivanovich Chulkov (1879–1939) (Bogomolov, 559).

6. This is a reference to Matvei Nikanorovich Rozanov (1858–1936), a literary scholar (Bogomolov, 559).

7. Bobrov's *New Work on the Versification of Pushkin* (Novoe o stikhoslozhenii Pushkina) was published in 1915. *Zemshchina* was a radical right-wing monarchist daily newspaper published in Saint Petersburg in the years 1909–1917. *Russian Land* (Russkaia zemlia) was a similarly right-wing publication.

8. Mudrost' Pushkina, 1919.

9. The Pythia was the name given to the high priestess of the Temple of Apollo at Delphi. She would go into trances and make prophecies said to have come from Apollo himself.

10. "K Chaadaevu," 1818.

7. SOLOGUB

1. Excerpt from Sologub's 1902 poem "When I was afloat on stormy seas . . ." ("Kogda ia v burnom more plaval . . .").

2. Excerpt from Sologub's 1917 poem "The Profligate" ("Rastochitel' ").

3. Sologub's real name.

4. An eight-line poetic form in which the first, fourth, and seventh lines are the same and the second and eighth ones are as well.

5. Zhemchuzhnie svetila, 1913.

6. The 1884 poem that Khodasevich refers to here is "To the Brook" ("Ruch'iu"). The 1888 poem is "July" (Iiul').

7. Excerpt from Sologub's 1898 poem "When the Judgment Day arrives . . ." ("Kak nastanet Strashnyi Sud . . .").

8. Full text of Sologub's 1907 poem "You know not how to kiss my earth . . ." ("Vy ne umeete tselovat' moiu zemliu . . .").

9. Plamennyi krug, a collection of Sologub's poetry published in 1908.

10. Rodine and Politicheskie skazochi, respectively.

11. Excerpt from Sologub's 1911 poem "Waking up not early . . ." ("Prosnuvshisia ne rano . . .").

12. Excerpt from Sologub's 1921 poem "My supreme will" ("Moia verhkovnaia volia").

13. Excerpt from Sologub's 1921 poem "I know with my last knowledge" ("Znaiu znaniem poslednim . . .").

14. Excerpt from Sologub's 1921 poem "In the cloudless heavens God the Father reigns . . ." ("V iasnom nebe—svetlyi Bog Otets . . .").

15. Excerpt from Sologub's 1921 poem "Why love? The earth does not deserve . . ." ("Zachem liubit'? Zemlia ne stoit . . .").

16. Phrases from Sologub's poem "Unhappy friend, do not condemn my path . . ." ("Pechal'nyi drug, moi put' ne prokliani . . ."), first published in 1921.

17. Excerpt from Sologub's *I. A Book of Complete Self-Assertion.* (Ia. Kniga sovershennogo samoutverzhdeniia), published in 1906.

18. Excerpt from Sologub's 1902 poem "Why say that life outlived itself . . ." ("Chto govorit', cho zhizn' izzhita . . .").

19. From Sologub's 1898–1901 cycle *The Star Maïr* Zvezda Mair.

20. Excerpt from Sologub's 1897 poem "Overcome joy . . ." ("Pobezhdaite radost' . . .").

21. In the original, this series of puns reads as follows: "*Nozh da vilka est', a nozhrezalka est'?*" (literally: "We have a knife and fork, but do we have a knife that cuts?" Here, the Russian phrase for "and fork" sounds similar to the word for a crushing instrument—so the speaker is asking for a knife that cuts rather than crushes); "*Ty Iliia ili ia Iliia?*" (literally: "are you Ilya or am I Ilya?," a pun which takes advantage of the Russian name Ilya's similarity to the sound of the phrase "or I"); and "*Ona Selenitochka—a na sele nitochka*" (literally: "She is [called] Selenitochka—and in the village there is a string." The first and second halves of the sentence sound alike in Russian).

22. "**The earthly grind, space and time**" is a reference to Sologub's 1902 poem "Elisaveta, Elisaveta . . ." ("Elisaveta, Elisaveta . . ."). The *Petty Demon* (Melkii bes) was Sologub's most famous novel, first published in a standalone edition in 1907. It tells the story of Peredonov, a morally corrupt schoolteacher going insane in a provincial Russian town.

23. For information on *Libra,* see note 8 in "Bryusov."
24. Excerpt from Sologub's 1898 poem "Life with others is a trial!" ("Byt' s liud'mi—kakoe bremia!").
25. Olga Kuzminishna Teternikova (1865–1907) was a midwife. She lived with Sologub for a number of years and he married only after she died.
26. Excerpt from Sologub's 1920 poem "You will recognize in the trembling darkness . . ." ("Uznaesh' v tumane zybkom . . .").
27. Excerpt from Sologub's 1921 poem "Once again, they've put their shrouds on . . ." ("Snova savany nadeli . . .").
28. A bergerette (shepherdess's air) is a form of early rustic French song related to the rondeau.
29. Excerpt from Sologub's 1921 poem "Thyrsis in the willow's shade . . ." ("Tirsis pod sen'iu iv . . .").

8. ESENIN

1. Stikhi (1920–24), 1924.
2. Sobranie stikhov i poem, 1922.
3. Russian peasant man.
4. From Esenin's 1922 autobiographical essay "About me" ("O sebe").
5. Radunitsa, 1916. Radunitsa is an Eastern Slavic religious rite: the dead are commemorated with a feast held on their graves in the first week after Easter.
6. Excerpt from Esenin's 1914 poem "Swamplands and morasses . . ." ("Topi da bolota . . .").
7. Full text of Esenin's 1914 poem "The Lord went out to test the people's love . . ." ("Shel Gospod' pytat' liudei v liubovi . . .").
8. Excerpt from Esenin's 1917 poem "Not in vain the winds did blow . . ." ("Ne naprasno duli vetry . . .").
9. **X** is Sergei Antonovich Klychkov (1889–1937), who went on to become a well-known peasant poet (Bogomolov, 560). In standard Russian, **unstressed *o*'s** are normally pronounced as [a] or [ə]. Pronouncing an unstressed *o* as [o] is a marker of certain provincial dialects. **Bova Korolevich** is a popular hero of Russian folklore.
10. This is a paraphrase of an excerpt from Georgy Ivanov's 1928 memoir *Petersburg Winters* (Peterburgskie zimy), a memoir noted for its rather fast-and-loose dealings with the facts.
11. The **Khlysts** were an underground ascetic sect that split off from the Russian Orthodox Church in the late seventeenth century. They were rumored to engage in ceremonies that culminated in sexual orgies and self-flagellation. For more information on the **Black Hundredists**, see note 40 in "Bryusov." **Mystical anarchism** was a current in Russian Symbolism founded and popularized by Georgy Chulkov (1879-1939) in the years 1906–1908. The

Socialist Revolutionary (**SR**) Party was a major Russian political party in the early twentieth century. Its platform was a brand of democratic and agrarian socialism. **Religious-philosophical societies** were designed to bring together theologians, philosophers, and other public figures for mutually beneficial and enlightening conversations.

12. Popular stock characters in Russian folklore, **Ivan the Fool** (*Ivan Durachok*) is usually portrayed as a simpleminded young peasant lad whose naivety leads him to great fortune, while **Ivan Tsarevich** is a hero whose patronymic means "son of the tsar."

13. This section refers to a policy instated by Tsar Ivan IV (better known as Ivan the Terrible, r. 1547–1584) in 1565. Ivan established his absolute power over the **oprichnina** region, while the noble Boyar Council was left to rule over the less prosperous **zemshchina** region. The tsar appointed a secret police force, known as the *oprichniki*, to carry out mass terror, public executions, and the confiscation of aristocratic lands.

14. This and the section that follows are excerpts from Esenin's 1917 poem "O, Rus', spread wide your wingspan . . ." ("O Rus', vzmakhni krylami . . .").

15. Excerpt from Esenin's 1916 poem "Farewell, dear virgin forest" ("Proshchai, rodnaia pushcha").

16. Chetyrnadtsatyi god, 1915.

17. Sent to him by Tsar Nicholas II.

18. For information on Free Aesthetics, see note 34 in "Bryusov."

19. *Red Wheat Field* (Krasnaia niva) was a Soviet literary journal that appeared as a supplement to *Izvestia* (Izvestiia), a daily broadsheet newspaper founded in 1917. It was published in the years 1923–1931.

20. Grigory Rasputin.

21. Esenin served neither at the front, nor in a disciplinary battalion.

22. Goluben', 1918.

23. Communist Party of the Soviet Union.

24. This and the two sections that follow are excerpts from Esenin's 1917 cycle Octoechos (Oktoikh). This title refers to the Ochtoechos, an Eastern Orthodox hymnbook arranged in eight parts.

25. The Russian Social Democratic Labor Party split into two factions, the more radical Bolsheviks led by Vladimir Lenin and the more moderate **Mensheviks**, led by Julius Martov, in 1903.

26. This and the following are excerpts from Esenin's 1917 poem "Singing Call" ("Pevushchii zov").

27. This and the two sections that follow are excerpts from Esenin's 1917 poem "Advent" ("Prishestvie").

28. "Inoniia," 1918.

29. This and the following verse section are excerpts from Esenin's 1917 poem "The Transfiguration" ("Preobrazhenie"), which is dedicated to Ivanov-Razumnik.

30. Excerpt from "Inonia."

31. The poetess K. is possibly a reference to **Elizaveta Yuryevna Skobtsova, née Pilenko, by first marriage Kuzmina-Karavaeva** (1891–1945), a poet, noblewoman, and nun (Bogomolov, 561). Known in the Russian Orthodox Church as Mother Maria, she spent the later years of her life in Paris helping the impoverished, refugees, and Jews. She died in Ravensbrück concentration camp and was canonized by the Russian Orthodox Church in 2004.

32. "Tovarishch," 1917.

33. The **RSFSR** is an acronym for the Russian Soviet Federative Socialist Republic, the official name for Russia in the Soviet period. **"My mother, my homeland! I am a Bolshevik."** is from Esenin's 1918 poem "Jordanian Dove" ("Iordanskaia golubitsa").

34. For information on War Communism, see note 23 in "Andrei Bely."

35. Excerpt from Esenin's 1919 poem "The Mare Ships" ("Kobyl'i korabli").

36. "Pugachyov," 1921.

37. This and the following are excerpts from Esenin's 1920 poem "Remembrance of the Departed" ("Sorokoust").

38. This and the following are excerpts from Esenin's 1921 poem "O secret world, my world primeval . . ." ("Mir tainstvennyi, mir moi drevnii . . .").

39. This and the following two sections are from Esenin's 1922 poem "Don't abuse [me]! It's just the way things are! . . ." ("Ne rugaites'! takoe delo! . . .").

40. Excerpt from Esenin's 1922 poem "They drink again, fight here and cry here . . ." ("Snova p'iut zdes', derutsia i plachut . . .")

41. Excerpt from Esenin's 1922 poem "I won't fool myself that I've no foibles . . ." ("Ia obmanyvat' sebia ne stanu . . .").

42. Excerpt from Esenin's 1922 poem "Yes! Now it's decided . . ." ("Da! Teper' resheno . . .").

43. Excerpt from Esenin's 1923 poem "To the brutish go the joys . . ." ("Grubym daetsia radost' . . .").

44. A Russian post-revolutionary literary movement that favored poetry constructed as a series of striking images.

45. Excerpt from Esenin's 1923 poem "I've never before felt so tired . . ." ("Ia ustalym takim eshche ne byl . . .").

46. "Pis'mo materi," 1924.

47. An item of traditional female dress formerly worn in parts of northern and central Russia.

48. *Song Introductions* (Zapevki) was published in 1916. **Churilo Plyonkovich** was a dandified character in Russian folklore.

49. *Chronicles* was a journal edited by Maxim Gorky in the years 1915–1917. *Rusalkas* are water spirits in Slavic folklore. The Firebird is a magical bird in Slavic folklore. **"The Windmill in the Wood"** ("Mel'nitsa v lesu") was written in 1912.

50. Otto **Weininger** (1880–1903) was an Austrian psychologist who gained widespread fame after his suicide for the book *Sex and Character* (Geschlecht

und Charakter). Much of his work was anti-Semitic and misogynistic in character. Written by Anastasia Alexeyevna Verbitskaya (1861–1928), *The Keys to Happiness* (Kliuchi schast'ia, 1908–1913) represented a breakthrough in representations of women and sexuality in pre-Revolutionary Russia.

51. Traditional Russian oral epic narrative poems.

52. This and the following are excerpts from Esenin's 1924 poem "Return to the motherland" ("Vozvrashchenie na rodinu").

53. "Soviet Rus'" ("Rus' sovetskaia"), 1924.

54. For information on NEP, see note 53 in "Bryusov."

55. On November 20, 1923, Esenin, Klychkov, P. Oreshin, and A. Ganin were arrested by the military police following a scene in which anti-Semitic comments had been shouted in a restaurant. The **militsia** was the name given to the police force by the Provisional Government in 1917 in order to distance it from the imperial police force that had preceded it.

56. Reference to Esenin's 1923 poem "This street is familiar to me . . ." ("Eta ulitsa mne znakoma . . .").

57. Excerpt from Esenin's 1921 poem "Are you my country, my country! . . ." ("Storona l' ty moia, storona! . . .").

58. Excerpt from Esenin's 1920 poem "A Hooligan's Confession" ("Ispoved' khuligana").

59. Here, Khodasevich uses the archaic/dialect spelling *"Russiia"* as opposed to the standard modern *"Rossiia,"* which, unfortunately, would be rendered identically in English using transliteration and translation, respectively. The version I have given, Rusia, hopefully evokes the idea of Rus' while maintaining its closeness to the standard country name.

9. GORKY

1. Though most people know him by his pseudonym, the author Maxim Gorky was born Aleksei Maximovich Peshkov. In this section, Gorky is referred to either by his real first name and patronymic (Alexei Maximovich) or by his adopted surname, Gorky, while the name "Maxim" is used to refer to Gorky's son.

2. *The Lower Depths* (Na dne) was first performed on December 18, 1902. One of Gorky's best-known works, *The Lower Depths* presents a grim view of the lives of impoverished Russians. Its message is rather ambiguous, and one of its main themes is harsh truth contrasted with comforting lies. "**The Song of the Falcon**" ("Pesnia o sokole") was published in1895. Khodasevich's first book of poetry was *Youth* (Molodost'), which came out in 1908.

3. **Sail** (*Parus*) publishing house was cofounded by Gorky in 1915 and was a gathering place for people who shared Gorky's anti-war views. **Khodasevich's niece** was Valentina Mikhailovna Khodasevich (1894–1970), a painter and scenery designer.

4. For information on the World Literature publishing house, see note 1 in "Gumilyov and Blok."

5. **Prince Gavriil Konstantinovich Romanov** (1887–1955) and his wife, **Antonina Rafailovna Nesterovskaya, née Nesterovskaya** (1890–1950), a former ballerina, hid in Gorky's apartment on Kronverksky Prospect for several months in the summer and autumn of 1918 with their bulldog (Bogomolov, 563).

6. The **Pan-Russian Writer's Union** was a professional writers' organization that existed in the years 1920–1932. It was designed primarily for writers of the "older" (which is to say, prerevolutionary) generation.

7. Excerpt from Derzhavin's 1807 poem "To Eugene. Life at Zvanka" ("Evgeniiu. Zhizn' Zvanskaia").

8. *Messenger of Europe* (Vestnik Evropy) was the major liberal magazine of late nineteenth century Russia, published 1866–1918.

9. In this chapter, the name "Maxim" refers to the author Gorky's son; the author is referred to either by Alexei Maximovich, his real first name and patronymic, or Gorky, his adopted surname (see note 1 of this chapter).

10. Nadezhda Alexeyevna Peshkova (née Vvedenskaya) (1901–1971). She received the (masculine) nickname "Timosha" from her father-in-law after she cut her hair short.

11. "**Vladimir Ilych**" are Lenin's first name and patronymic. "**Felix Edmundovich**" is Felix Edmundovich Dzerzhinsky (1877–1926), nicknamed "Iron Felix," a Bolshevik revolutionary and Soviet statesman. He was known for his oversight of the Soviet secret police force and his involvement in the Terror.

12. A reference to the poem "The sun rises and sets . . ." ("Solntse vskhodit i zakhodit . . ."), which Gorky includes in *The Lower Depths* as a song of the Volga tramps.

13. In Russian, the word "Cacace" sounds like a comparative formed from the scatological cognate "caca." Therefore, Alexei Maximovich is suggesting that the situation couldn't be crappier.

14. The story referenced here is "About the siskin who lied and the woodpecker who loved the truth" ("O chizhe, kotoryi lgal, i o diatle—liubitele istiny"), first printed in 1893.

15. Mayakovsky made the declaration in question in his autobiography *I Myself* (Ia sam), written over the period 1922–1928.

16. French: "spoilsport."

17. Excerpt from Pushkin's "Fairy Tale about Tsar Saltan" ("Skazka o Tsare Saltane"), 1831.

18. The People's Commissariat for Foreign Affairs (*Narodnyi komissariat inostrannykh del*).

19. **Vladimir Pavlovich Paley** (1897–1918) was the son of **Grand Duke Pavel Alexandrovich** (1860–1919) and **Princess Olga Valerianovna Paley, née Karnovich** (1865–1929). He was killed by the Bolsheviks on July 18, 1918, along with other members of the imperial family. His father was shot less than a year later.

20. *On the Eve* (Nakanune) was a Berlin journal active in the years 1922–1924. The issue in question came out on November 6, 1923 (Bogomolov, 568). *A Guide to the Removal of Anti-Artistic and Counterrevolutionary Literature from Libraries Servicing the Mass Reader* (Vsem Gub. i Upolitprosvetam, Oblitam, Gublitam i Otdelam GPU: Instruktsiia o peresmotre knizhnogo sostava bibliotek k iz"iatiiu kontrrevoliutsionnoi i antikhudozhestvennoi literatury) was released in 1923.

21. A reference to Gorky's 1901 revolutionary poem "The Song of the Stormy Petrel" ("Pesnia o Burevestnike").

22. Gorky's birth name.

23. **"A Story about Cockroaches"** ("O tarakanakh") and *The Artamonov Affair* (Delo Artamonovykh) were published in 1926 and 1925, respectively.

24. *Discourse* (Beseda) was a Russian-language literary journal published by Epoch (*Epokha*) publishing house in the years 1923–1925. It was an attempt to publish writers both from the Soviet Union and abroad. **"A Story about a Hero"** ("Rasskaz o geroe") and **"About a Certain Novel"** ("Rasskaz ob odnom romane") were published in 1924. *Rudder* (Rul') was a Russian-language daily newspaper published in Berlin in the years 1920–1931.

25. Sovremennye Zapiski, a Russian-language literary journal published in Paris in the years 1920–1940.

INDEX OF NAMES

Nikolai Vasilyevich **Bugaev** (1837–1903), Andrei Bely's father, was a professor of mathematics at Moscow University. **50, 52, 53, 64, 239n**

Alexandra Dmitrievna **Bugaeva**, née Egorova (1858–1922), Andrei Bely's mother, was a celebrated beauty. **51, 239n**

Ivan Alexeyevich **Bunin** (1870–1953) was the first Russian writer to win the Nobel Prize for Literature. He is best known for his realist short stories and novels. **60, 216**

Pyotr Yakovlevich **Chaadaev** (1794–1856) was a philosopher who was labeled as insane and placed under house arrest due to the unflattering portrayal of Russia as a backward, isolated country in his *Philosophical Letters*. Gershenzon was his biographer, as well as the editor of his collected works. **120, 130**

Alexei Pavlovich **Chapygin** (1870–1937) was a writer best known for his historical novels about the peasant uprisings of the seventeenth century. He drew on Russian folklore in his work. **161**

Alexandra Nikolaevna **Chebotarevskaya** (1869–1925) was a translator and writer. She was the sister of Anastasia Chebotarevskaya. **148**

Anastasia Nikolaevna **Chebotarevskaya** (1877–1921) was a writer, translator, and Sologub's wife. **144, 146**

Kornei Ivanovich **Chukovsky** (born Nikolai Vasilyevich Korneichukov) (1882–1969) was a literary critic and essayist in addition to being one of Russia's best-loved children's poets. **109, 110, 195**

Georgy Ivanovich **Chulkov** (1879–1939) was a Symbolist poet and the brother of Khodasevich's second wife, Anna Ivanovna Khodasevich (née Chulkova) (1887–1964). **105, 243n, 244n, 246n**

Cima da Conegliano (c. 1459–1517) was an Italian Renaissance painter of the Venetian school who worked mainly on religious subjects. **23**

Georges **Delvari** was the stage name of Georgy Ilych Kruchinsky (1882–1942). He performed as a clown and acrobat. **198**

Anton Antonovich **Delvig** (1798–1831) was a poet and school friend of Pushkin's. **129**

Demyan Bedny was the pseudonym of Efim Alexeyevich Pridvorov (1883–1945), a poet and satirist of peasant origins. His pseudonym means "Demyan the Poor." **190**

Gavrila Romanovich **Derzhavin** (1743–1816) was one of the greatest Russian poets in the period before Pushkin. Khodasevich wrote an excellent biography of Derzhavin, which is available in an English translation by Angela Brintlinger. **16, 92, 202, 250n**

Alexander Mikhailovich **Dobrolyubov** (1876–1944?) was a decadent poet who went out "among the people" and founded a sect of "Dobrolyubians" ("*Dobroliubtsy*"). **28, 29**

Isadora **Duncan** (1877–1927) was an unconventional American dancer who toured Europe to great acclaim. She met Esenin in Moscow in 1921. They married in 1922 and divorced in 1923. Her infamous death in Nice occurred as a result of her extravagantly long scarf getting caught in the rear wheel of an open-top car. **185, 242n**

Vyacheslav Ivanovich **Ivanov** (1866–1949) was a Symbolist poet and playwright. **35, 130**

Lev Borisovich **Kamenev** (Rozenfeld) (1883–1936) was a Soviet politician. He was chairman of the Moscow Council in the years 1918–1919. **45**

Solomon Gitmanovich **Kaplun** (pseudonym Sumsky) (1891 or 1883–1940) was the head of the Berlin publishing house Epoch (*Epokha*). **73**

Nikolai Mikhailovich **Karamzin** (1766–1826) was a writer, critic, and historian best remembered for his *History of the Russian State*. His *Letters of a Russian Traveler* (Pis'ma russkogo puteshestvennika), written after a journey to Europe undertaken in the years 1789–1791, earned him instant literary fame. **40, 238n**

Boris Osipovich **Khariton** (1877–1941) was a journalist and editor. **101**

Nikolai Alexeyevich **Klyuev** (1884–1937) became the leader of the "peasant poet" movement. He was a close friend and mentor to Esenin. **152, 157, 158, 159, 160, 161, 162, 166, 173, 175, 187, 188**

Henrikh Aaronovich **Koiransky** (1883–?) was a doctor and one of three literary brothers. He published poetry under the pseudonym G. Tverskoy. He treated Nina Petrovskaya for her drug addiction and nervous disorders on numerous occasions. **47**

Alexei Vasilyevich **Koltsov** (1809–1842) was a cattle merchant's son who wrote poetry inspired by the Russian peasantry in secret in his youth. He later attracted a wide audience and has been called the Russian Robert Burns. **161**

Ivan Ivanovich **Konevskoy** (born Oreus) (1877–1901) was an erudite Symbolist poet and critic. **28**

Anatoly Fyodorovich **Koni** (1844–1927) was a famous lawyer and man of letters. He was extremely popular in literary Saint Petersburg at the beginning of the 1920s. **100–101**

Lavr Georgievich **Kornilov** (1870–1918) was a general in the Imperial Russian Army who was arrested and charged with attempting a coup d'état against the Provisional Government in 1917. Following his escape from prison, he became a military commander in the anti-Bolshevik Volunteer Army during the Russian Civil War, in which he was killed. **170**

Nestor Alexandrovich **Kotlyarevsky** (1863–1925) was a literary scholar. **101, 103**

Leonid Borisovich **Krasin** (1870–1926) was a Soviet public official. **196**

Sergei **Krechetov** was the pseudonym of Sergei Alexeyevich Sokolov (1878–1936), a Symbolist poet, publisher, and lawyer. He was founder and editor-in-chief at Griffin and was married to Nina Petrovskaya in the years 1903–1905. **41, 234n**

Mikhail Petrovich **Kristi** (1875–1956) was a Soviet public figure. In 1921, he was chairman of the Academic Center in Saint Petersburg (then Petrograd). **102**

Pyotr Petrovich **Kryuchkov** (1889–1938) was a lawyer and personal secretary to Maxim Gorky. He later became a victim of political repression. **196**

Nadezhda Konstantinovna **Krupskaya** (1869–1939) was a Bolshevik revolutionary, politician, and the Soviet Union's Deputy Minister of Education in the years 1929–1939. She was also the wife of Vladimir Lenin. **225**

Alexander Ivanovich **Kuprin** (1870–1938) was a naturalist prose writer whose most famous works focused on the social ills of his day. **60**

Ekaterina Dmitrievna **Kuskova** (1869–1958) was a political activist and publisher who opposed the Bolsheviks. **215, 221**

Boris Mikhailovich **Kustodiev** (1878–1927) was a painter and stage designer. He painted a portrait of Sologub in 1907. **132**

Mikhail Mikhailovich **Lashevich** (1884–1928) was a military and party official. **200**

Nikolai Semyonovich **Leskov** (1831–1895) was a novelist and short story writer known for his formal experiments and innovative use of dialect. **225**

Konstantin Abramovich **Lipskerov** (1889–1954) was a poet, translator, and friend of Khodasevich. **43**

Colonel Dmitry Nikolaevich **Loman** (1868–1918) was a journalist, military officer, and personal aide to Empress Alexandra Fyodorovna Romanova. **164**

Vera Osipovna **Lourié** (1901–1998) was a poet and student of the Acmeist Nikolai Stepanovich Gumilyov. **73**

Anatoly Vasilyevich **Lunacharsky** (1875–1933) was the first Soviet People's Commissar of Education. He was an active critic and journalist throughout his bureaucratic career. **108, 147**

Nadezhda Grigoryevna **Lvova** (1891–1913) was a poet who killed herself following an unhappy love affair with Bryusov. **xi, xxxii, xxxiv, 15, 30, 35, 36, 237n**

Pavel Nikitich **Makintsian** (1888–1938) was an Armenian historian and translator who aided Bryusov in the compilation of *Poetry of Armenia*. **42**

Sergei Konstantinovich **Makovsky** (1877–1962) was a poet and art scholar, as well as the second husband of Khodasevich's first wife. He was the son of noted painter Konstantin Egorovich Makovsky (1839–1915). **51, 239n, 243n**

Osip Emilyevich **Mandelshtam** (1891–1938) was a major Acmeist poet and essayist who perished in a prison camp. **105, 106, 108**

Vladimir Vladimirovich **Mayakovsky** (1893–1930) was a major Russian Futurist poet. Best known for his Revolutionary poetry, he had a complicated relationship with the Soviet state—and his legacy in the Soviet Union remained complicated after his suicide in 1930. **216, 250n**

Wilhelm von **Mirbach-Harff** (1871–1918) was the German ambassador assassinated by Yakov Grigoryevich Blyumkin (1898–1929) in an attempt to provoke war with Germany. **179, 254**

Muni was the pseudonym of Samuil Viktorovich Kissin (1885–1916), a Russian poet. See the essay "Muni." **x, xv, xxiv, xxxiv, xxxv, 81, 82, 83, 84, 85, 86, 87, 88, 90, 91, 92, 93, 94, 95, 155, 157, 242n**

Pavel Pavlovich **Muratov** (1881–1950) was an art historian, writer, and editor of the literary journal *Sofia* (Sofiia). **207, 235**

Vladimir Ivanovich **Narbut** (1888–1938) was an Acmeist poet. **105, 243n**

Ivan Fyodorovich **Nazhivin** (1874–1940) was a writer and Tolstoyan. His novel about Rasputin was published in 1923. **203, 204**

Sergei Evgenyevich **Neldikhen** (1891–1942) was a primitivist poet. **106, 107, 108, 243n**

Maria Solomonovna **Nemenova-Lunts** (1879–1954) was a pianist and educator. **39**

Mikhail Vasilyevich **Nesterov** (1862–1942) was a Symbolist painter associated with the Wanderers (*Peredvizhniki*) and World of Art (*Mir Iskusstva*) movements. He was known for his religious themes. **178**

Nikolai Platonovich **Ogaryov** (1813–1877) was a poet, historian, and political activist best known for his close relationship with the writer and social reformer Alexander Ivanovich Herzen (1812–1870). **120, 129**

Abram Rubimovich **Palei** (1893–1995) was a poet and science fiction writer who was in correspondence with Gorky. **224**

Vladimir Pavlovich **Palei** (1897–1918) was the son of Grand Duke Pavel Alexandrovich (1860–1929) and Princess Olga Valerianovna **Palei**, née Karnovich (1865–1929). He was killed by the Bolsheviks on July 18, 1918, along with other members of the imperial family. **223, 224**

Boris Leonidovich **Pasternak** (1890–1960) was a poet, novelist, and literary translator, best known internationally for his novel *Doctor Zhivago* (Doktor Zhivago), published in 1957. He was awarded the Nobel Prize for Literature in 1958, which caused a scandal in the Soviet Union; he was forced to decline the prize. **xviii, 64**

Nadezhda Alexandrovna **Pavlovich** (1895–1980) was a poet who was very close to Blok in the final years of his life. **114**

Father Vladimir Sergeyevich **Pecherin** (1807–1885) was a Romantic lyricist poet, memoirist, and Catholic religious thinker. **129**

Maxim Alexeyevich **Peshkov** (1897–1934) was Gorky's son by Ekaterina Pavlovna Peshkova. **207, 229, 249n**

Ekaterina Pavlovna **Peshkova** (née Volzhina) (1876?–1965) was a Soviet human rights activist and humanitarian, as well as Gorky's first and only legal wife. **207**

Nina Ivanovna **Petrovskaya** (1879–1928) was a writer and memoirist. See the essay "The Death of Renate." **x, xi, xv, xxiv, xxxii, xxxiii, xxxiv, 3, 5, 6, 8, 9, 10, 11, 13, 16, 18, 31, 35, 36, 55, 57, 58, 59, 61, 69, 73, 80, 195, 234n, 236n, 239n**

Nikolai Efimovich **Poyarkov** (1877–1918) was a writer and critic. His decadent poetry was disparaged by, among others, Alexander Blok, who once referred to him in a letter as "a button off of Balmont's drawers." **88**

Kozma Petrovich **Prutkov** was a collective pseudonym used by Alexei Tolstoy and the three Zhemchuzhnikov brothers to publish humorous works during the reign of Nicholas I (1825–1855). Prutkov's trademark style was a sort of cleverly pompous stupidity. **72, 87**

Ivan Nikolaevich **Rakitsky** (1883–1942) was an artist. **198, 207, 208, 219**

Grigory Efimovich **Rasputin** (1869–1916) was a controversial self-proclaimed holy man of peasant origins with close ties to (and significant influence over) the imperial family. He was assassinated by a group of conservative noblemen. His death was surrounded by as many fantastic rumors as his life had been: he was reported

Sergei Mikhailovich **Solovyov** (1885–1942) was a Symbolist poet, critic, and theologian. He was a nephew of Vladimir Sergeyevich Solovyov and a second cousin of Alexander Blok. He was also a close friend of Andrei Bely. **24, 62, 103, 240n**

Vladimir Sergeyevich **Solovyov** (1853–1900) was a religious philosopher, poet, and literary critic who had a tremendous impact on the Russian Symbolist movement. **xix, xxiii, xxxiii, 54, 225, 234n**

Vera Oskarovna **Stanevich** (1890–1967) was an anthroposophist, poet, translator, and critic. She was married to the poet Yu. P. Anisimov (1886–1940), and their home was something of a literary salon. She was known for her masculine habits, which included walking around in short pants in her home. Thus, Bely, with whom she was in love, would tease her by calling her "Shtanevich"—a combination of her last name and the Russian word for "trousers" (*"shtany"*). **64, 240n**

Arseny Viktorovich **Starkov** (1874–1927) was a doctor and anatomist who lived in Sorrento in the years 1924–1925. **207**

Rudolf **Steiner** (1861–1925) was an Austrian philosopher, social reformer, and architect who founded anthroposophy, an esoteric spiritual movement rooted in German idealist philosophy and theosophy. **64, 70, 71, 72, 241n**

Nikolai Ilych **Storozhenko** (1836–1906) was a literary historian, Shakespeare specialist, and professor at Moscow University (now Moscow State University). **23n**

Pyotr Berngardovich **Struve** (1870–1944) was an economist, philosopher, and editor. Originally a Marxist, he later cofounded the liberal Constitutional Democratic Party. Finally, during the Russian Civil War, he became active with the pro-imperial Whites. **42**

Ekaterina Pavlovna **Sultanova**, née Letkova (1856–1937) was a writer and translator in addition to being considered a great beauty. **51**

Valentin Pavlovich **Sventsitsky** (1881–1931) was a writer as well as a Russian Orthodox priest and theologian. **157**

Hippolyte **Taine** (1828–1893) was a French critic and historian. He was associated with French naturalism, sociological positivism, and historicist literary criticism. **225**

Olga Kuzminishna **Teternikova** (1865–1907) was a midwife and Sologub's sister. She lived with him for a number of years and he married only after she died. **246n**

Alexander Nikolaevich **Tikhonov** (pseudonym Serebrov) (1880–1956) was a literary figure, one of the heads of World Literature, and a close friend and collaborator of Maxim Gorky. **109, 196, 222**

Alexander Ivanovich **Tinyakov** (1886–1934) was a poet, publicist, and literary critic. **27, 28**

Alexei Nikolaevich **Tolstoy** (1883–1945) was a writer known primarily for his science fiction and historical novels. He was also a distant relative of Lev Tolstoy (1828–1910). **105, 130, 179**

Ivan Ivanovich **Troyanovsky** (1855–1928) was a doctor, art collector, amateur botanist, and cofounder of Free Aesthetics. **39**